Point

COLLECTION 8

A terrifying trio in one!

Have you read these other fabulous Point Horror Collections?

COLLECTION 1

Mother's Helper, The Invitation, Beach Party

COLLECTION 2

My Secret Admirer, The Accident, Funhouse

COLLECTION 3

April Fools, The Waitress, The Snowman

COLLECTION 4

THE R.L. STINE COLLECTION:

The Baby-sitter, The Boyfriend, The Girlfriend

COLLECTION 5

The Cemetery, Freeze Tag, The Fever

COLLECTION 6

THE CAROLINE B. COONEY COLLECTION:

The Cheerleader, The Return of the Vampire, The Vampire's Promise

COLLECTION 7

The Window, The Train, Hit and Run

Point Horror

COLLECTION 8

A terrifying trio in one!

The Dead Game
A. Bates

The Stranger
Caroline B. Cooney

Call Waiting
R.L. Stine

■SCHOLASTIC

Scholastic Children's Books,
Commonwealth House, 1-19 New Oxford Street,
London WC1A 1NU, UK
a division of Scholastic Ltd
London ~ New York ~ Toronto ~ Sydney ~ Auckland

First published in this edition by Scholastic Ltd, 1996

The Dead Game
First published in the USA by Scholastic Inc., 1993
First published in the UK by Scholastic Publications Ltd, 1994
Copyright © A. Bates, 1993

The Stranger
First published in the USA by Scholastic Inc., 1993
First published in the UK by Scholastic Publications Ltd, 1994
Copyright © Caroline B. Cooney, 1993

Call Waiting
First published in the USA by Scholastic Inc., 1994
First published in the UK by Scholastic Publications Ltd, 1994
Copyright © R.L. Stine, 1994

ISBN 0 590 13481 7

Printed by Cox & Wyman Ltd, Reading, Berks.

10 9 8 7 6 5 4 3 2 1

The right of A. Bates, Caroline B. Cooney and R.L. Stine to be identified as the authors of
this work has been asserted by them in accordance with the Copyright,
Designs and Patents Act, 1988.

Contents

The Dead Game   *1*
A. Bates

The Stranger   *169*
Diane Hoh

Call Waiting   *369*
R.L. Stine

THE DEAD GAME

*To Grover, who will never read this book,
and to Shirin and Wesley Grover, who will . . .
with thanks, love, and hope.*

Chapter 1

"Almost," Linnie said glumly.

She stuffed a piece of pizza crust into her milk carton.

The background noise — trays banging on table-tops, and several hundred voices complaining, joking, talking — went on all around her, ignored as she focused on her thoughts.

"Almost what?" Jackson asked.

He grabbed Linnie's milk carton and looked in the top. "I could have eaten that," he said sadly.

Linnie barely heard him. She frowned, stabbing her potato triangle with her fork, rubbing it back and forth in the ketchup on her tray as she worked at putting her thoughts into words.

She felt Jackson's hopeful stare and glanced up. "Oh, sorry. Here." She handed him the triangle, fork and all. "I almost had a good senior year," she explained, wiping her fingers on a napkin. "It was almost fun. It was almost memorable."

She wadded her napkin. "I'm almost glad I was here."

"You're disasterizing," Ming told her.

"I'm what?"

"Making a mountain out of a molehill," Ming said, tossing her dark hair back. "Maybe you aren't going to get an A in Studio. Maybe you're not going to be world-famous for your ceramic pots. That doesn't make the whole year a disaster. One class, maybe. But not the whole year."

"It makes my whole career plan a disaster!" As soon as she said the words, Linnie wished she could grab them back. Ming's disappointment was much worse than hers, and she'd hardly said a word about it.

"It's been a fine year for both of us," Ming said firmly. "And finally we're almost out of here. Out of Hollander High is where we've wanted to be since tenth grade, right? So we're doing great."

She sounds like she's giving a pep talk, Linnie thought. All that fake enthusiasm. But who is she trying to pep up — herself or me? She glanced thoughtfully at her friend, ignoring the people who stopped by to say hello to Jackson and offer any lunch they had left over. Jackson usually ate three lunches — one that he bought, two that were donated piecemeal — so the steady stream of offerings was commonplace.

Ming's earlier words hung unspoken over the table. *Graduating number three means nothing. It's not valedictorian. It's not salutatorian. It's nothing.* That was all Ming had said about the situation, and she'd said it back in January when Austin and Adler had transferred to Hollander and Ming's class

4

rank plummeted immediately from first to third place.

Linnie said, "Maybe a meteorite will fall out of the sky and smash both the transfer twins in one crashing blow."

Ming gave a small grin, but it was only a fraction of her usual smile.

She's really hurting, Linnie thought, feeling helpless as she watched her sober-eyed, too-quiet friend. I've never been number one, but I know how it feels to be cut down!

"Maybe my real problem is I never had a real problem before," Ming said. "So when this hit, I didn't have any experience. I'm still kind of numb and it's been, what? Most of the semester?"

"Seems like forever," Jackson said.

"I've been thinking about it," Ming went on. "I realized how easy I've had it all my life. Getting good grades was never hard for me, and I'm naturally athletic. Making friends has always been easy because I'm not shy and I always liked everybody."

"Even Austin and Adler?" Jackson asked.

"I was talking past tense," Ming said. "No, I do not like the transfer twins. My point was I'm not handling this well. I think if someone had transferred here who had really worked hard for their grades . . . I think I'd feel better. At least I'd know they'd earned it. It's just so hard when Austin and Adler — well . . ." Her voice trailed off. "I think it's really sinking in now. Once the numbness wears off, it hurts."

Linnie stared at her lunch tray, empty except

for ketchup smears and a crinkled straw paper. It's not fair, she thought. If Hollander High doesn't offer Advanced Placement and Honors courses, why do they give extra rating points to people who take them somewhere else? Why is my friend hurting, and Austin and Adler, the cheats, are doing just fine?

Jackson licked his fingers. "I heard they researched," he told Ming. "The story I heard is they were ranked number eight and number ten at their prep school so their folks went looking for a place like Hollander — a place that has a good reputation but doesn't offer AP or Honors classes."

"Which automatically guarantees top ranking to anybody who just happens to have a bunch of AP classes on their transcripts," Linnie added. "And that stinks!"

"It's clever." Jackson crumpled his milk carton and tossed it into the bin across from the table. "So simple. Wonder why my folks didn't think of it."

Ming grinned again, a little wider this time. "Jackson, you wouldn't know an Honors course if it sat in your lap. The story is true, by the way. I heard Austin bragging. He and Adler think it's funny. Their parents are rich enough to move anywhere, and they picked here for A and A's final semester just so the boys can take top honors. Austin will graduate number one, and Adler is number two."

And you're number three, Linnie thought grimly. Not valedictorian. Not salutatorian. Nothing.

Jackson sighed. "Maybe we could manufacture a meteorite," he said. "We could spend evenings after track practice on the roof of the school building it, and when it's big enough to do mortal damage, Bam! We just roll it over the edge — at the exact moment the A and A boys are walking by, of course."

"That could be fun," Ming said, sounding less glum.

Linnie had smoothed out her napkin and was staring at it. I should have guessed, she thought. She's been so quiet lately. I should have known what was bothering her. The closer graduation gets, the worse it's going to hurt.

She felt Jackson's eyes on her and looked up. "What?" she asked. "Can I shred my napkin or do you want to eat that, too?"

"Go ahead and shred," Jackson told her. "I'm full for now."

"Thank you." Linnie solemnly tore a strip off the edge of her napkin, then a second one.

"I think we should do *something*," Jackson announced. "Something as nasty and underhanded as what they did."

"That's not possible," Linnie said.

"It's too late to transfer somewhere, even if I wanted to," Ming said. "And first I'd have to look for another school with no Honors classes and where no one already has a 4.0 grade point, which I might be willing to do if that meant getting even with Austin and Adler. But it wouldn't mean that. I'd just be hurting someone else. That would be pointless. If I were going to hurt someone, I'd want it to be the transfer twins."

"I didn't mean pull the same trick they did," Jackson said. "I just meant there has to be something we could do."

"All that's left is to hope someone kills them," Ming pointed out. "And soon. They're here. They have a higher grade-point average than I can ever get. It's over. They win. There wasn't even a battle. I lost without a fight."

"Actually," Linnie said slowly, "that's not a bad idea."

"What isn't?" Ming asked.

"Killing them," Linnie said.

Jackson and Ming looked doubtful, as if they weren't certain they'd heard right.

"Ax them, ice them, knock them off," Linnie said. "Bump them off. Chop." She made a chopping motion with her hand against the edge of the table.

Ming laughed uneasily. "You're kidding, right?" She and Jackson both turned to stare at Linnie.

Linnie tore off another shred of napkin and shook her head. "Nope," she said. "Death. I'm completely serious. It's the perfect solution."

Chapter 2

The pottery studio with its wheels and kilns and clay-stained tables was in the farthest corner of the school from the lunchroom, and Linnie hustled. Her art teacher was great, but she had the traditional artistic temperament and her pet peeve was people who were late to *her* class.

Linnie could recite the tirade from memory. "Nothing is more important than art. Artists may forget to eat, to sleep, to breathe, even, but they do not forget to come to class. On time!"

She did make it on time — barely — and spent the class alternately muttering at the vase that wouldn't soar artistically into being, and grinning as she remembered the expressions on Ming's and Jackson's faces as she'd left them in the lunchroom.

They'd mirrored each other, looking shocked, horrified, disbelieving, and just a tiny bit excited.

Linnie hadn't explained her idea, had suggested, instead, that they meet in the parking lot right after school to discuss it.

She turned her thoughts back to her vase. "It

just won't GO," she moaned to the teacher, who had paused at her table.

"Because you don't have any concentration today," the teacher replied, eyeing the vase critically. "Your fingers are like sausages poking at the clay."

Stung, Linnie stared at her hands, feeling clumsy. People do that to me, she thought. They find all my little sore spots and push on them. Just like my sister. Now I'm afraid to touch the clay. Maybe I'm not an artist at all. Artists have a different vision; I have . . . sausage fingers.

The teacher moved on to Brenda at the next table, murmuring a few words that, to Linnie, sounded like encouragement. But Brenda started crying. "You're right!" she yelled. She lifted her hand, made a sudden fist, and smashed her vase. "It was no good!" She raised clay-muddied hands and covered her face.

Oh, that was a good touch, Linnie thought, her lips compressing in disgust. Very carefully done. I wish I'd thought of it. It'll take her all of three minutes to dab the clay off her face and redo her lipstick. If she'd happened to touch a single hair on her head during her little fit I'd have been more impressed since that would have been a lot harder to fix!

She watched the teacher as she comforted Brenda, murmuring soothingly.

Now she'll get an A for her artistic temperament, Linnie thought, poking at her own vase. And she won't even have a project to turn in. I'll turn in a decent vase and get a C for sausage fingers. We'd better build a big meteorite because it's got to have room for Brenda under it, too.

Then she brightened. We don't have to limit ourselves to Austin and Alder! We can make up a hit list.

She laughed aloud, sobering almost instantly at the teacher's startled, hopeful stare.

No, I did not have a burst of artistic inspiration, she thought in silent answer to the teacher's look.

Her fingers molded the clay, feeling the cool dampness, the graininess, the way the clay responded to her touch. I love clay, she thought. It's so clean and fresh, like a baby, ready to be whatever I make it. I am the creator and the clay follows my thoughts and my hands.

The wheel spun and her fingers worked. The sides of the vase flared upward, forming into a graceful shape that reminded Linnie of an urn.

Maybe I did get inspired, she thought, watching the urn take shape. A hit list. Austin, Adler, and Brenda. I'd put my sister on it, too, but she lives too far away.

She grinned, admiring her urn, smiling over it at Brenda.

Chapter 3

Jackson and Ming were not waiting for her in the parking lot as they usually did when Linnie arrived after school. She waited, but it was not until she had given up and started walking home that she saw them, coming toward her.

Jackson, tall and muscular, stood nearly a foot taller than Ming. He walked with the aggressive gait of a defensive back on the football team, which he was. Ming, looking frail and tiny beside him, walked with the light and graceful step of a dancer, which she was not. She played volleyball, basketball, and was on the summer softball team, but she often said her dance skills had gotten stuck on basic fast and basic slow.

They both looked wary. And determined.

"Can't do it," Jackson said firmly, before Linnie had a chance to say anything. "And we can't let you do it, either. I can almost believe they deserve it, but I can't let it happen."

"You idiots!" Linnie said, laughing. "Is that why you're late? You've been trying to figure out how to stop me from killing people? I can't believe you took me seriously! I thought you understood . . . well, how could you? I didn't explain I meant a game. I just . . ."

She couldn't help laughing at the embarrassment and relief on their faces. "You guys are too much!" she said. "After all the years you've known me you actually think I could turn into a murderer? You know I don't like blood. It's messy. Anyway, I've got a much more practical idea. Come on, let's go get a taco or something and I'll explain."

The taco stand was half a block up from the school, on the other side of the street, and after ordering, they took their food back across the street to the park that adjoined the school grounds.

"Let's eat down by the river," Ming suggested. She led the way to where the river lined the north edge of the park. The banks had been fenced in tall chain-link to keep people from wading in and possibly drowning, but there were benches facing the water and they sat together on one, watching the calming, almost hypnotic flow.

"I'm sorry," Ming said finally. "I should have known you couldn't really mean it . . . even though you said you were serious." She glanced at Linnie.

Linnie nodded. "I did say that," she agreed, apologizing. "I was being dramatic. It never occurred to me you'd think I was really serious, though. I can't imagine either of you suddenly planning murders, and I guess I thought you'd automatically know I didn't really mean it."

"It's because . . . that's what I've been wishing," Ming admitted softly. "It's so unfair! I sent out all my college and scholarship applications with number-one class rank on them. I've had to write to everyone and say I'm only number three now, and some of the scholarships were only for valedictorians and salutatorians. It's so humiliating to have to explain."

She sighed and unwrapped the burrito. "I've been writing letters and hating Austin and Adler, wishing they were dead. So when you said let's kill them . . . well. I believed you really meant it because I kind of really wanted it to happen. You must think I'm a real baby, whining about things not being fair."

"Don't be silly." Linnie licked hot sauce off her fingers. "Only what I really had in mind will seem pretty tame now, compared to what you imagined."

Jackson had been busy eating as he listened. He jumped up and put his trash in the barrel, then came back. "Let's hear it," he said.

"It's a game my sister played at a retreat once," Linnie said. "The Dead Game. The way they did it, everyone played and they all knew the rules. We can't play it like that, of course, because we certainly don't want to tell A and A what we're up to. But it's a good starting point."

Ming took small bites of her burrito, listening attentively.

Jackson's watching each bite she takes, Linnie thought. Is he gauging whether there'll be any left for him? "In the real game," she went on, "everyone had an assigned target. And each player was a target, too. So while you were trying to kill your target, someone else was trying to kill you.

"Basically, you had to get your target alone, and then you said, 'You're dead,' or something like that, and then you had to take their target and try to kill that person, too, so the last one left alive was the winner."

She glanced at Jackson. He looked interested. So did Ming.

"What I was thinking," Linnie said, "was that we could do something to A and A. Something that would sting a little, and maybe be symbolic, like . . . oh, I haven't figured that out yet. But they'd know it when they got hit, only they wouldn't know who did it, or why."

"A kind of bloodless vengeance," Jackson muttered. "I like the idea. Only what would we do? How would it actually work?"

"We'd have to do something that had impact," Ming said, frowning.

"What would impact them?" Jackson asked. He stretched his legs out in front of himself, resting his hands on his thighs. "They're not hurting for anything. They've got looks, money, top class rank, huge egos, and successful images."

"That's it!" Ming said, bouncing on the bench. "If we could dent their image we might sting them a little. I have a feeling that's what they value most, anyway. It LOOKS good to graduate first and second. It LOOKS good to go to an Ivy League college. I think they value looks more than anything."

"That's a good point," Linnie said. "What they

value. If we really want to sting someone, it makes sense to figure out what's most important to them and somehow target that." She handed Jackson her crumpled taco wrapper.

He looked at it. "It's empty." He sounded disgusted.

Linnie nodded. He wadded it into a tight ball and tossed it into the bin.

"Austin's hair," Ming said thoughtfully. "He must use a can of hairspray a week on it. It has to look perfect. He probably wouldn't come to school if it didn't look perfect. I wish we could buzz-cut it all off. He'd stay home, and his grades would drop."

"He'd hire a tutor," Linnie said. "Besides, I can't see him sitting still while we cut off his hair. And how would we do it without Austin knowing who'd done it?"

Ming brightened. "His letter jacket!"

"It's certainly important to him." Jackson grinned and stood up, restless. "He makes a big deal out of it, anyway. He's always kind of running his fingers over it, and he hassles anyone who touches it. But what would you do to it?" He took a few steps, came back, glanced toward the river, then at his watch. "I've got track practice pretty soon," he told them.

"I will steal the jacket," Ming announced. "That ought to make an impression on him. He might even get so upset he goes around accusing people and looking like a fool."

She looked over at Linnie, her expression darkening. "Did you know he had the nerve to ask me out?"

Linnie saw Jackson's eyes swing to Ming, his jaw tightening.

Oh! Linnie thought. If I were in a cartoon, light bulbs would be going on above my head. Jackson likes Ming!

"He made it sound like he was doing me a favor," Ming said. "He stood there in his jacket acting like he was granting his attention to a peasant. After what his coming here cost me I could have . . ."

She shook her head, giving a half-laugh. "I almost said I could have killed him," she admitted.

Chapter 4

Linnie, Ming, and Jackson sat at their lunch table the next day, staring across the room at Austin.

"I don't see how you could have done it," Linnie said doubtfully. "He's got it on."

"I feel like a fool," Ming said.

"Are you sure you got the right jacket?" Linnie asked.

"Of course I'm sure! How many prep school letter jackets are there around here? I'm telling you, I took his jacket yesterday and I put it in the woods." Ming glared at Austin. He was sitting sideways to them, obviously wearing the same letter jacket he always wore.

"Tell us what happened," Linnie suggested. "Step by step. Maybe there was another jacket similar to his and you got it by mistake."

Ming rolled her eyes. "There was no mistake. I was going home after we split up. Jackson went to practice, you went back toward the front of the school, and I cut on through the park. I usually go home that way if the sprinklers aren't on."

"Right," Linnie said.

"I went past the stairs and into the woods and then I heard voices murmuring, kind of quiet. I didn't feel like interrupting anyone, so I was going to turn around and go back the other way, but that meant going up all those stairs and I decided I could probably just sneak by whoever was talking because it sounded like . . . well, it sounded like a guy and girl in private conversation. And it was."

She rubbed her forehead. "It was Austin and Brenda. The jacket was behind them on a rock, with their books and stuff. They were too busy kissing to notice me, and besides, I was very quiet. I couldn't believe my luck! I decide to steal Austin's jacket and there it is, right in front of me. It was like a sign. I just grabbed it and kept on going. It was his jacket! I know it was!"

"What did you do with it?" Jackson asked.

"I hung it in that old graveyard," Ming told them, her eyes crinkling as she smiled. "I hung it over a tombstone. It was still there this morning. I checked."

"Well, I guess he found it after you checked, then," Linnie said. "Because he certainly has it on."

"Let's go look," Jackson suggested.

They quickly finished eating and Ming led the way out the back door of the cafeteria, past the huge trash bins, down the steep stairs onto the grassy park grounds, and into the woods. The sun warmed their shoulders until they got into thicker trees. They followed a path, scurrying noises darting ahead of them, then falling silent as squirrels and chipmunks hustled away from the intrusion.

"Over here," Ming said, pointing. "See? That's where I found the jacket. I just picked it up. I didn't even have to stop. I figured they'd go back to school since they both had cars in the lot so I went on this way. I have to admit I was feeling pretty good about the whole thing working out like that. I felt sneaky, but it felt good, like I was finally doing something instead of just giving up."

A slight breeze made the branches creak, and Linnie was suddenly glad it was bright daylight. Their feet scuffled in the layer of old leaves as Ming led them onto a fainter, less well-traveled path. She stopped and pointed.

The clearing ahead was bright, but shadowed in spots. Straight ahead the sun shone on half a dozen ancient tombstones.

"That's fabulous," Linnie said, stepping nearer. "Very artistic."

The tombstone looked as if it were wearing the jacket.

"And that *is* his jacket." Ming sounded almost relieved.

"How long did this take you?" Jackson asked.

"Not very long," Ming said. "The rocks and sticks were all around here. I just had to arrange them." She knelt next to the grave, knelt outside the ring of stones she'd spaced around the mound. "I thought if he went looking for the jacket, it would be nice and spooky for him to find this."

She straightened the rock that was the head, patted the side of the mound and fussed with the sticks she'd laid as bones on top of the grave. "I was very careful to make the bones as realistic as I could. Here's the femur, patella, tibia, fibula . . ."

Linnie shivered. The effect suddenly looked too real. Rocks and sticks, she told herself. That's not really bones. The real bones are six feet under and a hundred years old. "Let's go back," she said. "We saw the jacket. Lunch is almost over."

Ming nodded. She gave the leg bones a final twitch and stood up.

"He's rich," Jackson said as they headed back. "I'll bet he just went out and bought another jacket."

"You can't just go buy a letter jacket," Linnie said. "Especially one from a school in another state."

"I guess if you're rich enough you can do anything, because he's got another jacket on," Jackson pointed out.

"So much for denting his image," Ming said, tossing her hair back. "We didn't even scratch it. I really feel stupid, going to all that effort. I kept imagining his face when he saw the grave and realized it was his jacket. I was hoping he'd have a bunch of people with him and he'd lose his poise in front of them. Instead, I'm the fool."

"You had the right idea," Jackson said, holding a branch out of their way. "We just need to carry it further. There's no point in hitting a target if the target has no idea he's been hit. We should have planned the grave. We should have lured Austin out to see it. Then he'd have felt the hit."

"It's kind of lost its impact, now, since he already has another jacket," Ming pointed out.

They hurried across the grass as the warning bell sounded from above them. From behind them a *ti-ti-ti-ti-whirrrr* sounded and Linnie jumped. "Oh," she said. "The sprinklers. We're going to get wet — unless you want to go back through the park and around the front?"

"We'll just run," Jackson said. "We'll barely get sprinkled."

"Run?" Linnie asked. "Up those steps?" She put a hand on the railing and stared up the steep flight of concrete steps.

"I do it for football training," Jackson said. "Watch." He ran up the stairs, stepping on each stair with first one foot, then the other, as if he were running through staggered tires on an obstacle course.

"I guess I'll be late to pottery if I don't run," Linnie said, laughing as the park sprinkler whirred in their direction, spattering her and Ming as they dashed up the stairs.

At the top, resting briefly, Jackson said, "Listen, Ming. The grave was great. It was our idea that was dumb, not your execution. We should have thought it out better. Let's try again. We'll meet for hamburgers and talk about it. After school."

"And I have someone else to add to the list," Linnie said. "I thought we could make a hit list. But I better run. See you later."

She did run, the *tick-tick-hiss* of the sprinklers

fading as she entered the building. But she was late, anyway. She had to meekly endure the "artists may forget to eat, sleep, and breathe" lecture, but the teacher did admire her vase.

"It's got an intriguing shape," the teacher commented critically. "It's almost a statement. I think it might be one of your better efforts."

Linnie's pleasure was only slightly dimmed when the teacher was just as generous praising Brenda's lump of clay.

That's okay, you're on the list, Linnie thought, winking at Brenda. But Brenda was looking the other way, watching her own reflection in a little pocket mirror she had pulled from her purse, and fussing with her hair.

Chapter 5

"First, it was too easy," Ming said. "And second, it didn't work because it didn't have any effect."

"There needs to be an effect," Linnie agreed. She opened the bag and handed Ming a shake, took the iced tea she'd ordered, and gave the rest to Jackson.

They'd met at the hamburger joint at Jackson's suggestion, carrying their food outside for privacy while they plotted.

"So we know what was wrong with our idea," Jackson said, unwrapping his first burger. "How can we make it right?"

"I've been thinking about that," Ming said. "All games have rules, right? And they have goals. You know when you've won. This is a game. We need rules. Tell us about the real game's rules."

"My sister was at a resort hotel when she played it," Linnie said, idly watching the cars that turned into the lot.

"One of the rules was you had to be alone with your target to kill him, but alone meant that no one else in the group could be within eyesight. Other people from the hotel could be there, but not one of the other group people. And you couldn't use force to get someone alone. Like you couldn't drag your target away from people to get him alone. And you couldn't kill him in his own hotel room, or during the retreat functions."

"So it was actually kind of hard to kill someone," Ming said.

Linnie nodded.

Jackson played imaginary drums on his knees while he chewed his hamburger. "I don't see how that helps us much," he said, taking a drink of water. "All we know so far is we're not stealing any more jackets. And I'm not telling anyone, 'Bang, you're dead.' They'll have to figure it out from what we do. But what are we doing?"

Ming turned to Linnie.

"We need something more than a jacket," Linnie said, thinking. "I liked the idea of something symbolic. And we need it to be more public than the jacket was."

"Something that's more humiliating to the target than to me," Ming said.

"Humiliation is more humiliating if it's public," Jackson announced, drumming it.

"I like the sound of that," Linnie said. "That can be one of our rules. Whatever we do, we have to cause a public humiliation for it to be a hit. Don't forget, I have someone to add to the list."

Jackson unwrapped his last burger. "Who?"

"Brenda," Linnie said. "Because she fakes herself into an A in Studio. The teacher doesn't give very many A's, so Brenda's cheating someone else out of a grade they've actually earned, just by having artistically temperamental fits."

"So there's another rule," Ming pointed out. "The people on the list have to be cheating, somehow, and their cheating has to be keeping the people who earned something from having it."

"Then Karl DeBerg qualifies," Linnie said. "Remember the seventh-grade science fair?"

"I do," Jackson said. "Karl won it with a study of cannonball and bullet trajectories. It was great."

"He won," Linnie said. "But it wasn't really his project. His older sister did it. She was in tenth grade then, which I'd say gave Karl a slight edge over the competition!"

"You took second!" Jackson said. "You should have gotten first place."

Linnie nodded. "First-place winner got their picture in the paper, got out of school to go to the state competition, and won forty dollars. Second place got a ribbon. I still have the ribbon."

"He's on the list." Jackson wrote his name in the air. "We're up to four targets."

"John," Linnie said.

"Stalley?" Ming asked. "Absolutely. John Stalley is the biggest sleaze to ever hit this school. He not only passes on dirt; he makes it up. He threatens to spread rumors about any female who turns him down . . . and then he does, whether she turns him down or not."

Jackson was watching Ming out of the corner of

his eye. "I hope you're not speaking from experience," he said.

Ming looked up, surprised. "Of course I am," she said. "He told me he'd heard I got my grades because I kissed up to the teachers and if I didn't go out with him, he'd send a letter to the school board exposing me."

Jackson's eyebrows lowered.

"I told him to go ahead," Ming went on. "I said the worst they'd do would be to make me take a few tests to see if I knew my work and I could ace any test they could find. I told him he'd be exposed, not me. So he started a bunch of disgusting rumors about me that eventually died down, and all was well again. But he's a sleaze."

Jackson looked even angrier and Linnie wondered how Ming could be missing all the cues. He really likes her, Linnie thought. And she doesn't seem to notice a thing.

"Speaking of rumors," he said finally, "the one about Price is true."

"What rumor?" Linnie asked, rattling the ice in her cup, trying to decide if she was thirsty enough for a refill.

"Let's just say his performance is not all natural," Jackson said.

"I heard he's on steroids," Ming said. "It's true?"

"I never heard that," Linnie said. "Why do you hear everything? I thought I heard everything that went around, but obviously not."

"Sports," Ming said loftily, flexing her arm. "We

athletes are the true source of all knowledge."

"You're not even in track," Linnie said, flicking an ice cube at Ming.

"I am," Jackson said, glancing at his watch. "And I'm due at practice any minute."

"A lot of my basketball and volleyball buddies are on the track team," Ming said. "I still have my sources, even if I'm not active. I hear a lot about Price because people are afraid. If he gets caught, not only do they lose their ace performer, but the coach will be investigated for contributing — which he isn't, but they'll check anyway — and the team will probably get stripped of its past wins and be disqualified from competition this year."

"What I hate is what he's doing to himself," Jackson muttered. He stood up, leaned over the table. "I can't stop him. I keep giving him things to read about how bad steroids are. I don't know if he even reads them. He just tells me to get off his back. I try to talk to him and he goes nuts. He's unpredictable and I'm worried. In a way, I want him to get caught because maybe they'll make him stop. He's killing himself this way. I just hate to see the team go down with him."

"We'll walk you to practice," Linnie offered, jumping up.

Jackson, his natural restlessness erupting, jogged ahead of them for a minute, then returned, almost running in place as he kept pace beside them.

"Price makes an interesting target," Ming said, looking thoughtful.

"He fits the rules," Linnie said. "He profits by

cheating. He's keeping people from winning fairly because he's winning unfairly."

"And he's doing the same thing to himself, too," Ming pointed out. "Which makes him both the victim and the victimizer." She shifted her book bag to her other shoulder. "Is that our list then? Austin, Adler, Brenda, Karl, John, and Price?"

Jackson stopped jogging momentarily. "I want to add two names," he said. "But I don't want to explain why." He flushed. "I guess that's not fair."

"It's okay with me," Ming said. "I trust you. As long as they fit the rules, I'm willing to add them."

"Rafe Gibbons," Jackson said. "I thought he was perfect and he wasn't. And Julie Clay."

He sounds so grim, Linnie thought. It's only a game, right?

Chapter 6

Eight people, Linnie thought.

Austin, Adler, Brenda, Karl, John, Price, Rafe, and Julie.

Eight cheats. Eight fakers. Eight people who got something by cheating someone else out of it.

She programmed the CD player to randomly mix songs from all five CD's she'd chosen, and settled in at the table to study. Her books were strewn around her, a glass of ice and a can of Sprite within reach.

She read the English assignment. *Change this paragraph from passive to active voice.*

Easy, she thought. Cut all the *ing* endings and make them all *ed*.

Instead she scribbled a list of people.

Austin, Adler, Brenda, Karl, John, Price, Rafe, and Julie.

Then she listed the rules they'd worked out before and after Jackson's practice.

— Pick a name from a hat.

— You have approximately two weeks to do your hit.

— If you can't do it within a reasonable amount of time, put the name back and let someone else try.

— A successful kill is a public humiliation.

— The more appropriate the humiliation, the more humiliating and the more public, the better the kill.

— Work alone. No telling whose name you have. No help from the group, no telling the game to anyone else. You can get help from others outside the group, but only if you do it without letting anything slip about the game, the purpose, or the group.

— After everyone's been hit, we'll vote on the best kill and treat the winner to something.

Linnie turned her attention back to the English assignment. It wasn't as simple as she'd thought. Changing the endings made the paragraph nonsense. I think I was thinking of participles or something, she decided. There must be more to passive voice than I thought. When in doubt, look it up.

But instead of looking in her English book, she found herself writing a different paragraph.

My first victim: John. The womanizing sleaze. What do I know about him? I know he's eighteen. He's probably going to be a con

*man when he grows up. He's already a con
man. He looks for weak spots and pushes on
them until you cave in. He's probably dated
every female at Hollander who's good-looking,
popular, or rich. Including me, so I guess I'd
better stretch the list to include every female
who's afraid of being laughed at by good-
looking, popular, or rich kids, too.*

She shuddered, remembering their date. She'd
been flattered when he asked her out. They'd both
been in tenth grade, but unlike John, she wasn't
very self-assured. He'd fed her a few lines, which
she'd believed. She met him as arranged, and he'd
taken her directly to the place everybody called
Beer Can Hill. She'd known, then, exactly what he
had in mind.

*I had real-life training in being humiliated even
before that day,* she thought, idly X-ing out English
endings. *Thanks — I guess — to my sister. She
was an expert at humiliating me. I guess I figured
out pretty early the only way to win was to run
away. That's humiliating, too, because then they
laugh and tell everyone what a coward you are. But
it's less damaging in the long run than staying and
letting them work you over.*

Linnie drew dark, heavy lines under John's
name.

You told everyone I didn't know how to kiss, she
thought, drawing a little coffin under his name. *You
told them I was so ugly you weren't interested, and
you said I cried because you took me home.*

You ruined a whole year of my life.

She drew a skull in the coffin.

Nothing happened. I got out of your car and I walked home. That's what really happened. But nobody would believe me by the time you got done spreading rumors . . . just like you did to Ming and all the others.

It's our turn to get back at you. Victim's revenge. I have to think of a fitting punishment. I owe it to all of them — all of your victims. What if . . .

Smiling, she drew little rocks around the coffin, like Ming had put around the grave. She felt like an avenging angel.

She had an idea.

Something public.

And very humiliating.

"I need a small microphone," Linnie explained to the clerk. She'd left her unfinished English homework and had driven twenty miles to the next town, to a different mall from the one she usually went to. She hadn't seen anyone she knew.

"The recorder has to be small, too, but the microphone can't be any bigger than a quarter or so. We just have small writing surfaces in the lecture hall, and my books and things take up most of the space. I can't set up a microphone and still have room to take notes. And I sit in the back of the hall. It has to be a good microphone."

"We've got some excellent microphones," the clerk assured her. "I'm afraid they're kind of expensive."

"If I flunk, I lose my scholarship," Linnie said. "The microphone will be cheap compared to a semester of college!"

"I see." The clerk looked sympathetic. "If you don't want to worry about setting the mike up, you might want to consider a wireless. You could pin it on your collar, or even stick it on the professor's desk and still pick up the whole lecture from your desk in the back of the room. You don't even have to take the tape recorder out of your book bag, especially this model. It's particularly designed to be sensitive to the human voice."

Perfect, Linnie thought.

The recorder and microphone cost plenty, but she bought them, taking them home and playing with them all evening until she was fairly confident of their range and sensitivities. She'd been assistant to the assistant sound-and-lighting-control person for the Thespian Society — working the control panel for sound and lights for the school plays for a whole year — so she already had a basic understanding of distance, clarity, and tonal quality when recording music and the human voice.

She found the miniature system satisfactory, able to pick up music from the stereo from twenty feet or more with no distortion.

Perfect, Linnie thought again. I'm now prepared to commit the perfect "murder."

Chapter 7

Ming finished her homework quickly and neatly.

Her parents were at meetings, but they'd brought home a pizza, leaving it in the fridge with a note.

Enjoy. Left the Mazda if you need a car. Back late. Hugs and kisses.

She wondered how many X's and O's they would have written if they were still signing with X's and O's. Kisses and hugs, she thought, folding the note. X's for kisses, O's for hugs. I used to get five each when I was little. Unless I'd done something special. Then I'd get eight. And an exclamation point. I used to put the note under my pillow at night to help me get to sleep.

She put two pieces of pizza on a plate and stuck it in the microwave. When it buzzed, she took the plate to the table, stacked her books, got milk, a napkin, and a fork.

While she ate, she thought about Rafe, the name she'd drawn.

Jackson only said he thought Rafe was perfect and he wasn't. What does that mean? He sounded pretty grim, so Rafe must have done something pretty bad. But what kind of thing?

She cut a bite of pizza off with her fork. John would be easy. I wish I'd drawn his name. I know what he does, so I'd know how to humiliate him — make him look like the lying, rumor-spreading creep he is. What a strange idea, that I could humiliate someone by showing the world what he actually is. That's ironic. Would it work with everyone? Is that the key? Not really, I guess. Obviously exposure is only humiliating if a person is ashamed or embarrassed by what he is.

When she finished eating she drank her milk, then rinsed her dishes and put them in the dishwasher. She got out a piece of paper.

How can I expose Rafe for what he really is when I don't know what he really is?

She stared at the blank paper for a while, then wandered around the house, looking for inspiration. In the den, she turned the TV on, then back off, looked through their collection of movies, thumbed through the tapes and CD's.

Wait a minute, movies! Bad guys and problems and resolutions. There may be an idea there.

She thought back over her favorite movies, then laughed at herself, realizing she mostly watched high-action adventure shows where the hero was always in great physical danger, performing impossible feats by the end of the show.

I'm afraid my problem isn't that dramatic, she decided, recalling some of her favorite fight scenes, fiery crashes, and incredible rescues. When I was little I used to reenact the good parts over and over, she remembered. I'd practice karate on trees, I'd wrestle anybody who'd come close enough to challenge . . . what a little terror I was. Maybe I should forget movies and try something less dramatic. I go to school. I should be able to think of something!

She headed back to the kitchen, and the blank piece of paper, which she stared at again.

Darn it! I have a very simple problem here and I don't have the faintest idea how to solve it. Why don't they teach us anything practical in school?

Chapter 8

Jackson drummed on his knees, staring at the name *Brenda*.

Brenda, Brenda, he thought. Fluffy hairdo. Lots of makeup. Fancy clothes. One of those bouncy types — always talking and flirting. Brenda who smashes pots in Studio Art class. Brenda, who has artistic fits to impress the teacher.

Jackson stood up and wandered into the kitchen to check for lemonade. The beasts — his half brothers, ages five and three and a half — were setting up a last-ditch effort to escape bedtime.

"But I'm hungry!"

"I didn't get no dessert!"

"Any dessert," Jackson told the little one, patting his head.

"You're not so smart," Wesley, the five-year-old, told Jackson. "Daddy said so."

"Hush," his mother said, giving Jackson an apologetic and harried glance.

I'm no genius, Jackson agreed silently. He poured the lemonade, told the beast-children good night, and escaped back to his room, closing his door on their protests.

No great genius, no great athlete. Not even a great son, stepson, or stepbrother.

He turned his radio on, keeping the sound low.

Okay, so I'm not great. I can live with that.

Still, remembering the harried look in his mother's eyes, he sighed. I'm not helpful. I could at least be helpful.

Sighing again he went back to the kitchen and swooped up the beasts — one in each arm. The boys shrieked happily, pounding on his shoulders.

"Muscles!" Wesley crowed. "Carry us up!"

"Up!" the little one echoed.

"They've had their baths and brushed their teeth," his mother said, smiling gratefully. "It just remains to get them in bed and keep them there long enough to fall asleep."

Jackson carried the squirming boys up the stairs, bouncing on each step. He plunked them in the wrong beds, to their delight, and would only let them switch back when they promised to hug tight to their teddy bears and not let them loose till morning.

That'll keep their hands occupied, he thought.

"Story!" Wesley demanded.

Jackson thought for a moment, then told them a story about Brenda, a pretend person who thought she was real and spent all day bothering people so they would notice her.

Chapter 9

"So how goes the hunt?" Jackson asked. He'd just come through the line but his tray was nearly empty.

"Why aren't you eating?" Linnie asked. "Don't you like the school's burritos?"

"I like everything if it's food," Jackson informed her. "I ate my burrito already."

"Between the kitchen and the table?" Linnie shook her head. "How are things going for you?"

Jackson shrugged. "I'm not sure. The only thing I'm sure of is that things seem very different lately. There's a new slant on the world, and on the way I see things."

"I'll say!" Linnie agreed. "I keep finding myself thinking about and noticing all kinds of different things, and I zone out on the stuff I'm supposed to be doing."

"Me, too," Ming said, joining them at the table. "I've never had to remind myself to pay attention in class before. It's kind of fun being an airhead."

She sliced her burrito in half and gave half to Jackson.

"I've got a plan of attack!" Linnie announced, leaning forward, keeping her voice low. "I'm so excited! Did you notice anything different about me today?"

Jackson and Ming both looked at her carefully, finally shaking their heads.

"Good!" Linnie said smugly. "Then it's working."

"I have a fairly good idea what I'm going to do," Ming told them. "It kind of depends on the lunch menu, but they all look reasonably good."

Jackson raised an eyebrow.

"No fair asking questions," Linnie reminded him.

"I didn't say a word."

"You looked like you were going to."

Ming smiled. "I feel like a crook," she said. "Planning a job. A bank job, maybe. It's so much fun to walk around knowing I get to murder someone and they don't know anything about it!"

"Well, I haven't got a plan of attack," Jackson admitted. "I'm having a terrible time coming up with an idea. But it is fun stalking the victim. It's like on TV where the bad guy stakes out a place and learns the victim's habits, like what time she's due home and when and where she shops. Maybe I'll be a detective after I graduate."

"You'll have to learn how to plan attacks, then," Ming said. "And how to be more discreet. You just said 'she,' so now we can guess which names you didn't draw."

"Oops. Maybe I was just using *she* the way most people use *he*."

"Maybe." Ming grinned. "But since you're having so much fun stalking, I'm going to guess it's a she."

"Um . . . excuse me. Jackson, do you still want this? It's cold now. Sorry."

Jackson smiled at the girl who had interrupted them. "Cold burritos are my favorite," he said. "Thank you very much."

When the girl was gone, Linnie said, "I wanted to mention that since we're all kind of busy researching our new project, maybe we should arrange to meet regularly outside of school or something."

Ming nodded. "I was going to bring that up, myself. I'll need to be absent during lunch one of these days. Well, not absent from school, just absent from our group. And it might look better if I joined other tables at lunch between now and then so it's not so obvious."

"Gotcha," Jackson said, tapping on the tabletop. "How about we meet Mondays after track practice — say five? At the field? I have to get home pretty quick after practice but let's try it. If it doesn't give us enough time we can work something else out."

And I need to find the chink in Brenda's armor, he told himself. Linnie and Ming both have plans of attack laid out and I haven't the foggiest idea how I'm going to do Brenda in.

Chapter 10

The next week, on Tuesday, Ming examined her "R-Notes."

> *Rafe's last class before lunch — Chemistry.*
> *East wing. Always arrives at IN door: 11:59.*
> *Brings lunch from home. Eats with: blond guy*
> *in leather jacket and dark-haired guy, very*
> *short hair.*

She'd arranged the information in graph form, with M-T-W-Th-F along the side, and headings across the top.

This is what I'm good at, she thought, eyeing her graph. Gathering, compiling, organizing, and re-membering information. I can write reports, re-member facts, understand the relationship of one table of data to another.

But DO something with it?

I'm afraid.

Rafe will walk through that door within the next five minutes, paper bag in his jacket pocket, two friends — one on either side — and he'll walk directly to that table there. One friend will sit with him, the other will go buy milk for everyone.

She laughed, almost choking on the grape she'd been chewing.

Milk! she thought. If he's the bad guy, it doesn't seem right for him to be drinking milk! Somehow that makes him seem more like a little kid. Little kids don't have egos like his, though. And little kids act real.

She was standing near the OUT door, watching the hall, holding her tray. Fruit cup, spaghetti, buttered bread, corn, milk.

She'd picked the grapes out of the fruit cup, nibbling nervously while she waited, making herself watch for Rafe and not try to locate Jackson or Linnie, not try to catch their attention or see if they were watching her.

She waited until 12:07, then gave up, sitting with a crowd from her Math Analysis class, watching the door.

Rafe never came.

That really messes up my graph, Ming thought. Now I'll have to redo it and add some new headings.

Linnie paused, a few feet behind John.

Initially she'd been worried about picking up the hall noise and voices other than John's. But it seemed that whenever John Stalley moved in, everyone else got quiet. The tapes had been excellent so far.

"So, baby." John made the words last a long time,

as if he enjoyed the sound of them. "How's things?"

The poor sophomore, Linnie thought. She's overwhelmed. She can only smile adoringly. Poor baby! She's going to wish she'd never met this creep. And the sad thing is, she probably knows that already!

"You sure you can get out tonight?" John asked.

The girl nodded eagerly, then frowned. "I thought . . . I heard Brenda . . . she says you've got a date with her."

"She'll wait," John said. "They all wait. Tonight it's you I want."

He leaned closer to the girl, running his left hand down her right arm, ending at her fingers. He grasped her hand. "Tonight?"

"Oh, yes!" she said. "I can get out. I'll tell them I have a baby-sitting job."

Beautiful! Linnie thought. Perfect!

Doesn't she ever get tired of shopping? Jackson wondered, leaning against the wall just outside the store where Brenda was selecting items to look at and try on. Suddenly he stiffened. Blinked.

Did I see that? I think I did. Yes, I did. I saw it.

Gotcha! he thought. Oh baby, I found the chink in your armor!

How can I use it?

Chapter 11

Wednesday, Ming waited, watching through the OUT door to see if Rafe passed by.

When he did, at 11:59, she could feel her muscles tense, her mouth go dry.

She took a step, felt her knees trembling.

Rafe turned right, instead of left, standing in the hot lunch line.

With a mixture of relief and disappointment, Ming joined the Classics Discussion group, trying to immerse herself in the argument about Silas Marner.

I'm a coward, Ming thought. I was so relieved that he went the other way! He has to turn this way or else I'd have had to crowd around all those tables to get near him. He ruined my plan and I'm kind of glad, but I'm a coward because I'm not doing anything. I'm using the Dead Game as an excuse to feel better about Austin and Adler, but I'm not getting a hit on Rafe, either.

* * *

Thursday Rafe showed up at 12:09, a girl clinging tightly to his arm. While Ming hesitated, Rafe and the girl sat at a table.

I'm running out of time, Ming thought. The two weeks is up pretty soon. I have to be ready for these changes. I have to be more flexible. Just because he's a few minutes later, or turns the wrong way, or has another person with him doesn't mean I couldn't do it anyway. I'm looking for excuses.

Maybe tomorrow. Maybe Friday will be my day.

Chapter 12

"Now I've been with girls and I've been with women," John said. He'd gone into what Linnie called his confidentially-speaking-doesn't-my-deodorant-smell-good pose, leaning on the girl's locker with one arm extended in front of her, and one arm draped loosely over her shoulders.

"It's not the age that makes a woman, you understand. It's the attitude."

The girl — another sophomore — looked unblinkingly into his face.

Mesmerized by the sheer force of his personality, no doubt, Linnie thought.

"Now, Mary Ann . . . you know Mary Ann, don't you?"

The girl nodded.

"Mary Ann, well, she's a real sweet little girl. There's that word, *girl*. I thought . . . well, you know. She told me she loved me so I thought . . . well. She's just too young. She'll grow up one of these days. Now, you. You're different. I can tell. Are you sure you can get out tonight? Maybe your folks won't let you out, even if it is Friday. Maybe you have to stay home Friday nights?"

"I'll get out. I'll meet you. Eight o'clock, right?"

He doesn't even change his lines, Linnie thought, absently patting her book pack. I've heard this a dozen times already.

"I could go to the party with you," the girl said hopefully.

"Oh, we'll see," John said. "Who knows what'll develop by then."

I know what will develop by then, Linnie thought. Nothing. It's Brenda's party. No way is he going to show up with a sophomore! Especially since I happen to know Brenda invited him as her date.

Wait! The party! Linnie thought. I have enough! I can edit tapes after school, make my final tape, show up at the party, and make sure it gets played. Almost everyone who'll be there is mentioned on one of my tapes — Brenda especially. And it's HER party!

This is going to be good!

Chapter 13

Jackson watched Brenda all day Friday.

The girl is a total fake, he thought. She hasn't got a real feeling, emotion, opinion, or action in her entire being.

He watched her invite people to her party, then turn around a minute later and say, "Oh, I'm sorry. I forgot you didn't make the cheerleading squad. Well, never mind about the party. You wouldn't feel comfortable there, I'm sure." She shrugged apologetically. "Oops."

Or, "You didn't get accepted at Yale, after all," or "I forgot you can't dance."

Why? Jackson wondered, shaking his head. Why do people hurt each other like that? She has to know what she's doing.

Brenda noticed Jackson eventually and turned her charm on him.

"Football," she said definitely. "I know I've seen you on the field with a football. It's Jackson, isn't it?"

"I think I heard someone say that," Jackson said, mentally checking his defenses.

"Such a . . . different name. Wherever did your parents find it?"

"In the Bible," Jackson said solemnly.

Her eyes widened. "Oh! A Bible name. How special."

"Not so special," Jackson said. "Lots of names are in the Bible. Matthew, Mark, Luke, John, Brenda."

"You're kidding!"

"Probably," Jackson agreed.

"You know I'm having a party tonight," Brenda said, leaning toward him.

"No!"

She nodded. "And I'd like you to come."

"Oh, I couldn't." Jackson grinned shyly, leaning forward, as if in response to her. "I have to wash my hair." He walked off quickly before Brenda could say anything back. He had to bite his lip to keep from laughing.

He caught quite a few admiring glances and knew two things — he'd just made himself quite a few friends, and he'd just made himself one ruthless enemy.

It's okay, he thought. Because I've got her.

Chapter 14

Friday at lunch, Ming waited.

The menu was spicy barbecued beef on a bun, french fries, Jell-O, and milk.

She'd loaded her fries with a mound of ketchup, had opened her milk carton. The sandwich was open face, both sides covered with sauce and thin slices of meat. The Jell-O quivered in response to the shaking of her knees.

She saw Rafe through the OUT door, saw him and his two friends. Saw the end of the paper lunch bag in his pocket. No girl.

For Jackson, she thought, forcing herself to step forward, to walk the imaginary line she'd drawn that would intersect Rafe's path.

One step. Two.

For Jackson and all the other people you hurt.

Three steps.

Six.

Ming managed to bump Rafe perfectly. His elbow knocked the tray from her hands. Barbecued beef slid down the front of his shirt, leaving brownish-red smears. Great slops of milk, ketchup, and Jell-O went flying.

Rafe wiped at his shirt, muttering angrily. He took a step back as Ming's tray hit the floor.

Then the people behind him surged forward and Rafe fell forward. Off balance, his arms flew out.

Ming had been pushed backward in the odd surge, but she reached out automatically to grab at Rafe's arm, to try to steady him.

This isn't part of the plan, she had time to think.

Then, rapid-fire, Rafe — still off balance and flailing for a handhold — stepped in Ming's tray, and propelled by the people behind him, who were also falling, he went sliding and tumbling into a crowd of people. Several of them held trays; some tripped over Rafe, some dropped trays on him. It seemed like Rafe fell in silence, in single-frame slow motion.

The startled yells hit Ming like a fist as sound and movement erupted.

Ming tried to push forward to the pile of fallen trays and people. Rafe was on the bottom. She'd seen the whole thing, and it played in reverse as the pile began to undo itself, revealing a silent, un-moving Rafe, on the floor, smeared with food.

Ming had almost reached him when the first teacher finally took over, ordering people to sit at a table. NOW!

What have I done?

Ming's chest hurt, her knees threatened to col-lapse, her teeth were clenched so tightly that the muscles in her jaw quivered. She pushed forward.

The crowd began to thin as people found chairs and got out of the way. A lot of people were spattered with food. A couple were limping. Only Rafe was lying still, uncomplaining, unmoving.

He . . . I saw . . . someone kicked him in the head, Ming thought. And then his neck snapped back. He looked . . . shocked.

She wiped her eyes, but the scene kept replaying, forward this time, from the beginning.

Someone landed on him, hard. I saw knees hit him in the chest . . . his head snapped back from the kick . . . and then someone fell right across his back. What happened to his face? People were falling all over him.

What have I done?

"You! Miss!"

Dumbly Ming realized the teacher was talking to her.

"Go to the office. We need an ambulance. Can you manage?"

Ming nodded.

"Fast!"

The cafeteria had cleared out enough so Ming could run.

I didn't mean for that to happen.

She gave her message at the office, then ran back to the cafeteria where she sat, tears running down her face, until the ambulance arrived and a pale, silent, motionless Rafe was taken off on a stretcher.

Chapter 15

*We're at the theater tonight. We knew you'd
have plans since it's Friday. Left you the
Mazda. Home by 1:30. Hugs and kisses.*

The note was taped to a Chinese takeout dinner in
neat, white boxes with metal handles, which meant
Ming had to dump the food on a plate before she
could microwave it.

Her parents worked in the city, commuting an
hour each way. They wanted their daughter to grow
up in the suburbs, but they never spent any time
there, themselves. They left the house before Ming
got up, and like true bankers, got to work by six
A.M., brought something home for her for dinner
around three-thirty, then went back into the city
almost every night for dinner, the theater, more
work, shopping, or whatever. They slept most of
the weekend to make up for their frantic schedules.
Ming wondered why they didn't just move into the
city. Maybe they would after Ming went away to
college.

She tried to remember when she'd last seen her parents — actually seen them or talked to them for more than five minutes.

She decided it had been almost six years ago at her twelfth birthday party, but she knew she was exaggerating, trying to divert her thoughts from the lunchroom.

At first it worked just right, she thought. Rafe got ketchup and barbecue sauce on his jacket. He looked disgusted. He looked messy. That was perfect.

Then, that surge of people.

What happened?

The phone rang. It was Linnie.

"What happened?" Linnie asked.

"I don't know." She doesn't know I picked his name, Ming thought. But she can guess, I suppose.

"I heard there was a riot in the lunchroom and Rafe got beat up by Sheila's boyfriend because he'd been flirting with her."

Ming sighed. I wish, she thought. "No riot. It was . . . an accident."

"Oh. That's not as interesting."

"I suppose not." Ming wanted to explain her part in the accident. She also didn't want to explain it. I'll have to tell sooner or later, she thought. And I might feel better. But not yet. I can't talk about it yet.

"Are you going to Brenda's party?" Linnie asked.

"She invited me," Ming said. "But I'm not particularly interested."

"I think you should come," Linnie said. "And I

have a very good reason, which I don't want to go into right now. I have the car. Will you go with me?"

I'm not exactly in a party mood, Ming thought. But then, I'm not in the mood to stay home alone, either. "Thanks," she said. "Give me a half hour to get ready."

Ming and Linnie wandered through Brenda's house and yard, then wound up in the shadows alongside the house, watching the party develop around them.

Brenda had a huge backyard, with large bushes and trees, benches, outdoor lights, and a sound system plugged in outside. The food was indoors, the drinks on the deck, and people went from the yard to the deck, into the house, and back out in a constant stream.

Brenda kept checking her watch and looking annoyed.

Your precious John, Linnie wanted to tell her, is out with a tenth-grader. And I'm just as eager as you are for him to get here. Then I'll play my tape and go home.

Actually, he ought to be here pretty soon, she decided, reaching into her purse.

Brenda turned off her look of annoyance when Austin stopped by to talk to her, but as soon as he left, she frowned again.

Linnie couldn't feel the tape. She rummaged around in her purse, feeling again.

"Why do you keep doing that?" Ming asked. "Do

you need something? I have Tylenol. I have tissues."

"I need something, all right," Linnie muttered. "And I know I put it in here."

"Look, there's Jackson." Ming waved. Jackson joined them, hugging them both. Surprised, Ming hugged him back quickly. I needed that, she thought.

"It's so nice to be around *real* people," Jackson said. "You can't imagine!" He pointed at the groups of people scattered across the lawn. "Do you realize the fake-cheat-fraud ratio out there? I'll give you a hint. Brenda invited them."

"She invited me," Ming told him, half smiling.

"You've got status," Jackson said. "You are Most Likely to Succeed, Hollander High's success story — all in capital letters."

"Number three," Ming said.

Jackson grabbed her by the forearms. "Don't DO that!" he said. "Nobody's counting. Nobody who matters, anyway. You've got everything in front of you — engineering school, medical school, anything you want, no matter which number anyone gives you. Don't fall into that number trap. You're good!"

Startled and grateful, Ming tried to think of a response. She felt short of breath, and drew in air, trying to fill her lungs.

"I can't believe this!" Linnie said. "I know I put it in here, but I can't find it!"

"What?" Ming asked.

"Oh . . . something. I came here tonight to do something and I can't find it."

She has a hit planned for the party, Ming thought. Who? Brenda? But almost everyone else on the list is here, too. It could be any one of them, I guess.

The thought of a hit reminded her of Rafe, slipping slow-motion, the kick to his head, the legs twisted, people thudding on him as they fell, the head snapping back too fast and too far.

"Do you know how Rafe's doing?" Ming asked Jackson.

"It's kind of weird," Jackson said. "I can't believe he could get hurt like that in the lunchroom. I heard all kinds of things — he got hit in the chest and the doctors are worried that he might have bruised his heart, he's in a coma, his brain is bruised, he has a concussion — you name it, I've heard it. I don't know what to believe."

Ming felt suddenly smaller as if she'd contracted inward upon herself. It's bad, she thought. I really hurt him.

"I can't believe this!" Linnie said. She knelt down in the arc of light from the back porch and dumped her purse upside down. "What could have happened to it? Did I leave my purse unattended somewhere? Yes, darn it. I did. I left it in the kitchen while I got food and stuff . . . how stupid can I get?"

"What is going on?" Jackson asked her.

Linnie replaced her wallet, bottle of pain reliever, keys, coins, notebook, receipts, gum. "It's gone. Someone took it."

"Took what?" Jackson asked.

Linnie looked both horrified and excited. "Took

my hit," she said. "I was going to do my kill tonight and it's gone. But why would someone take a tape from my purse?"

"A tape?" Ming asked.

"Yeah. Like a tape-recorder-type tape."

"Maybe someone thought it was music," Ming suggested. "Maybe you dropped it."

"Oohhh!" Linnie moaned. "Look, there's John. There's Brenda. Everybody's here! And my tape's gone."

"I knew it would be a very dramatic evening," Jackson said, nodding. "That's why I came, anyway — despite the fact that Brenda invited me."

Chapter 16

Monday morning in homeroom, at precisely 7:42 — as it did every school morning — the PA system clicked on.

"Good morning," the principal's voice said. "This is Monday, April sixth. There are forty-one days of school left, thirty-six days for seniors. The announcements this morning are . . ."

The sound of paper rustling, then a click.

"I've been with girls, and I've been with women."

The voice permeated the school. The principal could no longer be heard. Linnie sat up straight, her eyes wide.

"It's not the age that makes a woman, you understand. It's the attitude." The voice was clear, seductively conversational.

My tape! Linnie thought. That's my tape!

"Brenda now. She's a senior, but she's a baby. I know fourteen-year-olds who are more mature . . .

"They'll wait. They all wait . . .

"Oh, no, Brenda, there's no one else. Just you . . .

"Baby . . . baby . . . baby."

I don't believe this! Jackson thought. Is this Linnie's hit? It's got to be. If it is, she just won. This is spectacular!

"She told me she loved me. I thought . . . well, you know . . . you know. I've been with girls and I've been with women — women — women."

Linnie glanced from side to side, eyeing people, checking their reactions, hoping her own guilty knowledge didn't show. Heads had gone up in attention, faces lit with recognition. A few girls giggled. The guys looked gleeful.

"It's John Stalley!" someone said, and everyone broke up laughing.

"Who did this?"

Once the question had been asked, Linnie was sure everyone was looking at her. She wanted to shrink in her seat, but she was afraid to do anything that might draw attention to her.

"I wonder why they're letting it play?"

"The principal probably wants to hear the lines."

"Brenda's a baby," the tape continued. *"She's not that good-looking, either. She's a baby. Not like you. Not like you. You. You."*

I knew it was a good tape, Linnie thought, listening to the hoots around her.

The homeroom teacher had seemed as startled and amused as the students, but he finally stood. "Keep yourselves out of trouble," he told the class. "I'll bet someone tapped into the system and the front office can't turn it off. As entertaining as this may be for the school, I guess it's my civic duty to help stop it."

When he opened the door to the hall, Linnie could hear hooting and laughter from all over the school.

The tape played on, with a new voice saying, "*I can get out. I'll tell them I'm baby-sitting.*" A series of different voices followed, "*I'm sure I can get out. I'll find a way. I love you, John.*"

I'm not half bad at editing, Linnie thought smugly. This is better than I realized. It shows him perfectly.

"I should copy down some of these lines," a guy behind Linnie said dryly. "They obviously worked for John."

"I don't think they'll work after today," someone else told him.

The tape played for another few minutes and then the PA system clicked, popped, gave one shrill shriek, and went dead.

The groans from students resounded through the halls.

Linnie sighed.

"Anybody want to take any bets on how soon John gets another date?" someone asked, grinning.

The school buzzed with laughter and comments the rest of the day. Linnie heard that John had been seen at school that morning before homeroom, but no one had seen him since.

She had no way of knowing whether he'd heard the tape, since he hadn't been in his homeroom class, but as Tuesday and Wednesday went by with no sight of him, she guessed that he had.

I guess my tape worked better here than it would have at the party, she decided. If it was in the hands of fate, the fates couldn't have done a better job. I wonder if I'll ever get it back, though.

Rumors had flown throughout school. Linnie heard that John had left town, that he was hiding out in his basement with the twenty-six girls who'd been absent that Monday — making them the only ones who hadn't heard the tape. She heard he'd developed laryngitis trying to plead his case with Brenda.

By Wednesday afternoon she'd heard that someone had rigged a timer to the tape player in the auditorium, then had run a wire from the tape player to the master panel, bypassing the office and tapping into the PA system, there.

Rumors flew, too, about who was responsible, but since the rumor changed minute by minute, Linnie figured no one really knew who had done it, and whoever really had done it wasn't stepping forward to claim credit.

Chapter 17

"Thank you," Ming said quietly, hanging up the phone. She turned away from the booth, turned out of the phone alcove, and headed upstairs to class.

Thank you for nothing, she thought, nodding automatically at the people who greeted her. What does it mean, no change? What was he like before? What condition is it he hasn't changed from? How is he doing? Will he be okay? I know I'm not family, but why can't they tell me anything? It can't be good that he's in intensive care. Maybe that rumor was true, then. He's in a coma. Maybe he's going to die.

She almost walked into the wall instead of into class, mumbled a startled, "Thanks," at the person who grabbed her arm and aimed her at the doorway.

If he dies, I'm a killer. That's a whole lot worse than losing scholarships and being number three! That's a whole new level of categories — murderer, killer, criminal.

I don't want him to die!

For the first time in her life Ming did not have

the answer when the teacher called on her.

She looked vaguely at the board, not even certain which class she was in.

"Are you okay?" her teacher asked. "Maybe you should go to the nurse's office."

Ming felt tears well up in her eyes, slide down her cheek. She didn't know if she was crying for Rafe or because the teacher didn't understand.

What if he dies?

What good can the nurse do for that?

What if he lives, but he has brain damage and has to be fed and can't even say his name anymore? I'll have to go to nursing school instead of engineering school so I can take care of him. I'll have to take care of him. It's my fault!

She saw again the surge of people, surging forward almost as if they'd been suddenly pushed from behind, falling on Rafe . . . saw the foot as someone stumbled, kicking him in the head, saw his head snap back, saw the pile collapse on him in a mess of barbecued beef and Jell-O and bright red that was not ketchup.

The school nurse sent her home and Ming covered a sheet of paper with X's and O's, put it under her pillow and finally fell asleep, crying.

Chapter 18

On Wednesday, Jackson's plan was ready to be put into action. He slid a folder into his backpack, feeling smug. I'm no great artist, he thought, but I did okay.

Now for the fireworks. Whenever the situation is ripe.

He was so pleased he called hello to people he barely recognized, did his tire-obstacle step up the stairs, and raised his hand in class.

He was disappointed when he saw Brenda at lunch. Conditions weren't ripe.

He was doubly disappointed that he didn't see Ming, but since they'd discussed needing time at lunch to plan and arrange hits, he figured she was busy. But he didn't see her in the halls, either. After asking around, he finally discovered she'd gone home sick. His fabulous mood evaporated.

People get sick, he told himself, trying to concentrate in his afternoon classes. It's no big deal. And it's not like she's your girlfriend or anything. She's just a friend. And co-hitperson.

At that thought he brightened, thinking of the hit on John. That had been fabulous. He hoped his hit went over as well. He wondered what Ming had planned. Ming.

It isn't like her to go home sick, he thought.

He had Phys Ed last hour, and hurried to the gym, looking for the teacher — who was also his track coach. "I'm skipping Phys Ed so I can make practice," Jackson said.

The coach eyed him for thirty solid seconds, his eyes measuring, weighing.

"You have forty-five minutes after school, before practice."

"I don't know if that'll be enough." Jackson waited patiently, keeping his expression determined. He knew the coach was weighing the situation. Should he conspire to allow Jackson an unreported absence, or make him come to class knowing he would then miss practice?

"I understand you will be unavoidably detained for Phys Ed last hour," the coach finally said. "Knowing that in advance, I will not mark you absent. This time."

"Thanks," Jackson said, meaning it.

"Good time last week on the fifty meter," the coach said. "But your kick wasn't its best. Could do better."

"Gotcha." Jackson understood. He'd have to work at bettering his time in the fifty meter in trade for skipping class.

He jogged slowly to Ming's, using the run as a warmup for practice. He rang her doorbell, waited.

He knocked on the door. He rang again, worrying now. What if she'd been too sick to make it home? What if she was lying in the shrubbery somewhere between school and her house? What if she'd cut through the woods and had fallen somewhere off the path? How would he ever find her?

The door opened.

She's been crying, Jackson thought. Her eyes were swollen, her face pale. "What's the matter?" he asked.

Ming blinked hard. "Rafe," she said.

Oh, no! Jackson thought. She's in love with Rafe! He's hurt and she's worried about him.

Without planning it, or even quite knowing how it happened, Jackson found himself hugging Ming, comforting her in her doorway, patting her back, and murmuring, "It's okay. He'll be all right."

"It's my fault," Ming said, sniffing back sobs. She leaned into him, hugging him back.

"It's not your fault. Everyone says he knocked the tray out of your hands." Jackson felt a sweet warmth filling his arms, running into his chest. He remembered hugging his little brothers, how warm and clean-smelling they were after their bath.

This is better, he thought, his arms tightening. This is as nice as it gets.

Ming pulled free, and embarrassed, Jackson dropped his arms. She's smart, he thought. I'm not. There is the whole story in four words. She's-smart-I'm-not. Besides, it looks like she's in love with Rafe.

"Please come in," Ming said formally. "It was

nice of you to come. Would you like a soft drink or something?"

"Water," Jackson said automatically. "I've got track practice later. I have to run faster. Kick better. I'd better stick to water."

"Ice?" Ming asked. "Please sit down." She pointed to the couch.

"No ice, thank you," Jackson said, sinking onto the surprisingly comfortable, modern-looking sofa. He looked around the room while Ming went after water. The house was about as opposite from his as it was possible for a house to get.

There was no clutter at all. No shoes, balls, books, half-eaten sandwiches, crumpled lunch bags, Nintendo games, stray dishes, game pieces, sweatshirts, or forgotten race cars. No remote controls waiting to be reunited with vehicles, no Lego pieces, no crayons. Nothing in the living room was out of place.

The two couches faced each other like enemies, trying to be polite for the sake of the formal flower arrangement, the dramatic, knotted drapes, the framed artwork on the walls.

It was a formal room, looking unused and unfriendly, as if people themselves would clutter it . . . a room to look at, not to use.

No one fidgets in here, he thought, smiling thanks as Ming handed him a glass of cool water, no ice.

"What are you doing out of school?" Ming asked. "It's early."

"You went home sick," Jackson blurted out, then wished he could stuff the words back into his mouth and try again.

Ming smiled, but it was a formal, polite half-smile that crumpled as he watched.

Jackson looked around desperately for a coaster. It was obvious that no one actually put a glass down on these tables — not without a protective barrier. Finally he put the glass on the hearth and stood to face Ming.

"Let's walk," he suggested, almost running to the door and pushing it open. "Come on. You need some exercise."

You idiot! he told himself. She needs exercise? That's a great line. Great. Try to do something right!

"Okay," Ming said obediently. She stepped out onto the porch. "I killed him, you know."

"Rafe? He's not dead."

"He will be." Ming set off at a brisk pace, glancing back at Jackson. "It's only a matter of time."

"But he's doing better!" Jackson said, catching up to her, taking her arm.

"How do you know? No one will tell me anything. I know he's in intensive care and I hear all the rumors, but no one tells me when I call the hospital."

"Our families are friends," Jackson said. "I know his mom. Rafe and I used to be friends. I hear every day how he's doing. He's supposed to get his own room tomorrow."

Ming stood in front of him, looking as if she

wanted to believe him, but couldn't. Abruptly she sat on the curb and wrapped her arms around her legs. "No one would say," she said. "No change. Intensive care. And I did it. It was my hit, Jackson. I put him in the hospital."

"Oh, no," Jackson said softly.

"I just wanted him to look ridiculous!" Ming wailed. "I planned and planned it. It was such a messy lunch. I opened my milk carton and everything. I thought . . . I just wanted him to slip and get messy and look dumb. I didn't want him hurt, not even a little!"

Jackson found his arms around her again, hoping that maybe she wasn't in love with Rafe after all. Quickly he turned his thoughts to fifty-meter dashes and getting his kick right. It was safer.

"It's not your fault," he whispered, slowly dropping his arms. "I nominated him, remember? If it's anyone's fault, it's mine. See, he was perfect. At least, I thought he was. He was a good athlete and a good friend and he could really run. He was the reason the track team took third place at state my sophomore year. He was good."

Jackson paused, swallowed, remembering. "Then he dropped out of track. He just dropped out. Quit the team. He wouldn't talk to me about it or listen or anything. My junior year without him, we didn't even place."

And then Price came along, he thought. Price with his steroids. We're doing well this year, but at what cost? What price for Price? We could all be disqualified.

"Why did Rafe quit? Did he ever say?" Ming asked.

"There was no good reason," Jackson said, casually draping one arm over her shoulder, though he wanted to wrap Ming in both arms again. "He said his image was too important to waste on the track. He said motorcycles were more his style than hurdles and high jumps. He said track bored him."

Jackson took a deep breath, letting it out carefully. Rafe's defection still stung, especially since their friendship had ended at the same time. "I've been thinking about it since . . . since he wound up in the hospital. I nominated Rafe because without him, the team couldn't win. He stole himself from the team, and stole our chance at being state champions. He stole our wins . . . the team wins.

"He had a responsibility to the team. He had a skill. He had to use it. But now I don't know. Just because he could save the team, does that mean it was his duty to? Even if he didn't want to?"

Ming wiped her cheeks carefully with the backs of her wrists.

"I don't know anymore," Jackson admitted, feeling the truth tighten his insides. "I was mad at him for quitting when he was so good. He wasn't just good, he was perfect. But maybe perfect isn't all there is.

"I feel . . . whole when I run," he finally managed to explain. "Maybe Rafe didn't feel that way. I nominated him for a hit because he was better than I am, but he wouldn't run. And I added Julie's name because she . . . because when Rafe bought his motorcycle, Julie dropped me and went with him.

"I thought they were wrong," Jackson said. "But maybe I was the one who was wrong. Do you understand now? It isn't your fault. It's mine."

Chapter 19

Ming was back at school Thursday looking a little pale, but determined. Jackson said hi, and was disappointed at her polite response.

So what did you expect? he asked himself. For her to jump into your arms and never let go? Get real. You are a person who is hoping for a sports scholarship to a decent college, and then hoping you can keep a C average and manage to hang onto the scholarship. She is a person who can get a merit scholarship to practically any college in the country. She is intelligent. She's not going to waste her life on a jock.

He tried to tell himself it didn't matter, but he knew he was lying. I didn't notice it before, he thought. But there's something really special about her.

He went on saying hello to her, when he saw her in the halls, and again Friday morning, listening and watching each time to see if her eyes warmed, or if her smile was broader.

Maybe, he thought Friday morning. Maybe that

was a warmer hi. He almost walked into Brenda, then almost laughed out loud when he saw her. Conditions are ripe, he thought. Yeah!

He shadowed Brenda off and on, and at lunch the situation went beyond ripe to perfect. He watched as Brenda stopped by table after table, leaving behind unhappy, silent faces.

"A sleepover for your seventeenth birthday?" he heard her say. "Oh, gosh! I haven't done that since I was twelve. Sounds like fun . . . in a twelve-year-old sort of way." She moved on, turning back now and then to see her effect in action.

She's like one of those harvest machines, Jackson thought. Only instead of mowing down wheat, she mows down egos.

He looked around to see if Linnie or Ming was in the lunchroom to witness his hit. He couldn't see either of them, but the room was crowded, as usual.

Oh, well, he thought. They'll hear about it. He moved to the sleepover table, pulled the folder out of his backpack, and tossed it on the table. "This will never make the yearbook," he said. "But I want your honest opinion. What do you think?"

The girls at the table were slow picking up the folder, but once the first person had seen the sketches and gasped, the table came to life, eyes brightening.

"I don't believe it!" one of the girls said.

"I do," Jackson said. "I saw it."

"You saw Brenda . . . stealing this bracelet? She has it on!"

That's what I was waiting for, Jackson thought.

I saw her slip it off the counter into her book bag and walk out without paying for it. I just needed a day when she was wearing it at school.

My sketches aren't bad, he thought, considering the fact that I'm a jock, not an artist. He'd done six of them, showing Brenda in stages — eyeing the bracelet, with a dozen pieces of jewelry in front of her on the counter, knocking the bracelet into her bag, pushing the jewelry in a bunch back to the clerk, walking out of the store, and putting the bracelet on her wrist, a smug, triumphant smile on her face.

The same bracelet she was wearing today.

The table erupted in laughter. The girls passed the sketches back and forth, laughing and talking louder and louder.

The noise drew Brenda back, like a moth toward the light it will burn its wings on.

"What is so funny?" Brenda asked.

The girl who had the folder held it closer to her chest, but another girl grabbed it, dropping it on the table.

Brenda picked up the sketches. She looked at the first one, tossing it on the table. The second sketch made her frown. At the third — showing her slipping the bracelet into her bag — she cried out. She threw all the sketches onto the table, grabbed them back up, and looked at the rest.

She crumpled the pictures, dropped them. She glanced wildly at the table, cried, "Oh!" and ran.

The girls broke into laughter. They smoothed the sketches out and passed them to the next table.

Jackson felt his triumph fading. Suddenly he understood how Ming had felt.

Vaguely he heard a door slam and his mind registered that it was the back door out of the lunchroom, the door to the back lot with the trash containers. The sketches made the rounds at the next table over, then were grabbed by someone passing by who stopped, stared, carried them to his table.

"Wait," Jackson said. He wiped his hand across his forehead, thinking, uncertain whether to try to stop what he had put in motion or to let it run its course.

She deserved it, he reminded himself, remembering the parade of hurt and embarrassed people Brenda managed to leave behind everywhere she went.

But he remembered, too, Brenda's face — crumpling, falling apart, horrified, and guilty. I did it to her, he realized. I did to her what she does to everyone else. That should make it fair. Why doesn't it seem fair?

Maybe if I gave her the pictures . . .

He sprinted across the lunchroom and grabbed the sketches from the eager crowd.

"Hey!" someone protested. "I was looking at those."

Jackson stared at the protestor. "They're mine," he said. "And I'm taking them back."

The guy grumbled, but he turned away.

Jackson stuck the sketches back in their folder and headed for the back door. He stepped out, but there was no one there. He stood and listened, but all he could hear was the *ti-ti-ti-hiss* coming from the sprinklers in the park below him. He saw no one.

He waited outside until the bell rang, then went slowly back inside to his first afternoon class.

As Jackson headed for his last afternoon class, he heard a shrill, semihysterical voice near the office. He detoured toward it.

A large crowd had gathered, with the office aide in the center of it. The aide was crying one moment, eerily calm the next as she told her story. "They found her at the bottom of the stairs . . . the ones that lead down to the park," she was saying.

"The sprinklers were on so they couldn't really see what it was at first. One of them said they thought it was a doll. But the closer they got, the bigger it was, until they were close enough to see that it was a person."

"It was Brenda," someone near Jackson said. "Dead."

No! Jackson thought. No!

"I think she was running away from something," someone else said. "I saw her run out of the lunchroom. She must not have been watching where she was going. She fell right down the stairs. It's always slippery when the sprinklers are on."

"They thought it was a doll." The office aide was repeating herself.

Jackson ran from the hall, into the lunchroom, but the back door was blocked off by police banners and an officer, looking solemn and suspicious. Jackson ran toward the front of the school, the story running through the halls and through his head like lava down a hillside and into the sea, flaming and deadly, consuming everything in its path. Brenda . . . dead.

The police had both sides of the school blocked off so no one could get to the back.

Jackson ran up the street and into the park from the front, his mind one resounding voice, screaming, NO!

Chapter 20

Ming and Linnie found him in the park hours later, found him huddled in the woods where he could see the yellow police ribbon — CRIME SCENE DO NOT CROSS — found him staring, staring at the place where Brenda had died.

"It's all going wrong," Ming said quietly, wrapping her arms around Jackson. He felt like a stone to her, cold and unyielding. "Brenda should have laughed off those pictures. She should have come up with some scathing remarks and bluffed her way out of things."

"She didn't," Jackson said dully.

"Things keep going wrong," Ming repeated. "I told you how all I wanted was for Rafe to get covered with food, maybe sit in it, even, and look like an idiot. And he wound up in the hospital."

"She's dead," Jackson said. "I humiliated her and she ran out and fell. She's dead."

"Listen," Ming said firmly. "You're not responsible for what other people do. You didn't tell her to slip and fall. You didn't chase her out here. That was her choice. She could have bluffed her way out of this. I've seen her get away with worse. In fact, if you'd told me what you were going to do, I'd have said don't bother; it won't work."

"I killed her," Jackson said. He shivered.

"It was an accident," Linnie told him. "Now listen. Do you want to go to jail?"

Jackson shivered harder, as if his whole body were spasming. He shook his head.

"You thought you saw her taking a bracelet . . . stealing a bracelet," Linnie said, speaking slowly and clearly. "You weren't positive, so you couldn't say anything to the clerk. But you didn't feel right just forgetting it, either. So you decided to draw the pictures."

"How do you know?" Jackson asked, looking up for the first time.

"We've been busy," Ming said. "Putting pieces together. Guessing. Figuring. Looking for you."

"Why are you telling me this?"

"Be quiet and listen," Linnie ordered. "And remember. You thought you'd show the sketches to Brenda and see what she said. You thought she'd probably laugh and call you a few names and that would be that, but you were hoping she'd get so flustered you could maybe catch her in a lie. You hadn't really thought beyond that."

Jackson looked at Ming, then back at Linnie. "What's going on?" he asked.

"You hadn't really thought beyond that," Linnie repeated firmly. "Then you heard her making fun of some girls at lunch so you tossed the pictures down. It was just an impulse. You felt sorry for the girls."

"I did," Jackson agreed, nodding. Though he knew he was imagining it, he still couldn't get the picture of a too-still, broken Brenda out of his mind.

"Brenda saw the pictures and ran off. You figured she was embarrassed, and you figured that meant she really had stolen the bracelet. So now you didn't know what to do. You couldn't go to the police, even after her reaction at lunch. That wasn't proof of anything. You thought maybe if she had stolen it, you could talk her into returning it, once she calmed down."

"I never thought of that," Jackson said sadly. "It would have been a good idea. Instead, I killed her."

"Don't even THINK that!" Ming ordered, her arms tightening around him.

"And certainly don't SAY it!" Linnie added. "You had no idea she was going to run to the park. You thought she was just running outside to get away from the laughter, and even that surprised you because usually she just bluffs and laughs and that's the end."

"Repeat it," Ming told him.

"Why?" Jackson asked. "We know what really happened."

"Tell me what Linnie said!" Ming said fiercely. "That's what happened!"

"Why?" Jackson asked again.

"Because the police have already heard about the sketches. They know you brought them and passed them out. They know Brenda saw them, got upset and ran out the back door, and fell to her death."

Jackson thought he might never stop shivering again.

"And now," Ming told him, her cheeks streaked with tears, "they want to talk to you."

Chapter 21

It was after midnight when the police finally quit asking questions, quit going over the story again and again. It seemed to Jackson that he'd get half-way through telling it and they'd jump back to the beginning, then jump forward to the end, and he was so confused he didn't know which lunchroom table he'd started or ended at, didn't know for sure who had died. He thought it might have been himself.

But they let him go.

His mother was in her car, waiting in front of the station, her brow creased with worry, her eyes huge, and he had to go over everything again.

"If you don't mind," he told her when he'd finished. "I've heard enough about this and answered enough questions about this to last me the rest of my life. If you would just talk and talk so I could listen and not think I'd be forever grateful."

After a moment's thoughtful silence, his mother started talking about his half brothers, and kept telling stories until they were home.

She cut the engine in the drive, and they sat, listening to the heat clicks of the engine for a few minutes in silence.

It doesn't make sense, Jackson thought. Brenda should have laughed at me. It shouldn't have worked. I don't know why she got so upset, but the sketches can't be the real reason . . . or not the only reason. Something else must have been going on in her life. I didn't kill her.

He said it aloud. "I didn't kill her."

"Of course you didn't," his mother said. "No one thinks you did. Everyone always feels guilty when the police finish with them! Let's go in. I promised the little guys you'd hug them good night no matter how late you got in. I hope you don't mind. They've gotten used to you and your stories, and I'm just not as good."

Jackson sighed, feeling — for the first time since he'd dropped the sketches on the lunchroom table — that maybe, just maybe, he wasn't a totally rotten human being.

Chapter 22

Monday, they met after track practice, all three faces solemn. They met at the field as planned, but wound up on the bottom row of the bleachers, alone, staring soberly at each other.

Ming shook her hair back, then ran her fingers through it as if making sure it would stay away from her face. "It was a surge of people," she said again. "Like . . . I keep thinking about it and I swear it's like someone was back there pushing."

"Rafe remembers hitting your tray with his elbow," Jackson pointed out. "And then falling. He doesn't remember a surge."

"Like a tidal wave," Ming insisted. "Do you hear me? Someone pushed people forward. At least that's what it seemed like."

"I'd say you were nuts," Linnie said thoughtfully. She stood, stretched, then sat on the grass at the foot of the bleachers. "But think about it. I had a tape and it disappeared. I was going to play it at Brenda's party — which would have been bad enough! Everybody was there. But it wound up playing on the school's PA system. How? Why? Who took it?"

"Who even knew about it?" Ming asked.

"I didn't say a word to anyone," Linnie swore, holding her hand up like a Girl Scout. "I didn't even tell you guys. I certainly didn't tell anyone else."

They all looked at each other, Jackson's gaze softening as it crossed Ming's.

"I drove twenty miles to a different mall, and then I told the clerk some story about needing to tape a lecture," Linnie told them. "He couldn't have figured out the whole plan from one conversation! And he's the only one I talked with at all."

"And Brenda," Jackson said sadly. "You guys were right. She fell apart too easily. She should have bluffed her way out of that the way she bluffs her . . . bluffed her way out of everything else. Something was odd."

Linnie picked clumps of grass and scattered them on her legs, then brushed them off. She picked up a few stray blades and began twisting them together. "You know," she said. "It's not possible, but it seems like someone else is involved somehow."

"Think," Ming ordered. "Did you say anything at all to anyone? Maybe someone said they hated Rafe and you smiled funny because you were thinking that his name was on our list. It could have been something as simple and innocent as that."

They sat, thinking, and one by one shook their heads.

"I never showed the sketches to anyone," Jackson said.

"It seems pretty impossible that the clerk where I bought the tape recorder would know anyone who goes to Hollander," Linnie said. "That's the only way I can think of that someone might have known I was making a tape. But it's too farfetched. I don't believe it happened."

"I said nothing to anyone," Ming said. "And I didn't need to buy anything. I didn't need any sketches. I had no help of any kind from anyone. I did make a chart of Rafe's movements, but I can't see how anyone could have seen it.

"Your tape is easy to explain," she went on, glancing at Linnie. "If someone knocked your purse over while you weren't watching it, and went to put things back in and found the tape, they could have been curious enough to take it and listen to it privately. Once they figured out what they had, it could have seemed like too good an opportunity to pass up."

Jackson found himself shivering again.

"It had to have been coincidence and circumstance," Ming said. "Circumstance that caused the opportunity for disaster, and coincidence that it was our three hits that were made worse by the disaster."

"I quit," Jackson said suddenly.

Ming looked relieved. "Me, too," she said. "This is too . . . I don't know. It sounded great to start out with, but it wasn't so good the way it worked out."

Linnie nodded. "It got too ugly. I vote let's officially disband. No more getting even. Julie, Austin, Adler, Karl, and Price are safe from us! Let's all quit!"

Ming giggled. "I never thought it would feel so good to be a quitter," she said. "But I am happy. I am so relieved!"

They grinned at each other.

"Tomorrow let's go get a pizza to celebrate the end of the Dead Game," Jackson suggested.

"And I know what the toast should be," Linnie said. "To Austin, Adler, Karl, Julie, and Price . . . I can't help wishing you bad luck, but I wish that someone else deals it out to you!

"I feel reprieved," she admitted. "Like I should have gotten in trouble, and didn't."

Jackson had been sitting still for a long time. He joined Linnie on the grass, his head propped on his hand, watching Ming.

"Me, too," Ming said. "Though I've never been in trouble. Don't laugh! I wasn't perfect, it's just there wasn't anything I wasn't allowed to do."

"You could break windows and run wild?" Jackson asked.

"I never would have wanted to," she said. "I never wanted to do anything my parents might have said no to."

Jackson sat up, still looking at Ming. "It's a good thing I didn't have your parents! I wanted to do everything I ever thought of doing, felt like doing, or saw anyone else do."

"Maybe my parents weren't as generous as it

sounds," Ming said slowly. "They expected me to learn from my mistakes and make things right if I created a problem. But I had a phobia about doing the wrong thing or making mistakes."

"I never did anything else," Linnie said, twisting grass blades again. "If people are supposed to learn from their mistakes, I should be a genius by now. And I'm not."

"You can't have been that bad," Jackson told her.

"I was, according to my sister. She had the same phobia Ming had about doing the wrong thing. Only instead of being good like Ming, my sister just blamed all her mistakes on me. I thought the family baby was supposed to be spoiled, but no one spoiled me. It was my older sister who was cute and smart and talented. I was the scapegoat." She jumped to her feet, scattering grass debris. "It's time to get going."

They all headed back toward the school, walking slowly, enjoying the fact that it was their last Dead Game meeting.

"I have to admit I learned a lot from my sister," Linnie said thoughtfully. "She put me down to make herself feel better. I realized that people act like that because they feel second-rate on the inside."

"Whoa!" Jackson said. "You're telling me Austin and Adler feel second-rate? They've got the biggest egos I've ever seen."

"To hide how inferior they feel," Linnie told him. "Maybe not that exactly. It's more like somewhere buried inside they suspect they really aren't as good as they want people to believe they are. And in a way I feel sorry for people like that."

"Do you feel sorry for Austin and Adler?" Ming asked.

Linnie smiled slowly. "Well . . . my feeling sorry is as deeply buried as their feeling inferior!"

Chapter 23

Tuesday, Hollander High had a memorial service for Brenda.

Jackson sat hunched, uncharacteristically still, wishing he'd skipped the service. He did smile briefly at Ming when she slid in to sit next to him. He remembered the conversation she and Linnie had had with him in the park the day Brenda died, remembered the feel of Ming's arms around him.

Ming took his hand.

The artistically tempered art teacher broke down suddenly, sobbing. One of the other teachers helped her from the auditorium.

Linnie looked around at all the faces and wondered how many people were genuinely sad about Brenda's death.

Not that they're glad she's dead, she thought. But who will actually miss her? Besides the art teacher. I'm sure Brenda's family will miss her. But even all the people who went to her parties — will they miss her?

She shivered, wondering how many people in the

auditorium would miss her, Linnie, if she died, too.

The thought was sobering.

A handful of people, she told herself. Ten? Twenty? If I died, ten or twenty people in the whole world would actually care and actually miss me. What kind of epitaph is that?

The principal was finishing his eulogy, his voice emotional.

What's really sad, Linnie thought, is that the same is true for almost everyone. Ten or twenty . . . maybe even fifty people if you have a big family, will miss you when you die, and that's it.

Unless you're famous. No wonder people want to be famous! This is a sad way to end things. It would be nice to matter . . . to really do something for the world.

She filed out of the auditorium with everyone else, trying to decide whether to go home, or hang around for forty-five minutes until track practice started and watch.

She could see Ming and Jackson pause together at Ming's locker, talking quietly and seriously together.

Linnie sighed, knowing Jackson still felt responsible for Brenda's death. She hoped Ming was having some success talking him out of it.

I'll leave her to it, Linnie decided. We were supposed to go for pizza tonight, but I think I'll just go home. I don't think any of us are in the mood for a celebration, anyway.

* * *

The rest of the week seemed to drag by. The police evidently accepted Jackson's story, for they didn't call anyone back in for another round of questions. Word was going around school that the official ruling was accidental death.

Linnie, Ming, and Jackson sat together at lunch again, but all three ate silently. Jackson seemed preoccupied and distant.

Ming threw herself back into her studies, reading while she ate.

Linnie endured the silence as long as she could, finally getting exasperated in the middle of the second silent week.

"Will you two quit it?" she snapped. "I'd rather eat lunch with Brenda than with you ghouls."

Jackson looked up. "Brenda's . . ." He didn't finish.

Linnie raised her eyebrows. "My point, precisely. She's dead and she'd make better company. You're alive, but you act like you died instead of her."

Ming looked almost dazed, as if she were having trouble pulling herself back from her textbook.

"I really feel out of it," Jackson admitted. "I can't even tell bedtime stories to the beasts because I used to make up stories about . . . her. You know how I ended the stories? I said in the end Brenda faded so completely she wasn't there at all."

"Beasts?" Linnie asked.

"My little brothers."

Jackson's jaws clamped shut and he looked

blindly at his half-full tray. "It was bad enough that I contributed to her dying, but . . . it's almost like I knew, somehow. That's what I told the kids. She faded away until she wasn't there at all. I can't forget that. And then, what Linnie said the other day about people like that, how they only put people down to make themselves feel better. I didn't realize that. All she was trying to do was feel better."

"Oh, Jackson!" Ming looked as upset as he did. She put her hand on his arm, trying to comfort him. "You helped me feel better about Rafe and I can't seem to help you back. I wish I could make you believe it wasn't your fault. I wish there was something I could say."

Abracadabra, Linnie thought, watching her friends. A magic word that makes everything okay. Nobody's found one that I know of. She looked more carefully at Jackson, frowning at the sharpness in his face. She realized people had stopped by with food, but she couldn't remember if he'd taken any. She didn't think he had. "How much weight have you lost?" she asked.

He didn't answer.

Ming looked concerned. "How much?" she echoed.

"I don't know. Some," Jackson mumbled.

"It has to stop," Linnie said firmly. "You've got to shake this off."

"A dead girl?" Jackson said sharply. "You think I can just shake off a dead girl?"

"Jackson, you were no more involved than if you'd never heard of her and just read about it in the paper. You didn't really know her. You didn't like her. And you didn't cause her death." Linnie jabbed the table edge with her forefinger, emphasizing each point. "Brenda is dead. You aren't. So quit acting as if you were."

Jackson lowered his eyes.

"What about track?" Linnie asked. "Your classes? You're letting everything fall apart, aren't you?"

He didn't respond.

"You can't tell your brothers stories. What good does that do you or them? What good does it do the track team if you act as if you're dead? What good does it do anyone for you to act like this?"

"I know," Jackson said finally. "But telling me doesn't do any good, either. I wish, sometimes, there was someone else to blame. It's so senseless. If I could blame someone else, maybe I could quit blaming myself. I guess I just need some time."

Chapter 24

The next day, Thursday of the week after Brenda's memorial service, Linnie was again hurrying to Studio Art class after lunch, her mind on reaching class early enough to avoid the standard lecture. Gradually she realized that the chatter she was hearing in the halls was a little more excited than usual, a little less subdued. She slowed, moving her attention to the halls, the people, the conversations.

She could tell by the expressions on people's faces that something had happened, so she slowed even more, listening.

"It was Austin," someone said.

"It was not. It was Adler. They found a copy of the test in his book."

"Austin, Adler. What's the difference? You know they both had to be in on it."

Linnie vaguely knew the people who were having the conversation. It didn't matter — she'd have eavesdropped even if she'd never seen them before.

"What happened?" A third person joined the group and Linnie stayed just a few feet in front of them to hear better.

"Either Austin or Adler dropped his books at the top of the stairs. Everything went flying. One of the teachers stopped to help him pick things up and found a copy of next week's science test in with the twin's stuff. And guess which teacher it was? Mr. Byre! The science teacher. It was HIS test he found a copy of! Can you believe it?"

Talk about dumb luck! Linnie thought. Any other teacher might not have realized what it was, but Mr. Byre! He'd certainly recognize his own test! She laughed out loud. Maybe this will help Ming! she thought. If the transfer twins are cheating on their tests, maybe they'll lose their rank. They should get F's for cheating, and that'll bring their grades down in a hurry!

After school Linnie and Ming watched track practice together, frowning critically at Jackson's performance.

"I don't think he's as fast as he used to be," Ming said.

She sounded worried, and Linnie wondered if she and Jackson had admitted how they felt about one another.

"You heard about the transfer twins and the test?" Linnie asked.

Ming nodded. She was leaning on the wire mesh fence that ran around the track, her forearms resting on the metal pole that formed the top.

Linnie noticed that Ming's fingers had curled into fists, but she couldn't tell if the reaction was due to the mention of Austin and Adler, or to Jackson's efforts in the sprint he was running.

When practice ended, Jackson joined them and Ming suggested they go get something to eat.

"Sounds good to me," Linnie said. "And Jackson, whatever it is, we'll cut it up and force-feed you if you don't eat."

Jackson looked startled. "You sound just like Coach," he said. "He got on me, too. But I can't go anywhere. It's almost dinnertime. I have to go home."

"What did Coach say?" Ming asked. "Did you listen?"

Jackson grinned slightly, looking guilty at the same time. "Told me I had to shape up or I'm off the team," he admitted. " 'Eat,' he told me. 'Run.' Life at its simplest, huh? Eat and run. As if that could fix everything."

He picked up his book bag and his jacket, and they started toward the front of the school where they would split up and go their separate ways. Ming no longer walked home through the park, not if it meant going down the way Brenda had gone.

Jackson kept watching Ming and his expression made Linnie want to cry. He looked yearning, hungry, and hopeless. She could tell he hadn't said anything to Ming and that he didn't know whether she felt anything back or not.

Linnie watched Jackson, wishing that someone would look at her like that, love her that much. I just want to matter, she thought.

She shook her head to clear the thoughts away.

"No what?" Ming asked.

"Nothing," Linnie said. "I wonder what will happen to A and A? Do you think they've been cheating all along?"

"We don't actually know they were cheating this time," Ming said.

"From what I hear," Jackson said, "they say they don't know anything about the test at all."

"Of course they'd say that, but who'll believe it?" Linnie asked. "They had a copy of it!"

"Austin says it was planted in his papers after he fell."

"Oh, right," Linnie said.

"I was in class already," Ming said. "I heard the noise and looked out in the hall. I didn't see anyone drop papers in with Austin's, but it could have happened. I didn't see everything."

"I was there, too," Jackson said. "I was getting a drink and the landing was crowded. I remember that. I was thinking only an idiot would put a drinking fountain at the top of the stairs where there's always a traffic jam."

"Did you see the whole thing?" Ming asked.

"Not really." Jackson slowed his steps as they neared the cement benches in the front of the school. "I just heard the noise, and when I turned around Mr. Byre was already helping pick up papers."

"Adler was there, too," Ming added. "I saw them both picking up papers, shoving them all together. And then I went back to class."

"I'm glad they got caught," Linnie said. For Ming's sake, she added silently.

Chapter 25

Friday morning, as Linnie approached the school building, she saw Jackson and Ming on the sidewalk, obviously talking about something important because Jackson kept making broad, expressive gestures and Ming was holding herself very still, staring at nothing.

Linnie hurried, almost running, afraid of something unnamed. Something was wrong. "What?" she asked, grabbing Jackson's arm. Close up he looked worse than she'd imagined he would, pale and shaken.

"Price," he said numbly. "Didn't you hear?"

"Hear what? Did I hear what?"

"Price has been disqualified from everything," Jackson said, sitting abruptly on one of the cement benches near the front stairs. "From the state meet, from the team, from sports, period. Everything."

Linnie glanced sharply at Ming's shocked expression, then her eyes went back to Jackson. "That's bad news for the track team," she said. "Will the team be disqualified?"

Jackson shook his head. "It wasn't steroids," he said. "He'd been drinking. He got disqualified for drinking."

Linnie sat down next to Jackson. "That's actually better, then, isn't it? The whole team won't be under suspicion if Price didn't have any steroids with him. The coach won't be investigated for contributing. Price will get the counseling he needs. I mean, I'm sorry. I'm especially sorry it's going to be so hard on you. But it kind of sounds like what you were wanting."

Jackson got up abruptly and grabbed Linnie by the arm, pulling her away from the crowded front steps. Ming followed them. When they were out of the main traffic flow, Jackson turned Linnie so she faced him.

"That's kind of the point," Jackson said soberly. "It is what I wanted — when we set up that stupid game. And it happened. I just think it's a little odd."

Linnie looked perplexed. "What do you mean?" she asked.

"Doesn't it seem a little too convenient that Austin and Adler, who are on . . . who WERE on our list when we had a list, get publicly humiliated? And then Price, who was also on our list, also gets publicly humiliated."

"I don't think it's too convenient at all," Linnie said. "I think any form of disaster for the transfer twins is simply nicely convenient, not TOO convenient. And as for Price, that just has to be a coincidence, doesn't it? What else could it be?"

Chapter 26

Monday morning, Linnie approached the school reluctantly, almost afraid to see Jackson or Ming. I'm glad A and A got in trouble, she thought. I'm glad Price got disqualified. And it was just coincidence. Austin and Adler were cheating and got caught. And poor Price — he's been using bad judgment for so long it's a miracle he didn't get himself in trouble years ago.

And if all that's true, why is it I'm not very eager to get to school today?

Because something else is going to happen, she thought, looking around at the various crowds of people. Everything seemed normal. Nobody acted too excited, or too serious.

But it's not over, Linnie thought. Not yet.

She saw Ming coming in her direction.

She saw Jackson catch sight of Ming and wave.

"Has anything else happened?" Linnie asked Ming.

"Nothing I've heard about," Ming said, looking brighter, hopeful. "And that's good news . . . as long as you haven't heard of anything."

"Not a thing!" Linnie said, smiling. She felt like cheering.

"I have heard more about Price, though," Ming said, sobering again.

Jackson joined Linnie and Ming in time to hear Ming's remark. "What else about Price?" he asked.

"He says he doesn't know where the liquor came from," Ming said. "He remembers getting off work and it was in his car."

"Where'd you hear that?" Jackson asked. "I haven't heard anything."

"His sister was on the Junior Varsity volleyball team," Ming said. "I used to help coach them sometimes so I got to know her. I called her this weekend. It's been a big topic of discussion at her house, obviously."

"Do you think he's telling the truth, or trying to cover for whoever bought it for him?" Linnie asked.

Ming shrugged. "Hard to tell. It was at least secondhand information by the time I got it. He told his parents, his sister was eavesdropping, and she told me."

"It's inconclusive," Jackson said. "We can't tell from that whether someone set him up or not."

The bell rang and they wandered into the school. Everyone was grabbing papers from the table inside the door. "Oh," Linnie said. "It's the 'Vine." She hurried over to pick up copies of the school newspaper, handing one to Jackson and one to Ming.

"This has got to be the last issue," Ming said. "That means it'll have the Senior Will column in it."

She looked at the index on the front page.

Jackson thumbed through his copy, looking for the column that was a tradition every year. "What did you guys leave to posterity? I left my skill on the football field to Jason Royal so he can dazzle the fans like I did." He found the column, scanned it, looking for his quote.

"I left my soaring artistic vision . . ." Linnie stopped. She nudged Jackson. He glanced up, then followed her gaze. Ming stood totally still, staring blankly. Her copy of the *'Vine* had slipped to the floor at her side.

Jackson, looking as if he'd already heard bad news but couldn't quite remember what it was, reached over and tapped Ming. "What is it?" he asked.

Ming jumped. "It's in the *'Vine*," she said.

Linnie didn't know where to look or what to look for, so she crowded Jackson, reading over his arm.

Jackson pointed to a line in the Senior Will column. It read: *Julie Clay leaves Rafe Gibbons and jumps on the back of Karl DeBerg's motorcycle. It looks as if she's left Rafe for dead and gone after the guy with the biggest bike. Once a flake, always a flake. But will she will her flakiness to anyone? Will Karl leave his sister's science fair projects to anyone else, or is he the only one who gets to use them?*

"You can kiss coincidence good-bye," Jackson said, crumpling the newspaper. "And circumstance. This is deliberate. Everybody on our list has been hit. Everybody!"

He threw the paper on the floor. "Maybe that's the end," he said. "Since everyone's been hit, maybe we can all sleep easy now."

Linnie and Ming looked at each other.

"How did it get in the paper?" Ming asked.

Linnie shrugged, shaking her head.

"We quit and the game didn't," Jackson announced. He eyed Linnie, then Ming, looking stern and suspicious.

"You suspect me or Ming," Linnie said. "That's logical. I suspect you or Ming. If someone kept playing the game, one of us is the logical suspect. One of us did it."

"Not necessarily," Ming said. She bit her lower lip. "I've been thinking it over. I can't think about anything else, in fact. We haven't been as careful as we thought."

"What do you mean?" Linnie asked. "I know I didn't tell anyone. We've been through this before."

"We didn't have to tell anyone," Ming pointed out. "It's all we talked about. We were pretty careful at our planning sessions, but even then we didn't actually check to make sure no one was around. And we discussed it over and over at lunch, at track practice, even on the bleachers. Did either of you look to be sure no one was under the bleachers? I didn't."

"We'd have noticed if someone was around," Jackson said. "Especially if it was always the same person, and it would have to be the same person."

Ming shook her head. "There could have been several people in on it together. And besides, whoever it was wouldn't have to be there every time we talked about it, just often enough to get the names and the general idea."

"If that's true, then they've been watching us," Linnie said. "I followed John Stalley around for a whole week. That's certainly out of character for me! So anyone keeping an eye on us would have known John was my target. That means showing up at Brenda's party was pretty stupid. I might as well have announced what I was doing. It was obvious I had a hit planned, and no big problem for anyone to search my purse, find the tape, and take it."

Ming nodded. "And I did the same thing. I followed Rafe around, and then I stood in the cafeteria every day, holding my tray and watching the OUT door. It was pretty obvious I was watching Rafe, and that I was planning to do something to him with my lunch tray. And even I knew who Jackson's target was because I saw him following her around."

Jackson ran his hands through his hair. "I guess you're right," he said finally. "We were pretty obvious."

"So we can quit suspecting each other," Ming said. "And the good news is, I think the game is finally over. There aren't any names left on the list. We may never know who else played the game with us, but at least it's over."

Chapter 27

"Linnie?" It was Monday night, and Ming's voice over the phone sounded shaken, almost frightened.

"What is it?" Linnie demanded. "Has something else happened?"

"Nothing else," Ming said. "It was enough already."

"Then what's wrong?" Linnie asked.

"I . . . I thought of something," Ming said. "I called Jackson already and he said we should meet tomorrow morning before school. We have something to discuss. Something we didn't figure out before."

"What?"

Ming sighed. "There's something we missed," she said. "And it bothers me."

"What?" Linnie asked again.

"It's Brenda," Ming said. "And the sprinklers."

"Yes?" Linnie listened intently.

"Brenda could hear the sprinklers," Ming said. "They're noisy. You can hear them from the back of the school. Brenda was upset — more than she should have been — and she ran out the back door. We can presume she ran to get away from everyone who was laughing at her and she ran out the nearest door. That makes sense."

"Go on," Linnie said.

"Once she got out that door and heard the sprinklers, she'd have done what anyone else would have done . . . gone any direction except toward the park."

"I don't get it," Linnie said.

"Remember her dramatics in art class, Linnie? She was very careful of her hair," Ming went on. "She was automatically careful of her hair. I just can't see Brenda running toward the sprinklers when the water would have ruined her hair. So why did she do it?"

Linnie had no answer.

Chapter 28

Ming woke — snapping awake — without knowing why. She felt totally alert, yet she was afraid to move, even to turn her head so she could see her clock.

After a full minute of motionless fear, she realized she'd left all the lights on. That awareness helped because it meant she wouldn't have to face anything in the dark, but it made things worse, too, because it meant her parents weren't home. They'd have turned the lights off if they were.

She was alone.

She had awakened for some unknown reason and she was afraid.

She finally looked over at her clock. A few minutes before eleven-thirty. Surely her parents would be home soon.

Home to what? What would they find? What had she heard?

Heard? she asked herself.

Yes. I heard something.

She covered her ears with her hands, then realized she couldn't shut out a sound she'd already heard. She dropped her hands.

What if the noise was just her parents coming home? But if it was, they'd be making more noise now, coming in, turning off lights. Why was a high school senior still such a fanatic about lights and locks, anyway?

She'd had that conversation with herself often before, and oddly, it reassured her. She knew she was a fanatic about lights and locks for the simple reason that she'd been left alone at night since she was little and it scared her.

Of course, she thought, grabbing a robe, they only left me alone because I told them I was too old for a sitter, and then I was too stubborn to tell them I was afraid to stay by myself.

Since all the lights were already on, Ming had only to walk from room to room, checking, and she did, finding nothing and hearing nothing but her heart.

She checked the bedrooms upstairs, both baths, then went slowly down the stairs, listening, certain she could hear something below . . . a rustling flap, flap, flap.

She reached the bottom of the stairs, heard a sudden *whirr*, and screamed, then recognized the noise of the refrigerator compressor kicking on, sounding ten times louder than usual.

Ming took a deep breath to slow her heartbeat, then turned into the doorway of the living room where the flapping seemed to come from.

A drape rustled in the breeze, flapping back against the wall.

Ming almost crossed over to close the window, but stopped, clutching her robe shut at the top.

I closed the window already. I always close all of them.

Then she saw the glass — a hundred shards glittering on the carpet.

She saw a paper-wrapped rock.

Stepping gingerly, Ming bent and picked up the rock, slid off the crisscrossed rubber bands, smoothed the paper.

Just like one of those old-fashioned kidnapping notes, she thought. They always used to cut letters from the newspaper and glue them on the ransom note.

The piece of paper read, *BACK OFF. DROP IT*.

Ming folded the note and put it in her robe pocket, then, even though her mind was whirling, she went to the garage to find the shop vacuum to clean up the mess.

Chapter 29

Jackson woke when the five-year-old beast brother snapped on Jackson's bedroom light and announced, "Your stupid friend didn't have to break the window. I'd have noticed her if she just knocked."

Jackson rolled over and glared. "What are you doing out of bed?" he mumbled, fishing for a T-shirt.

"I hadda get a drink," Wesley explained. "But she threw a rock and it almost hit me!"

"What?" Jackson demanded. "What are you talking about?"

His brother held out his hands, showing a rock, several rubber bands, and a crumpled piece of paper. "It came right through the kitchen window," he said solemnly. "I hadda duck or it woulda hit me. Now there's glass everywhere."

Jackson grabbed the paper. It reminded him of fourth grade, when he and a friend had laboriously cut letters from magazines and newspapers and pasted them on pieces of paper, spelling out every dirty word they could think of and tucking the papers into all the girls' desks.

Only this piece of paper said, *FORGET IT. IT'S NOT YOUR PROBLEM*.

"Did you see who did this?" Jackson asked.

The child shook his head.

"Then why did you say it was a girl?"

"It hadda be," Wesley said. "The girl in the story. Trying to get someone to notice her so she'd be real. It hadda be Brenda." He yawned. "I didn't get my drink. And I'm thirsty."

"What were you doing in the kitchen? Why didn't you get a drink in the bathroom?" Jackson asked.

His brother's eyes opened wider and he looked both amazed and disgusted at Jackson's stupidity. "You can't get chocolate milk out of bathroom faucets!" he explained.

Chapter 30

Linnie woke on time, which meant she was going to be late if she wanted to talk with Jackson and Ming before school started. She rushed her shower, ran downstairs to grab a box of crackers to eat on the way, and stopped short at the sight of her parents, arguing as they swept glass from the entryway.

"What happened?" Linnie asked.

"Vandals, I guess," her father said. "Now I'll be late to work. I have to nail something over this and call the insurance agent."

"I'll call the agent. You just nail," her mother said.

"Nail what?" her father asked, exasperated. "Do you think I keep pieces of wood around already cut to the exact size to fit each window in case one of them gets broken?"

"It wouldn't hurt to have some wood around," her mother said. "I believe it's called being prepared."

Linnie saw the wad of paper and rubber bands.

She picked it up, felt the rock beneath the paper. She slipped it all into her pocket.

"Dad!" she said, interrupting the argument. "Call Mr. Marl next door. Tell him I'll cut his lawn next weekend if he'll watch the house until someone gets here to replace the glass. Then call the insurance agent from your office. He'll know what to do."

She ran off, but not before seeing her father's face light up with recognition of a perfect solution. She felt a warm, pleased glow for the first block, which faded as she jogged on.

Too little too late, she thought. My sister was the shining light. I was just the little lamp that kept burning out bulbs too fast till they threw the whole thing away.

She jogged into the schoolyard and saw Ming pacing, waiting nervously.

Jackson came running up as Linnie arrived, yanking a piece of paper from his pocket, holding it up. "I don't like being told what to do!" he said, his face red from anger as well as from the exertion of running.

Linnie pulled the rock from her pocket and Ming and Jackson froze.

"You, too?" Ming asked.

"Through the window?" Jackson asked.

"We all got one, then," Ming said woodenly.

Linnie freed the paper and smoothed it. *YOU DON'T NEED ANYTHING MORE TO WORRY ABOUT* stared up at her.

She held it out to the other two, who examined her note, and passed theirs around.

Linnie shivered. "I want to go home," she said. "I want to go back to bed and forget the whole thing."

Ming half laughed. "But you have a broken window at home," she said. "Anyone could get in."

"My little brother said Brenda did it," Jackson said.

They all hunched their shoulders against the chill of Brenda's name.

"But he didn't see anyone," Jackson added.

"I wonder if anyone else got anonymous notes last night," Ming said thoughtfully, snugging her windbreaker around her shoulders. "Or if it was just us."

"I'll give you one guess," Jackson said. "We have to face it. Someone is still playing the game."

"I don't want to face anything," Linnie said.

"Me either," Ming agreed. "Let's just drop the whole thing. This is creepy. I don't like middle-of-the-night messages. I don't like broken windows and night noises. I don't like being invaded!" Her hands clenched. "I like boring, peaceful days and nights. I like things to be predictable!"

"Just exactly what do you think the notes mean? What are we supposed to back off from and forget about?" Jackson asked.

Linnie and Ming looked at him. "The game, I suppose," Linnie said.

"We already quit the game," Jackson pointed out. "If you recall, the last thing we were discussing was the fact that Brenda would have run away from the sprinklers, yet she didn't. We were wondering why, and then we all got these notes telling us to forget it."

"I'm ready to forget the whole thing," Ming said. "All I want is my normal life back. I just want to study and do homework and sleep peacefully without rocks through the window."

"You're either missing the point, or ignoring the point," Jackson said. "Somebody died." His hands curled into fists. "We can't just forget that. I was involved in that death. As soon as we started to realize there might be more to it than we'd thought, we got rocks through our windows and warnings to back off."

He looked at both of them, in turn. "I don't like being pushed around. I don't like it when someone I know pushes me around, and I especially don't like it when the person who's trying to push me around won't even show his face."

"Nobody likes being pushed around," Linnie said.

Jackson pounded at the air, too frustrated to speak. Finally he said, "You still don't get it! Put it together! *Why* did Brenda run TOWARD the sprinklers?"

He looked at Linnie, then Ming, his teeth clenched. "I've gone over it and over it in my mind. Brenda ran TOWARD the sprinklers because somehow she was lured there. And now someone is trying to warn us off thinking about it."

"Now wait a minute," Linnie said. "I agree that it was odd for Brenda to go toward the park when the sprinklers were on. But lured?"

"Her car was in the lot," Ming said. "She should have run for her car if she just wanted to get away."

"That's right. Cars offer the best and fastest escape," Jackson agreed. "From school, anyway. So what else can we think? She would have gone toward the parking lot, and since she didn't, I say someone made her go the other way."

"You went out there right after she did," Linnie said. "Did you see anyone?"

Jackson shook his head. "I didn't follow right away, though. Maybe five minutes later. It doesn't take long to fall down the stairs . . . maybe five seconds. That still leaves time for someone to lure her over there and . . ."

"And what?" Linnie asked.

"I don't know," Jackson said. "Somebody knows a lot more about Brenda's last few minutes than we do. A lot more."

Ming looked at him, her eyes dead-sober. "Are you saying someone pushed Brenda? Are you saying she was murdered?"

"I don't know," Jackson said again. "I'm saying there's someone else involved. I'm saying our three hits were a lot worse than we intended, which could have been what someone else intended. We do know someone kept on playing the game once we quit. I'm saying someone lured Brenda over toward the steps. I'm not saying it was murder. Not yet. I need to look at it from a lot more angles than I have so far. It could have been an accident, even if there was someone else there . . . but getting warnings like this makes me think otherwise."

"So now what?" Linnie asked.

"I don't know," Jackson said for the third time. "What I do know is that this is too much. I can't take it and I won't take it."

The school grounds were filling up with people. Jackson stood silently, looking around. Then he walked away from Ming and Linnie without saying good-bye, and without looking back.

Chapter 31

It can't be murder, Linnie thought, trying to look as if she were paying attention in class. There's got to be another explanation.

Linnie kept sinking into her thoughts, then jerking back to an awareness of her surroundings.

My sister started this whole mess, she thought. She should never have told me about the Dead Game. There are a lot of things she should never have done.

Linnie heard someone ask a question, and tried to focus on the teacher's answer, but she kept remembering the summer when she was five years old and her sister twelve. That was the summer Linnie had finally realized what game her sister was playing.

Each summer had two highlights, two special days — the Fourth of July and the county fair in August — days filled with crowds, excitement, food, noise, games, music, carnival rides, streamers, and fireworks. Linnie always had a glorious time.

Linnie had actually believed the accident on July third was accidental. Her sister had run through the living room with her friends, knocking over Mom's antique vase. She didn't notice, didn't stop, so Linnie picked up the pieces and took them to show her sister, who started screaming about Linnie being in big trouble now. She'd suggested burying the vase — had even helped.

Of course, their parents noticed right off that the vase was missing, and Linnie's sister confessed — that Linnie had broken it. Linnie's protests only made things worse. She'd not only broken the vase and hidden it, she'd lied about it.

She had to go to a baby-sitter the Fourth of July and miss the celebration. She was miserable, but at least she believed it was a sincere mistake on her sister's part.

But the day before the August fair their mother discovered money missing from her purse — money that was found tucked into a pair of Linnie's clean socks. Then Linnie knew her sister had deliberately framed her. There was no other explanation. But the more she tried to get her parents to see what had really happened, the more convinced they were that Linnie was making up lies about her sister.

My parents had us mixed up, Linnie thought. *They thought I was what my sister really was. Now my sister's done it again and she's not even here. I wish she'd never told me about the Dead Game, and I wish I'd never mentioned it to Ming and Jackson! The last thing they needed their senior year was to* be caught in the middle of playing a game that doesn't want to end, and wondering whether one of our victims was murdered!

When the bell rang she followed the crowd into the hall, stopping at her locker to trade books. She waved at Jackson, but he didn't wave back.

We're all a little preoccupied, she told herself, settling into her desk in her next class. The teacher started his lecture, and Linnie's thoughts wandered.

I realized a lot of things that summer, she thought. I realized my sister was a fake. Fakers don't really feel, and they don't think. Since they don't feel, it doesn't bother them to hurt other people, and since they don't think, they're impulsive. They just grab at whatever opportunity comes along and then make up a scheme or a lie so other people have to pay for their mistakes.

Austin and Adler are a lot like my sister. They didn't see anything wrong with cheating Ming out of what she'd earned. They wanted it, and they saw a way to take it, so they took it. The same with the others on our list.

Okay, smartie, she told herself. If you know so much about people, use it. Figure out how to get this mess cleaned up. Figure out what we can do.

We have to do something. We can't just wander around accusing each other. There has to be a solution to all this.

She sighed, then remembered she was in class. Everyone else was thumbing through their books.

Linnie heard a whispered, "Page 213," and gratefully turned to the page, paying attention during the rest of the class.

At lunch she sat with Ming. Jackson sat across the room from them and ignored them.

Ming looked at Linnie sadly. "He won't talk to me."

"Same here, I guess," Linnie said. She opened her milk. "I've been thinking."

Ming didn't have to ask about what. She nodded.

"We've got to do something," Linnie said. "I can't think what, yet, but we're the only ones who can do anything, so we have to. We can't go around not talking to each other, being suspicious, and thinking about murder. Wait a minute! I think I know why Jackson won't talk to us."

Ming leaned forward. "Why?"

"Jackson thinks this whole mess is the result of someone listening in on our conversations," Linnie told Ming. "Of someone, somehow, hearing all of our plans."

"So if we don't plan, that person can't hear anything!" Ming said. "I see. You could be right."

Linnie spread her roll with butter and took a bite. "We have to talk again," she said, whispering. "Whether Jackson wants to or not. But we should think things over first. We should look at this from all sides. Get your mind going in some different directions from murder and see what you can come up with."

Chapter 32

Murder! Ming thought, hurrying home after school. She clutched her books tightly to her, as if they could provide a barrier . . . could keep the word away.

Murder.

It's an ugly word, she thought. A big, final word. It means the end of a person . . . the end of all the hopes and laughter, all the smiles and thoughts and jokes. It means an end to function, to eating and drinking, wanting, thinking. Stopped. Dead.

On purpose.

She thought about Jackson, his attentiveness to her, his kindness, his guilt.

Her head snapped up and she stopped, the thought knocking her out of her hurry. Guilt?

He said all along he was responsible. What if he meant it literally? What if he's so sure Brenda was murdered because he . . .

She set off again. No, she told herself. I will not believe that about Jackson.

She remembered Jackson skipping class to make

certain she was okay. She also remembered how guilty she'd felt after Rafe's injury. It's only natural to feel guilty when you're involved, she decided, and that's why Jackson feels guilty — because he's involved — not because he is guilty.

She turned up the sidewalk to her house, noting that the window had been fixed, the new white putty standing out, the manufacturer's decals still decorating the new pane. She fished out her keys and unlocked the front door, remembering the feel of Jackson's comforting arm on her shoulders.

As she thought of him, the pictures flashed through her mind like a slide show — Jackson, always hungry, his look of concern, his almost-constant motion, telling about his little brothers, playing drums on his legs, on the table, on the ground.

I really like Jackson, she thought. He can't be guilty.

And if my mind has to go off in new directions to think of solutions, it isn't going to go in that direction. Jackson isn't guilty of anything except playing the game in the first place. And we all did that.

She felt her face heat up as she recalled how eagerly she'd joined the game, how ready she'd been to humiliate Austin.

I haven't thought about being number three in ages, she realized. It doesn't matter like it used to. Rafe . . . that's what did it. When I thought I'd killed him — that just couldn't compare with something like class rank. The problems are on completely different levels.

So, if I'm not going to think about Jackson being guilty, what am I going to think about?

I got myself into this mess because I was too stupid to see how small my problem really was, and I was too eager for revenge. We didn't really think this through before we started. If we're going to get out of this mess, we've got to be clear-sighted and careful.

She got an apple and a knife, grabbed a plate, carried everything to the table, and started slicing.

Define the problem, she told herself.

Someone died.

No, the problem is more basic than that. That's the result. The problem is, the game got out of control.

What are the factors?

The game players. Known: Jackson, Ming, Linnie. Plus at least one unknown. X. Or maybe X and Y.

She grabbed a piece of paper and a pencil and scribbled the names.

The original victims were: Rafe, John, and Brenda. The intended action (Ia) was complicated by either coincidence (C) or by the action of the possible unknown or unknowns (X, maybe Y). Ia + Rafe × C, or Ia + Rafe × X + Y. Which one?

But there was no intended action for Austin, Adler, Price, Julie, or Karl. We never drew their names or planned any hits.

The equation for the whole thing, she thought, is GOOC. Game out of control.

She crumpled the piece of paper and threw it in the trash. She cut more apple slices.

It's not a math problem, she thought. I can't reduce this to plus and minus.

She thought about their hits. John had come back to school three days after the incident. Ming had witnessed a couple of confrontations between the girls on the tape and John. John had just shrugged and laughed, saying, "There's nothing wrong with going after what you want in life."

Rafe had returned to school after missing three weeks, walking with a slight limp, looking a little paler, talking a little quieter, but joking about the accident. He insisted he'd be back on his bike in no time, and his limp attracted plenty of sympathetic female attention. Plus, Jackson felt responsible since he'd nominated Rafe in the first place, and had begun working at rebuilding their friendship.

And Brenda was dead.

So our hit made no difference at all to John, Ming thought. Rafe shouldn't really have been on the list, and he was hurt. He lost three weeks of his senior year, but he'll be okay.

And Brenda is dead.

Chapter 33

Brenda is dead, Jackson thought, jogging home after practice. His sneakers slapped the letters out on the asphalt, D-E-A-D, D-E-A-D.

For a second he thought he heard an echo, and realized he'd been hearing it for some time. He stopped, but heard nothing. After a second he started off again.

I'm spooked, he thought. Or maybe it was my heart pounding. Death is not my favorite subject.

He remembered when his father died. Jackson had been eight. He remembered neighbors crowded into their house, lots of food, people crying.

Industrial accident.

Things had blurred. He'd seen death before — dead birds, cats, dogs. He'd seen mice caught in traps. But Dad?

It didn't seem possible that someone so big, so good at shuffling cards and cooking stir-fry and cracking dumb jokes could be dead. It couldn't be real. Grown-ups did strange things sometimes, muttering about taxes, IRS, parking tickets, stock markets. This was just another one of those hazy, hard-to-understand grown-up things. It wasn't real.

Not even the funeral had seemed real.

The casket had been closed, and that big black box was not his father. Jackson had been positive his father was not inside. He remembered deciding his father was probably working late, and would come home later. He would be sorry he missed this funeral, since it was supposed to be for him.

But of course, Dad never came home. Things kept on changing, and then one day Jackson was a senior in high school with a stepfather and two little stepbrothers.

And Brenda's death seemed more real than his own father's had.

Because I didn't believe Dad died, Jackson thought. And I know Brenda did. But just because her death is more real, doesn't mean I understand it any better.

He remembered, with sudden guilt, the expressions on Ming's and Linnie's faces when he'd ignored them earlier. I hope they figured out why, he thought, speeding up his pace. The echo he'd heard before sped up, too, and he knew it was his heartbeat, haunting him because he was alive and Brenda wasn't. Her heart would never beat again.

He jogged up the front sidewalk and opened his front door, making it all the way into the kitchen without being mobbed by the beasts. The television blared from the back room so Jackson figured he was temporarily safe. His brothers seldom heard anything other than the TV when they were watching cartoons.

He made a ham sandwich and checked the oven to see what was cooking for dinner. It looked like chicken and smelled Italian.

What went wrong? he wondered. Why does it feel like the game took over and played itself? Like it didn't need us anymore. Games don't play themselves. People play games. Which people, though? That's the question.

The beast-children didn't discover him until dinner, so he had time to think, but he didn't reach any further conclusions. He only reached more questions.

Or the same questions over and over.

Who? Why?

I can't figure it out alone, he finally decided.

He woke the next morning with the same thought. I can't figure it out alone. We have to talk.

Chapter 34

Jackson waited near the front door of the school, waving at Ming and then at Linnie. "We have to talk," he said.

Ming looked relieved. Linnie nodded.

"But we can't talk here and we can't talk now. Somehow, someone knows too much," Jackson said. "We'll have to make sure we don't let him hear anything else we say."

Linnie and Ming exchanged glances, nodding in agreement.

Jackson grinned suddenly. "I almost forgot," he said. "Austin finally found his jacket."

Ming looked blank for a second, then said, "What happened?"

"I heard about it in Phys Ed," Jackson told her. "I guess another guy found the grave and knew it was Austin's jacket. So instead of telling him, he got a few people, including Austin, to help him look for something he'd supposedly dropped in the woods."

Jackson's grin widened. "He led Austin to about

fifteen feet away from the graveyard and everyone started looking. Austin's the one who saw the path and decided to check in that direction."

Jackson shook his head in admiration. "It must have been beautiful! There's Austin, wearing his jacket, staring at its twin on the gravestone in front of him. The way I heard it, he turned all kinds of colors and then ran off without saying a word. He just ran. It sounds like a perfect hit to me."

"I wish I'd seen it," Ming said wistfully. "That might have been the only moment of triumph in this whole mess."

"Where did the new jacket come from then?" Linnie asked.

"It's Adler's," Jackson said. "So simple. We should have realized they both had one, even if Adler never wore his. Austin just borrowed it and ordered a new one.

"But that's not all." Jackson sounded glum. "I heard that Austin and Adler were cleared of stealing that science test."

"What do you mean, they were cleared?" Linnie demanded. "They got caught red-handed!"

"I heard about it, too," Ming said. "Mr. Byre said he had the copies of the test made before homeroom. He took the copies as they were made, put them in a stack, and put the stack in his briefcase. During the whole time Austin and Adler were in the counselor's office, talking about college."

"But if Mr. Byre carried the tests around in his briefcase, then Austin or Adler could have opened it and taken the test later," Linnie said.

"Mr. Byre said he only left his briefcase unguarded once, at the end of homeroom," Ming said. "He went to get a cup of coffee, then came back and remembered the tests. He's pretty sure whoever took the test, did it then. And Austin and Adler have an alibi."

"Darn it!" Linnie said. "I was hoping they'd get F's."

"They do have to take a different test," Jackson said. "They have to take it in the principal's office and be monitored and all, but if they pass, they're off the hook. What's ironic is the hit we thought didn't work at all, is the one that worked best. The jacket."

"They must have a guardian angel," Linnie said, looking disgusted.

"Well, at least the jacket story will be all over school tomorrow," Jackson said.

Ming giggled. "I wish I'd seen his face!" she said.

"Look," Jackson said, serious again. "We can't talk here. This is too public. It's too easy for people to overhear our conversation."

"I've been looking over my shoulder for several days," Linnie said. "But I still think this whole thing was an accident. This is high school. People don't murder each other in high school."

Jackson shrugged.

"It's strange that just one person died." Linnie swallowed hard. "I mean, if we presume it's the same person behind everything, then why would he kill one and not the others? That's why I think it was an accident."

"When Brenda died, we quit," Jackson said, keeping his voice low. "Dying's pretty serious! But the game didn't quit. That's why I think it was murder, because whoever kept playing wasn't bothered by Brenda's death. He kept right on playing."

"Personally, I don't like thinking about murder," Linnie said. "I think we're just talking ourselves into this. We talked ourselves into the game, and now we're talking ourselves into thinking murder. Besides, if someone killed Brenda, what's to stop that person from killing us to keep it quiet?"

Ming's eyes darkened. "We have to tell the police."

"They won't believe us," Linnie said.

"That's the problem," Jackson said glumly. "Especially since I went to great effort to convince them I didn't know anything. I'm not sure how smart that was."

"I don't think it'll be too hard to convince the police we withheld information," Ming said. "The problem will be getting them to believe our new version."

"I'm having trouble believing it," Linnie said.

"I think we have to try, anyway," Jackson said, jamming his hands in his pockets. "I agree with Ming. I say we've got to tell."

"When?" Linnie asked. "After school?"

Jackson shook his head. "We've got the state meet coming up. I really can't miss practice. We don't have Price anymore, so the rest of us really have to work if we're going to have any chance at all. How about later? After practice? No, that's dinnertime. After dinner?"

"I've got a dentist appointment at six-thirty," Ming said.

"We should all go together," Linnie said. "Otherwise I might chicken out and not go at all. I'm going to feel like a real fool!"

"I think we need to be together," Jackson said. "For moral support, if nothing else."

"I should be back from the dentist by around eight," Ming told them.

"I do typing for my father," Linnie said. "Usually on Thursdays, but he's got letters that need to be done tonight. It'll probably take me till nine or nine-thirty depending on how many letters he has for me to do."

"How about ten?" Jackson suggested. "I know it's late, but I don't want to wait another day. There's too much chance of more things happening. I think we should do it tonight."

They agreed to meet at ten at the gas station up the street from the police station. Then they would walk over together to tell the police their story.

Linnie started smiling, then she laughed. "That means the game that wouldn't quit might finally be over," she said. "We couldn't end it ourselves, but if we can get the police to believe anything we say, it might finally happen! The Dead Game will be dead for good."

Chapter 35

Linnie ate dinner with her parents, trying to tune out their conversation. It wasn't working very well.

She ate carefully, knowing after years of practice precisely how much food she could take, eat, and leave on her plate without attracting notice or comment.

"Did your Western Literature test go okay, dear?" her mother asked.

I took Western Literature last year, Linnie thought. "Yes, Mom," she said. "It went fine."

"Oh, good. It's such a relief when things are fine."

Things are just fine, Linnie thought. Jackson thinks Brenda was murdered. He thinks people have been eavesdropping on us and . . . wait! We made our plan to meet at the gas station! If someone was listening to us . . .

What if someone gets there ahead of us?

I have to get there first and look around.

"Dad? Can I type your letters right after dinner?" she asked. "I have plans for later."

Her father frowned, then nodded. "I suppose so."

"Oh, dear," her mother said. "You have plans? Your sister is coming over this evening. I was saving the news for a surprise. You won't want to miss her."

My sister? "How can she come over?" Linnie asked. "She isn't here."

"No, dear," her mother said. "She isn't here, but she will be."

Linnie felt confused. "Where is she now?" she asked carefully.

Her mother sighed. "I've told you every night for weeks, dear. I do believe you weren't paying attention. I suppose you have a lot of schoolwork to worry about."

"Where is she now?" Linnie repeated.

"She's been working day and night, I guess, setting up new accounts for her boss. He's expanding, and she gets to move home again."

"Here?" Linnie couldn't keep the alarm from her voice.

"No, no, she's not moving to the house. She's living near that new mall. I did tell you all of this before. She and your father and I have all had lunch and it was lovely and tonight she won't be working so late so she's coming to visit and I'm sure you won't want to miss her."

What a perfect evening this will be, Linnie thought bleakly. I get to go to the police and see my sister, too!

"I won't miss her, I promise," Linnie said. I won't miss her at all!

Chapter 36

The police station was on Delano, with River Street on the west end of the block, and 12th Street on the east. The gas station they'd agreed to meet at was on 12th, up a block and around the corner from the police station.

Linnie drove around the area first, covering three blocks on River and 12th, two blocks on Delano, Eleanor, and Franklin, weaving in and out, trying to figure out where someone would hide . . . if someone were planning to hide and wait for them.

The police station and the library took up the long side of Delano, and Linnie thought the library grounds would be perfect for a hidden watcher until she realized the only place with a good view of the route they would take from the gas station was the library parking lot. It was too brightly lit.

Not there, then, she decided. River Street would be great for hiding on — a person could hide in the trees, or slide down the embankment and wait. But no, the police station isn't really visible from River

Street . . . and anyone hiding there couldn't get to us in time to stop us from reaching the police.

Is that what I'm worried about? she wondered. Will someone try to keep us from going to the police?

She sighed. I'm past thinking what anyone else is going to try to do. I'm just looking for places someone might hide.

She drove on. Both sides of the long street behind the police station were filled with businesses that were closed for the night. Quite a few had security lights on, and their parking lots were lit.

That leaves this section here along 12th, she decided, between the gas station and the corner. She parked near the gas station, cut the lights and engine, and sat, listening to the silence.

It was nine-fifteen. She hoped that was early enough.

She hadn't recognized any of the cars she'd seen on her reconnaissance drive, but that didn't mean much. Cars could be borrowed from friends, grandparents, even neighbors.

She sighed and pulled out her flashlight. She didn't really want to go around on foot checking shadows, but she had to. She'd known she would have to. That was why she'd dressed all in black, from her jeans and windbreaker to the scarf she'd tied around her hair . . . and why she had brought the flashlight.

She climbed out of the car and closed the door with a quiet *thunk*, trying to put together a mental schematic of the area between the gas station and the front of the police station.

Gas station, driveway, pharmacy, street. Medical supply building, driveway, end of police station, around corner, front of police station.

Two driveways. The one by the police station is the back way into the station. A cruiser could come by at any time.

The other driveway?

Linnie slid from shadow to shadow, watchful and alert, using the light sparingly. It was one of those rechargeable flashlights, metal and heavy, and Linnie's arm felt weighted. As she passed the driveway by the gas station, she realized it was actually an alley. She listened for a minute, then continued on, looking closely at the route they would take, checking all the shadowy areas. She paused for a moment in front of the police station. The station and ground lights blazed, bright and cheerful, but Linnie shuddered, wondering what kind of reception their story would receive.

She returned to the alley. She couldn't remember seeing a matching driveway on the other side of the block. Did that mean this was a dead-end alley?

Somehow that possibility made the alley seem darker and more frightening.

Linnie hesitated.

It's getting late, she reminded herself. The others will be here soon. I need to be sure. . . .

She drew in a deep breath and slipped into the alley.

Was that a noise?

She froze, certain she could hear something . . . something like breathing?

The flashlight, she thought. But Linnie hesitated to turn it on. It might show her what was in the alley if she managed to get it aimed in the right direction. What it would do for sure was show anyone who might be waiting exactly where she was.

She left the light off, breathing quietly, trying to shrink into the shadows and decide what to do next.

Her senses felt alive and heightened, her hearing unnaturally acute. Her fingers could feel each ridge on the handle of the flashlight. Her eyes peered into the darkness . . . seeing? Imagining?

She shook her head.

If anyone's here . . . there's nothing moving, she thought. Nobody attacking.

It's my turn, then. It's up to me.

Slowly, working on adrenaline and nerve and determination, Linnie inched forward. She thought she heard the noise again, and fell to her knees, then rolled quickly sideways, hoping to avoid the blow.

Chapter 37

Jackson and Ming both arrived at nine fifty-five, in separate cars but evidently on the same time schedule. Both cars parked and both sets of headlights faded.

Both car doors clicked open, clunked shut.

"Where's Linnie?" Ming asked, shivering slightly as she joined Jackson.

He shook his head. "We're early. She's not here yet. How are you doing? Are we nuts? Do we go through with this?"

"What else can we do?" Ming couldn't decide where to look. She tried meeting Jackson's eyes in the light of the street lamp, but the light fell on her over Jackson's shoulders. His eyes were shadowed, and even in the shadows they seemed too intense, burning.

She glanced, instead, up the street, then down, watching for Linnie.

Her eyes widened. She pointed. "That's Linnie's car," she said. "I mean, it's her parents' car. Who else would be driving it? She's already here."

Jackson looked where Ming was pointing. He nodded. "I've seen her in it before," he agreed. "Unless her parents are here. But that wouldn't make sense. She must have gotten here early . . . but where is she?" He glanced all around them without seeing Linnie.

"I should have gotten here early to look around," he said, hitting himself on the thigh in sudden frustration. "Why didn't I think of that? I'll bet Linnie thought of it. I'll bet she's here, checking around. She's probably on the next block over, hiding in the shadows and watching to see if anyone else shows up. It's what I would be doing if I'd thought of it."

"Then let's find her and tell her we're here," Ming said. "I can't just stand around waiting. I came here to DO something and I need to DO it, not stand around."

"Okay," Jackson agreed. "Come on. We'll go this way." He pointed left.

"You go that way," Ming suggested. "I'll go the other way and we'll meet in the middle."

"I don't think we should split up," Jackson said.

"I want to go to the police station, tell my story, answer a million questions, and go home," Ming said. "I don't want to spend half the night looking for Linnie. It'll be faster if we split up. I will not do anything stupid, Jackson. I will just walk around the block calling for Linnie and meet you halfway around."

Reluctantly Jackson nodded. It would be faster, he thought. I don't like it, but Ming's certainly able to think for herself. It's not my place to go all macho and insist on doing this my way. She obviously doesn't think she needs my protection.

"Okay," he said shortly.

Ming headed to her right, away from the police station, calling, "Linnie?" She turned the corner and was soon out of sight, though Jackson could still hear her calling.

"Linnie?" he called. He took off to his left, hurrying a little so he could meet Ming sooner. "Linnie? Where are you?"

A little way up from the gas station Jackson came upon the opening to an alley. He paused. "Linnie?" he called.

He heard something, but couldn't tell if it was a cat noise or a person noise. "Linnie?"

The sound was not repeated.

It's just a cat, he thought. Or a rat. He took one step into the alley. "Linnie?"

This time there was a definite noise beside him and Jackson spun, his right arm flinging up in an automatic attempt at protecting his face. "Wha — ?"

His question was cut short by a mountain crashing into his brain, splitting it apart into a million stars, into a million Jacksons, each one a tiny glittering spark in the night sky, each one giving a short, strangled cry of pain before fading into nothingness.

Chapter 38

"Linnie?" Ming's voice rang impatiently in the darkness. "Jackson?"

She'd been all the way around the block without seeing Linnie. Now she was almost back where she'd started from and she hadn't met up with Jackson, either.

"Jackson?" Ming waited a minute, then continued. She'd start from the gas station, she decided, and trace Jackson's route, in the same direction Jackson had headed. Maybe she'd missed something. Maybe Jackson had seen something across the street toward the police station and had gone that way. She reached a driveway of sorts just before the gas station, and paused, looking around.

"Hey." The voice was muffled. "My ankle. I fell."

The voice, even muffled, was familiar and Ming plunged gratefully into the darkness, immediately stumbling on some obstruction. She fell onto it, hearing a whistling past her ear as she landed on a body. She screamed, her hand brushing a face.

Ming rolled, drawing her knees up and leaping to her feet. Her heart pounded and her knees felt like Jell-O — the same way they'd felt when she'd waited for Rafe.

It's too dark! I can't see! she thought.

Then her shoulder burst into flames as a great weight smashed it, separating her right shoulder and arm from the rest of her. For a shocked second Ming held her breath, listening to hear her severed arm fall to the ground.

Instead, she fell, landing again on the body. Her right arm crumpled beneath her like a tissue, offering no resistance. She screamed in pain . . . a pain mixed with momentary relief as Ming realized her shoulder and arm were still attached. They wouldn't hurt like that if they weren't attached. The relief faded into a gray blankness as she fainted from the pain.

She woke, feeling motion.

With her left hand she felt for the ground, feeling instead the face again, a familiar face that slid away from her hand as Jackson slid steadily away.

Jackson!

Tears stung Ming's eyes as Jackson's body was smoothly towed from beneath her. Her face hit the dirt of the alley as the cushioning body disappeared. She stifled a sob. Jackson! He's gone . . . and I didn't get to tell him . . .

What?

Ming shook her head. The motion made her shoulder scream.

Shoulders can't scream, she thought dully. But she knew it had, even if it hadn't made a sound. The pain was a scream.

"I'm sorry," a voice said. "But you were going to tell. I can't let that happen. I'll be back after I take care of this."

"Wait!" Ming cried. She wasn't certain whether she'd actually made a sound. "Linnie, don't."

Linnie?

Ming's brain struggled against the pain and the gray, trying to piece the mental images of what had happened into a picture. Her right arm, crumpling onto a body, her left hand feeling a face as it slid from beneath her, a voice emerging from the darkness, a calm voice, promising.

The body is Jackson.

The voice is . . . Linnie.

Ming sobbed in despair. Her shoulder was still screaming without sound, burning, throbbing, and threatening to take over her mind. Pain was the strongest sensation, and it was drowning her.

Linnie.

Dragging Jackson.

With a sudden clarity Ming knew it was true. Linnie was really dragging Jackson away. Jackson . . . limp, unprotesting . . . dead? She felt overwhelmed by despair at the loss of Jackson.

No, she thought. She lurched, trying to get her left arm under her to push herself upright. No. You can't have him.

Her right arm flopped like a dead fish — a

screaming dead fish. She wriggled until she got her good arm beneath her chest and pushed herself back onto her knees, sitting. With her teeth, she bit onto the left wrist of her windbreaker, holding it while she pulled her hand up inside. She let go with her teeth, shrugged her shoulder loose, then awkwardly shook her arm free of the sleeve. She wanted something to tie her right arm with, something to keep it from flapping around.

The jacket worked, more or less.

Using her left hand, Ming pulled the jacket around behind herself, trapping her right arm, clenching her teeth to keep from screaming again as the jacket brushed free of her injured shoulder. From then on, she had to pause frequently to keep from passing out as she pulled her right arm along with the jacket, pulled it snug in front of her body, drew the empty sleeve up over her left shoulder, dropped it behind her, then stuffed the wrist of the jacket into her jeans.

She had a sling of sorts, and had more or less immobilized her shoulder. But how long had it taken her? Where was Jackson now? And was he still alive?

Ming gave a staggering lurch and got to her feet this time with no flapping arm to drag her back down. She headed after Jackson.

And Linnie.

Linnie?

Ming couldn't believe Linnie was doing this, hurting Jackson.

It is Linnie, Ming told herself firmly. She's going to take care of "this." "This" was Jackson. Dead? Or alive?

"Taking care of" either means getting rid of a dead body, or making a dead body out of a live person.

Ming tried to hurry.

Ahead of her, in the streetlight, she could see Jackson's head slithering around the corner, bumping, thudding. Going around the corner in the direction Ming had gone earlier . . . away from the police station. His jacket had ridden up behind him and fluttered on both sides of his head.

Linnie had been facing forward, towing Jackson behind her, holding one of his feet in each hand, towing him like he was nothing but a sled or a downed tree.

Ming hurried, whimpering as she tried to run. Scenes from all the fight and action-adventure movies she'd ever seen flashed through her brain. The heroes always kept going, even with mortal injuries. Bleeding from every inch of their broken bodies they kept going.

Ming gritted her teeth in fury and pain. She gave a low grunt as she hurried her pace, felt her legs gaining strength and spring as she almost ran now, gaining on Linnie, screaming as she ran, launching an attack on Linnie from behind. Ming kicked Linnie's leg, slashed with her left arm at Linnie's head, catching her across the cheek and nose.

Linnie dropped Jackson's legs, turned toward Ming, stumbled over Jackson. Ming kicked Linnie again, kicked her over and over, fury driving her.

Linnie lunged once more, but this time she slipped. Her head struck the pavement; her body fell limp.

Ming grabbed Jackson as Linnie had, but she only had one useful arm. She tried towing him away from Linnie, but the fight had cost her more than she'd realized. She slowed her pace. Jackson was very heavy.

She made it back around the corner and stopped, panting, her shoulder awash in agonizing pain.

Ming could see the gas station, closed, its night-lights shining gloomily against the night. A smaller light on the edge of the station's lot signaled a phone booth and Ming almost wept with relief.

Beautiful phone, she thought, letting Jackson's leg down gently. Dial 911. She hurried, panting with effort. Or is it 0 for operator? Are pay phones hooked into 911? She reached the booth, fumbled at the receiver, knocked it off the hook.

She felt for the dangling receiver, tried to drag it up to her ear. The fight and the towing had sapped her energy, and as the adrenaline drained from her body, so did her strength.

Can't stop, she told herself. Where is the dial tone!

She realized she had the receiver upside down. She tried to reverse it, dropped it again.

"Help me," she begged, fumbling at it again.

Then the world stopped again . . . crashed into her head. Ming was knocked against the wall of the phone booth, slumping, her sight fading.

Chapter 39

"No," Linnie said. "You may not call the police."

Ming could hear distinctly, though the world was gray-black or red pain.

"You may not tell on me," Linnie said. "Do you understand? How can I be famous if you call the police? How can I matter?"

"Jackson?" Ming asked. Her voice sounded feeble to her own ears, her tongue difficult to move.

"I'll take care of him," Linnie said kindly.

Does that mean he's still alive? Ming couldn't stop the surge of hope. "Linnie?" She sounded as if she were three years old . . . felt as if she were three years old. "Why?"

Linnie laughed. "Why? Why did my parents only like my sister? Why don't Austin and Adler think they did anything wrong? Why did Jackson decide we had to tell on ourselves?"

Sight returned slowly and through a red haze

Ming saw Linnie, holding a huge flashlight high, ready. Waiting.

Ming didn't move.

"I'm really sorry about this," Linnie said. "It's all my fault. I should have understood earlier. It was playing the game that made me start thinking."

Linnie waved the flashlight and Ming stayed motionless. She tried to deepen her vision, to see where Jackson was. She felt lightheaded, groggy and weak, and knew she was very near to being in shock.

"See?" Linnie was serious, wanting Ming to understand. "The fake people will win in the end if we let them because the real people have soft hearts. They'll never rise up and stop the Austins and Adlers. Real people can't hate!" She shouted the last three words, then went on in a softer voice, "But I can. I can hate."

She smiled. "I'm flawed. It's okay. If I were a fake person I'd be just like my sister. If I were a real person I'd be a victim like you and Jackson. I'm not really one or the other, and that's why I can do it. I saw that someone had to do it, and I'm the only one who can."

Ming felt tired and slow, faraway . . . fading. She broke my shoulder, Ming thought. And I'm too cold.

"You guys wouldn't even play the game unless it was nice. I could see that right away, so I let it be nice . . . only then I helped it along. All those fake people deserved a little more than you wanted to give them! Then Jackson needed someone else to blame. I figured if the game kept on playing, that would give him someone to blame. But he wasn't happy even then."

Linnie's voice had dropped . . . or else Ming's hearing had faded.

"The game would have ended once everyone on our list got hit," Linnie continued. "I was going to keep playing by myself, of course, but you two would think it was all over. Except Jackson wouldn't let go. I really thought the rock through the window would stop him. It would have stopped me!"

Linnie bowed her head slightly, the flashlight drooping. "Then you two decided to go to the police. You and Jackson will be sacrifices. I'm very sorry about that. I told you it was all my fault, but there's no other way."

We're all so ready to hurt each other, Ming thought tiredly. That's what this was all about. Getting even. Getting back at people.

"It's okay," Linnie whispered. "You won't feel it much. And you'll know . . . you'll know you'll be helping me. We'll get as many of the cheats as we can, Ming. For as long as I live, we'll be working together. We'll get them."

Linnie looked down on Ming. "You'll wait," Linnie said, her voice very kind. "I think you're in shock. Jackson isn't. He's just unconscious. I'd better take care of him first."

She reached over, grabbed the receiver, and

yanked it viciously, pulling it free from the phone box.

The silence, once Linnie had disappeared, was too loud. Ming listened, but even her own heartbeat seemed to have gone silent. Am I dead? she wondered.

Chapter 40

Ming sighed as softly as a leaf falling from a tree, letting go without anguish or thought.

She'll kill him.

I can't let her.

If she'd had the strength, Ming would have laughed at herself — a half-blind, staggering, barely conscious ninety-five-pound hospital case setting off to rescue Jackson.

If she'd had the strength, she'd have wept for Jackson, having nothing better than Ming between him and death.

Instead of weeping, she concentrated. She couldn't take a deep breath — it hurt her shoulder — so she took several shallow breaths. She felt distant and scattered, as if Linnie's blows had literally knocked her out of herself.

Pull yourself together.

Ming knew she'd heard those words before. They came from a past she couldn't really remember, and they sounded like good advice, but how was she supposed to do it? She took another breath, slowing when her shoulder protested, but continuing to inhale until her lungs felt full. She pushed with her legs, trying to grab something to help pull herself upright, and the pain in her shoulder and head acted like a focus for her awareness. If she didn't think of it as pain, it pulsed, like energy, urging her on.

She stumbled to her feet and out of the phone booth, going the same direction she'd gone before, figuring Linnie would not go toward the police station. She couldn't see very well. Her hair kept falling in her face. Shake it back? No. Shaking my head hurts.

She rounded the corner. Stay on the sidewalk, she told herself, because . . . because why? Shapes loomed, turned into a planter box complete with small tree. Ming remembered seeing it before. She edged around the box, feeling more and more vague with each step, feeling like Brenda in Jackson's story — as if she were fading and would soon fade completely away.

She staggered on.

She could hear nothing. She knew the street was lit, but it seemed very dim. There was a certain solid feel to the concrete beneath her feet and Ming felt very wise, knowing she'd answered an important question. Stay on the sidewalk because it feels solid and it leads somewhere.

Her hearing began to return, and she heard sobbing. Someone was sad. Weeping.

Her cheeks were wet. The sobbing was her own labored tears. She stopped sobbing and listened, hearing only a faint rushing of water. Her mouth was dry and her tongue seemed swollen, and the water sounded cool and welcome.

She stumbled into a planter, held onto the small tree trunk, kneeling at the planter's rim. She used the tree to help pull herself to her feet again.

The planter is almost at the corner, she remembered. There will be a street. She made a great mental effort and came up with the name — River Street. The water. The river. The same river that runs through the park where Brenda died. Brenda. Jackson.

The name acted as a focus appearing out of the night, wrapping the fuzz of her thoughts in a form she could recognize . . . Jackson!

She plodded on, reeling onto River Street. She felt off-balance, felt like she was moving too fast for her feet and would fall, but she couldn't stop herself. She almost ran across the street, tripped up over the curb on the far side, stumbled forward for a few yards and fell, jarred to her knees by the little stone wall that marked the edge of the embankment. The river lay below her.

Ming leaned against the wall, her lungs heaving. When she could see beyond her own pain, she leaned forward in horror, seeing the scene beneath her — Jackson, lying on the bank just at the water's edge, lying motionless except for the rise and fall of one leg as it rode the water. Linnie scrabbled around, looking.

Looking for . . . what? A rock, Ming thought dully. To smash his head, then push him into the water where he will float away and drown.

It was almost like watching a cartoon. Linnie and Jackson below Ming seemed only half real. Ming thought she should laugh, but it wasn't very funny. Why wasn't it funny?

She knew her brain wasn't functioning very well. It hurt to think. Bits of·scientific information kept floating into her awareness — mass times something, gravity plus something, inertia — but the bits never jelled into a whole.

She will kill him. Soon.

She can see me if she looks up.

Ming sighed herself into the fence, trying to become one with the rocks. Rock. Linnie was almost directly below her, tugging at a half-embedded rock, rocking it side to side to free it from the earth.

Ming could hear Linnie breathing, could hear the grunts of effort as she worked the stone.

Falling object . . . not enough height to reach maximum speed. Still, weight plus gravity . . .

Ming pushed her legs against the ground. I can, she thought. It's all I have left. I can give this to Jackson.

She leaned her good arm against the low wall, and pushed herself up far enough to sit on the wall, her back to the scene below. With enormous effort she lifted one leg, then the other over the wall, stood on the river side of the barrier, and leapt.

She dropped into nothingness, the moment suspended unbearably . . .

. . . until she landed. Ninety-five pounds falling from a height of . . .

They crumpled together, tangling, falling, disentangling, rolling, rolling into cool, damp oblivion.

Chapter 41

Noise and confusion, pain and lights, voices . . . finally settling into throbbing pain . . . two pains. Shoulder. Head.

Ming smiled, feeling absurdly pleased that she had put a name to what hurt. Then pricks and voices and light, and darkness passed, and more times of darkness passed and finally she opened her eyes, feeling human again, alive and almost normal.

"Jackson!" Her voice came out creaky and Jackson handed her a plastic cup full of ice water. She took a drink.

He smiled at her. "Hi. How do you feel?"

"Okay, I think," Ming said. "You?"

"Fine." He looked apologetic. "Last week I wasn't so fine, but now . . ."

"Last week!"

"Well, yeah." He drummed on his knees. "It's Monday. Last Wednesday we decided to go to the police."

Ming let the missing days sink in. Thursday, Friday, Saturday, Sunday, Monday. What month? April . . . May?

"May fourth," Jackson said.

Ming had a thousand questions, but didn't ask any.

"It was Linnie all along," Jackson said, understanding what she wasn't asking, what she needed to know. "She . . . she didn't plan for this to happen. It started out all right, except she thought the people on the list deserved worse than we were planning for them. She watched us, figuring out what we were up to. She said she didn't really plan what happened to Rafe. She was trying to push her way forward to see exactly what you had in mind and she caused the surge of people. That made her realize she could improve on our hits."

Ming sighed.

"I know," Jackson said. "Her own hit was next. She'd worked with the sound-and-light director for school plays so she'd learned all about the PA system. She played a little part herself, at Brenda's party, making it look like her tape had been stolen, but she had it all planned. She spliced into the system herself and set her tape to play at announcement time."

"Brenda?" Ming asked.

"She thinks it was an accident." Jackson closed his eyes. "She's not real clear on this part. She told Brenda someone had a videotape of her doing something illegal. She told Brenda it would all be made clear soon. She saw me pass out the pictures and she figured since we were near the back door,

Brenda would run out the back door. Linnie went out there to wait."

Jackson opened his eyes, but he stared at his hands. "When Brenda saw the sketches, she thought Linnie was hinting there was a videotape of her stealing the bracelet. A videotape is pretty damaging evidence. She ran outside, saw Linnie, and ran to her. Linnie says Brenda was screaming at her, and either Brenda reached out to hit Linnie, or else Linnie reached out to shake Brenda to make her stop screaming, but all of a sudden Brenda was at the bottom of the stairs. I don't think we'll ever know more than that. I'm not sure Linnie knows."

Ming shook her head.

"The science test was simple," Jackson went on. "Linnie saw Mr. Byre make copies and put them in his briefcase. She waited, watching, and when he left them alone, Linnie was ready. She grabbed one, and then bumped into Austin at the top of the stairs. She dropped the test in with his things and no one even saw her. And the articles in the *'Vine* . . . she planted those, too. She just told the editor she had a last-minute change for her Senior Will, and no one looked at it closely. No problem at all."

"Price?" Ming didn't think about what Jackson was telling her. She just wanted to hear everything. She would think about it later.

"She took the liquor from home," Jackson said, "put it in his car, and made an anonymous call to the coach. And then, the final installment . . . last Wednesday night. She was really afraid I had thought of getting there early. She was afraid I'd be there, waiting for her. I should have been. I was so stupid."

Ming shook her head. Jackson paced back and forth for a minute, and Ming almost smiled. Restlessness, the need to move . . . it was so typical of Jackson.

"When you landed on her . . . I was waking up about then. I saw you fall, saw you both go rolling toward the river. I crawled over and I grabbed your arm. I just let Linnie go. She rolled into the river and floated away and I was glad. I was glad!"

"I would have been glad, too," Ming said. "She hurt us. She would have gone on hurting us. She was going to kill us."

"She didn't die," Jackson said. "She was only stunned. She came to and swam ashore downstream. Some people were walking by the river and saw her crawl out. They insisted on taking her home to dry out and get warm. While they were doing that, I crawled up to the road and flagged a car. The police came. I talked till I was hoarse, explaining what I knew. They believed me, after seeing you."

"Why did she do it?" With everything Linnie had told her, and all that had happened, Ming still didn't know the answer to that question.

Jackson shrugged. "Who knows?" He tapped idly at the edge of Ming's hospital bed. "I only know all this because Linnie's parents told me. They talked to me for an hour, trying to explain what Linnie had told the police and the psychiatrist. They told me he said things about paranoid delusions, delusions of grandeur. It all boiled down to Linnie feeling persecuted, and thinking she could save the world, and being . . . like two people in one.

"They were trying to convince me I shouldn't be angry, I think. I think they're afraid we'll sue them, in addition to all the legal problems they already have now.

"But I'm not angry. I'm just very sad." Jackson looked out Ming's hospital window, looked at the view of the roof on the next wing over. "I've felt like she did, Ming. Persecuted and like I could save the world, and feeling as if I were more than one person. I was big brother, son, student, athlete — and sometimes all those Jacksons felt like separate people who didn't belong together. But I never killed anyone. So . . . what happened with Linnie? She wasn't evil, Ming. Was she?"

Ming's shoulder and her head were throbbing again. She remembered the many faces of her friend, smiling, planning the Dead Game with them, talking, laughing, holding a flashlight over her head, ready to strike, dragging Jackson.

"She wasn't evil. She was just Linnie," Ming finally said. And somehow, that said it all . . . except for one thing.

"Jackson?"

He looked at her.

Ming held his gaze. There was so much to say, about his tenderness, his caring, his attention, the way he cared about his brothers and told them stories, the way he was always so hungry, so restless . . . how could she put it into words?

Jackson looked into Ming's eyes.

You're smart I'm not, he thought.

Ming waved her hand, reading his objections and waving them all away.

Jackson smiled.

THE STRANGER

Chapter 1

It was cold in the music room. Somebody had cracked the windows to freshen the stale school air. But Nicoletta had not expected her entire life to be chilled by the drafts of January.

"Nickie," said the music teacher, smiling a bright, false smile. Nicoletta hated nicknames but she smiled back anyway. "I called you in separately because this may be a blow. I want you to learn the news here, and not in the hallway in front of the others."

Nicoletta could not imagine what Ms. Quincy was talking about. Yesterday, tryouts for Madrigal Singers had been completed. Ms. Quincy required the members to audition every September and January, even though there was no question as to which sixteen would be chosen. Nicoletta, of course, as she had been for two years, would be one of the four sopranos.

So her first thought was that somebody was

hurt, and Ms. Quincy was breaking it to her. In a childlike gesture of which she was unaware, Nicoletta's hand caught the left side of her hair and wound it around her throat. The thick, shining gold turned into a comforting rope.

"The new girl," said Ms. Quincy. "Anne-Louise." Ms. Quincy looked at the chalkboard on which a music staff had been drawn. "She's wonderful," said Ms. Quincy. "I'm putting her in Madrigals. You have a good voice, and you're a solid singer, Nickie. Certainly a joy to have in any group. But . . . Anne-Louise has had voice lessons for years."

Nicoletta came close to strangling herself with the rope of her own yellow hair. Madrigals? The chorus into which she had poured her life? The chorus that toured the state, whose concerts were standing room only? The sixteen who were best friends? Who partied and carpooled and studied together as well as sang?

"I'm sorry," said Ms. Quincy. She looked sorry, too. She looked, to use an old and stupid phrase, as if this hurt her more than it hurt Nicoletta. "Since each part is limited to four singers, I cannot have both of you. Anne-Louise will take your place."

The wind of January crept through the one-inch window opening and iced her life. How could she could go on with high school if she were dropped from Madrigals? She had no activity but singing. Her only friends were in Madrigals.

I'll be alone, thought Nicoletta.

A flotilla of lonely places appeared in her mind: cafeteria, bus, hallway, student center.

Her body humiliated her. She became a prickly mass of perspiration: Sweaty hands, lumpy throat, tearful eyes. "Doesn't it count," she said desperately, trying to marshall intelligent arguments, "that I have never missed a rehearsal? I've never been late? I've been in charge of refreshments? I'm the one who finds ushers for the concerts and the one who checks the spelling in the programs?"

"And we'd love to have you keep doing that," said Ms. Quincy. Her smile opened again like a zipper separating her face halves.

For two years Nicoletta had idolized Ms. Quincy. Now an ugly puff of hatred filled her heart instead. "I'm not good enough to sing with you," she cried out, "but you'd love to have me do the secretarial work? I'm sure Anne-Louise has had lessons in that, too. Thanks for nothing, Ms. Quincy!"

Nicoletta ran out of the music room before she broke down into sobbing and had the ultimate humiliation of being comforted by the very woman who was kicking her out. There had been no witnesses yet, but in a few minutes everybody she cared about would know. She, Nicoletta, was not good enough anymore. The standards had been raised.

Nicoletta was just another ordinary soprano.

Nicoletta was out.

There was a narrow turn of hall between the music rooms and the lobby. Nicoletta stood in the dark silence of that space, trying to control her emotions. She could hear familiar laughter — Madrigal friends coming to read the list of the chosen. She thought suddenly of her costume: the lovely crimson gown with the tight waist and the white lace high at the throat, the tiny crown that sat in her yellow hair. People said that the medieval look suited her, that she was beautiful in red. And beautiful she always felt, spun gold, with an angel's voice.

Ms. Quincy followed her into the safety zone of the dark little hall. "Go down to Guidance, now, Nickie," she said in a teachery voice. "Sign up for something else in the Madrigal time slot."

I'll sign up for Bomb-Making, thought Nicoletta. Or Arson.

She did not look at Ms. Quincy again. She walked in the opposite direction from the known voices, taking the long way around the school to Guidance. In this immense high school, with its student body of over two thousand, she was among strangers. You had to find your place in such a vast school, and her place had been Madrigals. With whom would she stand now? With whom would she laugh and eat and gossip?

Of course in the Guidance office they pretended to be busy and Nicoletta had to sit forty minutes until they could fit her in. The chair was orange plastic, hideous and cold, the same color as the repulsive orange kitchen counters in Nicoletta's repulsive new house.

Her parents had gotten in too deep financially. Last autumn, amid tears and recrimination, the Storms family had had to sell the wonderful huge house on Fairest Hill. Oh, how Nicoletta had loved that house! Immense rooms, expanses of windows, layers of decks, acres of closets! She and her mother had poured themselves into decorating it, occupying every shopping hour with the joys of wallpaper, curtains, and accessories.

Now they were in a tiny ranch with ugly, crowded rooms, and Nicoletta was sharing a bedroom with her eleven-year-old sister, Jamie.

In their old house, Jamie had had her own bedroom and bath; Jamie had had three closets just for herself; Jamie had had her own television and *two* extra beds, so she could have sleepovers every weekend.

The ranch house had only two bedrooms, so now Jamie slept exactly six feet from Nicoletta. The seventy-two most annoying inches in the world. Nicoletta had actually liked her sister when they lived in the big house. Now the girls could do nothing except bicker, bait, and fight.

Fairest Hill.

Nicoletta always thought the name came from the fairy tale of Snow White: *Mirror, mirror, on the wall, who is the fairest of them all?*

And in those pretty woods, on top of that gentle sloping hill in that lovely house, she, Nicoletta, had been the fairest of them all.

Now she could not even sing soprano.

It was difficult to know who made her maddest — her parents, for poor planning; the economy, for making it worse; Ms. Quincy, for being rotten, mean, and cruel; or Anne-Louise, for moving here.

Within a few minutes, however, it was the guidance counselor making her maddest. "Let's see," said Mr. Parsons. "The available half-year classes, Nicoletta, are Art Appreciation, Study Skills, Current Events, and Oceanography." He skimmed through her academic files. "I certainly recommend Study Skills," he said severely.

She hated him. I'm not taking Current Events, she thought, because I sit through television news every night from five to seven as it is. I'm not taking Oceanography because deep water is the scariest thing on earth. I'm not taking Study Skills just because he thinks I should. Which leaves Art Appreciation. Art for the nonartistic. Art for the pathetic and left-behind.

"I'm signing you up for Study Skills," said Mr. Parsons.

"No. Art Appreciation."

"If you insist," said Mr. Parsons.

She insisted.

That night, as a break in the fighting with Jamie, Nicoletta received three phone calls from other Madrigal singers.

Rachel, her sidekick, the other first soprano next to whom she had stood for two lovely years was crying. "This is so awful!" she sobbed. "Doesn't Ms. Quincy understand friendship? Or loyalty? Or anything?"

Cathy, an alto so low she sometimes sang tenor, was furious. "I'm in favor of boycotting Madrigals," said Cathy. "That will teach Ms. Quincy a thing or two."

Christo, the lowest bass, and handsomest boy, also phoned.

Everybody, at one time or another, had had a crush on Christopher Hannon. Christopher had grown earlier than most boys: At fifteen he had looked twenty, and now at seventeen he looked twenty-five. He was broad-shouldered and tall and could have grown a beard to his chest had he wanted to. Nicoletta was always surprised that she and Christo were the exact same age.

"Nickie," said Christo, "this is terrible. We've all argued with Ms. Quincy. She's sick, that's what I say. Demented."

Nicoletta felt marginally better. At least her friends had stood by her and perhaps would get Ms. Quincy to change her mind and dump this horrible Anne-Louise.

"I have to take Art Appreciation instead," she said glumly.

Christo moaned. "Duds," he told her.

"I know."

"Be brave. We'll rescue you. This Anne-Louise cannot possibly sing like you, Nickie."

She entered the Art Appreciation room the following day feeling quite removed from the pathetic specimens supposed to be her class-mates. Christo, Cathy, Rachel, and her other friends would turn this nightmare around. In a day or so she'd be back rehearsing like always, with a cowed and apologetic Ms. Quincy.

Without interest, Nicoletta took her new text and its companion workbook and sat where she was told, in the center of the room.

A quick survey of the other students told her she had laid eyes on none of these kids before. It was not a large class, perhaps twenty, half boys, which surprised her a little. Did they really want to appreciate art, or were they, too, refusing to take Study Skills?

The teacher, a Mr. Marisson, of whom she had never even heard let alone met, showed slides. Nicoletta prepared to go to sleep, which was her usual response to slides.

But as the room went dark, and the kids around her became shadows of themselves, her eye was caught not by the van Gogh or the Monet painting on the screen but by the profile of the boy in front of her, one row to her left.

He had the most mobile face she had ever seen. Even in the dusk of the quiet classroom, she could see him shift his jaw, lower and lift his eyes, tighten and relax his lips. Several times he lifted a hand to touch his cheek, and he touched it in a most peculiar fashion — as if he were exploring it. As if it belonged to somebody else, or as if he had not known, until this very second, that he even had a cheek.

She was so fascinated she could hardly wait for the slide show to end.

"Well, that's the end of today's lecture," said Mr. Marisson, flipping the lights back on.

The boy remained strangely dark. It was as if he cast his own shadow in his own space. His eyelashes seemed to shade his cheeks, and his cheeks seemed full of hollows. His hair was thick and fell onto his face, sheltering him from stares.

Nicoletta, who had never had an art-type thought in her life, wanted to paint him.

How weird! she thought. Maybe Mr. Marisson put him in the class just to inspire us. Perhaps this is how van Gogh and Monet got started, emotionally moved by a stranger's beautiful profile.

Never had the word *stranger* seemed so apt. There was something genuinely strange about the boy. Essentially different. But what was it?

Nicoletta could not see straight into his eyes. He kept them lowered. Not as if he were shy but as if he had other things to look at than his surroundings.

Class ended.

People stood.

Nicoletta watched the boy. He did not look

her way nor anybody else's. He did not seem aware of anyone. He left the room with a lightness of step that did not fit his body: His body was more like Christo's, yet his walk might have been a dancer's.

Nicoletta rarely initiated friendships. She tended to let friendship come to her, and it always had: through classmates or seatmates, through group lessons or neighbors. But she wanted to look into this boy's eyes, and unless she spoke to him she would not have the privilege.

Privilege? she thought. What a strange word to use! What do I mean by that? "Hi," she said to his departing back. "I'm Nicoletta."

The boy did not register her voice. He did not turn. He might have been deaf. Perhaps he was deaf. Perhaps that was his mystery; his closure from the rest. Perhaps he really was hidden away inside his silent mind.

She stopped walking but he did not.

In a few moments he vanished from sight, blending with crowds and corridors.

After school, Nicoletta saw Christo, Cathy, Rachel, and several of the others. She ran up to them. They would have spoken to Ms. Quincy again. She could hardly wait for their report.

"Hey, Nickie," said Christo. He rubbed her

shoulders and kissed her hair. Affection came easily to Christo. He distributed it to all the girls and they in turn were never without a smile or a kiss for him. But that was all there was. Christo never offered more, and never took more.

Nor did he say a word about the first Madrigal rehearsal in which Anne-Louise, and not Nicoletta, sang soprano.

"So?" said Nicoletta teasingly, keeping her voice light. She was mostly talking to Rachel, her sidekick. Her fellow sufferer in soprano jokes. (Question: A hundred dollars is lying on the ground. Who takes it — the dumb soprano or the smart soprano? Answer: The dumb soprano, of course. There's no such thing as a smart soprano.)

Rachel looked uncomfortable.

Cathy looked embarrassed.

Even Christo, who was never nervous, looked nervous.

Finally Rachel made a confused gesture with her hands, like birds fluttering. Awkwardly, she mumbled, "Anne-Louise is really terrific, Nicoletta. She has the best voice of any of us. She is — well — she's — " Rachel seemed unable to think of what else Anne-Louise might be.

"She's Olympic material," said Christo.

Rachel managed giggles. "There's no soprano divison in the Olympics, Christo."

But it was very clear. Anne-Louise was miles better than Nicoletta. Nicoletta was not going to get back in. She was not going to be a Madrigal again. Her friends had put no arguments before Ms. Quincy.

"But come with us to Keyboard, Nickie," said Rachel quickly. "There's so much to talk about. You have to tell us about Art Appreciation. I mean, is it wall-to-wall duds, or what?"

Keyboard was the city's only ice-cream parlor with a piano. Perhaps the world's only ice-cream parlor with a piano. For years and years, before Nicoletta was even born, the high school Madrigals had hung out there, singing whenever they felt like it. They sang current hits and ancient tunes, they sang Christmas carols and kindergarten rounds, they sang rock or country or sixteenth-century love songs. In between, they had sundaes, milk shakes, or Cokes, and stuck quarters in the old-fashioned jukebox with its glittering lights and dated music.

Okay, thought Nicoletta, trying to breathe, trying to accept the slap in the face of Anne-Louise's superiority. We're still friends, I can still —

Anne-Louise joined the group.

She was an ordinary-looking girl, with dull brown hair and small brown eyes. But the other singers did not look at her as if *they* saw anything ordinary. They were full of admiration.

She'll wear my crimson gown, thought Nicoletta. She'll put my sparkling crown in her plain hair. She'll sing my part.

Christo rubbed Anne-Louise's shoulders and kissed her hair exactly as he had Nicoletta's. Anne-Louise bit her lip with embarrassment and pleasure, and said, "Are you sure you want me along?"

"Of course we do!" the rest chorused. "You're a Madrigal now."

And I'm not, thought Nicoletta.

Rachel and Cathy protested, but Nicoletta did not go to Keyboard with them. She claimed she had to help her mother at home. They knew it was a lie, but it certainly made things easier for everybody. With visible gratitude, the new arrangement of Madrigals left in their new lineup.

Nicoletta headed for the school bus, which she rarely took. Christo had a van and usually ferried Madrigals wherever he went. But she did not get on the bus after all.

Walking purposefully down the road, knowing his destination, was the dark and silent boy from Art Appreciation.

The high school was not located for walking home. It had been built a decade ago in a rural area, so that it could be wrapped in playing fields of the most impressive kind. No student lived within walking distance. Yellow buses awaiting their loads snaked around two roads, slowly filling with kids from every corner of the city.

Yet the boy walked.

And Nicoletta, because she was lost, followed him.

Chapter 2

The first two blocks of following the boy meant nothing; anybody could reasonably walk down the wide cement.

But then the boy turned, and strode down a side street, stepping on every frozen puddle and cracking its ice. DEAD END said the sign at the top of the street. Nicoletta had never even noticed the street. The boy surely knew everybody on his street, and he would also know that she did not live there, had no business walking there. That she had no destination at the DEAD END.

At no other moment in her life would she have continued. Nicoletta was conventional. She was comfortable with social rules and did not break them, nor care to be around people who did.

But all the rules of her life had been broken that day. She had lost her circle, her pleasure.

She had been found lacking, and not only that, she had been replaced by someone better.

The sick humiliation in her heart was so painful that she found herself distanced from the world. The rules were hard to remember and not meaningful when she did remember them. She was facing a terrible empty time in which the group she loved forgot her. If she filled the time by going home, she'd have a crabby sister, a small house, and a nervous mother. She'd have television reruns played too loud, a fattening snack she didn't need, and homework she couldn't face.

So Nicoletta crossed the road, and followed the boy down the little lane.

She had his attention now. An odd, keep-your-back-turned attention. He didn't look around at her. At one point he paused, and stood very still. She matched him. He walked on; she walked on. He walked faster for a while; she did, too. Then he slowed down. So did Nicoletta.

Her head and mind felt light and airy. She felt as if she might faint, or else fly away.

She was mesmerized by the task of making her feet land exactly when his did. He had long strides. She could not possibly cover as much ground. She was carrying her books, hugging them in her arms, and they grew heavy. She hardly noticed. Her head was swimming and there was nothing in the universe but the rhythm of their walking.

The houses ended.

The road narrowed.

The trees that had neatly stayed inside hedges and yards now arched over the street. Latticed, bare branches fenced off the sky. In summer this would be a green tunnel. In winter it was grim and mean.

The asphalt ended. The road became dirt ruts.

Nicoletta would have said there were no dirt roads in the entire state, let alone this city. Where could the boy be going?

Trees grew as closely as fence posts. Prickly vines wrapped the edge of the woods as viciously as concertina wire. Stone walls threaded through the naked woods, the lost farms of early America. For a moment, she felt their souls: the once-breathing farmers, the vanished field hands, the dead wives, and buried children.

At the end of the dirt lane, an immense boulder loomed like a huge altar from some old-world circle of stones.

Nicoletta had the strangest sensation that the stone greeted the boy. That the stone, not the boy, changed expression. They knew each other.

Nicoletta kept coming.

Some boys would have readied for combat. They would have slipped into the athletic stance used for obstructing or catching. This boy was simply there.

Very, very slowly he turned to see whose feet had been matching his, what person had trespassed on his road. Dark motionless eyes, falling heavy hair, smooth quiet features. Not a word. Not a gesture.

People often asked Nicoletta if her shining gold hair was really hers. They often asked her if her vivid green eyes were really hers. The general assumption was that extremely blonde hair and very green eyes must be the result of dye and contact lenses. She hated being asked if parts of her body were really hers.

And yet she wanted to ask this boy — *Is that really you?* There was something so different about him. As if he wore a mask to be pulled off.

There were about twenty paces between them. Neither he nor she attempted to narrow the distance.

"Hi," she said at last. She struggled for a smile, but fear gave her a twitch instead.

He did not ask her what she was doing, nor where she was going.

"I followed you," she said finally.

He nodded.

A flush of shame rose up on her face. She was a fool. She was utterly pathetic. "It was just something to do," she offered him.

Still his face did not move.

She struggled to find explanations for her ridiculous behavior. "I had a bad day. I lost all my friends. So — you were walking — and I walked, too — and here we are."

His face did not change.

"Where's your house?" she said desperately.

At last he spoke. But he did not tell her where his house was. He said softly, "You can't have lost *all* your friends." His voice was like butter: soft and golden. She loved his voice.

"No," she agreed. "Probably not. It just feels like it. It turns out I'm not as important as I thought."

He said, "I'll walk you back to the road while you tell me about it."

She told him about it.

He simply nodded. His expression never changed. It was neither friendly nor hostile, neither sorry for her nor annoyed with her. He was just there. She wondered what his mouth would look like smiling. What his mouth would feel like kissing.

Nicoletta talked.

He listened.

She poured out her feelings as if he were her psychiatric counselor and she was paying by the hour. She had to face this boy tomorrow, and every day for the rest of the school year! And yet here she was describing the workings of her heart and soul, as if he were a friend, as if he could be trusted.

It was horrifically cold. She had not worn clothing for a hike in the outdoors. She shifted her books, trying to wrap her cold hands inside one another.

The boy took off his long scarf, which was plain, thin black wool, with no fringe and no pattern. He wrapped it gently around her freezing ears, brought the ends down and tucked them around her icy fingers. The wool was warm with his heat. She wanted to have the scarf forever.

She had to know more about him. She wanted to see him with his family, standing in his yard. She wanted to see him in his car and in his kitchen. She wanted to see him wearing jeans and wearing bathing trunks.

"Will you be able to get home from here?" he asked instead. They were standing next to the bright yellow DEAD END sign. A few hundred yards ahead, traffic spun its endless circuit.

She could not let their time together end. In fact, standing with him, they did not seem to be in normal time; they were in some other time; a wide, spacious ancient time. "Were you just going for a hike or do you live down there?" Nicoletta said.

He regarded her steadily. "It's a shortcut," he said finally.

He's very, very rich, thought Nicoletta. He lives on an immense estate by the ocean. Acres of farm and forest between us and his circular drive. Perhaps his mother is a famous movie star and they live under another name. She said, "I'm Nicoletta Storms."

"Nicoletta," he repeated. How softly he sounded each consonant. How romantic and European it sounded on his lips. Antique and lyrical. Not the way her classmates said it, getting the long name over with. Or switching without permission to Nickie.

"What's your name?" she said.

For a while she thought he would not tell her; that even giving out his name to a classmate was too much personal expression for him. Then he said, "Jethro."

"Jethro?" she repeated. "What an odd name!

Are you named for an ancestor?"

He actually smiled. She was lifted up on that smile like a swallow on a gust of summer wind. His smile was beautiful; it was wonderful; it was buried treasure, and she, Nicoletta, had uncovered it.

Their city was one of the oldest on the East Coast. She had never previously met a native, but there had to be some. Perhaps Jethro was a descendant of the *Mayflower*. That was the kind of name they gave boys back then. Jethro, Truth, Ephraim.

"Ancestors," he agreed. The smile slowly closed, leaving behind only a sweet friendliness.

"How did you like Art Appreciation?" she said. She did not want to stop talking. "Do you know a lot about art or were the slides new to you?"

"Everything is new to me," the boy answered, and gave away the first tiny clue. Slightly, he emphasized *everything*. As if not just art were new — but everything. The world.

"Let's have lunch together tomorrow," she said.

He stared at her, eyes and mouth flaring in astonishment. And blushed. "Lunch," repeated Jethro, as if unfamiliar with it.

"Meet me in the cafeteria?" said Nicoletta. She wanted to kiss him. Rachel would have. Rachel would have stood on her tiptoes, leaned forward, and kissed long and slow, even the first time. Rachel felt kissing was the world's best hallway activity. Teachers were always telling Rachel to chill out.

Instead the boy touched her face with his fingertips.

And Nicoletta, indeed, chilled.

It was not the hand of a human.

Chapter 3

"Of course he's a human," said her sister Jamie. Jamie was absolutely disgusted with the end of the story. "Nick, you blew it. I cannot believe you turned around and ran!" Jamie was always convinced that she would handle any situation whatsoever a hundred times better than her older sister. Here was yet more proof.

Nicoletta hated defending herself to a child of eleven. But it happened constantly. There was no decision Nicoletta made, including, of course, being born, which met with her sister's approval. "I was scared."

Jamie flung up her hands in exasperation. "If you had enough guts to follow him into the dark and dank and dreary woods . . ."

"They weren't dark or dank or dreary. The sun was shining. There was still snow on the ground in the forest. It was more silver than dark."

"My *point*," said Jamie, with the immense disgust of younger sisters who were going to get things *right* when *they* started dating, "is that he started talking to you! Flirting with you. You even invited him to meet you for lunch. Running away from him was stupid, stupid, stupid, stupid, stupid."

Their father said, "Jamie. Please. You are entitled to your opinion, but saying it once is enough."

The worst thing about this minihouse was the way they had to function in each other's laps. There was no privacy. All conversations and confrontations became family property. Nicoletta thought of their lovely house on Fairest Hill, and how she should have had an entire suite in which to be alone and consider her — well, Jamie was right — her stupidity.

"Besides," said their mother, "of course the boy's hands were cold. You'd been in the woods for hours and he didn't have any gloves on and it's January." Mother sniffed. She did not like fantasy, and when the girls were quite small, and liked to make things up, their mother put a stop to it in a hurry. "Not human," repeated Mrs. Storms irritably. "Really, Nicoletta."

Nicoletta had told them about Jethro because it was easier than telling them about Madrigals. She could not bring herself to say that part out loud. *I'm not in it anymore. You won't go to concerts anymore. You won't have to iron my beautiful medieval gown ever again. Somebody else — somebody named Anne-Louise — gets to dress up and sing like an angel and hear the applause from now on.*

"Speaking as the only man in this family, . . ." said Nicoletta's father. He looked long and carefully at his hands, as if reading the backs instead of the palms. "I want to say that if some girl followed me home, walked after me for miles through the woods, and told me she had a crush on me, and then I walked her all the way back to the main road, I would certainly have been hoping for a kiss. And if instead of throwing her arms around me, the girl *fled* . . . well, Nickie, I would feel I'd done something incredibly stupid or had turned out to be repulsive close up. I'd want to change schools in the morning. I'd never want to have to face that girl again."

Wonderful, thought Nicoletta, wanting to weep. Now I'll never see him again.

She struggled with tears. In the other house, she could have wept alone. In this one, she had witnesses. The small-minded part of her tried to hold her parents responsible, and hate them instead of herself, for being a complete dummy and running from Jethro.

She remembered the cold touch of his hands. I don't care what Mother says, thought Nicoletta. Jethro's hands were not normal. He scared me. There really was something strange about him. Something terribly wrong, something not quite of this world. I felt it through his skin. I can still feel it. Even though I have washed my hands, I can still feel it.

"So," said her father, his voice changing texture, becoming rich and teasing, "what'll we do tonight, Nickie? Want me to play my fiddle?"

Jamie got right into it. Nothing brought her more satisfaction than annoying her big sister. "Or we could slice up a turnip," Jamie agreed. "That would be fun."

Right up until high school, Nicoletta had loved the *Little House* books. How unfair that she had to live now where the family could go to McDonald's if they got hungry, check out a video if they got bored, and turn the thermostat up if they got chilled. A younger Nicoletta had prayed every night to fall through a time warp and arrive on the banks of Plum Creek with Mary and Laura. She wanted a covered wagon and a sod house and, of course, she wanted to meet Almanzo and marry him. In middle school, Nicoletta had decided to learn everything Laura had to learn; quilting, pie making, knitting, stomping on hay. Nicoletta's mother, who hated needlework and bought frozen pies, could not stand it. "You live in the twentieth century and that's that. Ma Ingalls," Nicoletta's mother said, "would have been thrilled to live like you. Warm in winter, snow never coming through the cracks, fresh fruit out of season."

When she was Jamie's age, Nicoletta had made her fatal error. "Daddy never gets out his fiddle and sings songs for me when it's snowing outside," she'd said.

Her father laughed for years. He was always making fiddle jokes.

The second fatal error came shortly after, when Nicoletta tried eating raw sliced turnip because the Ingalls considered it a snack. Nicoletta's mother had never in her life even bought a turnip because, she said, "Even the word gives me indigestion."

Only last Christmas, Nicoletta's stocking had included a raw turnip and a paring knife. "Instead of potato chips," said the card. "Love from Santa on the Prairie." It was Jamie's handwriting.

Nicoletta's *Little House* obsession ended with Madrigals: The singing, the companionship of a wonderful set of boys and girls from tenth to twelfth grade, the challenge of memorizing the difficult music filled Nicoletta the way her pioneer fantasies once had.

She thought of her life as divided by these two: the *Little House* daydream years and the Madrigal reality years.

And now Madrigals were over.

She was not a Madrigal singer. She was just another soprano, good enough only for the ordinary non-audition chorus.

Unwillingly, Nicoletta looked at the photograph of herself on the mantel. Every few years these photos were replaced, when the old one began to seem dated and ridiculous. Nicoletta's portrait had been taken only last fall, and she stood slim and beautiful in her long satin skirt, crimson fabric cascading from her narrow waist, white lace like sea froth around her slender throat. Her yellow hair had just been permed, and twisted like ribbons down to her shoulders. In her hair glittered a thread of jewels. She seemed like a princess from another age, another continent, dressed as a Nicoletta should be dressed.

Now she hated the portrait. People would come to the house — Rachel, Cathy, Christo — and there it would sit, pretending nothing had changed.

I don't want this life! thought Nicoletta, her throat filling with a detestable lump. Who needs high school? It hurts too much. I don't measure up. I'm not musical and I'm a jerk who runs away from boys and makes them wish they attended school in another town. I don't care what my mother says. Laura Ingalls had it good. Blizzards, starvation, three-hundred-mile hikes, scary badgers, and flooding creeks.

She thought of Jethro. His profile. His odd, silent darkness. His quiet listening while she poured out her pain.

"I got kicked out of Madrigals," Nicoletta said abruptly. "Ms. Quincy tried everybody out again, and a new girl named Anne-Louise is better than I am, so I'm out and she's in and I don't want to talk about it."

Chapter 4

She did not dream of Madrigals.

She dreamed of Jethro.

When she awoke much earlier than usual it was quickly and cleanly, with none of the usual muddleheaded confusion of morning. She arose swiftly and dressed without worry.

That in itself amazed Nicoletta. Choosing clothing normally took her half an hour the night before, and then in the morning half an hour to decide that last night's choice would not do, and yet another half hour to find clothing that would fit the day after all. It was amazing how an outfit that had been absolutely the right choice for last Thursday was never the right choice for the following Thursday.

She did not brush her hair; Nicoletta's permed curls were too tight for a brush to manage. She ran her fingers through it, fluffing and smoothing at the same time. She put on a simple black turtleneck, a plain silver necklace, and narrow dangling silver earrings. She wore a skirt she rarely touched: It had two layers, a tight black sheath covered by a swirl of filmy black gauze. The skirt was dressy, but the plain turtleneck brought it down to school level.

She did not look romantic. She looked as if she were in mourning. For Madrigals? Or for the boy she would not meet for lunch after all?

Jethro.

Her school bus did not pass the strange little country lane she had never before noticed. When she got off the bus, she looked for him, but she had never seen him wandering around the school before, and she did not see him now. In the halls, her eyes scanned the taller people, searching for him, both aching and scared that she would actually spot him.

First-period history, she covered a page in her notebook with the name Jethro. It looked historical. Where did it come from? It sounded Biblical. Who was Jethro and what had he done? She wrote it in script, in plain print, in decorated print, in open block letters. She wrote it backhand and she wrote it billboard style, enclosed in frames.

Second-period English, the other person in her life with an O name sat beside her. Christo. "Hi, Nick," he said cheerfully.

She had always admired Christopher's endless cheer. It seemed an admirable way to face life: ever up, ever smiling, ever optimistic and happy.

Now it seemed shallow. Annoying.

Am I comparing him to Jethro or am I angry with him for still being in Madrigals, for making peace in a single day with the fact that I have been replaced? "Hi, Christo," she said. He had not even noticed how she skipped a beat before answering him.

The teacher had visited England last year and, sad to say, taken along his camera and several million rolls of film. Today he had yet more slides of where famous English authors had lived and gone to college and gardened. It was the gardening that most amazed Nicoletta. Who could possibly care what flowers bloomed in the gardens that no longer belonged to the famous — and now dead — authors? In fact, who could possibly have cared back when the famous authors were alive?

Nicoletta sat quietly while the teacher bustled — fixing his slides, flipping switches, lowering screens, focusing.

Christo murmured in her ear. "Nicoletta?"

His use of her whole name startled her. She turned to look at him, but his face was so close to her they touched cheeks instead.

"There's a dance Friday," whispered Christo. "I know it's late to be asking, but would you go with me?"

Nicoletta was stunned. Christo? Who showed affection to everybody equally? Christo, who never appeared to notice whether he was patting the shoulder of Nicoletta or Rachel or Cathy, or — now — Anne-Louise? Christo, for whom girls seemed to be just one generic collection of the opposite sex?

Christo. Who was certainly the best-looking and most-yearned-for boy in school.

She absolutely knew for a fact that Christo had never had a date.

One of the things Madrigals spared you was dating. You had your crowd; you had your portable group. You had people with whom to laugh and share pizza. Rarely did any of them pair up, either within or without the group.

On the big white screen at the front of the class, appeared a dazzling slide from inside a cathedral. Great gray stones held up a gleaming and terrifying stained glass window. The glass people were in primary colors: scarlet arms, blue gowns, golden heads. If Jethro were hers, she, too, would be as vivid as that: Together they would blind the eye.

If I go to a dance with Christo, how can

Jethro ask me out? Nicoletta thought. I want to be with Jethro.

Christo's hand covered hers. She dropped her eyes, and then her whole head, staring down at his hand. His hand was afraid. She could feel uncertainty in the way he touched her. Christo, who touched everybody without ever thinking of it, or knowing he was doing it, was fearful of touch.

The slide changed and a gargoyle appeared on the screen. Carved stone. An unknowable man-creature stared out from oak leaves that were both his hair and his beard, which grew into him and, at the same time, grew out of him. *It's Jethro*, thought Nicoletta.

"That sounds wonderful," she murmured, mostly to Christo's hand. "I'd love to go. What dance is it?"

"Fund-raiser," said Christo. "It'll be at Top o' the Town."

A famous restaurant where in years past her father had taken her mother for special occasions, like Valentine's Day or their anniversary. Nicoletta had never been there. It was not a place that people wasted on children.

I'm not a child, thought Nicoletta. I'm a young woman, and Christo knows it. Christo wants me. He doesn't want any of the others.

Not Rachel or Cathy. And not this Anne-Louise. But me.

She looked nervously at Christo in the half-dark of the classroom. He was truly nervous. His easy smile puckered in and out. He had needed the dark to do this; he had chosen a place where they could not possibly continue the conversation or else people would hear, and because lights would come on in a moment, and the teacher would begin his lecture.

She was amazed at the discovery that Christo was afraid of anything at all, let alone her.

But when she looked at him, she still saw Jethro.

Who is Jethro? thought Nicoletta, that he has consumed me. Who am I, that I am letting it happen? Mother is right; daydreaming and fantasy are silly and only lead to silly choices. I'll stop right now.

Then came chemistry.
Then came French.
Then came lunch.
And Jethro was there.

He had come. He was waiting. He did mean to meet her.

She saw him from far across the room. Her whole body shivered, and she did not understand him the way she had to her surprise understood Christo. She could not imagine who that person Jethro was. He was as hidden to her as the gargoyle in its mask and crown of oak leaves.

She could not smile. There was something frightening about this boy who also did not smile, but who stared at her in his dark and closed way. She walked toward him, and he moved toward her, exactly as they had in the lane, surrounded by thorns and vines and boulders that spoke.

They were only a table's distance apart when Christo caught Nicoletta's arm.

Nicoletta could not have been more astonished if an army had stopped her. She had thought her coming together with Jethro was inevitable, was destined, was a part of the history of the world before it had even happened. And yet Christo, who touched anything and whose touch meant nothing, had stopped it from happening.

"I'm over here, Nickie," Christo said eagerly. "You didn't see me."

She looked up at Christo.

She looked back at Jethro.

Jethro had already turned. There was no face at all, let alone the smile she wanted.

There was only a back. A man's broad back, unbent, uncaring. Departing.

Jethro! her heart cried after him.

But this time she did not follow him. She sat with Christo, and within moments everybody that Christo and Nicoletta knew had learned that Christo had arranged his first date ever. With Nicoletta.

The attention was better even than Madrigals. Better even than solos or applause.

And she didn't want it.

She wanted Jethro.

Chapter 5

After lunch, Jethro did not come to Art Appreciation.

Nicoletta stared, stunned, at his vacant seat.

"Is Jethro absent?" asked the teacher.

"He was here at lunch," said Nicoletta. Her lips were numb.

"He's cutting," said Mr. Marisson disapprovingly. He pressed down hard with his pencil in the attendance book.

He cut class because I cut him, thought Nicoletta. Oh Jethro! I was going to explain it to you — I was going to —

But what was there to explain? She had behaved terribly. She had arranged to meet Jethro in the cafeteria. He had done so and then what had she done? Walked off with another boy.

His empty seat mesmerized her as much as the occupied seat had.

His name filled her head and her heart, as if it really were her heartbeat: *Jeth-ro. Jeth-ro.*

Like a nursery rhyme her head screamed Jeth-ro, Jeth-ro. And of course, after school up came Chris-to, Chris-to, smiling and eager and offering her a ride home.

It was by car that romance was established. When a boy gave you rides, or you gave him rides, it meant either you lived next door and had no choice, or you were seeing each other. If you didn't want the school to make that interpretation, you had to fill your car with extras. Christo had always filled his van with extras. But now he stood alone. He must have told them already that they had to find another way home. For the usual van crowd was not there and the much-complimented Anne-Louise was not in evidence.

But Nicoletta could not go home with Christo.

She had to find Jethro. She had to go back down that lane, follow that shortcut he took to his house, and locate him.

How many lies it took to make Christo go on without her! How awful each one of them was. Because, of course, he had to believe her lies, or else know that she was dumping him. Know that she did not want to be alone with him and go for a ride with him.

When you're in love, the possibility that the object of your love has better things to do is the worst of all scenes.

So Christo just smiled uncertainly and said at last, "I'll call you tonight."

"Great," said Nicoletta, smiling, as if it were great.

They did not touch. For Christo it was the not-touching of a crush; physical desire so intense it pulled him back instead of rushing him on. For Nicoletta, it was a heart that lay elsewhere.

But Christo did not know.

Love rarely does.

Nicoletta waited inside the lobby until she saw Christo's van disappear.

And then she gathered her books and her belongings and ran out the school doors, up the road, across the street, and down the quiet lane.

There was no Jethro ahead of her. Of course not. He had left at noon, abandoning his lunch and his classes. Because of her.

She ran, and was quickly out of breath.

Today there was no sun. The last of the snow had vanished into the brown earth. The words Jamie had used were now, horribly, the right ones. These woods were dank and dark.

At the end of the lane she saw the boulder,

big and scarred and motionless. Of course it's motionless, she said to herself, it's a rock. They're always motionless.

And yet the huge stone sat there as if it had just returned from some dreadful errand.

The stone waited for her.

It's a rock, she said to herself. Put there by a glacier. That's all it is.

She might have come to the end of the world instead of the end of a little dirt road. The sky lay like an unfriendly blanket over a woods that was silent as tombs.

She clung to her books as if to a shield. As if spears might come from behind that great gray stone and pierce her body. It took all her courage to edge around the boulder.

On the other side of the rock was a footpath of remarkable straightness. In a part of the world that was all ups and downs, crevices and hills, rocky cliffs and hidden dells, here was an utterly flat stretch of land and a trail from a geometry test: The quickest way between two points is a straight line.

What are the two points? thought Nicoletta. Is his house at the other end?

Jethro, she thought. I'm coming. Where are you? What will I say to you when I find you? Why am I looking?

She walked down the trail.

When she looked back over her shoulder, the boulder was watching her.

She whimpered, and picked up speed, running again, trying to turn a corner, so the stone could not see her. But there were no corners and no matter how far she ran, the stone was still there.

The silence was complete.

She could hear nothing of the twentieth century. No motors, no turnpikes. No doors slamming, no engines revving, no planes soaring.

The only sounds were her own sounds, trespassing in this dark and ugly place.

Abruptly the trail descended. She heaved a sigh of relief as mounded earth blocked her from the terrible boulder. She wondered where she would come out, and if perhaps she could return to her own home from another direction. She did not want to go back on that path.

The trees ended, and the vines ceased crawling.

The ground was clear now, and the path became a narrow trail on top of a man-made earthen embankment. Suddenly there were lakes on each side of her, deep, black, soundless lakes with a thin, crackled layer of ice. She could go neither left nor right. Not once had there been a choice, a turning place, a fork in the road. Now she could not even blunder off into the meadow or the forest, because the trail was the only place to put a foot.

The trail ended.

She could not believe it.

It had stopped. Stopped dead. It simply did not go on.

In front of her was a rock face, a hundred feet high. Behind her lay the narrow path and the twin lakes.

She was being watched. She could feel eyes everywhere, assessing her, wondering what she would do next. They were not friendly eyes.

She wanted to scream Jethro's name, but even drawing a breath seemed like a hostile act in this isolated corner. What would a shout do? What horrible creatures would appear if she screamed?

She put a hand out so she could rest against the rock face, and her hand went right through the rock.

She yanked her hand back to the safety of her schoolbook clasp. Tears of terror wet her cheeks. Mommy, she thought. Daddy. Jamie. I want to go home. I don't want to be here.

It was a cave.

It was so black, so narrowly cut into the cliff, that at first she had not seen it. It was nothing natural. It had been chipped by some ancient tool. The opening was a perfect rectangle. She did not even have to duck her head walking in.

The wonder was that she did walk in.

Even as she was doing it, she was astonished at herself. She — a girl who hated the dark, or being alone in the dark, or even thinking of the dark — was voluntarily entering an unknown cave. Was she so terrorized that terror had become an anesthetic, flattening her thoughts? Or was she finally getting a grip on her ridiculous, fabricated fears and handling them like an adult?

She stepped into the cave.

She had expected absolute black darkness, especially with her own body blocking whatever weak sunlight might penetrate at this angle, but the cave walls themselves seemed to emanate light. They were smooth and polished like marble. She slid a bare hand over them and the texture was rich and satisfying. The cave was not damp or batlike. It seemed more like an entrance to a magnificent home, where she would find beautiful tapestries and perhaps a unicorn.

She followed a shaft of light. Even when the cave turned and the opening to the world behind her disappeared. Even when the cave went down and she had to touch the wall for support.

Part of her knew better.

Part of her was screaming, *Stop this! Get out! Go home! Think!*

But more of her was drawn on, as all humans are drawn to danger: the wild and impossible excitement of the unknown and the unthinkable.

She did not know how far she went into the cave. She did not know how many minutes she spent moving in, deeper in, farther from the only opening she knew.

She paused for breath, and in that moment the cave changed personality. Gone was the elegant marble. In a fraction of a second, the walls had turned to dripping horrors.

Holes and gaping openings loomed like death traps.

Whistling sounds and flying creatures filled her ears and her hair.

She whirled to run out, but the cave went dark.

Completely, entirely dark.

Her scream filled the cave, echoing off the many walls, pouring out the holes like some burning torch.

"Jethro!" she screamed. "Jethro!"

She touched a wall and it was wet with slime. She fell to her knees, scraping them on something, and then . . . the something moved beneath her.

She was not falling. The earth was lifting, arranging itself against her, attaching itself to her. She actually tried to fall. Anything to free herself from the surface of the underworld that clung to her, sucking like the legs of starfish.

"Jethro!" she screamed again.

Tentacles of slime and dripping stone wrapped themselves around her body.

I will die here. Nobody will know. Who could ever find me here? Nobody has been in this cave in a hundred years. This is some leftover mine from olden days. Abandoned. Forgotten.

And Jethro — he could live anywhere. What on earth had made her think that the walk through the woods necessarily led to Jethro's house? What on earth had made her think that she would find Jethro by following a path that led only to a cave?

Nothing on earth, she thought. Something in hell. This is an opening to some other, terrible world.

The creatures of that other world were surfacing, and surrounding her, dragging her down with them.

"Jethro!" she screamed again, knowing that there were no creatures, there was only a mine shaft; she must stay calm, she must find her own way out. She must stop fantasizing. She must be capable.

She tried to remember the calming techniques that Ms. Quincy used before Madrigal concerts. Breathe deeply over four counts. Shake your fingertips. Roll your head gently in circles.

It turned out that you had to be pretty calm to start with in order to attempt calming techniques. Screams continued to pour from her mouth, as if somebody else occupied her.

I'm the only one here, Nicoletta told herself. I must stop screaming. This is how people die in the wilderness. They panic. I must not panic. I am the only one here and —

She was wrong.

She was not the only one there.

The cave filled with movement and smell and she was picked up, actually held in the air, by whatever else was in the cave with her.

A creature from that other, lower, darker, world.

Its skin rasped against hers like saw grass. Its stink was unbreathable. Its hair was dead leaves, crisping against each other and breaking off in her face. Warts of sand covered it, and the sand actually came off on her, as if the creature were half made out of the cave itself.

She could not see any of the thing, only feel and smell it.

It was holding her, as if in an embrace.

Would it consume her? Did it have a mouth and jaws?

Would it carry her down to wherever it lay?

Would it line its nest with her, or feed her to its young?

She was no longer screaming. Its terrible stench took too much from her lungs; she could not find the breath to scream, only to gag.

And then it carried her up — not down.

Out — not in.

And spoke.

English.

Human English.

"Never come back," it said, its voice as deep and dark as the cave itself.

She actually laughed, hysteria crawling out of her as the screams had moments before. "I won't," she said. I'm having a conversation with a monster, she thought.

"It isn't safe," it said.

"I could tell."

The walls became smooth and they glowed. The beautiful patterns of the shiny entrance surrounded them.

She looked at what held her and screamed again in horror. She had never had such a nightmare, never been caught in such a hideously vivid dream. The features of the thing were humanoid, but the flesh dripped, like cave walls.

Old sayings came true: There was literally light at the end of the tunnel.

Real light. Sunlight. Daylight!

She flung herself free of the thing's terrible embrace. Falling, slipping, running all at the same instant, Nicoletta got out of the cave.

Never had a gray sky been so lovely, so free, so perfect.

Never had dark lakes and bleak woods been so appealing, so friendly.

She held up her hands to the real world, incredibly grateful to be back. The sight of her bare hands reminded her she no longer held her schoolbooks.

The thing stood slightly behind the mouth of the cave, so that its shadow but not itself was visible. The books sat neatly in a pile by the opening. Had Nicoletta set them down like that?

"Don't come back," the thing said again, with a sadness so terrible that Nicoletta dissolved from fear into pity. Nicoletta knew what loneliness was, and she heard it in that awful voice.

It lives down there, she thought. It's caught forever in that terrible dark.

How ridiculously petty to be fretting for a larger house and a separate room. She could be sentenced to *this*, whatever this was! She would never have gotten out without this creature's help. She would have died down there.

She felt a strange bond between them, the bond of rescuer and rescued. Her need to run and scream had ended with the sunlight. "Are you alone?" she asked.

"No," it said sadly. "Alone would be better."

What terrible company it must have, to think alone was better.

"Don't come back," it whispered. "Not ever. Don't even think about it. Not ever. *Promise*. Promise me that you will never even think about coming back here."

Chapter 6

A strange and difficult promise. *Don't even think about it.*

A promise not to go back would be easy to keep. Neither wild horses nor nuclear bombs could have made Nicoletta go back.

But not even *think* about it?

Not wonder who or what it was? What sort of life it led?

Not wonder about its name, or gender, or species?

It had saved her life. Who could forget such an event?

A strange evening followed that weird and inexplicable afternoon.

She walked through a house which only that morning she had hated. But how wonderful it was! For it had walls and warmth, lamps and pillows. It had love and parents and food and music.

Her sister did not infuriate her. Jamie actually seemed beautiful and even worthy. She was alive and giggling and pesky, which was how little sisters are meant to be. What did Jamie have to do with caves and monsters?

Nicoletta had always told her family everything. Other girls who said they could not communicate with their families confused Nicoletta. What could they mean? Nicoletta simply arrived home from school and started talking. So did Jamie. So did Mother and Dad. Not communicate?

For the first time in her life, she did not communicate.

She did not tell them about the quiet lane, the staring stone, the straight path, the descending cave. As for the creature who brought her up from the depths, by the time she had reached home, she could no longer believe in him herself. He could have been nothing but an hallucination. She had not known her imagination was so active; in fact, Nicoletta thought of herself as having little or no imagination.

Such a thing could not have happened, and therefore it had not happened.

And so she remained silent, and shared none

of it, and it swelled in her mind, filling her with confusion and disbelief.

Several times she drew a deep breath to begin the story somewhere. Each time she looked away and said nothing. She did not want a lecture on safety. Safety alone could consume weeks of scolding. Just the idea of Nicoletta walking alone into an unknown woods would outrage her parents. But when she told them she walked straight into an abandoned mine shaft — well, please.

But what kind of mine could it have been? Who had mined it? Who had smoothed those lovely walls, and what mineral caused the elegant glow?

A monster lives in it, she imagined herself saying to her father. The monster has cave skin: sand skin: rock skin. It has calcified leaves for hair and crumbling stones for fingers.

It occurred to Nicoletta that her family might just laugh.

She did not want anybody laughing at the creature. It had saved her. It had carried her out.

And yet — she wanted to talk about it. She was a talker and a sharer by nature.

And more than anything, she wanted to go back.

On that very first evening, sitting quietly at

the dining table — while Jamie did geography homework and Nicoletta pretended to do algebra — while her mother balanced the checkbook and her father finished the newspaper — Nicoletta thought — *I want to go back.*

Jethro was familiar with the path. Surely he had followed it to its end at least once. Jethro would not have flinched from entering that shining cavern. He would have walked in as she had.

That's why Jethro didn't want me to follow him any farther, she thought. He's met the monster, too! The monster asked Jethro never to tell either!

In school tomorrow she would ask him about it. She would see if his eyes flickered when she said "cave." It would not be breaking a promise if you talked with a person who already knew.

When the phone rang and it was Christo, Nicoletta could hardly remember who that was. She could barely remember Madrigals, her group of friends and her great loss. Christo wanted to know what color dress she would wear. Nicoletta actually said, "Wear to what?"

Christo laughed uneasily. "The dance Friday, Nicoletta."

She detested rudeness in people. She was ashamed of herself for not having her thoughts where they belonged. Quickly she said, "I was kidding. I'm sorry. It was dumb. I have this lovely pale pink dress. Are you getting me flowers? I adore flowers."

Nobody had ever given her flowers. Why was she implying that she had had the honor often?

Christo said his mother was recommending white. Roses or carnations.

Nicoletta said she would love white roses.

But before her eyes was the blackness of caves.

And inside her mind was a slipperiness. She had a secret now, she who had never had a secret. The secret wanted to be in the front of her mind, consuming her thoughts. She had to push it to the rear, and behave like a normal human being, and flirt with Christo and miss Madrigals and study algebra.

"Let's have lunch again tomorrow," Christo said.

She hesitated. What about Jethro? Well, she would talk to Jethro in Art Appreciation. Or follow him again.

"Yes," she said. "Lunch was fun today." She couldn't even remember lunch today.

And lunch the next day blurred as well.

She had difficulty paying attention to Christo. Everything she did was a fake. She was sufficiently aware to know that, and be appalled at herself. She knew that Christo half-knew.

She knew he was thinking that perhaps this was what girls were like: that easy friendship evaporated, to be replaced by hot and cold flirtation. And she knew that while he was hurt by her distance, he was also fascinated by it. He had never experienced that with a girl; all the girls adored him. Christo was thinking more about Nicoletta than he had ever thought about a girl.

And am I flattered? thought Nicoletta. Am I falling in love with him? Am I even thinking about my first formal dance and my first bouquet?

No.

I am thinking about a boy in art whose last name I do not even know. I am thinking about a cave in which I thought I might die and a monster in whom I no longer believe because there is no such thing as a monster.

Lunch ended and she rushed to Art Appreciation, barely taking time to wave good-bye to Christo.

"He would have kissed you," whispered Rachel as the girls rushed up the stairwell together. "He wanted to kiss you in front of everybody, I can tell. I know these things."

Two days ago, Nicoletta had thought that the loss of her girlfriends in Madrigals would kill her. Now she just wanted Rachel to vanish so that she could concentrate on Jethro.

And because passing period was only three minutes, Rachel had no choice but to vanish, and Nicoletta entered Art Appreciation.

Jethro was present.

She was filled with exuberance. It was like turning into a hot-air balloon. Flames of delight lifted her heart and soul.

"Jethro," she said.

His body stiffened in his seat but he did not turn.

She knelt beside his chair and looked up into his face.

He remained frozen. How perfect he was. Like a statue — sculpture from some Dark Age. She wanted to stroke his face and hair, as if he were artwork himself, and she could study the curves and surfaces.

He relented and looked down at her.

"I'm sorry about lunch," she said, keeping her voice so soft that nobody could share their words. "But I have to talk to you. Something happened yesterday, Jethro. I have to tell you about it."

She stared into his eyes, looking for a clue to his thoughts.

Jethro wet his lips, as if she were frightening him.

"After school?" she said. "Let's walk down the lane together."

He was shocked.

She might have suggested that they bomb a building.

"Just a walk," she whispered. "Just a talk. Please."

He shivered very slightly.

She could not imagine what his thoughts were. His eyes gave her no more clues than a sculpture would give and he used no words.

The teacher cleared his throat. "Uh — Nicoletta? Excuse me?"

She got to her feet, and in the moment before she slid into her seat she stroked the back of Jethro's hand.

He spent the entire class period looking at his hand.

As if nobody had ever touched him before.

Chapter 7

They stood where they had stood before, beside the stone. With Jethro beside her, she was not afraid of the stone. It still seemed alive, as if left over from another world, it held a spirit. A woodland power. But it no longer threatened her.

"And you promised?" said Jethro.

How measured his speech was. How carefully he pondered each word before he actually put it in his mouth and used it. Nicoletta realized that everybody else she knew used speech cheaply: It meant little. To Jethro, every syllable was precious. He squandered nothing.

"I didn't actually make any promises," said Nicoletta. How she wanted to touch him again. But he was more like the stone than like a boy. He was entirely within himself, and only the few spare syllables of speech escaped his control. "I left," explained Nicoletta. "I was afraid."

Jethro nodded. "I can understand that you were afraid." His eyes looked down into an emotional cave of their own.

"I want to go back," said Nicoletta. She felt light and bright, as if she were the flame of a candle.

He was shaken. "Caves are dangerous, Nicoletta." He had never used her name before. She took his hand as if it were her possession, as if they had both agreed that she might have his hand, and again he stared at the way her fingers wrapped around his. He seemed caught in emotion so deep that there were no words for it. Perhaps even a person used to speech, like Nicoletta, could not have explained his emotion.

"Please don't go back," said Jethro. His voice was meant only for her. It was not a whisper, and yet it did not carry; it was intended to travel only as far as her ears and then stop. He sounded as if he had had a lifetime of practice at preventing his speech from being heard. It was the opposite of what anybody else did with speech. "It's dangerous, Nicoletta."

"Then you do know!" she said. "You *have* been in there, Jethro. You know what I'm talking about."

He looked at the stone and drew himself together, becoming more remote, more taut. "I know what you're talking about," he admitted.

"Let's go together," she said. She tried to pull him around the stone to the straight and silken path that lay beyond.

But he did not cooperate. "You must go home," he said. "You must not come this way again."

Nicoletta did not listen to him. She did not want warnings. She wanted Jethro. "Where do you live?" she said. "Tell me where you live!" She explored his fingers with hers, slipping between them, pressing down with her thumb, feeling his bones and sinews.

This is what falling in love is, thought Nicoletta. It's looking at a boy and wanting to know every single thing there is to know about him, and wanting to know every inch of him, and every emotion of him, and every word in him.

Jethro's eyelids trembled, closing down over his eyes as if he could shutter himself away, and then they opened wide, and he stared back into her eyes.

He loves me, too, thought Nicoletta. Still holding his hand in one of hers, she lifted her other hand to his face. As if reading mirrors, he did exactly what she did. Fingertips approached cheeks. Nicoletta and Jethro shivered with the heat of first love's first touch.

His hand slid cupped over her chin and around her face. His fingers went into her hair. He drew the gleaming yellow locks through his fingers, and wound them gently over his palm. "You have beautiful hair," he said in a husky voice. His lips pressed together, coming to a decision, while her lips opened, ready.

Kiss me, thought Nicoletta. Please kiss me. If you kiss me, it will seal this. It will be love. I can tell by the way you're standing here that you want to be in love with me. Kiss me, Jethro!

But a car came slowly, noisily, down the road.

They were jolted by the sudden sight and sound of the vehicle.

This had been a place in which the twentieth century did not come, and now it was driving right up.

She knew the car.

It was Christo's.

Jethro's breathing was ragged. "Do not tell him!" whispered Jethro with a ferocity that frightened her. "You must not tell him!" Nicoletta was stunned by the force of Jethro's command. "You have promised to keep a secret! You must keep the promise, Nicoletta!"

Christo swung out of the van, leaving the motor idling.

"*Promise*," breathed Jethro, with a terrible force, as if his lungs were going to explode.

But she did not answer him.

"Hi, Christo," she said. "Do you know Jethro?"

Christo shook his head. She introduced them, using only first names, since she did not know Jethro's last name. The young men stared at each other warily. Christo extended his right hand. They shook hands, also warily, as if they were about to be contestants in some duel.

"I'm glad you came," said Jethro. His voice calm now, even bland. "Would you mind giving Nicoletta a ride home? She shouldn't be down here. We were arguing about it. The woods are dangerous. Nobody should be in these woods without a compass."

Christo was amazed. "You don't seem like the outdoor type," he said to Nicoletta. "Do you hike? Do you camp?"

"No. Never."

"That's why I told her to stay away," said Jethro. "It's dangerous for somebody who's ignorant about it."

"I love the woods," said Christo happily. "I'll teach you, Nickie. That's what we'll do this

235

weekend! We'll go to the state forest and hike down to the waterfalls! They're so beautiful in winter." Christo led Nicoletta to his van as he gave her a long, lyrical description of frozen waterfalls and gleaming ice.

How easily he used words! Not like Jethro, who could hardly bear to let a syllable out of his mouth. "Nice to have met you," Christo called cheerfully back to Jethro.

How strange romance is, thought Nicoletta. I was following Jethro and Christopher was following me. To Christo this is the beginning of a beautiful romance in which we share the great outdoors. I don't care about the outdoors at all. I don't care about Christo either. I care about Jethro.

And I wonder about the cave.

And the monster.

And the promise that mattered so much.

To whom was I making that promise? she thought suddenly, frowning. To the creature? Or Jethro?

Christo, backing his van down the narrow rutted lane, suddenly lifted his right hand from the wheel and stared at it. He shook his hand slightly.

"What?" said Nicoletta. Her eyes were glued to the place where Jethro had stood. He stood there no longer. He had circled the stone, and must even now be tracing the straight path. Even now Jethro was going toward the cave, on a path that seemed to go nowhere else, a path he had wanted her to promise she would never follow again.

But I will, thought Nicoletta. I will follow Jethro forever.

"There's sand on my hand," said Christo. "That guy's hand was all sandy."

Chapter 8

Never before in her life had Nicoletta intentionally done something stupid and dangerous. Her parents were cautious in all things but money. They had taught Nicoletta and Jamie to steer clear of strangers, to look both ways before crossing streets, to be home before dark. They were full of warnings and guidance, and Nicoletta had spent a lifetime listening carefully and obeying completely.

But not today.

The snow was falling lightly when she left the school building. She had hidden in the library stacks until Christopher had definitely driven away. Hidden among the dusty pages and unread texts until there was not a single soul left in the school whom she knew.

Little homework had been assigned for the night. Nicoletta was able to leave her bookbag in her locker. How strange to be unburdened, to have hands and arms free. She ran all the way, feet flying, hair streaming behind her, heart filled with excitement.

How lovely the woods were, dusted with snow, crisp and clean and pure in the fading afternoon.

The snow was dry and separate. Snowflakes touched her cheeks like kisses.

The road narrowed and she had to slow down, unable to find easy footing on the snow-hidden ruts of the dirt lane. At first she did not even see the boulder; snow had draped it like a cloak. It did not look like a stone, but like an igloo, a place that would be cozy inside. She patted the stone as she rounded it and her glove left a perfect five-fingered print.

On each side of the slim, straight path, the dry weeds stood up like snow bouquets. Ice flowers.

The snow came down more heavily.

There was no sky anymore; just a ceiling of white.

When she came to the place where pools of water lay below each side of the raised pathway, snow had covered the ice, and had Nicoletta not seen the lakes before, she would have thought they were fields; she would have thought it was safe to run over them, and dance upon them.

The cliff wall was hung with frozen water from springs deep in the earth. Snow danced in gusts, spraying against the cliff like surf and falling in drifts at the foot of the rocks.

A piece of the cliff moved toward her.

Nicoletta held out her palm like a crossing guard, as if she could stop an avalanche that way.

It was stone, and yet it walked. It was snow, and yet it bore leaves. It was a person, and yet —

It was the creature.

She could see its eyes now, living pools trapped in that terrible frame.

She could see its feet, formed not so differently from the huge icicles that hung on the cliff: things. Dripping stalagmites from the floor of the cave.

She felt no fear. The snow, falling so gently, so pure and cleanly, seemed protection. Yet snow protected nothing but ugliness. Ugliness it would hide. Filthy city alleys and rusted old cars, abandoned, broken trikes and rotting picnic tables — snow covered anything putrid and turned it to perfect sculpture.

Even the thing, the monstrous thing that had stank and dripped and scraped — it was perfect in its softly rounded snowy wrap.

"Go away," it growled. "What is the matter

with you? Don't you understand? *Go away!*"

"I want to find Jethro."

It advanced on her.

She backed up. What if I fall off the path? she thought. What if I fall down on those ponds? How thick is the ice? Will I drown here?

"Go away," it said.

"I know Jethro lives here somewhere," she said. "You must know him. He takes this path. The path stops here! Tell me where he turns off. Tell me where he goes. Tell me where to find him." She could no longer look at the thing. Its face was scaly, like a mineral, and the snow did not cling to its surface, but melted, so that it ran, like an overflowing gutter. She looked past the thing and saw the black hole of the cave. It wanted her. She could feel its eagerness to have her again. She tore her eyes away and wondered how she would get past the cave to wherever Jethro was.

"Why does he matter?" asked the thing.

Why does Jethro matter? thought Nicoletta. I don't know. Why does anybody matter? What makes you care about one person so deeply you cannot sleep?

She said, "He wasn't in school today."

The creature said nothing. It turned around and moved toward its cave.

"Don't go!" said Nicoletta. "I'm worried

about him. I like him. I want to talk to him."

It disappeared into the cavern.

Or perhaps, because it was stone and sand itself, it simply blended into, or became part of, the cliff.

She followed it. She ran right after it, inside the flat and glowing walls of the entrance.

"Stop it!" the thing bellowed. Its voice was immense, and the cave echoed with its deep, rolling voice. "Get out!"

"I love him," said Nicoletta.

In the strange silence that followed, she could see the thing's eyes. They had filled with tears.

Only humans cry. Not stones.

"Who are you?" she whispered.

But it did not answer.

The only sound was the sharp unmistakable report of a rifle. Nicoletta whirled.

"Hunters. They think I'm a bear," whispered the thing. "They'll come in here to shoot me. Poachers."

"Have they come in before?" she whispered back.

"They don't usually find the cave opening. Sometimes they see me, though, if I'm careless, and they follow me."

She could hear the loud and laughing voices of men. Cruel laughter, lusting for a kill.

"If they see you move, they'll shoot you," it told her. "They shoot anything that moves."

"I'll go down in the cave with you," said Nicoletta. "We'll be safe together." No snow remained on the humanoid creature. Its stink increased and its stone skin flaked away. Its hair like dead leaves snapped off and littered the floor. As long as she didn't have to touch it, or look too closely, she was not afraid of it.

"No," it said. "You must never, never, never go down in this cave."

"I did before."

"And you only got out because I brought you out. If you go any farther into the cave, the same thing will happen to you that happened to me."

"What happened to you?" she said. She forgot to whisper. She spoke out loud.

From out in the snow came a yell of satisfaction. "I see the cave!" bellowed a voice. "This way! We'll get it this time! Over here!"

The thing grabbed Nicoletta and the horrible rasp of its gruesome skin made her scream. It put its hand over her mouth and she could taste it. A swallow of disease and pollution filled her throat. She struggled against the thing but it lifted her with horrifying absolute strength. She was carried down the tunnel and into a small low-ceilinged pit beside the shaft.

"Don't make any sounds," it breathed into her ear. Its breath was a stench of rot.

She was weeping now, soaking its ghastly skin with her tears. The acid of her very own tears dissolved the thing. Its coating was soaking off onto her.

I've been such a fool, thought Nicoletta. My parents will kill me. I deserve anything I get.

She fought but the thing simply pressed her up against the back of the dark pit. When the slime of the wall came off on her cheek, Nicoletta sagged down and ceased struggling. She tried to crawl right inside herself, and just not be there in mind or in body.

But she was there. And all her senses — smell, sight, sound, touch — all of them brought her close to vomiting with horror.

If I can let the hunters know I am here, thought Nicoletta, they will save me. They'll shoot this horrible animal and take me home.

The hunters came into the cave.

There were two of them.

They had a flashlight.

She saw the light bobble past her little cavern but she knew that if they glanced in her direction, they would see only the stony side of the creature. To their eyes, the thing gripping her would look like cave wall.

She took a breath to scream but the thing's

handlike extension clapped so tightly over her mouth she could taste it, toxic and raw.

"This is neat," said one of the hunters. His voice was youthful and awestruck. "I can't imagine why I've never heard of this place. Never even seen the opening before."

"Me either," said the other one. "And I've come around here for years. Why, it's — it's — "

"It's beautiful! I'm calling the TV stations the minute we shoot that bear."

"Let's put the body right outside of the cave opening," agreed the other one. "It'll make a great camera angle."

Their voices faded. The creature's grip on Nicoletta did not.

They walked more deeply into the cave. No! she thought. They mustn't go in farther! The cave will turn! I've been at that end of it! It isn't beautiful, it's the opening to some other terrible place. I've got to warn them. I've got to stop them.

She flung herself at her captor, but its strength was many multiples of her own. Nothing occurred except bruising against its stony surface.

Her heart pounded so hard and so fast that she wondered if she would live through this.

Perhaps her own heart would kill her, giving up the struggle.

So distantly that Nicoletta was not confident of her hearing, came two long, thin cries. Human cries. Threads of despair. Cries for help.

The final shrieks before the final fall.

The two hunters, plunging down the black end of the shaft. Hitting bottom, wherever that might be.

She knew what they felt. The textures and the moving air, the shifting sands and the touching walls.

The thing released her. Her mouth and lips were free. Shock kept her silent. The entire cavern was silent.

Silence as total as darkness.

No moans from the fallen pair. No cries of pain. No shouts for help.

They had hit bottom. They were gone. Two eager young men, out for an afternoon of pleasure.

The monster's sand clung to her face and wrists. She could not move. She could not run or fight or think.

After a moment, it picked her up like a pile of coats and carried her out of the cave.

The snow was now falling so heavily that the world was obliterated.

If there was a world. Perhaps this horrible

place was the only place on earth, and it was her home.

She wept, and the tears froze on her cheeks.

"I'm sorry," it said. "I had to do that."

"How will they get out?" she said, sobbing.

"They won't."

How matter-of-factly it gave an answer. How will the hunters get out? *They won't.*

She backed away from him. "You *are* a monster," she said, and she did not mean his form, but his soul. "You let them go down in there and fall. You knew they would fall! You knew they would come to a place where there was no bottom." She began to run, slipping and falling. The path was invisible. The snow came down like a curtain between them. When she fell again, she slid periously close to the ice over the deep, black lake.

He picked her up out of the snow and set her on her feet. "I'll go with you some of the way. In this weather there will be no more of them."

He held her gloved hand and together they walked between the lakes. On the straight and slender path they could not walk abreast, and he walked ahead, clearing the snow for her.

She had given him gender and substance. Her mind had taken him out of the neuter-thing category. The monster was a he, not an it.

They reached the boulder. "Promise you

won't come back," he said. His voice was soft and sad.

Her hair prickled. Her skin shivered. Her hands inside the gloves turned to ice.

"You must go home. You must not come this way again."

She looked into the eyes. Deep, brown, human eyes. And a human voice that had said those same words to her once before.

Chapter 9

Her first real dance. Her first real date.

And Nicoletta was as uninterested as if her parents had gone and rented a movie that Nicoletta had seen twice before.

"What is the matter with you?" yelled Jamie.

True love is the matter with me, thought Nicoletta. Jethro is the matter with me. Instead of having Jethro, I'm almost the captive of Christo.

It wasn't that Christo had taken her prisoner. Christo was his usual gentlemanly self. It was more that she was not arguing about it. She was not saying no. She was allowing events with Christo to take place because they did not matter to her at all.

"I don't think you even care about Christo," said Jamie, flicking a wet towel at her half-dressed sister. "Even the middle school knows that Christo asked you out."

"They only know because you told them," said Nicoletta. "How else could they know who Christo is?"

"Nicoletta, you're so annoying. He's a football star, isn't he? Me and my friends went to every game last fall, didn't we? We won the regional championship, didn't we? He has his picture in the paper all the time, doesn't he?" Jamie made several snarling faces at her sister.

Nicoletta never thought of Christo as an athlete. She thought of him exclusively as a baritone in Madrigals. She thought of him, not in a football uniform, but in the glittering turquoise and silver he wore for concerts, a king's courtier, a royal flirt.

Christo was a football player, and she did not even know, had never attended a game, never considered his practice schedule. And Jethro. Did he play sports? What was his schedule? Where did he live?

"You don't even care what you're wearing!" complained Jamie. "You didn't even ask Mom to buy you a new dress for this!"

Her dress lay on the bed, waiting for her to put it on.

She felt as if there were a veil between her mind and her life. The veil was Jethro. She was as consumed by him as if he had set her on fire. It was difficult to see anything else. The rest of the world was out of focus, and she did not care whether she saw anything clearly but Jethro.

Jamie held the dress for her and she stepped carefully into it. It was Jamie who exclaimed over the lovely silken fabric, the way it hung so gracefully from Nicoletta's narrow waist, and dropped intoxicatingly at the neckline, like a crescent moon sweeping from shoulder to shoulder. Nicoletta had borrowed her mother's imitation ruby necklace. The racing pulse at her throat made the dark red stones beat like her own blood.

"You're in love, aren't you?" whispered Jamie suddenly.

Nicoletta turned to see herself in the long mirror.

I'm beautiful, she thought. She blinked, as if expecting the beauty not to be there at the second glance. But it was. She was truly beautiful. She had to look away. It felt like somebody else in that gown.

And it is somebody else! thought Nicoletta. It's somebody in love with Jethro, not somebody in love with Christo.

Jamie was also reflected in the mirror: a scrawny little girl, still with braces and unformed figure — a little girl utterly awestruck by her big sister. For the first time in their lives, Nicoletta was worth something to Jamie. For Nicoletta was in love, and beautiful, and going to a dance with a handsome boy.

"Do you think you'll marry Christo?" said Jamie, getting down to basics. "What's his last name? What will your name be when you get married? I'll be your maid of honor, won't I?"

But Christo's last name did not matter. Only Jethro's.

Who is he? thought Nicoletta. *Where* is he?

Love was like clean ice.

Nicoletta skated through the evening. All things were effortless, all motions were gliding, all conversations spun on her lips.

Christo was proud of her, and proud that he was with her.

And if she glittered, how was he to know she glittered for someone else?

They left the dance shortly after midnight.

Snow had begun again.

There was a full moon, and each snowflake was a falling crystal. The night world was equally black and silver. Even the shadows gleamed.

They drove slowly down the quiet streets, rendered perfect by the first inch of snow.

"Where are we going?" said Nicoletta.

"That road," said Christo. He smiled at her.

"I never noticed that road before. It looked quiet."

He wants to kiss, thought Nicoletta. He is going to drive me down Jethro's road, to park at the end of the lane where Jethro's stone will see us. What if the stone tells? I know they talk. I don't want Jethro to find out about Christo.

She was dizzy with the magic of her thoughts. There is no stone, she told herself, and if there is one, nobody talks to it.

Jethro had not been in school. The gloomy skies and early dark of winter had been a perfect reflection of Nicoletta's emptiness when there was no Jethro in Art Appreciation. He was the only art she appreciated.

How she wanted Jethro to see her in this gown!

For she was beautiful. She had been the princess of every girl's dream at that dance. She had been as lovely as if spun from gold, as delicate as lace, as perfect as love.

She saw herself in the snowy night, floating down the path, her long gown flowing behind her, her golden hair glittering with diamonds of snow. She saw herself untouched by cold or by fear, dancing through the dark like a princess in a fairy tale to find her prince.

O Jethro! she thought. Where are you? What

are you thinking? Why weren't you in school? Are you ill? Are you afraid of me? What promises do you have to keep? What does the stone know about you that I do not?

Driving with his left hand, Christopher touched her bare shoulder with his right. He was hot and dry, burned by the fever of wanting Nicoletta.

She thought only of Jethro, and of Jethro's hand. The first time he touched Nicoletta, his fingers had not felt human. The first time he touched Christo, he had left behind grains of sand.

A strange and terrible thought had formed in Nicoletta's mind, but she refused to allow it a definite shape.

Christopher kissed her once, and then again. The third time he shuddered slightly, wanting a hundred times more than this — wanting no car, no time limit, no clothing in the way. The calm young man who easily flirted with or touched any girl because it meant nothing, was not the one driving the van tonight.

Touching meant a great deal to Christo tonight.

Think of Christo, Nicoletta told herself, accepting the kisses but not kissing back. But she could not think of him at all. She could hardly see him. He felt evaporated and diffuse. She felt sleazy and duplicitous. What have I done? thought Nicoletta. What have I let happen? How am I going to get out of this? "Good night, Christo," she said courteously. "And thank you. I had a lovely time."

She put her hand on the door handle.

Christo stared at her. "Nickie, we're in the woods, not your driveway."

But she was out of the van, standing in her fragile, silver dancing slippers on the crust of the snow. She knew she would not break through, she would not get snow in these shoes. She touched the ruby necklace. The moon came out from behind the snow-laden clouds, and rested on her face and her throat. The ruby and the red rose of her cheeks were the only heat in the forest.

Like a silver creature of the woods, she found the path, swirling and laughing to herself.

"Nickie?" said Christo. He was out of the van, he was following her. He could not stay on the surface of the crusted snow, as she could. His big feet and strong legs slogged where she had danced. "You don't even have a coat!" he cried.

The boulder carried a shroud of snow. Nicoletta was a candle flickering in the dark. She quickstepped around the immense rock. The boulder shrugged its shoulders as Christo passed and dropped its load of snow upon him. Muffled under layers of white, his cry to Nicoletta did not reach her ears. "Wait up!" he said to her. "Don't do this, Nickie. Nickie, what are you doing?"

She was in a dance choreographed by an unknown, moonlit hand. She had a partner, unseen and unknown, and the only thing was to keep up, to stay with the rhythm, her skirts making scallop shells around her bare stockinged legs, her feet barely touching the white snow, her hands in synchrony, touching, holding, waving.

Christo struggled free from the snow and circled the boulder.

He could see her, her gown luminous as the stars, her hair like golden music. He could not imagine what she was doing, but he did not care. She was too lovely and the evening was too extraordinary for reason. He simply wanted to catch up, to be with her, to see her eyes as she danced this unearthly dance.

When he caught up to her, she was dancing on a balance beam between two black-iced ponds. The path was so narrow his heart stopped. What if she fell? What could she be thinking of? He was too out of breath to shout her name again, he whose breath control and athletic strength were his strong assets. The stillness of the night was so complete it was like crystal, a call from him would shatter the glass in which they danced.

A black, black hole at the end of Nicoletta's narrow danger opened wide, and opened wider.

Christo stared, fascinated, unable to think at all, unable to shout warnings if warnings were needed.

From the side of the ice-dripping, rock walked rock. Moving rock. The rock and Nicoletta danced together for a moment while Christo tried to free himself from ribbons of confusion. What is going on? he thought.

It was possible that the night had ended and he was deep in a dream, one of those electrical-storm dreams, in which vivid pictures leap and toss like lightning in a frightened sky.

"Nicoletta?" he said at last.

She spun, as if seeing him for the first time, and the rock spun with her, and it had a face.

The rock was a person.

Chapter 10

"You brought him here," it said to her.

She knew who he was now, but not why or how. She wanted to talk to him. Not just this night, but every night and forever. She wanted him to be the only person she ever talked to.

But he was not a person. He was a thing.

"When do you change?" she said to him. "When are you one of us?"

"I am always one of you," he said desperately. "How could you have brought Christo? How could you betray me?"

"I would never betray you. I love you."

He released her, and the rough granite of him scraped her painfully. There was more red now under the moon: her rubies, her cheeks, and her one drop of blood.

"Go!" he breathed. "Go. Convince him I am not."

Convince him I am not.

Not what? Not who?

She was alone now between the lakes and Christo was trying to join her, his large feet clumsy on the tilting ice and snow. "I'm coming, Christo!" she said, and ran toward him, but she was clumsy now, too. Her partner of the silence and snow was gone; her choreography failed her.

She slipped first, and Christo slipped second.

They were a yard apart, too far to touch, too far to catch.

At first she was not afraid, because she knew that even falling through the ice, the creature would save her, lift her, carry her out.

But the sharp tiny heel of her silver shoe punctured the ice at the same moment that Christo's big black shoe cracked it, and as the frigid water crept up her stockings, she realized that the creature would not save her, any more than it had saved the hunters. What mattered most to it was being unknown, and being untouched, and being safe itself.

Christo and I will drown, she thought. We will fall as far beneath the black water as the hunters fell in the black shaft. We will die in ice and evil cold.

She thrashed desperately, but that only made the hole in the ice larger.

Christo said, in a normal high school boy's

voice, "I can't believe I have done anything as stupid as this. Don't tell anybody, that's all I ask." He was crouching at the water's edge, having pulled himself back. He grabbed her hand and waist and yanked her unceremoniously to dry land. "Let's get out of here before we get frostbite." He hustled her along the straight path and back into the woods and back around the boulder.

Nicoletta was afraid the boulder would roll upon them, would crush their wet feet beneath its glacial tons, but it ignored them. Back in the van, Christo turned on the motor and then immediately the heat, with the blower on high.

After a moment he looked at her, reassessing what had happened and who she was.

He knows now, thought Nicoletta. He knows who I love and where I go and what matters most.

But he did not know. People in love seldom do.

"You," said Christo finally, "are not what I expected." He was laughing. He was thrilled. Nicoletta had proved to be full of well-kept secrets, a girl whose hobbies were not the usual, and he was even more proud of being with her than he had been at the dance.

Christo started to list the things they would do together — things he probably thought were unusual and exciting. To Nicoletta they sounded impossibly dull. They were of this world. They were commonplace.

Nicoletta had a true love now, from another world, a world without explanation or meaning, and she did not care about Christo's calendar.

The light was on in the bedroom Nicoletta shared with Jamie when Christo pulled into the Storms's driveway. Jamie had definitely not gone to bed. Her little face instantly appeared, and she shaded the glass with her two hands so that she could see into the dark.

Christo grinned. "We have to give your little sister a show for her money," he said.

No! thought Nicoletta, shrinking. I can't kiss you now. I'm in love with another — another what?

Man? Boy? Rock? Thing? Beast?

Or was she in love with a murderer?

She thought of the two men falling to the depths of the cave.

Where are we going? they would have said to each other.

Down.

Down forever, down to certain death.

He could have prevented the hunters from dying, she thought.

Then she thought, No, he couldn't. They

would have killed him first, shot him, it was self-defense, in a way.

Her thoughts leapt back and forth like a tennis ball over a net.

It came to her, as black and bleak as the lakes in the dark, that she had forgotten those two men. They had fallen out the bottom of her mind just as they fell out the bottom of the cave.

Love is amoral, she thought. Love thinks only of itself, or of The Other.

There is no room in love for passersby.

Those hunters. They had passed by, all right.

Did they have wives? Children? Mothers? Jobs?

Nobody will ever find them, thought Nicoletta. They will never be buried. They will never come home. Nobody will ever know.

Unless I tell.

"Good night," said Christo softly. He walked her up the steps, dizzy with love. Together they stared at the blank wooden face of the door, at the bare nail where last December a Christmas wreath had hung.

Christo's kiss was long and deep and intense. His lips contained enough energy to win football games, to sing entire concerts. When he finally stopped, and tried to find enough breath to speak, he couldn't, and just went back to the car.

Behind Nicoletta the door was jerked open and she fell inside, her heart leaping with memories of caves and black lakes, of dancing in front of rock faces that opened like the jaws of mountain spirits.

"Ooooooh, that was so terrific!" squealed Jamie, flinging her arms around her sister. "He really kissed you! Wow, what a kiss! I was watching through the peephole. Oooooooh, I can't wait to tell my friends."

Nobody could ever accuse a little sister of good timing.

"Get lost, Jamie."

"Forget it. We share a bedroom. I'll never be lost. Tell me everything or I'll never let you sleep. I'll borrow all your clothes. I'll get a parakeet and keep the cage over your bed. I'll spill pancake syrup in your hair."

"Go for it," said Nicoletta. She walked past her pesky sister and into the only room in the teeny house where you were allowed to shut the door and be alone. In the bathroom mirror she stared at herself.

Mirror, mirror, on the wall, who is the fairest of them all?

There were answers behind the silvered

glass. If she could only look in deeply enough, she would know.

I didn't look deeply enough into the cave either, she thought.

I have to go back.

Further down.

Deeper in.

Chapter 11

"Daddy and I are going to see the Burgesses today," said Mother. "This is the first free Saturday we've had in so long!"

Mr. Burgess was Daddy's old college roommate. It was a long drive and when Mother and Daddy went to see Sally and Ralph, they stayed all afternoon and sometimes long into the night.

Yes! thought Nicoletta. I'll have the time to scout out the cave. Nicoletta tightened her bathrobe around her and thought of the long, unsupervised day ahead and what yummy food she would eat to sustain herself. Doughnuts, she thought, Gummi bears, ice cream, chocolate chips out of the bag, and barbecue potato chips. She would take some to Jethro. She would wear a backpack filled with junk food, and —

"Nicoletta," said her mother, in her high,

firm, order-giving voice, "you'll stay home and baby-sit for Jamie."

"Baby-sit for Jamie?" Nicoletta repeated incredulously. She needed to get out there in the snow and find Jethro! And they were making her stay home and baby-sit her stupid sister who was perfectly capable of taking care of herself?

Nicoletta tipped way backward in her wooden breakfast table chair, rolling her eyes even farther backward, to demonstrate her total disgust.

Luckily Jamie felt the same way. "Baby-sit?" she shrieked. "Mother! I am eleven years old. I do not need a sitter and I am not a baby. Furthermore, if I did need one, I would want one more capable, more interesting, and more worth your money than Nickie."

It was agreed that the girls could take care of themselves separately, as long as they promised not to fight, not to argue, and not to do anything foolish.

"I promise," said Nicoletta, who had never meant anything less.

"I promise," said Jamie, who lived for fights and arguments and would certainly start both, the minute their parents were out of sight.

Their car backed out of the driveway, leaving deep lacelike treads in the snow. The sky was a thin, helpless blue, as if its own veins had chilled and even the sky could no longer get warm.

But Jamie did not start a fight.

"Make pancake men," she said pleadingly to her sister. This was one of the few episodes out of the *Little House* series that Jamie considered worthy. Nicoletta was excellent at it, too. Nobody could pour pancake batter like Nicoletta.

So Nicoletta made pancake men and then struggled with pancake women, although skirts were harder to pour. They ate by cutting away limbs with the sides of their forks: having first the arms, then the legs.

Jamie drowned some of her men in syrup, pouring it on until their little pancake heads were under water, so to speak.

There was nothing quite so filling as pancakes. When you had had pancakes for breakfast, you were set for a hard day's work. Nicoletta dressed, carefully hiding her excitement from Jamie. Jamie loved Saturday morning cartoons and with luck would not even hear the door close as Nicoletta slipped out. With extremely good luck, she would still be cartooning and junk-fooding when Nicoletta returned in the afternoon.

There had been enough money last year for

Nicoletta to purchase a wonderful winter wardrobe. She wanted to be seen against the snow. A scarlet ski jacket with silver trim zipped tightly against the cold. Charcoal-gray pants tucked into white boots with furry linings. She wore no hat. The last thing she wanted to do was cover her hair.

She loosened it from its elastics and let it flow free, the only gold in a day of silver and white.

"Where are you going?" yelled Jamie, hearing the door open after all.

"Out." Nicoletta liked the single syllable. The strength of it pleased her. The total lack of information that it gave, increased the sense of secrecy and plotting. She stood for a moment in the doorway, planning her strategy. She'd be warm inside her puffy jacket, but the pants were not enough and the boots were more for show than snow. She needed earmuffs in the fierce wind, but would die before wearing them.

"Nicoletta!" screamed her sister, who never called her that. The scream soared upward with rising fear. "Nicoletta!" Loud. Louder than it should be for anything less than blood. "Nicoletta, come here!"

She flew through the house, remembering emergency numbers, fighting for self-control, reminding herself to stay calm. Was Jamie bleeding? Was Jamie —

Jamie was fine. Curled in a ball on the easy chair, with Mother's immense purple velour bathrobe draped around her like Cinderella's gown.

"This better be good," said Nicoletta. "Talk fast before I kill you."

"Kill me for what?" said Jamie.

"Frightening me."

Jamie was gratified to have frightened Nicoletta. Nicoletta could think only of time lost, time she needed to find and talk to Jethro. Time in the winter woods, time behind the swollen boulder. Get to the point! she thought, furious in the wake of her unreasoning fear.

Jamie pointed to the local news channel.

"You called me in here to look at something on TV?" shouted Nicoletta.

"Shut up and listen."

A distraught woman was sobbing. "My husband! My husband Rob!" she said. "We don't know what happened to him! He never came home last night. Or Al either. They must be hurt." The woman's shoulders heaved with weeping. "I don't know," she whispered. "They're lying out there in the snow. I know they are. Too weak to call for help. Or maybe they fell through unsafe ice. I don't know. But Rob didn't come home."

As if she, too, had fallen through unsafe ice, Nicoletta grew colder and colder, sinking to the depths of her soul.

"See," said Jamie, "what happened is, these two hunters went out yesterday morning and they never came home. Isn't that creepy? They took a day off from work to go hunting *and they never came home.*"

I forgot them, she thought. I forgot them right away. I yelled at the monster once and then I forgot again. But those were people. Real people.

"What if she never finds out?" said Jamie in a low, melodramatic voice. "You missed it, Nick, but they showed her little kids. The kids are too little to know what's going on. They just held hands and stared at the camera. You know, that goopy, gaping look little kids have."

Children, thought Nicoletta. I went back and danced on the snow while little children waited for a daddy who is not coming home. And I knew, I knew all along.

Something in her congealed. She felt more solid, but not flesh and blood solid. Metallic. As if she were no longer human, but more of a robot, built of wires and connections in a factory.

Because I didn't react like a human, she

thought. A human would have gone to the police, called an ambulance, taken rescue teams to the cave to bring the hunters up. And what did I do? I obeyed a voice telling me to keep its secrets.

The reporter's face became long and serious. "In this temperature," she said grimly, "in this weather, considering tonight's forecast, there is little hope that the men will survive, if indeed they are alive at this moment. They must be found today."

Nicoletta's stomach tried to throw up the pancake men.

She forced herself to be calm. She supervised every inside and outside muscle of herself. It seemed even more robotic. And it worked. She knew from Jamie's glance that her body and face revealed nothing.

"Search teams are combing the areas where the men are thought to have been," said the reporter. "We will return with updates." The long, grim face vanished into a perky smile, as if the reporter, too, were a robot programmed for certain expressions. "Now," she said cheerily, "back to your regular programming!"

Jamie, who always preferred regular programming, and never wanted interruptions, sighed happily and tucked herself more deeply into her mother's robe.

Nicoletta backed out of the room. She stared down at the bright, sparkling outfit she had chosen to shine in the snowy woods, so Jethro would see her.

I know where they are . . . but if I tell . . . his secret . . . my promise . . .

Anyway, they're dead. It isn't as if anybody could rescue them now. They have a grave, too — farther underground than an undertaker would put them.

It was not funny. Not funny at all. And yet a snickery laugh came out of her mouth and hung in the air like frost. She had to pull her mouth back into shape with both hands.

What shall I do? Does a promise to a monster count when wives are sobbing and children have lost their father? Of course not.

But in her heart, she knew there had been no promise to a monster. The promise had been to . . .

But even now she could not finish the sentence. It was not possible and she was calm enough to know that much.

But it was true, and she had seen enough to know that as well.

First, I'll find him, she told herself. We'll talk. I'll explain to him that I have to notify authorities. Then —

A small, bright yellow car whipped around

the corner, slipping dangerously on the ice, and zooming forward to slip again as it rushed up her driveway. Rachel, who aimed for every ice patch and shrieked with laughter at every skid. Rachel, coming for a Saturday morning gossip.

Nicoletta could not believe this was happening to her. First she had to make breakfast with her sister. Now she had to waste time with her best friend.

Rachel leapt out of the driver's side and Cathy from the passenger side. It wasn't enough that she would be saddled with one friend; now there were two. They slammed their doors hard enough to rock the little car and purposely leapt onto untouched snow, rather than using the path, tagging each other and giggling.

She was framed in the doorway anyhow; there was no escape; so she flung it open and said hi.

"Nickie!" they cried. "You have to tell us everything. We're dying to hear about it."

Her heart tightened. *How could Rachel and Cath know?* She had said nothing! Only Christo had been there, and he'd had no sense of what was going on. He'd been too in love with Nicoletta to see anything.

And yet Rachel and Cathy knew.

Nicoletta struggled to remain composed.

She could not talk to anybody until she had talked to Jethro. That was all, that was that.

Rachel flung her arms around Nicoletta. "It's terrible not to see you all the time," she said. "We're so out of touch. Now get inside where it's toasty-oasty warm and tell us all about it." Rachel shoved Nicoletta into her own house.

Cathy tap-danced after them. "You're so lucky, Nickie," she said, admiring her own steps. "Did you dance all night?"

They even knew that she had danced under the moon and across the snow!

"Hi, Jamie," said Rachel. "Are you still worthless or have you improved since we saw you last?"

"I'm flawless," said Jamie. "Get out of my living room. I'm watching television. But if you pay me, I'll describe Christo's good-night kiss. It was very long and — "

Christo.

This was about Christo! The dance at Top o' the Town. Not the dance to find Jethro.

Nicoletta surfaced. It was sticky coming up, as if, like the pancake men, she had drowned under syrup.

How quickly can I get rid of them? she wondered. She would have to give them every detail, assuming she could remember any details; and then what excuse could she use to make them leave her alone? She wondered if there was any way she could get Rachel to drive her to the dead-end road, save her that long hike. She could think of no way to explain being dropped off there.

"And then," said Jamie, accepting a pack of Starburst candy in payment, "Christo staggered back to the car like a drunk. Except he was drunk with Nickie." Jamie laughed insanely. "Men," she said, shaking her head in dismay. Clearly she had expected men to have higher standards in love than her own sister.

"Oh, that's beautiful," sighed Cathy. "Come on, Nickie, into your room for your version. We've already had Christo's and now Jamie's."

"You've already had Christo's?"

"Of course. We had an extra rehearsal this morning. At Anne-Louise's. She has the most wonderful house, Nickie. It's on Fairest Lane, as a matter-of-fact. Her family bought the house three down from your old one, and her living room is huge. The whole chorus can fit in easily. Plus she has a grand piano, not to mention a fabulous electric keyboard. There's nothing that keyboard isn't programmed to do."

"Cathy," muttered Rachel. "I don't think Nickie is thrilled to hear that."

Cathy apologized desperately.

"It doesn't matter," said Nicoletta. It didn't. All that mattered was getting to the boulder, the path, the two lakes, the cave.

And Jethro.

Is he the monster? She thought. How can he be? How can anybody be?

"So," said Rachel, hugging herself with eagerness. She lowered her voice. Excitedly she whispered, "Are you in love with him?"

Nicoletta stared into the faces of her former friends. Still friends, she supposed. Friends because they had not forgotten her . . . and yet, friends she'd forgotten.

Am I in love with him? she thought. Which him do we mean?

She told them many lies. At the time she uttered each sentence, she swore to remember it, so they wouldn't know she was lying, but she tripped continually. She could not remember one lie even through the following lie.

Cathy and Rachel thought it was wonderful. "You're so dizzy with love, you can't even keep your first date straight," accused Rachel. She hugged Nicoletta, cementing something, but Nicoletta did not know what.

"I'm jealous," added Cathy.

The doorbell rang.

"Get it!" yelled Jamie. "I'm busy."

Nicoletta went to the door. In this tiny

house, everybody was adjacent to everything and everyone.

It was Christo.

No, she thought. No, not now. I've told enough lies. I can't tell more.

Just seeing her brought a laugh to Christo's lips. "Hi, Nicoletta," he said, trembling over these simple words. It was not a tremble of nervousness, but of sheer pleasure to see her. But of course, it was not only Nicoletta he saw. With a touch of disappointment, he added, "Hi, Cathy. Hi, Rachel."

"We're just leaving," said the girls, nudging each other, pushing the romance along.

Don't leave me alone with Christo! How will I ever get to Jethro if Christo is here? I don't mind lying to you two. If I could explain everything to you, you wouldn't mind. But Christo! He would mind.

For there is no explanation for loving somebody else.

Chapter 12

"Let's all go to the mall!" said Nicoletta. "That would be fun." She clapped her hands like a moron and twirled to make her hair fly out in a golden cloud.

Christo was truly in love. Anything Nicoletta said sounded heavenly to him. "Great idea," he said. He ran his hand up her shoulder and caught at her thick, blonde hair. "You're already in your coat. Were you just leaving with the girls?"

"Yes," said Nicoletta.

Cathy and Rachel looked confused.

"We were talking about Anne-Louise," said Nicoletta. Cathy and Rachel were even more confused.

Christo, however, thought that Nicoletta was a wonderful, generous, and truly forgiving person. He could not get over how easily she had accepted Anne-Louise's presence in the

Madrigals, and how well she had dealt with her own loss. He complimented her profusely on her greatness of heart.

Cathy and Rachel looked skeptical.

Christo actually wanted to know if, on the way to the mall, they should swing by Anne-Louise's and pick her up and bring her along. "So the whole gang is together," he said eagerly, as if Nicoletta were part of the gang. Rachel cringed. Cathy held her breath. Boys were so thick.

"Sure," said Nicoletta. "I'd love to get to know her better." Who is saying these things? she thought. The only thing I'd love to do right now is shake you off, Christo, so I can find Jethro.

They clambered into the van. Christo turned the radio up higher, and then they talked louder, and he turned the radio up even more, and then they shouted and laughed and the interior of the van was a ringing cacophony of music and talk and giggling.

Nicoletta thought of unrequited love. It was dreadful. She could not believe she was a part of it. And yet, it was not unrequited, because Christo did not know. Once he knew, it would qualify. I'm sorry, Christo, she thought.

And then she heard the radio.

The update.

" . . . get a pizza," said Christo, taking Nicoletta's hand. "A new brick-oven pizzeria opened down by the highway exit. Want to go?"

" . . . rather go to the movies later on," said Cathy. "Let's all go, the way we used to. There's a fabulous fantastic cop-chase comedy playing."

Their voices were jackhammers in Nicoletta's skull.

" . . . rescue efforts," said the radio, "are to no avail. The fate of the two missing hunters remains unknown. On the economic front . . ."

"Isn't that scary?" shrieked Rachel. "I mean, those guys just walked off the face of the earth."

Walked off the face of the earth.

It was true. They had. The hunters had fallen down the gullet of the earth, and lay within its bowels.

"I wasn't inviting you for pizza, Cath-Cath," said Christo, friendly and flirty as ever. "Just Nicoletta." He smiled sweetly at Nicoletta and she ducked, as if the smile were a missile.

I was there when they walked off the face of it, she thought. *I know where the face of the earth ends.* And Jethro — what does he do? Cross the boundaries? Go between the face of the earth and whatever lies beyond?

The van whipped on well-plowed roads toward the city and the mall. Suddenly she saw the little dead-end road, and felt as if her eyes were being ripped out of her head in their effort to see all the way down it, and through the woods, and into the face of the cliff, and down the falling, falling cave.

"Nickie and I had the weirdest adventure the other night," said Christo, laughing and pointing. He turned down the volume of the radio and addressed the other girls. "We were going to park down at the end of that road. It dead-ends, you know, in a forest."

"We know," said Rachel in a sultry voice, implying that she, too, had parked a hundred times. Everybody laughed at her.

"Well," said Christo, in an introductory voice, as if he had much to say. "We go running through the woods. Nick and I. In the middle of the night! Ice and snow and moonshine. And we're running. Past boulders and trees and icicles hanging from the sky."

"Icicles hanging from the sky?" said Cathy, pretending to gag. "Christo you are getting altogether too romantic here. Next thing you know, you'll be writing greeting cards."

"Nickie?" repeated Rachel incredulously. "In the woods after dark? Come on."

"Nicoletta loves the outdoors," Christo told her.

"Nicoletta?" said Rachel.

"And," said Christo, "we spotted a thing. A Bigfoot. A monster. A Yeti. Something."

"I'll bet," said Cathy, giggling. "If I were running around in the woods in the middle of the night in the snow, I'd be seeing monsters, too."

"I'm serious," said Christo. He pulled into Fairest Lane without slowing for the curve, and the van spun momentarily out of control. "Oops," said Christo, yanking it back. He missed a tree by inches.

What if we had been killed? thought Nicoletta. Jethro would never know what happened to me.

She sneaked a corner-of-the-eye look at Christo. He had an excited look to him; not a preconcert look, but a prefootball game look. He was an athlete right now.

A hunter.

She had thought he had been confused or too swept away in his emotions to retain the memory of the stone that danced with Nicoletta between the lakes. She had thought he'd forgotten the warts of sand that covered its humanoid features, and its hair like old bones of thin fingers. Instead he had been making plans.

Christo pulled into the driveway of a house so similar to Nicoletta's old one that for a moment she thought she had fallen backward two years, the way the hunters had fallen backward into their particular hole. He honked the horn in a lengthy musical rhythm that must have made the neighbors crazy. Especially the neighbors Nicoletta remembered. It was a Madrigals' call. The hunters, she thought. What were they originally hunting? Ducks? Deer? Did they have a call, too?

I must make Christo hunt *me*, she thought, not Jethro. Christo must not go back. I betrayed Jethro once before. I can't let it happen again.

Anne-Louise came running out, laughing. "Want to go to the mall with us?" shouted Christo. She signaled yes and ran back for her coat and purse. "So what I'm going to do," said Christo to his three passengers, "is go back there and catch it."

"Catch what?" said Rachel.

There, thought Nicoletta. I admitted it. It's Jethro.

"The thing," said Christo. "Bigfoot. The monster. Whatever it is."

Rachel and Cathy exchanged looks. Give-us-a-break looks. This-nonsense-is-annoying-us looks.

Good, thought Nicoletta. If they laugh at him enough, we can get away from it. We'll make him forget it. I have to make him forget it.

"Or shoot it," said Christo, his voice as relaxed as if he were deciding on a flavor of ice cream for a sundae. "Whatever."

Shoot it? Nicoletta's heart felt shot. It isn't an "it," she thought, it's Jethro, you can't shoot him, *I won't let you shoot him!*

"I'd be the only person in North America who ever actually caught one." Christo beat out a rhythm on the steering wheel with his fists. "What a trophy, huh? Can you imagine the television coverage? I bet there's not a TV show in America I couldn't get on." His grin was different now. Not the sweet tremulous smile of first love, but a hard calculating grin.

A hunter. Ready to hunt.

Anne-Louise came running out of the house.

"After I shoot it, I guess I could have it stuffed," mused Christo.

Nicoletta clung to the seat belt.

"Christo," said Rachel. "Enough. Anne-Louise thinks we are civilized and interesting. Talking about shooting monsters in the woods will not do."

But Cathy was interested. She leaned forward. She tapped Nicoletta's shoulder. "Did you see it, too, Nickie?" she whispered, as if "it" were there, and might overhear, and so she needed to be careful.

Anne-Louise climbed into the van and yanked the sliding door shut after her. The van rocked when it slammed. She sat down breathlessly in the back with Cathy and Rachel and then, recognizing the front seat passenger, cried, "Nicoletta! Oh, what a pleasure! I've heard so much about you!"

"Nice to see you, too," said Nicoletta.

Cathy said louder, "Did you see it, too, Nickie?"

"Yes," said Nicoletta frantically. "I said hi. Nice to have Anne-Louise along."

"The monster," said Cathy irritably.

"No," said Nicoletta. "I didn't see anything. Of course not. There wasn't anything to see. Christo was seeing shadows."

Christo was genuinely angry. "I was not! You actually touched it, Nickie. Remember? Right there by the water and the cliff? Before we fell in?"

"You guys were running around in the dark in the woods where there were cliffs to fall off and water to fall in?" shrieked Rachel. "That sounds like the most horrible night on earth. Christo, remind me never to go on a date with you."

"It was Nicoletta's idea," said Christo defensively. "She knows the people who live around there."

"Who?" demanded Rachel. "Who lives around there?"

Nicoletta tried to shrug. "Nobody. Nothing. There wasn't anybody there."

"There was so a monster!" said Christo. He was really annoyed that she was not backing his story up. "And there was a cave! You were there, Nickie. You know I'm not making it up."

"A cave?" said Anne-Louise. "I wonder if that's what happened to those poor hunters. Where is this cave?"

Nicoletta was colder than she had ever been in the ice and snow.

Anne-Louise put a heavy, demanding hand on Nicoletta's shoulder. "Where is this cave?" she repeated. "We must notify the authorities. Who is this friend of yours who lives near there? He must show the rescue teams where to look."

Nicoletta heard her voice climb an octave and become brittle and screamy. "Christo is just being silly, Anne-Louise. Keep going to the mall, Christo. I need to buy . . . I need to look for . . . I'm out of . . ."

But she could not think of anything she needed or was out of.

Except time.

Chapter 13

At the mall, the teenagers gathered around a large, slablike directory of stores and entertainments. Christo was giving orders. First, he decreed, Anne-Louise was to stop her noise about the authorities. This had nothing to do with the two missing hunters. He was not going to tell her where the cave was. It would not become her business until she saw him on television. He was going by himself tomorrow morning to capture it. It would be his personal trophy. Second, Cathy and Rachel were to stop nagging and asking questions and not believing him. Third, Nicoletta was to tell him Jethro's last name and phone number, so he could get in touch with this person who undoubtedly knew the woods best.

Cathy and Rachel said they didn't know what anybody else was going to do about Christo's sudden personality change into staff sergeant, but they personally were going to try on shoes. Good-bye. And they would be happy to see Christo again once he turned back into a fun person.

Anne-Louise said that if Nicoletta and Christo wanted to hunt monsters and leave hunters to their hideous deaths, it was on their consciences not hers, and she was looking for shoes, too. So there.

Nicoletta was thinking that although her grasp of local geography was not great, the rear mall parking lot might back onto the woods. She might be able to walk through from this end and find the path, the two lakes, and Jethro. She waved good-bye to the other three girls.

What do I think will happen if I find the cave? Do I think Jethro will explain this away. Do I believe there could be an explanation? Do I expect to haul the hunters' bodies up so they can be found, and meanwhile hide Jethro? Do I expect to bring Jethro home with me, in whatever form he exists today, and ask my parents to let him sleep on the living room couch for a few years?

The mall was its usual bland self. Nothing ever changed there. The shiny, dark floors, the softly sliding escalators, the windows full of shoes and toys, the people sitting beneath indoor trees eating frozen yogurt. For a moment Nicoletta did not know which world was more strange: the world of the cave or the mall.

Christo, however, was not bland. He was full of the hunt. His muscles, his stride, his speech — they all talked together. He wanted this capture. He wanted this television coverage. This fame. This triumph.

It came to her in an unusual moment of understanding that he was not only hunting the thing he had seen in the forest; he was also hunting Nicoletta herself.

He was going to bring her a trophy she could not refuse.

He was going to show off his physical prowess, not on the football field where she had never even bothered to look, but in the forest, which she had claimed to love.

It was deeply flattering. She could not prevent herself from basking in this. Christo — admired by every girl in town — Christo wanted to impress only Nicoletta.

And she, after all, was not thinking only of Jethro. She wanted to impress Christo right back. But later. Much later. Right now she had to get to Jethro first. Warn him. Save him. Keep him.

As if, she thought in another moment of unwanted clarity, as if Jethro is *my* trophy before he's Christo's trophy.

She could think of nothing to say that was not stupid. Let's get French fries. Let's go with the others and try on sneakers. Let's check out the new videos and T-shirts and perfumes and pizza toppings. This nonsense when Christo was saying: Let's shoot the monster. And stuff it. Let's go out there and get the thing. "You don't want to come," he assured her. "You'd get squeamish." He laughed a strong male laugh, full of plans and promises. "In the morning," said Christo, "I'll take my father's shotgun."

The hunters had had shotguns. And what had happened to them?

She had a third all-too-clear vision.

It was not Jethro she had to worry about. Jethro was safe. The cave was his and he knew it.

It was Christo — innocent, show-off, excited Christo.

What had happened to the hunters would happen to him. He, too, would fall forever down. If she let Christo go on this expedition, she would betray him as well. She knew the length and depth of the fall Christo would take. She knew where he would hit bottom.

She knew he would never come out.

Never again sing or play ball. Never flirt or grow old.

Now as she looked at Christo, he seemed infinitely desirable. Perfect in every way. A person the world must have, a person who must live out his life span.

Christo, looking down at her, saw emotion in her eyes. He saw desire and fear and hope but he read it as love. Not a wish that he would live, but a wish that he would be hers.

Right there in the blandness of the encircling mall, among tired mothers pushing strollers and bored teenagers sipping soda, he kissed her with the sort of passion reserved for movies. The sort of intensity that belonged on late night drama.

He was embracing her with a ferocity she did not expect from a Madrigal singer. Perhaps this was Christo the football player, perhaps she was a goalpost he was trying to reach.

But no. He was kissing with the ferocity of a hunter.

When it ended, people were smiling softly and indulgently, enjoying this glimpse of true love. Christo was dizzy, backlit with the glow of his crush on her. He pulled slightly back from her to admire her from a distance of several inches instead of eyelashes against eyelashes.

But Nicoletta only wondered if Jethro would ever kiss her like that.

The day passed as, unbelievably, all days do.

It was a fact of life that fascinated Nicoletta. Even the worst days draw to a close. Sometimes a day seems to have the potential of lying there forever, trapping its victims as if they were treads on a circling escalator. But it never happens. The shopping ends, the van brings you home. The sun goes down, and the table is set for supper.

She endured her family. She swallowed her meal. She stared at a television screen. She held a book on her lap.

Outside, the snow fell yet again. They had never had such a winter for snow. The wind picked up, singing its own songs, sobbing its own laments. It dug tunnels in the drifts, as if hunting for its own set of hidden bodies.

Nicoletta undressed for the night.

Naked, she examined her body. What body did Jethro possess, he of the sandy hands and the granite face?

If I wait till morning, she thought, Christo will already have left on his hunt.

So I cannot wait till morning.

Chapter 14

The night was young. She had heard that phrase and never understood it. But now at one in the morning, she knew the meaning. She ran easily over the crusted snow, jumping the immense piles the plows had shoved against the curbs. She, too, was young. They had been born together, she and the night.

But the dirt road was far and the roads, with their walls of hard-packed, exhaust-blackened snow, obstructed her.

She was afraid of being seen. If a police car happened by . . . if grown-ups returning from parties noticed her . . . would they not stop? Demand to know why a lone girl was running down deserted streets at such an hour?

But the snow loaned Nicoletta enough hiding places to last a lifetime. Every pair of headlights caused her to bend a knee, and wait patiently behind a snow mountain until the vehicle passed by, and then she rose to her feet and ran on.

The night grew older. After one it became two, and was fast reaching three when finally she came to the end of the paved road, and found herself in the woods she wanted. She was exhausted. When the running ended, the trembling of legs and joints began, as if her body wanted to give up now, before its goal.

The boulder waited for her. It had gained in stature, for the snow had drifted upon it, increasing its height and breadth. As she trudged wearily up to it, snow fell from its stony mouth like words she did not comprehend.

She stopped walking. She had a sense of the boulder taking aim.

The moon was only a sliver, and the stars were diamond dust.

It was not enough to see by. And yet she saw.

And was seen.

In the pure, pure black of the night, she felt eyes. A thousand eyes, searching her like a thousand fingers. "Jethro," she whispered.

She wet her lips for courage and the damp froze and her mouth was encrusted with ice, the way Jethro's body was encrusted with sand. "Jethro," she cried, louder.

There was not a breath of wind. Just icy air

hunched down against the floor of the forest as if it planned not to shift for months. She waded through the cold and it hung onto her pants legs and shot through the lining of her jacket.

When she reached the boulder, she put her mittened hand against it for support. But there was no support. There was not even any rock. She fell forward, her hand arriving nowhere at all. She screamed, remembering her brief fall in the cave.

But this fall, too, was brief.

There was so much snow that her arm went through white right up to the elbow and then she touched rock. But under its blanket, the rock was not warm and friendly. It seemed to lunge forward, as if to hurtle her away from itself.

"Jethro!" she shrieked.

The trees leaned closer and listened harder. She pressed her back against the great rock, even though it did not want to shelter her. "Jethro!"

Her voice was the only sound in the silent black. It lay like an alien in another atmosphere. Nothing answered.

She would have to go to the cave in this terrible dark.

She remembered that first portion of her life when every day she had acted out *Little House on the Prairie.* She preferred being Laura, of course, because Laura had more fun, but every now and then it was her turn to be Mary. Nicoletta had always wanted to change the course of history and give Mary antibiotics so she didn't go blind. That was the only really awful thing in *Little House.* Oh, you could have your best friend read aloud to you for ten minutes and be your eyes for half an hour, but then you lost interest and had better things to do, and you didn't really like to think about Mary being stuck inside herself. Caught there in the dark. It used to make Nicoletta feel guilty and crawly that she could run away from blindness. Run into the sun and see and know the shapes and colors of the world, while Mary had to sit quietly at the table, forever and ever and ever in the dark.

The woods were so very dark.

She even thought she understood the meaning of forever, it was that dark.

If she did not find Jethro, she might lose her balance and slide into the black lakes and she, too, would be forever and ever in the dark.

A hand took hers firmly and guided her down the straight path toward the lakes. She was grateful for help and tightened her grip on the hand and even said thank you.

But there was no one there.

She was holding a stick. She could not even remember picking it up. It was weirdly forked, as if it really had once been a hand. She threw it hard into the trees to get it off her but it clung to her mitten and went nowhere. She began to cry soundlessly, because she was afraid the rest of the twigs and trees would attack if she made an ugly noise.

"Don't be afraid." The voice came from nowhere, from nothing. Now she screamed silently, twice as afraid. "They're trying to help," it said.

She was frozen. She had neither breath nor blood.

"It's me. I don't want you to look. I don't want you to know. You shouldn't have come, Nicoletta. Why do you keep coming when I keep telling you to stay away?"

Jethro. Oh, Jethro! "I had to warn you." She could not see anything. She knew his voice but he was not there. Nothing was there.

"Warn me of what?"

"Christo is coming back in the morning," she said. She began to cry again, and it was a mistake, for the tears froze separately on her cheeks and lay like rounded crystals upon her skin. "He wants to get you. Shoot you. Stuff you. He wants to take you for a trophy and go on television with you."

"Don't worry." Jethro's voice was consoling and gentle. "He won't find me. He'll find only the bottom of the cave."

The bottom of the cave.

Handsome, flirty, athletic Christo taking one step too many. Tumbling backward, screaming his final scream, hands flailing to stop himself, body twisting as helplessly as a pinecone falling from a tree.

Landing on the sharp spikes of stalagmites, dying slowly perhaps, his bones mingled with the bones of the hunters.

Oh, Christo! You don't deserve that!

He'll find only the bottom of the cave. How could Jethro say a thing of such horror in a voice of such comfort?

Fireworks of shock rocketed behind her blind eyes.

"Anyway," said Jethro, "the hunters will be glad to see him. They need company."

"What do you mean? Weren't they killed?"

"No one is killed by a fall into that cave."

"Jethro! Then I have to call the police! And the fire department! They'll bring ladders and ropes! We'll get the hunters out! We'll — "

"No, Nicoletta. No one gets out of the cave."

"You get out!"

"It took me a hundred years to learn how."

Exaggeration annoyed her. "Don't be ridiculous. Jethro, where are you? I can't really see you."

"I don't want you to really see me," he said quietly. "I don't want you to be as scared of me as you would be."

"I've seen you before! I know you in that shape. Jethro, *I need you.*"

There was no sound in the woods except the sound of her own breathing. Perhaps Jethro did not breathe. Perhaps he was all rock and no lungs. But then, how did he speak? Or did he not? Was she making it up? Was she out here in the woods by herself, talking to trees, losing her mind?

"You need me?" said Jethro. His voice quavered.

Humans have two great requirements of life. To be needed is as important as love. Now she knew that he was human, that he was the boy who sat beside her in art as well as the creature wrapped in stone. "I need you," she repeated. She slid her scarlet mitten off her hand and extended her bare fingers into the night.

The hand that closed around them rasped with the rough edges of stone. But the sob that came from his chest was a child's.

Chapter 15

They sat on the boulder, wrapped in snow as if in quilts. It was a high, round throne and the woods were their kingdom. The night was old now. The silver sliver of moon had come to rest directly above them, and its frail light gleamed on the old snow and shimmered on her gold hair.

She kept his hands in her lap like possessions. They were real hands. They had turned real between her own, as if the oven of her caring had burnt away the bad parts. "You are a real boy," she said to him.

"I was once. It was a long time ago."

She snuggled against him as if expecting a cozy bedtime story of the sort her parents loved to tell.

"Long ago," said Jethro. He told his story in short spurts, letting each phrase lie there in the dark, as if each must mellow and grow old like the night before he could go on to the next. "Long before the Pilgrims," said Jethro, "ancient sailors from an ancient land shipwrecked here."

The town was only a few miles from the sea, but she never thought of it that way. There was no public beach and Nicoletta rarely even caught a glimpse of the ocean. People with beaches were people with privacy.

"They found the cave," said Jethro slowly, "and explored it for gold."

Yes. She could believe that. Those gleaming walls and incredible patterns of royal rock — anybody would expect to find treasure.

"There was none. The men who went first fell to the bottom, and could not be rescued by the others." His voice waited until she had fully imagined the men in the bottom who could not be rescued. "They had to be abandoned," he said, his voice a tissue of sorrow.

"Still alive?" asked Nicoletta.

"Still alive."

Wounded and broken. Screaming from the bottom of a well of blackness. Hearing no words of comfort from above. But instead, words of farewell. *We're sorry, we have to go now. Die bravely.*

"In their society," said Jethro, "the soul could not depart from the body unless the body was burned at sea with its ship. But they, of course, could never return to the ship. And so the men at the bottom of the cave never died. Their souls could not leave. Their bodies . . . dissolved over the decades." His voice was soft. With revulsion or pity, she did not know. "Until," he said, "they became the cave itself. Things with warts of sand and crusts of mineral."

His hands took her golden hair, and he wove his fingers through it, and then he kissed her hair, kissed that long thick rope, but he did not kiss her face. "The ones who fell," said Jethro, "put a curse on the cave."

A chill of horrified excitement flashed down Nicoletta's spine. She had never heard a human being utter those words. *A curse be upon you.*

"What was the curse?" She whispered because he did. Their voices were hissing and lightweight, like falling snow.

"Whoever entered that cave," said Jethro, "would be forever abandoned by the world. Just as they had been."

Was he one of them? Ancient as earth? But the boy she knew from Art was her age. A breathing, speaking boy with thick, dark hair and hidden eyes.

"And did Indians fall in?" she asked.

"The Indians always had a sense of the earth

and its mysteries. They knew better than to go near the cave."

He seemed to stop. He seemed to have nothing more to say. She asked no questions. The moon slid across the black, black sky. "Then," said Jethro, "white men came again to these shores. To farm and hunt and eventually to explore." Now he was speaking with difficulty, and the accents of his voice were lifting and strange. "My father and I," he said, "found the cave. So beautiful! I had never seen anything beautiful. We did not have a beautiful life. We did not have beautiful possessions. So I stayed in the outer chambers, touching the smooth rock. Staring at the light patterns on the brimstone. Dazzled," he said. "I was dazzled. But my father . . ."

How softly, how caressingly, he spoke the word *father*. A shaft of moonlight fell upon the monstrous shape of him and she could see the boy inside the rock. His eyes might have been carved from a vein of gold. He smiled at her, the sculpture of his face shifting as if it lived. It was a smile of ineffable sadness.

"My father went on in."

She turned to look at him.

"My father fell, of course. He fell among the abandoned, and they kept him."

He stopped. The warmth of the great rock

dissipated. It was cold. She waited for Jethro to descend through the centuries and return to her.

"I didn't leave the cave. If I had run back out . . . things would have been different. But I loved my father," he said. His voice broke. "I offered myself in exchange. I told the spirits at the bottom of the cave that they could have me if they would give up my father. They were willing. My father was willing. He said he would come back for me. He emerged at the same moment that I fell into the cave on purpose."

Jethro paused for a long time. "I try to remember that," he told Nicoletta. "I try to remember that I stepped off the edge because I wanted to."

"Were you hurt?"

He smiled again, his sadness so great that Nicoletta wept when he did not. "I broke no bones," he said finally. He said it as if something else had broken.

"What did your father do? He must have run back to the house and the town and gotten everybody to brings ropes and ladders."

Jethro's smile was not normal. "There was a curse on the cave," he said. "I told you that." His words seemed trapped by the frost. They hung in front of his lips, crystallized in the air.

She had been listening to the story without listening. It was a problem for her in school, too. She heard but did not keep the teachers' words. She moved her mind backward, to retrieve Jethro's speech. *"Whoever entered,"* she repeated slowly, *"would be forever abandoned by the world. Just as they had been."*

Jethro nodded.

The moon was hidden by a cloud.

Jethro put a hand gently over her eyes. "Don't move," he said softly. "Don't look again."

His hand was heavy. Stonelike. "Your father?" she said. "Abandoned you?"

"He walked away. He walked out of the cave and into the daylight. He never came back. Nobody ever came back. I called and called. Day after day I called. He was my father! He loved me. I know he did. Even though there was nothing else beautiful in our lives, that was beautiful. He loved me."

She opened her eyes under the weight of his hands and saw only the underside of a rock. She closed her eyes again.

"Even though I gave myself up for him," said Jethro, his voice caught as if it, too, were falling to a terrible fate, "I didn't understand that it was forever. I was sure he would return and rescue me."

Rescue. A lovely word. Certain and sure. I will rescue you, Jethro, thought Nicoletta. I love you. I will rescue you from all curses and dark fallings.

"But he didn't, of course," said Jethro.

Jethro cried out. A strange terrible moan like the earth shifting. A groan so deep and so long she knew that he was still calling for his father to rescue him.

Being a monster was not as terrible as being abandoned by his father. Nothing on earth could be worse. Forgotten by your father? A child goes on loving a father who drinks too much, or beats him, or does drugs . . . but a father who leaves the son to endure horror forever . . . and even forgets that he did that . . . it was the ultimate divorce.

Abandoned. The word took on a terrible force. She could see his feet — that father's feet — as they walked away. Never to turn around. She could hear the cries, echoing over the years: that son, calling his father's name. Never to hear an answer.

"I try not to hate him," said Jethro. "I try to remember that there were no choices for him. The curse carried him away from me and kept him away. But he was my father!" The voice rose like the howl of a dying animal into the winter air. "He was my father! I thought he would come! I waited and waited and waited."

The voice sagged, and fell, and splintered on the forest floor.

"Oh, Jethro!" she said, and hugged him. He was sharp and craggy but the tighter she held her arms the more he softened. She felt him becoming the boy again, felt the power of her caring for him fight the power of the curse upon him. He removed his heavy hand from her eyes but she kept them closed for a while anyhow.

"You can emerge from the cave and be a real person some of the time," she said.

"It's a gift of the light. Sunlight, usually. I am surprised that the moonlight is giving me this now. Sunshine is a friend. It doesn't end the curse, but sometimes it gives me a doorway to the world. Haven't you noticed that I am only in school on sunny days? I cannot touch the world except on bright days."

"I will make all your days bright," said Nicoletta.

"You have," he said, his voice husky with emotion. "I think of you when I cannot leave."

For a long time they sat in each other's arms. Moonlight glittered on the fallen snow and danced on the icy fingers of trees. Very carefully she turned to look at him. He was Jethro. She sighed with relief. He had been in there all along, and she — she, Nicoletta Storms — has freed him with her presence. "At least I'll see you in school," she said.

"No. I can't go again."

"Why not? *Why not?* You have to! Oh, Jethro, you have to come back to school! I have to see you!" She gripped his arms and held him hard.

"You must forget about me."

"I can't. I won't. You don't want me to. I don't want to. We're not going to forget about each other."

He said nothing.

"Why do you come to school?" she asked him.

"To dream of how it might have been. You are my age when I fell. I hear human voices, I recognize laughter. I see human play and friendship."

Oh, the loneliness of the dark!

She pictured her family. How loving they were. How warm the small house was. She thought of Jethro, returning every time to the dark and the rage of the trapped undead. She kissed him, hungrily, to kiss away his loss. Around them the trees leaned closer and looked deeper. "Jethro, it feels as if the woods are alive," she whispered.

"They are," said Jethro. "We were all something else once. Every tree and stone. Every lake and ledge."

Horror surrounded her. She breathed it into her lungs and felt it crawl into her hair, like bats. She could not look into the woods.

"You must go home. You must never come again."

"But I love you."

He flinched. He pushed her away, and then could not bear that, because nobody had loved him in so very long. He held her more tightly than ever, cherishing the thought. *Somebody loved him.*

Love works only when it circles, and it *had* circled. It had enclosed them both. She loved him and he loved her back. He had to love her enough to make her stay away.

"Never come near the cave again. They know about you. They will look for you now, and guide your steps so that you fall. They will take you, Nicoletta. What else do they have to do for all eternity? Nothing. They will never be buried by fire at sea. You must go and never come back."

She was unmoved. Nobody would tell her never to do anything. Nobody would tell her that she could find true love and then have to walk away from it! No. She would always come back.

"Nicoletta," he said. His voice was hollow now, like a reed . . . or a cave.

"If you get too close, not only will you fall, I — cursed by the cave — I would do to you what my own father did to me."

She was looking into his eyes, eyes like precious gemstones. I love you, she thought.

He said, *I would abandon you.*

Abandon her? She could not believe it. He loved her. Love did not abandon.

"Abandon you forever, Nicoletta. In the dark. Turning to stone. Forgotten. I would not come back. Nobody would ever come back for you."

The moon hid behind wispy clouds. The night was too old to be called night. Jethro left. He had been there, and then he was not. She was alone on the stone in the dark.

For he did love her.

And to prove it, he had to leave. And so did she.

Chapter 16

It had taken great courage to walk into the woods.

It took none to walk out.

If Jethro was not afraid of what the trees and ledges had once been, how could she be afraid? She said good-bye to the boulder, but it said and did nothing, which surprised her. She had expected a response after the conversation and the agony it had heard; the loving it had seen.

When she reached the paved road, she would have to put away these things. Enter into her other life.

How distant it seemed — her other world.

Nicoletta touched the pavement.

Dawn was coming. Quickly the sun threw scarlet threads into the sky, and quickly the snow turned pink in greeting. As if they were flirting and blushing. Like me, she thought.

She smiled to herself, and then smiled at the sun.

She walked swiftly. She was happy.

What is there to be happy about? she thought. That the sun rises? That I love Jethro but he doesn't want me to come again?

And yet she was happy in a liquid way, as if she were still all one, a water glass of pure happiness, a crystal cylinder of delight.

Love, she thought. I know what it is now. It's every molecule of you. It connects you to yourself, even if you cannot be connected to the person who caused it.

Jethro. Oh, it was a beautiful name!

A car turned down the DEAD END road.

She had not wanted the other world to appear so soon.

A second vehicle followed it.

She considered hiding. Stepping off the road into the trees. She knew that the trees would take her in. Circle her, and blind the cars to her presence for Jethro's sake. Snow, its sides packed like a ski jump by a plow, and a little, green holly tree without berries were on either side of her. She could hunch down behind the sharp, leather leaves and not be seen.

The first vehicle was Christo's van. The second vehicle was a television network van.

Nicoletta had omitted the part that counted.

She had entertained herself. She had run to Jethro for talk and love and comfort and daydreams. But the important part of what she had needed to do before morning, she had skipped.

Christo, who was equally liquid and crystal with love. Christo, who was hot and surging with the need to show off, to hunt, to capture or to destroy.

Not only had Christo come. He had brought teams. Witnesses. Camera film. And, no doubt, weapons.

She thought of the cave. The long fall that Christo and his TV crew would take. The horrible slime and sand and narrowing walls of shining stone. The knowledge that they were doomed. Of course, they would not have that knowledge as they fell. They would think there was a way out. Or that rescue would come.

How many days, or weeks . . . *or years* . . . would they struggle against their fate? How long before they became, as Jethro had become, part of the cave? Just another outcropping of sand and rock and dripping water? Would she, Nicoletta, in that other world have grown up and had children and grandchildren and been buried herself by the time Christo understood and surrendered to his fate?

The van rushed down the narrow road.

Christo drove too fast, gripping the wheel of his car, leaning forward as if trying to see beyond the windshield and through the woods, behind the rock and into the cave. He looked neither left nor right, only ahead. He didn't see the packed snow and the holly, let alone Nicoletta. She had a glimpse of his profile as he sped past. How handsome he was. How young and perfect.

And how excited. He thought this would be an adventure. And oh! it would be. But not one in which he conquered.

She could not let him fall! Nor could she let those poor strangers in the van meet that fate.

The television van came much more slowly. Its driver was middle-aged and frowning, studying the road, the snow, the sky, as if he were worrying about a change in the weather, the studio deadline, his taxes, his wife, and his aching feet all at the same time.

He could have been her father.

He was surely somebody's father. Would he, like the hunters, end up forever fallen?

I have to do something, she thought. But what? I can't talk them out of it. The more information I give them, the more eager they'll be. The more I explain, the quicker they'll rush to see for themselves. And even if they stay away from the cave, even if I can convince them to stay in the meadow, or between the lakes, or among the trees . . . they'll try to shoot Jethro.

I have no control. I have no moves. I have no way to turn.

This is not the world of the ancient Indians who understood that there were mysteries, and that mysteries should not be touched. This is the world of the television networks, who think that everything on earth belongs to them and ought to be captured on their cameras.

Perhaps she owed Christo nothing; after all, she did not love him; it was he who loved her. Perhaps she should let them go, and let Jethro control what happened.

But love was too precious. Even if it was not hers, and would never be hers, how could she be part of its ending? She did not love Christo, but it counted that he loved her.

The television van was almost upon her.

She flung herself out from behind the piled snow and the little holly tree . . . directly under the wheels of the van.

"She jumped!" said the van driver constantly. "I swear it. The girl jumped right in front of me."

"I slipped," Nicoletta explained. It was not easy to talk because of the pain. The broken leg was so very broken. Pieces of bone stuck out of her flesh like long white splinters. "Snow," she explained. "Ice. No sand on the road yet. It's my fault. I should have been more careful."

Whatever spell Christo had cast to coax a network to send a crew, had dried up. The people who had been eager to film whatever this kid thought he'd seen, especially since it was near the disappearing point of the two hunters, were now interested in nothing but getting through a terrible day. The van driver was desperate to be sure everybody understood it was not his fault. He said this to Nicoletta's parents and to the doctors and the admitting secretary in the emergency room and to Christo.

Christo had questions of his own to ask Nicoletta, but being severely hurt provided its own camouflage. She need only close her eyes, rest her long lashes on her pale cheeks, and whisper. "I'm tired, Christo, visit me tomorrow." And he had to leave. No options.

The cast was big and white and old-fashioned. No vinyl and metal athletic brace for a break this bad; solid heavy-duty plaster and bandage was like a rock attached to her leg. She had always rather hoped to be wearing a cast one day, and attract lots of sympathetic attention, and have to use crutches.

But now she faced a new nightmare.

How will I go back to Jethro? thought Nicoletta. I can't get through the woods with this. I can't use crutches in the snow.

Not only had she stopped Christo and the TV crew from looking for Jethro, she had stopped herself.

People asked what she had been doing, anyway, on some remote road at the crack of dawn? There was only one acceptable excuse and she used it. "I've taken up jogging, you know. I've been running every morning."

Her parents had not known this, but then, they didn't get up before dawn and could not say she hadn't been.

Jamie was too jealous of the attention Nicoletta was getting to ask difficult questions. Jamie kept looking around for cute interns instead.

When Nicoletta woke up in the afternoon, she was alone in a quiet hospital room with pastel walls. The other bed was empty. There was something eerie about the flat white sheets and the untouched, neatly folded, cotton blanket on the other bed. It was waiting for its next victim.

The door was closed. She had no sense of noise or action or even human beings around her. She might have been alone at the bottom of the cave, she was so alone in the bare, pale room.

Her leg hurt.

Her head ached.

I'll never even be able to tell Jethro what I did for him, she thought, in a burst of self-pity. I'll hobble around by myself and nobody will care.

The door was flung open, banging heavily into the pastel plaster wall.

The Madrigals burst into the room, singing as they came. It was so corny. They were singing an old European hiking song: "And as we go, we love to sing, our knapsacks on our backs. Foll-der-oolllll, foll-der-eeeeee, our knapsacks on our backs."

She was so glad to see them that it made her cry. It was hokey, but it was beautiful. It was friendship.

"Now, now," said Ms. Quincy, "we won't stay long, it's too exhausting for somebody as badly hurt as you are. We just wanted you to be sure you know that you're among friends."

Nicoletta looked up, thinking, Ms. Quincy had a lot of nerve, when she'd kicked Nicoletta away from those friends. But out loud she said, "Hi, everybody. I'm glad to see you."

They all kissed her, and Christo's kiss was

no different from anybody else's. She wanted to catch his hand, and see if he was all right. Ask what he was thinking. But she didn't really want to know.

Rachel had brought colored pens so everybody could sign the cast. Rachel herself wrote, *"I love you, Nickie! Get well soon!"*

This meant everybody could write, *I love you, Nickie,* and they did. David and Jeff, whom she hardly knew, wrote, *"I love you, Nickie, get well soon."* Cathy did, Lindsay did, even Anne-Louise. *"Love you, Nickie!"*

Christo was last. She had to do something. She was out of action, but he might return to the cave anyway. She had to exert some sort of pull on him.

"Why were you there?" he breathed. "What were you doing? It was awfully far from home to be jogging."

"I knew you were coming, Christo," she murmured. "I wanted to watch you in action. I wanted to be part of it." She squeezed his hand. "Promise me you won't do anything unless I'm along to watch you, Christo?"

Everything about him softened. The love he had for her surfaced so visibly that the girl Madrigals were touched and the boy Madrigals were embarrassed. Nicoletta blushed, but not from love. Because he believed her. Because love, among all the other things it was, was gullible. Everybody had written, "Love you, Nickie," but he wrote on her cast, *I love you more. Christo.*

The Madrigals left, singing again, this time a burbling Renaissance song that imitated brooks and flutes. It was a lullabye, and Nicoletta slept, deep and long.

She dreamed that she was falling.

Falling in dreadfully icy cold, wind whipping through her hair and freezing her lungs. She dreamed that her hand was reaching for something to catch. Anything! A branch, a rock, a ladder, a rope —

— but found only sand.

The flat of her palm slid across the grit, finding nothing to hold, nothing at all, and the black forever hole below her opened its mouth.

In her sleep she screamed silently, because everything in that terrible world was dark and silent, and in one last desperate try she tightened her grip.

She found a hand. It held her. It saved her. She woke. It was Jethro's hand. He had come. He was safe. He had not been hurt, and nobody had hurt him. He was here in a pastel hospital room.

He leaned over her bed and found her lips. He kissed her as lightly as air and whispered,

"Nicoletta. *Oh, Nicoletta.* I love you."

Even when used by strangers like David and Jeff, or people at whom she was angry like Ms. Quincy, those three words remained beautiful. But from the lips of the boy she loved, those three words were the most beautiful on earth.

"I love you, too," she whispered.

A rare smile illuminated his face, momentarily safe from its terrible burdens. They held hands, and his was graveled and rasping, and hers was soft and silken.

Chapter 17

Jethro yelled at Nicoletta, albeit softly. "You could have been killed!"

"I know that now, but there wasn't time to think of that then."

"What were you thinking of?" he demanded.

"You."

The quiet of the hospital room deepened, and the pale colors of the walls intensified. Her hand in his felt warmer and his hand in hers felt gentler. "I can't stay long," he said.

"Why not? Stay forever."

He smiled sadly. He understood what forever meant. She had no grasp.

"Then I'll talk fast. Jethro, I have ideas." Her eyes burned with excitement. "The thing is," she said, "to bury them. Right?"

"To bury them?" repeated Jethro.

"The ancient souls! They didn't get buried. That's the problem, right? So we have to bury

322

them. We'll blast the cave! We'll dynamite them up! Or else we'll flood the cave! Or else we'll bring torches. We'll get toy wooden boats to count as their ships and set fire to those!"

He did not respond.

"Jethro! Don't you think those ideas are terrific?"

He said instead, "Who do you think you will have if you have me?"

Now she was the one to repeat words that meant nothing to her. "Who will I have if I have you?"

"Nicoletta," he said. "What if you have me . . . as a thing?"

She did not want to think about that.

"You screamed the first time I touched you. Because I am part of the cave. It's in me now. I don't even know why I came here, I could get caught in my other shape. There's no way out of my other being, Nicoletta." His sentences, normally so hard to come by, tumbled and fell on top of each other, like hunters in caves. "You told me yourself what your friend Christo wanted to do to me. Shoot me. Or exhibit me."

"Well, I won't let him."

"How many times do you plan to step in front of trucks?"

After the fact, Nicoletta was aware of what

she had done. She certainly did not want death. That was what this was all about! She wanted life, and she wanted it for both of them. Life and love, hope and joy. No. She did not plan to step in front of any more trucks. "Jethro, there has to be a way out for us."

His eyes looked into a deep distance she could not follow. Did not want to follow. Did not want to think about. "Think of rescue," she said urgently. "We have to work on this, Jethro." She gripped him with both her hands. "What's the point of love if we can't be together?"

His chest rose and fell. She wanted his shirt off, so she could touch his skin and rest her cheek against that beating heart.

His lips moved silently, but she could not read the words. Was he repeating that lovely word *rescue*? Was he imagining that it really could be done? That there really was a way out?

He said, "Love always has a point. Even if it stays within. Or is hidden. Or is helpless."

Nicoletta was angry with him. That was stupid. Who would want a helpless love? Who would want a hidden love?

"Okay," she said, "if you don't want to try anything drastic, what we'll do is tell my parents. We'll explain. They're wonderful people. We'll — "

"And think of what could go wrong," he interrupted. "What if your father fell into the cave? Or your mother? Or your little sister? To be lost forever instead?"

She wanted to joke. My little sister wouldn't be such a loss. But he knew nothing of jokes. "You don't even want to try dynamite?" she said.

"How would you get it?"

"My father bought some to blow up stumps in the backyard. But he never got around to it. It's just there in the garage."

He shook his head. The silence she had first found fascinating annoyed Nicoletta now. "We have to work out a strategy!" she said sharply. "We need to make plans."

But he said nothing, keeping his thoughts. Her hospital room darkened, more infected by his bleak hopelessness than her eager love.

A nurse bustled into the room. She was the sort of woman who called her patients "we." "How are we feeling, dear?" she said, thrusting a thermometer into Nicoletta's mouth so that answers were not possible. "Let's take our blood pressure," she said. She pumped the cuff up so tightly on Nicoletta's arm that Nicoletta had to hold her breath to keep from crying. She did not want to be a sissy in front of Jethro. She stayed in control by trying to read her blood pressure upside down, watching the mercury bounce on the tiny dial. She failed. "What is it?" she asked the nurse.

"Fine," said the nurse. "Keep the thermometer in your mouth."

"But what were the numbers?" mumbled Nicoletta. She hated medical people who kept your own bodily facts to themselves.

Reluctantly, as if answering might start a riot, the nurse said, "One-ten over seventy."

Nicoletta, who had studied blood pressure in biology last year, was delighted. "I'm in great health then," she said happily. The thermometer fell out of her mouth and onto the sheets. The nurse picked it up grumpily. Then she placed two cool fingers on Nicoletta's wrist.

Nicoletta looked at Jethro to share amusement at an old-fashioned nurse. Jethro was not there. A thing, a dark and dripping thing, like a statue leaking its own stone, was propped against the wall. Crusted as if with old pus, it could have been a corpse left to dry.

A scream rose in Nicoletta's throat. Horror as deep as the cave possessed her. He had changed right there, right in this room. In public, in front of people, he had become a monster. She could not look at him, she could not bear it that beautiful Jethro had turned into this.

"My goodness!" exclaimed the nurse. "Your pulse just skyrocketed. Whatever are you thinking about?"

I cannot scream, she thought. People will come. The nurse just has to leave quietly with her little chart and her little cart. I cannot scream.

She screamed.

The nurse followed Nicoletta's eyes and saw a monster.

In the split second before the nurse, too, screamed in horror, Nicoletta saw Jethro's eyes hidden beneath the oozing grit of his curse. Shame and hurt filled his eyes like tears. Fear followed, swallowing any other emotions.

Jethro was terrified.

Oh, Jethro! she thought. Your life isn't a life, it's a nightmare. Your body isn't a body, it's a trap.

Jethro vanished from the room before the nurse could finish reacting. Nicoletta heard his steps, lugging himself out of the room, down the hall, trying to escape.

There was nothing left of him there but a gritty handprint on a pastel wall.

The nurse was made of stronger stuff than Nicoletta had thought. She caught her scream and ran out of the room after Jethro, shouting for security.

No, thought Nicoletta, let him get away! Please let him get away!

She needed to run interference, needed to make excuses, think up lies, anything! Her leg lay on the mattress, heavy and white and unmoving. She literally could not get off the bed.

"Okay, okay," said a grumpy voice in the hallway outside Nicoletta's door, "We've phoned for security. Somebody will be up in a few minutes. Now what was the intruder doing?"

There was a pause. Nicoletta recognized it. The nurse had no idea what to say without sounding ridiculous or hysterical. "He was — he was just standing there," said the nurse lamely.

"What did he look like?" said the grumpy voice. "Race? Age?"

The nurse said nothing for a moment. Then she said, "I'm not sure. Ask the patient."

She's sure, thought Nicoletta. She knows what she saw. She saw a monster. But she can't say that. The words won't come out of her mouth.

Security never came in to ask Nicoletta anything. An aide, not the nurse, arrived later to finish charting Nicoletta's vital signs. Nicoletta said nothing about an intruder. The aide said nothing.

She thought of Jethro's journey home. How would he get there?

How could she ever refer to that cave as home?

Home. She knew now that a house was only a house; the building on Fairest Lane was a place to buy and sell, to decorate, and to leave. But a home is a place in which to be cherished. A home is love and parents, shelter and protection, laughter and chores, shared meals and jokes.

Home.

He had none.

And how with that curse upon him, could she bring him home? Find safety for him? Find release?

Her parents and Jamie burst into the room, loaded down with Nicoletta's schoolbooks and homework, a potted flower, a silly T-shirt from the hospital gift shop, and a balloon bouquet. The balloons rushed to the ceiling, dotting it purple and silver and scarlet and gold.

She wondered if Jethro had even seen a balloon bouquet. Or ever would.

"I'm so glad to see you!" cried Nicoletta. "Oh, Mommy! Daddy! Jamie!"

"You're even glad to see me?" said Jamie. "You *are* sick!"

"Darling," said her mother, hugging. "You look like you've had a good long nap. Feeling better?"

"Lots."

"You come home tomorrow," said her father. He looked worn and worried. He touched her cheek, as if to reassure himself that this was Nicoletta, his baby girl, his darling daughter.

"Tomorrow? I just got here." She thought of a father, years and years go, who left a son inside the earth and never looked back.

"Isn't it wonderful?" agreed her father. "Then just another day of rest at home and you're on crutches and back in school. Orthopedic decisions are very different from when I broke a leg. When I broke my leg skiing, back in the dark ages, why, I was in the hospital for ten days."

They talked about the dark ages: her parents' childhoods, in which there had been no fast food, no video games, no answering machines, and no instant replays.

Nicoletta thought of Jethro, for whom all ages were dark.

I know what I could do, she thought. I could do what Jethro did for his father. *I could offer myself to the spirits of the cave.* I could exchange myself for him.

How romantic that would be!

Greatness of heart would be required. She would step down and he would step up. She would take the dark and he could have the light.

Jethro would have his fair share of laughter and love; he would smile in the sun, with no fear of turning to horror and stone. He would have his chances, at last, for life, liberty, and the pursuit of happiness. The dark ages would end for him.

And she, Nicoletta . . . she . . . would inherit the dark ages.

Dark. Forever and ever, world without end.

Dark and all that *dark* meant. Unknown. Unseen. Things that crawled and bit and flew and slithered. Things that crept up legs and settled in hair. Things that screamed and moaned and wept in the entrapment of their souls.

Could she really do that? Was she, Nicoletta, strong enough to accept darkness and terror, fear and slime — *forever*?

But it would not be forever, of course. He would come back for her. He would —

He would not.

He would not even remember. He would abandon her. Everybody would abandon her.

She thought of the Madrigals. How quickly they had abandoned her for Anne-Louise. She thought of Ms. Quincy, who had praised her voice for so long, only to abandon her the instant she heard a better one. It would all be like that, she thought. My entire life. Except my life would not have a span. It would not end. There would be no way out. It would be eternal.

Oh, Jethro! Jethro!

I don't want you caught in your dark ages. I want you here on earth with me.

"Sweetie, don't cry," said her mother. "It isn't that bad of a break. All will be well. I promise."

She rested on her mother's promise.

She thought of Jethro going back, and down, and in. To become part of the walls and the fall and the blackness, to live among the spirits he would not describe because they were too awful for her to hear about.

"Don't cry," said her mother, rocking. "All will be well."

Chapter 18

"A snow picnic?" repeated Nicoletta.

"Yes!" said Anne-Louise. "It was my idea. And you'll be our mascot!"

Your mascot? thought Nicoletta. I get it. You're the soprano, Anne-Louise. I'm the puppy. The rag doll. The mascot. Drop dead, Anne-Louise, just drop dead.

Christo said, "I'm driving!"

Rachel said, "I packed the sandwiches."

Cathy said, "But I made them, so don't be afraid of food poisoning, Nickie."

Nicoletta had to laugh. She got her crutches. Christo's van was not large enough for so many Madrigals, but if they really squished and squashed, they could fit in a very uncomfortable but delightful way. The three leftovers followed in a leftover car. Nicoletta felt sorry for them, trailing behind.

Her white packed leg with its scrawls of

Madrigal names stuck out in front of her, between the two bucket seats.

Christo said, "We're going to that meadow you showed me, Nick. I thought I might climb the cliff."

Anne-Louise gave a little shriek of fright. "Christo! You might fall!"

Christo smiled arrogantly. Falling happened to other climbers. Not to Christo.

"It'll be icy," warned Anne-Louise. She patted Christo's knee excitedly.

Nicoletta definitely knew who had a crush on whom. Well, it was useful in a way. Christo would be deflected. It would free Nicoletta up for Jethro.

"Okay, Nickie," said Rachel. "The time has come. What is this crazy story Christo keeps telling us about rock people?" The packed singers burst into laughter and the whole van shook.

Christo just grinned. "You'll stop laughing when I catch it," he said.

"Actually," Anne-Louise said, turning to speak clearly, and be sure everybody knew that she knew first, "Christo brought his gun. He's not going to climb. He's going to hunt."

"I'm against hunting," said Rachel.

"I usually am, too," said Cathy, "but this is a rock he's after. The worst that can happen,

I figure, is there'll be two rocks after he shoots at it."

Nicoletta's brain felt as solid as the cast on her leg. She had plaster in her skull. What was happening? The cave and Jethro were becoming public territory. There were no taboos, there was no fear, there was no stopping them now. Even Cathy was laughing about hunting. It occurred to Nicoletta that she could not pretend Jethro was against hunting.

In fact, he and his companions in the cave were the most vicious hunters of all. For they hunted the hunters.

"I want a souvenir," said Anne-Louise, in a little girl singsong voice.

Nicoletta hated her. She hated the flirting, the silliness, the fakery. She hated every single thing about Anne-Louise. Drop dead, she thought. Out loud she said, "It won't be any fun picnicking there, Christo. Let's go to the state park or the town lake."

"Forget it," said Cathy. "He's told us and told us about this place, how romantic and weird it is, what strange things we'll see. We're on. This is it, Nickie."

They turned into the lane that said DEAD END.

They drove past the few houses and the high, winter-tired hedges.

They drove right up the dirt road and came to stop where the ruts were too deep for a suburban van. "How will we ever get through all this snow?" cried Anne-Louise, pretending fear. "How will we ever find our way in those woods?"

"Not to worry," said Christo, comforting her. He was completely sucked in by her acting.

Nobody except Nicoletta seemed bothered by Anne-Louise. The altos, tenors, and basses piled out, the leftover car with its leftover people caught up, the boys hoisted the coolers and then they were faced with the problem of Nicoletta's cast and crutches.

"See?" said Nicoletta. "I really think the town lake would be a good idea. That way you can prop me up on a bench right near where we park, and we'll still have a good view, and yet we — "

"Nickie," said Rachel, "hush. The boys are going to carry you. This is the most romantic moment of your life, so enjoy it."

Christo and Jeff made a carrying seat of their linked arms and David helped her sit. With David holding her cast at the ankle as if she were a ladder he was lugging, Christo and Jeff carried her.

They went past the boulder.

Straight as folded paper, the path led them through the snow-crusted meadow. Weeds from last summer poked out of last week's snow, brown and dried and somehow evil. The weeds tilted, watching the trespassers.

The two lakes were free of ice. They lay waiting. Tiny waves lapped the two shores like hungry tongues.

"Ooooh, it's so pretty!" squealed Anne-Louise.

The sound of their crunching feet was like an army. Jethro was surely hidden safely away; he would have heard them coming.

I couldn't stop them! Nicoletta thought at Jethro. It isn't my fault! I wouldn't have come, but I have to keep an eye on them.

The air was silent and the cave was invisible. They stopped walking. Only Anne-Louise found the place pretty. Rachel swallowed and wet her lips. "The water looks dangerous," she whispered. "It looks — as if it wants one of us."

Nobody argued.

Nobody said she was being silly.

Nobody tried to walk between the two lakes, either.

The boys set Nicoletta down. They set the big cooler down, too, and Nicoletta used it for a chair.

Ice had melted on the side of the cliff, and

then frozen again. It hung in thin, vicious spikes from its crags and outcroppings. There was no color. The stone was dark and threatening. The day was grim and silent.

Christo's voice came out slightly higher than it should have. "I'm walking between the two lakes," he said, as if somebody had accused him of not doing it. "The cave is over there. When the thing came out and attacked Nicoletta, it came out of there."

"Nothing attacked me," said Nicoletta.

"It touched you," said Christo.

"There was nothing here," said Nicoletta.

"I believe you, Christo!" sang Anne-Louise. "I know there was something here. I'll go with you, Christo!"

Anne-Louise and Christo walked carefully as if they were on a balance beam. The water reached up to catch their ankles. A moment passed before Rachel and Cathy and David and Jeff walked after them. Did they not see the cliff snarl? Did they not see the hunger of the cave, how it licked its lips with wanting them?

"There *is* a cave!" cried Rachel. "Oh, Christo, you were right! Oh my heavens! Look inside. It's beautiful!"

No, thought Nicoletta. No, Rachel, it's not beautiful. Don't go in, don't go in.

But now her tongue was also plaster and did

not move, but filled her mouth and prevented her speech.

No one went in.

A cave gives pause. Even with walls shining like jewels, the dark depths are frightening and the unknown beyond the light should remain unknown.

The Madrigals posed at the entrance, as if waiting for their cue to sing, needing costumes, or a director to bring them in.

"Anne-Louise," said a voice, "you go first."

Chapter 19

The screams of Anne-Louise were etched in the air, like diamond initials on glass. Indeed, glass seemed to separate the safe from the fallen.

The Madrigals were collected as if about to concertize. But it was horror that held them, not an audience. They, in fact, were the audience. They had aisle seats to the end of Anne-Louise.

Anne-Louise, whose voice was not so beautiful when screaming in terror, was on the far side of the glass.

The screams went on and on and then stopped. They stopped completely. The silence that followed was even more complete.

Nobody attempted to go in after her.

Nobody tried to rescue her.

Were they too afraid? Or too smart to risk the same ending?

Nicoletta had the excuse of an immovable

leg, a helpless body. None of the others had an excuse.

But Nicoletta had known what would happen. None of the others could have known. And so Nicoletta Storms was the one with no excuse at all, no excuse ever.

Whose voice sent Anne-Louise tumbling forever into the dark?

Was it me? thought Nicoletta. Did I shout *Anne-Louise, you go first*! I who knew what would happen to the one who went first? Did I want revenge that much? How sick and twisted I am, to destroy a classmate over a singing group.

I'm sorry! thought Nicoletta. As if being sorry would change anything.

Time stopped.

The sun did not move in the sky and the teenagers did not move beneath it.

Sound ceased.

Nothing cried out within the cave and nobody spoke without.

The glass wall broke.

Anne-Louise, babbling and twitching, fingers curling and uncurling, eyes too wide to blink, staggered out of the cave.

Still nobody spoke. Still nobody moved.

They were like a group photograph of themselves. A still shot of Madrigals from another era.

"It's in there," whispered Anne-Louise. "You were right, Christo. It's in there! It picked me up. It caught me."

Anne-Louise addressed Christo but did not seem to see him. Instead she staggered away from the cliff, hands out as if holding a rope nobody else could see. On an invisible lifeline she hauled herself in Nicoletta's direction. There was sand in her hair, as if she were a bride at some dreadful wedding. Her guests had not thrown confetti.

"It's there?" breathed Christo. Excitement possessed him. "It really exists? You saw it? You touched it?"

"Don't go in!" screamed Anne-Louise. Her voice was huge and roiling, nothing like a soprano's. It was ugly and swollen. "Don't go in!" she shouted. She did not let go of her lifeline, but kept hauling herself between the lakes, past Nicoletta. She fell to her knees, and Nicoletta saw that the kneecaps were torn and bruised from an earlier fall. Still Anne-Louise did not stop, but crawled, sobbing, trying to find the straight path and the way out.

"She's right, Christo," said Rachel. She sounded quite normal. "Don't go in there. What we'll do is come back with a truck and ropes.

Obviously it's slippery and the cave falls off. There are people who go into caves for hobbies. I've read about them. They're called spelunkers. We'll get in touch with a club and bring a group that knows what they're doing. We'll — "

"No!" said Christo. "It's my find! I'm getting it!"

Jethro saved Anne-Louise, thought Nicoletta. She wanted to call *thank you!* to him. She wanted to shout *I love you!* in his direction. She wanted to put her arms around him and tell him that he was good and kind.

How many people had he saved in the past? Nicoletta had been horrified because Jethro let the hunters fall. But he hadn't let Nicoletta fall. He hadn't let Anne-Louise fall.

He would let Christo fall. He would have to.

"Fine," said Christo in the furious voice of one who means the opposite. "Fine! I'll take everybody back to the van. Fine! We'll picnic at the lake. And then I'm coming back and I'm getting it."

Anne-Louise was walking upright now, a stagger to her gait as if something in her had permanently snapped. Rachel and Cathy were running to catch up and help her. The rest of the Madrigals, saying little, crept between the lakes, safely away from the stretching black elastic of the water, picked up the pace, and headed for the van.

For a moment, Nicoletta thought they would abandon her; that half the curse would come true. She prayed they would, because if she sat long enough, Jethro would come to her. Her Jethro. Jethro with the smooth quiet features, the heavy falling hair, the dark, motionless eyes.

But the boys remembered they had two burdens: a girl and a cooler. They hoisted her up, silently and with great tension, wanting to run, not wanting to admit it.

"You'll see, Nicoletta," said Christo eagerly. "I'll get it."

He wants "it" for me, she thought. "It" will be his trophy to lay at my feet, a golden retriever laying the gunshot duck before his master.

She knew now that Christo could never get "it." "It" would always win, because "it" had greater, deeper, more ancient and more horrible weapons.

She did not want Christo to fall, and not be saved.

She did not want Jethro to have to face that moment. To know that he could rescue . . . and would not.

She did not want coming here to be a hobby.

She did not want to think of the collection that would lie at the bottom of the cave. Or, if Jethro were caught on the outside, the collection he would be in, the display he would make.

The boys staggered in the snow, losing their footing.

Nicoletta looked back. The cliff face was nothing but rock and dripping ice. The lakes were nothing but dark surfaces. The hole in the wall was not visible.

And then part of the rock moved. Changed. Was light, and then dark. A dark wand rose upward. An arm. After a time in the air, like a flag without wind, the hand moved.

It was Jethro.

Terrible grief engulfed her. Was that his good-bye? Would she never see Jethro again? "Put me down!" she cried. "I have to go back!" Her heart was swept out of her, rushing like wind and desperation toward the last wave.

But the boys trudged on.

Chapter 20

Nobody would return anywhere that night.

The snow came down like a monster itself. It came in bulk, in dump-truck loads, smothering every car and bush and front step.

At least school would be canceled. At least Christo would be unable to get his van out of his driveway.

Long after Jamie had fallen asleep, Nicoletta raised the shades and sat up in bed, watching the beauty and the rage of the weather. The wind was not a single whooshing entity but a thousand tiny spinners. The night was dark with desperate clouds letting go, but yellow pools of streetlights illuminated the falling snow.

Jethro came.

She had not expected him. She had thought him gone forever. She had been in mourning, believing in his good-bye, sure that he had backed off for good.

"Jethro!" she cried, and then twisted quickly to see if she had awakened Jamie. Jamie slept on. She put a hand over her mouth to keep herself from speaking again.

When he moved, Nicoletta could see him. When he stopped, she could not. He was part of the landscape. He could have been a dark wind himself, or a heavy clot of snow on rock.

She looked at her sleeping sister. Jamie's mouth was slightly opened and in sleep she seemed glued to the sheets, fastened down by the blankets. She wouldn't wake unless Nicoletta fell right on top of her.

Nicoletta found her crutches, and slowly — far too slowly; what if Jethro left before she could get outside? — she made it down the stairs and reached the coat closet, wrapped herself tightly and hobbled to the back door to let herself out in the storm.

The wind aimed at her face. It threw pellets of ice in her eyes and tried to damage her bare cheeks. The three back steps could have been cliffs themselves. The distance between herself and the garage seemed like miles. "Jethro!" she shouted, but the wind reached into her throat first and seized the words.

"Jethro!"

Nobody could have heard her; she could not even hear herself.

She tried to wade through the snow but it was impossible. It would have been like swimming and the broken leg could not swim.

Why was he not at the door, waiting for her?

She gulped in snow, and put a hand blue with cold over her mouth. She should have worn mittens but she had expected to be out here only a moment before Jethro found her.

She launched the tip of her crutches into the snow ahead of her and attempted to get through the drifts.

There he was! By the garage door! She shouted his name twice, and he did not respond, and she shouted a third time, and he turned — or rather, it turned — and she waved the whole crutch in order to be seen.

He seemed to turn and to stoop. As if he were on an errand. Carrying something. When at last she knew Jethro had seen her, he looked away. What is this? thought Nicoletta. What is going on?

But she had been seeing things. Of course he came to her, white with snow. Snow purified and cleansed. Again he lifted her, and carried her this time into the garage, sitting her on the edge of her father's workbench, her good knee dangling down while the white plaster tip of her cast rested on the top of her mother's car. "You came," she said. "I knew you would come."

He said nothing.

For a frigid, suffocating moment she thought it was somebody else. Not Jethro. Some — creature — who —

She looked and at least knew his eyes: those dark pools of grief.

"Jethro, I don't want you to live like this."

"No," he agreed.

She could feel no pulse in him, no heartbeat, no lifting of a chest with lungs. He was stone beside her.

"You stay here and live. I will go down for you."

He did not smile, for there was no face to him that could do that. And yet he lightened and seemed glad. "No," he said again. The thing that was his hand tightened on hers.

"I don't want you to suffer anymore."

He said nothing.

"I've thought about it. It's your turn for life, Jethro. I will go down."

The words came as from a fissure in a rock. "No one should suffer what I have. Certainly not you."

"Aren't you even tempted? Aren't you even

daydreaming about what it would be like to be alive and well and normal and loved?"

"Always."

"Well?"

"Nicoletta, I will never be well and normal and loved."

"*I* love you!"

He was silent for a long time. The storm shrieked as it tried to fling the roof off the house. The snow whuffling into deepening drifts. "Thank you," he said finally.

"There won't be school tomorrow," she said.

He did not seem to know why.

"Canceled," she explained. "Snow is too deep."

He nodded.

Oh, tonight of all nights she did not want his silence! She wanted to talk! To know. To understand. To share. "When school begins again, will you be in Art?"

"No."

"Jethro, you have to come. Where else will I see you?"

His silence was longer than ever. She was determined to wait him out, to make him talk. She won. He said, "This is only pain and grief."

"What is?"

"Loving."

"You're wrong! It can end well! I want you to stay."

"Like this?" Bitterness conquered him. "Why would I want to be seen like this? What do you think will happen? Christo will exhibit me in a cage." He did not point out that if she had never come back to his cave, if she had never been followed by Christo, he would not be at risk. But they both knew it.

His voice rose like the wind, screaming with the pain of his nightmare. "I don't want anybody to see me. I didn't want you to see me!"

What would it be like, she wondered, to be so ghastly you did not even want the people who loved you to see you? What would it be like to look down at your own body and be nauseated? To be trapped — a fine soul; a good human — in such ugliness that another human would want to put you in a cage and exhibit you?

Nicoletta was freezing to death. It was not just Jethro's body in which she could feel no pulse, no heartbeat, no lungs. "I have to get inside," she said. "I'm so cold. I don't think I can move. Jethro, carry me inside?"

He said nothing, but lifted her. Her skin scraped against him and she hoped that it was deep, and would bleed, and leave a scar, so she would have something to remember him by.

He took her up the back steps and opened the door for her. He saw how she lived; the warmth and clutter, the letters and the photographs, the dishes and the chairs. The goodness of family and the rightness of life.

"I love you, too," he said, his voice cracking like old ice. "But try to see. I can't risk anything more, Nicoletta. You can't risk anything more. I can't be caught. I can't let Christo fall. He loves you. I care about anybody who loves you."

"You saved Anne-Louise," she said softly. "You're a good person. It isn't fair when somebody good suffers! Let me rescue you. I know there must be a way out of this."

His voice was oddly generous, as if he were giving her something. "When your leg is better," he said, "come to the cave. But don't come before that. Promise me. I need your promise."

"No."

"Nicoletta! Why won't you promise?"

"I love you. I want to see you."

"Don't come." He set her down. The one side of her was flooded with the warmth of her home and its furnace. The other side was crusted with snow turning to sleet.

She began arguing with him. Reasons why she must come, why they must get together, why they needed each other, and could think

of some way somehow to save each other, because that was what true love did; it conquered,
it triumphed.

She thought it was a wonderful speech.

She knew that she had changed his mind,
that he understood because she had said it so
clearly.

But when she put her hand out, there was
nothing there.

A snowdrift pressed against the door and a
snow-clumped branch from a heavy-laden fir
tree tipped over the railing and tried to reach
inside the kitchen. But no boy, no monster, no
rock.

No Jethro.

He had left her, and she had not even sensed
it.

He had gone, and she had not even heard.

"No!" she shouted out into the snow. "Who
do you think you are anyway? Don't you vanish
like that!"

Only the snow answered.

Only the wind heard.

"I don't promise, Jethro!" she shrieked.

The side door to the garage banged.

Jethro had not come to see her. She had been
right when she thought he stooped and carried.
He had come for the dynamite.

Tears froze on her cheeks but hope was resurrected. He had thought of a way out. He was going to use one of her suggestions. He would blow up the cave, and bury the curse, and when she came back to find him, they would be together!

Chapter 21

"Nicoletta, darling," said Ms. Quincy.

Nicoletta turned away, saw who was speaking, and very nearly continued on. How she yearned to be rude to the teacher she had once adored. She looked now at Ms. Quincy and saw not a friend, but a conductor who set friendship aside if she could improve the concert by doing so.

Nicoletta did not even know what was fair, let alone what was right.

In fairness, should the best soprano win? Or in fairness, should the hard-working, long-term soprano stay?

What was right? What was good teaching? What was good music?

Were the concert, the blend, the voices always first, and rightly so?

Or did loyalty, friendship, and committee time count?

She wondered if Ms. Quincy had wondered about these things, or if Ms. Quincy, like so many adults, was sure of her way? When she became an adult, would Nicoletta know the way?

She thought of Jethro, who knew the way but could not take it.

Of Jethro's father, who knew the way once but lost the memory of it.

Of Art Appreciation and Jethro's empty chair.

She said, "Hello, Ms. Quincy, how are you?" Manners were important. You always had them to go by. When you stood to lose all else, there were still manners.

"Fine, thank you, darling," said Ms. Quincy, relieved that Nicoletta was going to be polite.

Politeness is a safety zone, thought Nicoletta. She thought of Jethro coming out of her garage. The dynamite that no longer lay in the box on the shelf. Had he done what he had set out to do? She must go! She must see what had happened. She must find him and know.

Practically speaking, this meant she would have to get a ride from somebody. Who?

"Anne-Louise," said Ms. Quincy, "has let me down."

Down, thought Nicoletta. You have no idea,

Ms. Quincy, what the word *down* means to Anne-Louise now. You have no idea how far down Anne-Louise actually went. "I'm sorry to hear that," said Nicoletta politely. "But I'm sure it will work out in the end."

"No, darling. She has quit Madrigals! Can you believe such a thing?" Clearly Ms. Quincy could not. "And here we are in the middle of the winter season with several upcoming events!" Ms. Quincy was actually wringing her hands, an interesting gesture Nicoletta had never seen anybody do. "Nicoletta, please forgive me. Please come back. We need you."

Back to Madrigals.

Back in the group she loved, in the center of things, the whirl of activity and companionship and singing. Back, if she chose, as Christo's girlfriend, twice the center of things with that status.

But never . . . if she rejoined Madrigals . . . never again to sit in Art Appreciation. Waiting. Gazing on the boy she loved.

She knew Jethro was not coming back to school. He had said so quite clearly. And yet she knew she would see him again. She had to. A person you loved could not simply never be seen again. It was not fair.

In the end, things — especially things of true love — should be fair.

Three days of school since the roads were finally cleared, and each afternoon as she went to Art, her heart quickened, and a smile lay behind her lips. Let him come! Let me see that profile. The boy who was in darkness when they watched slides and remained dark when the lights came on.

He did not come.

If she did not continue in Art Appreciation, she would never know if he came back. If she did not rejoin Madrigals, she could not gather back those friendships and pleasures either. "I'll think about it, Ms. Quincy."

It had never occurred to the woman that Nicoletta might say no. There was a certain revenge in seeing Ms. Quincy's shock. "Nicoletta," said Ms. Quincy severely, "you are cutting off your nose to spite your face."

Nicoletta had never heard that saying before and had to consider it.

"You will hurt yourself more than you will hurt the group," said Ms. Quincy, putting it another way.

Nicoletta wondered if that was true. "I'll let you know on Monday, Ms. Quincy," said Nicoletta. "First I'll talk to Anne-Louise."

Anne-Louise was fully recovered. In fact, she was laughing about it. "I can't believe how

I behaved," she said. "Isn't it funny?"

If it's so funny, thought Nicoletta, why did you quit Madrigals?

"You know what let's do?" said Anne-Louise.

"What?"

"Let's go back to the cave," said Anne-Louise. "I mean, when I got home the other day, my mother said my eyes were glazed over. She thought I had cataracts or something. My mother said, 'Anne-Louise, what happened out there anyway?' And do you know what, Nicoletta?"

"What?"

"I can't remember exactly what happened. Let's go back and see. I'm curious. I don't understand what scared us all so much. It was only a cave."

"It's more than a cave. It needs victims," said Nicoletta. "You must not go back. You must never go back, Anne-Louise."

Anne-Louise shrugged. "I'm going back to the cave now, Nicoletta. I *have* to see it," said Anne-Louise. "Do you want to come?"

What way out, thought Nicoletta, would preserve us all? What way out saves Jethro, but gives him to me? Keeps us from exploring or falling? Gives Jethro life as a boy and not a monster?

But did it matter anymore? She thought she knew what way Jethro had decided would work.

No way.

The snow was so high it covered the DEAD END sign. The trees were like branch children with snow blankets pulled up to their shoulders.

Anne-Louise's car reached the end of the road. Here the immense amount of snow had been piled by the plows into sheer-sided mountains. The path was not visible. There was no way in to the boulder.

The road, indeed, was a dead end.

The girls got out of the car. Nicoletta had learned how to use her cast; it was just a heavier, more annoying leg than she had had before. She did not need the crutches for pain or balance.

They surveyed the problem. The snow was taller than they were. Shovels, possibly pick axes, would be necessary to break through. And beyond the snow-plowed mountains, it would still be nearly up to Nicoletta's waist. There was more snow here than elsewhere, as if the snow had conspired to conceal the path until spring.

Anne-Louise looked confused. She rattled

her car keys. She was losing touch with what she wanted to do, and thinking of leaving.

Yes, leave! thought Nicoletta. Leave me here. I'll get to him somehow; I know I will, because he needs me and I need him. He can't have left me forever. Jethro! she called through her heart and her mind. I'm coming!

Christo pulled in behind them. Oh, Christo, why do you always show up, as if I cared about you? she thought.

But he kissed her, because he knew nothing. "We'll just go around," he said.

She had never thought of that; never thought of just walking back to where the plows had not packed the snow so high. Christo went first, kicking a path. Anne-Louise went second, widening the path.

Nicoletta went third, dragging her cast.

The boulder had never seemed so huge. Snow had fallen from the surrounding trees, pitting the soft layers on the boulder. It looked volcanic, as if seething hot lava was bubbling just beneath the snow, waiting for them to put out a wrong foot.

But only to Nicoletta's eyes. To Christo they seemed the right places to step, where the snow was dented. He slogged forward, a football player with a goal in mind. A camera swung from his shoulder.

Nicoletta thought of the order in which they were going. Victims at the head of the line. "Stop," she said. "Stop, Christo!" It's dangerous for them, she thought. But not for me. Love will save me. Love always triumphs. I know it does! Jethro will save me, and we will be together.

"Nickie, I'm never stopping," said Christo. "I'm going to figure out what's happening here if it kills me."

The boulder moved.

It rolled right in front of them. The ground began to shake. Nicoletta had never known how terrible, how awe-full an earthquake is. Nothing in life was so dependable as the ground under her feet. Now it tossed her off, as if she were going to have to fly; she could no longer stand, the old order of human beings was ended.

Anne-Louise's scream pierced the sky, but the sky cared nothing for humans without sense and her scream flattened to nothing under the gray ceiling.

The stone rolled onto Christo's ankle and pinned him.

A huge and terrible noise came from beyond; greater noise than Nicoletta had ever heard; a shattering of rock and earth deeper than man had ever mined. Jethro had dynamited the entrance to the cave.

And then, and only then, Nicoletta knew what way out Jethro had thought of. Not one of hers. But his own.

For there was no way out that preserved them all.

Nicoletta was right that love triumphs. Jethro loved her. And he had put that first. He loved her enough to prevent her from coming back, from bringing her friends, from risking their lives.

He had closed his door forever. Himself inside.

They will all be buried this time, she thought. Every sorrowful spirit will find its rest. Buried at last. *Including Jethro.*

The shaking dashed Nicoletta against a tree.

Jethro gave me life, she thought. For the second time in his terrible life, he sacrificed himself for the person he loved. He wanted me to have my life: sharing a bedroom with a little sister, singing in Madrigals, and eating in the cafeteria.

He wanted no more hunters falling, no more Christos, no more Anne-Louises. He did not want me to risk myself again. He did not want another person on this earth to abandon, or to be abandoned.

Jethro. I love you.

The earth ceased its leaping. The stone rolled off Christo. He was only bruised. He got up easily.

The path through the meadow had received no snow. It was clear as a summer day, straight as the edge of a page. Christo and Anne-Louise led the way, Nicoletta following, her good leg walking and the other leg dragging.

There was no rock face left. There were no ponds. A jumble of fallen stone and rock lay where once a tall cliff and two circles of water had been.

"Wow," said Christo reverently, and lifted his camera. He got into camera athletics, squatting and whirling and arching for the best angle.

Nothing else moved.

Not a rock. Not a stone. Not a crystal.

"I didn't abandon you, Jethro," whispered Nicoletta. "I want you to know that. I came this afternoon to find you. So we could be together after all. I didn't know this was your plan. I swear I didn't. I thought you were only going to bury *them*."

There was only silence. The rocks that had made such a tremendous crash had made the only sound they ever would. They were done with motion and noise. And Jethro? Was he, too, done with motion and noise?

Jethro. I love you.

"Wow!" Christo kept saying. He bounded from rock to rock. "What do you think set it off? Was it an earthquake? I never heard of earthquakes in this part of the country. Wow!"

It was my father's dynamite, thought Nicoletta. But it was Jethro's courage.

Are you well and truly buried now, Jethro? Is the curse over? Are you safe in heaven?

Or deep within this cruel earth, are you still there? Your upward path closed? Still in the dark, forever and ever caught with the raging undead? Never again to hear laughter? Never again to hold a hand?

Oh, Jethro, I hope what you did for me worked for you, too!

I love you. Jethro! Be safe!

Christo finished the roll of film. "Let's go home," he said. "I want to call the television studio. The newspapers. I think my science teachers would love to see this, too."

Love, love, love. How Christo had misspelled that precious word. Only Nicolette knew what love was. And only Jethro had shown it.

"Jethro!" she screamed then. It was too much to keep inside herself. "*Jethro!*" she shrieked, trying to explode his spirit as the dynamite had exploded the rocks. She tried to run toward him, or where he had been, tried to find the place from which he had waved, his stone arm lifted to say farewell.

But of course she could not move, for the cast kept her in place, and the broken, destroyed surface of the earth presented a thousand rocky obstacles. "Jethro!" she screamed. "Jethro!"

She hated silence. How dare Jethro be silent? She wanted him to answer! She wanted him to speak!

Her tears spilled down her face and fell on her pleading hands.

It seemed to her as she wept, that the tears were full of sand, not salt, and that when they dried on her hands, she had some of Jethro in her palm.

"Be safe!" she cried. "Be at rest! Oh, Jethro, be safe!"

Christo said, "What are you talking about?" He shepherded the two girls toward the van.

Talking? thought Nicoletta. I am trying to be heard through hundreds of years of abandonment, and through thousands of tons of rock. I am screaming! I am screaming for the soul of a boy who loved me.

Anne-Louise rattled her car keys.

Christo rewound his film.

They reached the boulder. Nicoletta rested her hand on the snowcap it wore. There was nothing. Snow. Rock. Solidity. She put the same hand on her heart. It was as cracked as crystal thrown from the cliff. And no one knew, or heard.

"Jethro," she whispered.

It seemed to her that for a tender moment, the frozen trees of the woods, the lakes and ledges and stones of the earth, bent toward her and understood her sorrow.

Christo opened the van door for Nicoletta, and boosted her in. "Where does that Jethro kid live anyway?"

She looked into the silent woods and thought of Jethro, silent forever. "He moved," said Nicoletta. Let it be true, she prayed. Let him be safe wherever he moved to, wherever he lies.

Jethro, it was too much. To die for me was too much. I wanted you alive! I wanted us together! You can't do that with death. With death you can't be together.

Christo started the engine.

She looked down at her hand. Caught in the tiny cup of her curved palm was a grain of sand glittering like a diamond. She closed her fingers to keep her diamond safe. The way, with his death, Jethro had kept her safe.

They left in the little lane with its dwindling

ruts, and the trees closed around the road as if it had never been.

Her breath was hot in the icy van. It clouded the window. With the hand that held no diamond, she traced a heart in the mist on the glass. She wrote no initials within the heart, for she did not know Jethro's, and Christo would expect his initials to go beside hers.

They drove on, and the van heated up, and the warm air erased the heart.

But Jethro would not be erased. Jethro had lived and loved. He had loved *her*. Nicoletta Storms opened her hand. The diamond lay still and silent in her palm.

And always would.

CALL WAITING

Chapter 1

The frightening phone calls began less than an hour after Karen had the fight with Ethan.

One week before the fight, on a snowy, bone-chilling Saturday night, Karen Masters pulled her blue Corolla onto Jefferson, Ethan's street. The tires crunched over the salted pavement as Karen eased to the curb and cut the headlights.

She reached to turn the ignition key, but her friend Micah Davis grabbed her arm to stop her. "Karen, if you turn off the engine, we won't have any heat. We'll freeze."

Karen stared thoughtfully out the windshield, past the clicking wipers at the falling snow. "I know," she said. "But I'm nearly out of gas. If we have to wait a long time . . ."

Micah unlatched the seat belt so she could turn to Karen. "This is so crazy. I don't know what you hope to see," she said, shaking her head.

In the shadowy light, Karen caught Micah's disapproving frown. The wipers scraped across the windshield. The snowflakes were large and wet. Before they were brushed away, the light from the streetlamp made them glisten like teardrops.

"I don't know, either," Karen sighed, resting both gloved hands on the wheel.

"It's a rotten night for spying," Micah complained in a velvety voice. She tossed her blonde hair behind her shoulders. Then she ducked her head lower into the collar of her down coat. "I mean it. This is really crazy, Karen."

"I know," Karen agreed. "I just have to see . . ." Her voice trailed off.

"See what?" Micah demanded.

"I have to see if Ethan lied to me," Karen said. She turned off the engine. The wipers stopped halfway across their route, then slid into place. "Good. Silence. I can't stand that *click-click-click!*" she exclaimed.

"You're a nervous nut," Micah accused. "You've been a nervous nut for days."

"It's all Ethan's fault," Karen insisted. Her dark eyes stared straight ahead. She had parked at the top of the low, sloping hill that led down to Ethan Parker's house.

From this spot, she could see the Parkers' sprawling redwood ranch-style house and the short driveway that led to the garage at the side. A spotlight over the front door cast a bright rectangle of light over the snow-covered front lawn.

"Look at you," Micah said sharply, grabbing the sleeve of Karen's bulky sweater. "You're so pale, Karen. And you look positively anorexic."

"It's dark. How can you see if I'm pale or not?" Karen replied shrilly, tugging her sleeve free. "And I'm not anorexic. Everyone in my family is very thin."

She pulled off her wool ski cap and shook her short, dark hair free. And then she added pointedly, "Especially since we don't gobble down Kit Kat bars every minute."

Micah had a serious Kit Kat problem.

"Wish I had one now," Micah muttered. She gazed out at the falling snow. "I can't believe I agreed to come with you tonight!" she exclaimed.

Micah pushed her hair back with both hands. She had piles of curly blonde hair, and she was constantly playing with it, pushing at it, tugging at strands, twirling them around her fingers.

She shivered. "What do you think we're

going to see, Karen — before they find us frozen solid inside this car?"

"Ethan broke our date tonight," Karen replied, her voice revealing her emotion. She crossed her arms in front of her chest. "I want to see if he lied to me. I want to see what time he gets home."

"What's that going to prove?" Micah demanded. "If he gets home after midnight, is that going to prove he was out with Wendy Talbot?"

Karen started to reply, but the windshield suddenly glowed brightly. Headlights from behind them. An approaching car.

"Maybe that's him!" Karen whispered.

Both girls slid down low in their seats.

The bright lights rolled over the windshield. The car, a dark Taurus wagon, rumbled past them and kept going, moving slowly over the snow-slick street.

"False alarm," Karen said. She glanced at the dashboard clock, but it was a blank because the engine was off.

Micah sat up and tapped her long fingernails on the door. "You know, just because you saw him talking to Wendy in the hall after school doesn't mean they have a date or anything."

"I *told* you," Karen replied sharply. "It was the *way* he was talking to her. He was leaning over her. And when they laughed, she put her hand on his shoulder. Like she *owned* him or something."

"Karen — really!"

"Okay, okay," Karen muttered. "Not like she owned him. But she was definitely coming on to him. And he was loving it."

"So? Wendy is a flirt," Micah said, shrugging. "Everyone knows that. What does *that* prove?"

"Why are you defending her?" Karen demanded.

She immediately thought: Of *course* Micah would defend Wendy. Micah is a flirt, too. Micah is always coming on to boys, putting her hand on their arm as they talk. Micah always stands really close to boys, so close it makes them uncomfortable. And she's always purring at them with that sexy voice she has.

Micah is just like Wendy, Karen thought.

And then she scolded herself for thinking such cruel thoughts. Micah is my best friend, after all, Karen reminded herself. Micah is always there for me. She's here for me right now.

"I'm not defending Wendy," Micah insisted patiently. "I'm just trying to prove to you that you're crazy!" She laughed. "I mean, what are friends for?"

Karen didn't join in the laughter. "Don't you understand, Micah? This is the first Saturday that Ethan and I haven't been together."

"Karen — "

"The same day I saw him drooling all over Wendy Talbot in school, he called me and said he had to work the late shift at the Sizzler and couldn't see me Saturday night. Am I supposed to believe that?"

"Yes," Micah replied quickly. "Listen, Karen, you've got to stop acting so jealous. Really."

"If Ethan broke up with me — " Karen started. But the words caught in her throat. She couldn't bear to think about it.

"Oh, it's so *cold* in here!" Micah complained with a loud groan. "Feel my nose. Go ahead. Feel it. It's totally frozen, Karen."

"I can't feel your nose. I'm wearing gloves," Karen told her.

"Ethan isn't going to break up with you to start going with Wendy Talbot," Micah assured her. "But even if he does, Karen — " She grabbed Karen's sleeve. "Even if he does, it isn't the end of the world, you know? I mean, really. There are lots of other guys. You can't go totally to pieces — even *if* Ethan is interested in someone else."

Karen's dark eyes flashed. "You know

something — don't you!" she accused shrilly. "You know something about Ethan and Wendy, and you're not telling me!"

"No way!" Micah cried. "No way. I don't know anything. I'm just trying to help you. You know. I'm trying to give you a reality check, Karen. You're pretty. You're smart. Even if Ethan dumps you, you won't have any trouble — "

"Stop it!" Karen snapped, her voice trembling. "I don't want to talk about it."

Micah lowered her eyes and fiddled with the charm bracelet on her wrist. "Sorry," she murmured.

"No, *I'm* sorry," Karen replied quickly. "You're right, Micah. I'm a nervous nut. I didn't mean to snap at you. You're a true friend for coming along with me tonight. Really."

Micah traced her finger along the clouded-up passenger window. "Well, I just don't get it," she said softly. "I mean, if you think Ethan is out with Wendy, why aren't we parked in front of Wendy's house?"

"I don't want to see them together," Karen replied. "I really don't. I just want to see what time Ethan gets home."

Micah rubbed her hand in a wide circle on the passenger window, trying to make a peephole. "We can't see *anything* now!" she complained. "The windows are covered with snow, Karen. It's like being inside an igloo."

Karen only heard part of what her friend was saying. She had drifted into her unhappy thoughts. Once again, she pictured Ethan parked somewhere with Wendy. She pictured his arm around Wendy. She imagined them snuggling close, kissing, while the snow floated down over Ethan's car.

"You didn't hear a word I said," Micah accused, tapping Karen several times on the shoulder of her sweater. "Hey — snap out of it."

"Oh. Sorry." Karen glanced around. "I'd better scrape the windshield. I didn't realize."

She popped the trunk, pushed open the car door, pulled on her wool cap, and was immediately greeted by a blast of cold air and wet snowflakes. "I have a scraper in the trunk," she told Micah.

"Close the door!" Micah screamed. "It must be twenty below!"

Karen started toward the trunk, her boots crunching over the soft snow that blanketed the street.

The wet snowflakes tickled her face.

Soft as a kiss, she thought dreamily.

Ethan, where are you?

Leaning against the trunk, she gazed down

the hill to his house. The bright spotlight on the front of the house caught the falling snow, making the flakes white againt the low, purple sky. The slanted roof was blanketed with snow. The windows were all dark.

Sighing, Karen pulled up the trunk lid.

As the tiny trunk light came on, the boy's body came slowly into view.

The body was folded neatly in the trunk, the arms tucked underneath.

From out of the deep shadows, the boy's lifeless eyes stared up at Karen.

Karen opened her mouth to scream, but no sound came out.

Chapter 2

A low, terrified moan escaped Karen's throat.

In the dim light, the body in the trunk appeared to shift.

Or was that her imagination?

"Micah — help me!" Her cry came out a whisper, blown back in her face by a wet gust of wind.

And then Karen recognized the body.

A dummy. A mannequin.

The dumb department store mannequin her brother, Chris, had found years ago in a trash dump and had carried home to keep in his room.

Karen uttered an angry cry. She grabbed the plastic scraper and slammed the trunk lid shut, bouncing the car.

Chris and his stupid practical jokes!

He knew the mannequin would scare her to

death. Especially in the stressed-out state she'd been in.

Why did Chris think it was such a riot to frighten her?

He was older, bigger, smarter. He was already in college. He had a million friends and lots of girlfriends. So why did he have to prove how superior he was with all the dumb practical jokes he was always pulling?

I'll pay him back, Karen thought. I'll find a way to get him.

She slipped as she headed toward the windshield. Her feet started to slide out from under her, and she stumbled forward onto the hood of the car.

Pushing herself up with both hands, she quickly brushed the wet snow off the front of her sweater. Then she began scraping the windshield.

She felt cold droplets of snow in her hair that poked out from under the wool cap. Snowflakes clung to her eyelashes, making her blink as she worked to clear the windshield. Even three layers of sweaters couldn't keep out the cold.

Micah is right. This really is crazy, Karen thought.

We should have rented a movie and stayed in the nice, warm house.

But I couldn't, Karen realized. I couldn't just sit home thinking Ethan had lied to me, wondering where he was, wondering what he was doing — and with whom.

As she scraped the passenger side, Micah came into view. She was huddled low on the seat, staring out questioningly at Karen, her head buried in her coat collar, her hands shoved into her coat pockets.

I really took Ethan for granted, Karen thought, up until tonight. I guess I didn't realize how much he means to me until now. My life was really empty until Ethan and I started going together last year.

Karen and Micah had only been friends since the start of the school year. Before Ethan, Karen had spent a lot of lonely time. Her parents had had an angry divorce three years before. Karen's father had left home without even saying good-bye to her.

Karen had always had an intense personality. She took things seriously. She was always trying to figure out what people really meant by the things they said or did.

Her mother seemed to take the divorce better than Karen did. Karen had received only two letters from her father in three years.

Now the house was empty most of the time. Mrs. Masters had to work long hours at the department store where she was a floor manager. And Karen's big brother, Chris, was always busy with his college friends.

Ethan had saved Karen from her loneliness.

He was good for her. He was funny and outgoing and playful. He knew how to have fun. He kept her from getting too serious, too intense.

They took long bike rides along the river. They loved to ride to the high peak that overlooked town and gaze down at the tiny houses and shops below them.

They both loved trivia games. They played Trivial Pursuit until the cards were ragged and bent. Karen taught Ethan chess. They both enjoyed quiet, rainy evenings, staring at each other over the chessboard.

So many good times they had shared.

They had become so close, so close. . . .

But tonight he had dumped her for Wendy Talbot.

Karen knew he had. She just knew it.

And here she was, in the middle of a snowstorm, parked on the hill above his house, waiting — waiting for *what*?

Suddenly, the driver's window slid down, startling Karen from her thoughts. Micah, leaning over the seat, poked her head out.

"Hey — you don't have to scrape off the glass!"

"Oh. Yeah. Right." Karen hadn't realized the windshield was nearly cleared.

"Get in!" Micah called.

Karen obediently climbed in behind the wheel, quickly pulling the door shut. She dropped the scraper onto the floor beside Micah. "Ooh. I can't stop shivering," she said, brushing snow off her wool cap. "I have to turn on the heat. If we run out of gas — "

"I have an idea," Micah interrupted. "Let's drive to the Sizzler."

"Huh?" Karen hugged herself, trying to warm up. She was breathing hard, and her breath was steaming up the windshield.

"Drive to the Sizzler," Micah repeated. "If you see that Ethan is hard at work there, you'll feel better. Then we'll go to my house and make a fire, and try to warm up."

"But — but — " Karen hesitated, her mind spinning. "What if Ethan sees me? He'll know I was spying on him. Or . . . what if he isn't there, Micah? Really. I couldn't *stand* it if he wasn't there. I — "

"Karen, do you want to know the truth or not?" Micah demanded.

Karen couldn't reply. She wasn't sure *what* she wanted to know. "Maybe we should just go home," she muttered unhappily.

Micah started to reply, but bright lights against the windshield made her stop.

Both girls ducked low as white headlights shone through the car. A car roared past, speeding over the snow-covered street, down the hill.

At the bottom of the hill, its brakelights went on, and the car slid wildly, spun all the way around, then swerved into the Parkers' driveway. "It's him," Karen murmured, immediately recognizing Ethan's red Bonneville.

"Does he always drive like that?" Micah demanded, rolling her eyes.

"*Ssshhh,*" Karen whispered. Through the snow-dotted windshield, she could see Ethan climb out of his car and jog through the bright rectangle of light to his front door.

"Can we go now?" Micah whispered. "You saw him. You didn't prove anything. But you saw him."

"What time is it?" Karen demanded, her dark eyes peering down the hill. Ethan had disappeared into the house, but she kept staring at the front stoop anyway.

"It's too dark. I can't see my watch," Micah replied, holding her watch up close to her face.

Karen flicked on the overhead light.

"It's eleven-twenty," Micah told her.

"I *knew* it!" Karen cried unhappily. "He *was* out with Wendy!"

"Huh? How do you know?" Micah asked.

"The late shift at the Sizzler doesn't end until twelve. He shouldn't be home until twelve-twenty at the earliest."

"Karen!" Micah exclaimed. "You mean you were going to keep us sitting here another *hour*? I don't believe you! I really don't!"

Karen didn't reply. Her gloved hand trembled as she turned the ignition. The Corolla started right up. She jammed it into gear and slammed her foot down on the gas.

"Karen — not so fast! It's slippery!" Micah cried shrilly.

Karen ignored her and lowered her foot on the pedal. The tires spun as the car zigzagged down the hill.

Karen kept her eyes narrowed straight ahead as they sped past Ethan's house. She turned the wheel hard to pull out of a skid, then made a sharp right.

"Karen — slow down! I mean it!"

I don't feel cold anymore, Karen realized. I stopped shivering.

I'm too angry to feel cold. I feel only anger.

Anger and hurt.

"Karen — what is *wrong* with you?" Micah shrieked.

The white light appeared without warning. Twin headlights invading the car, momentarily blinding Karen.

She gasped and raised a gloved hand to shield her eyes.

The headlights grew brighter as the oncoming car roared closer.

"Slow down!"

Karen pumped the brake, but her car went into a skid, sliding toward the center of the street.

Her car slid sideways. Karen frantically spun the wheel, trying to straighten the car out.

Out of control. I'm out of control.

The white light rolled over her like an ocean wave.

"I — can't see!"

The crunch of metal and glass nearly drowned out her scream.

Chapter 3

Karen and Micah were both screaming as the car slid crazily over the street.

Karen's foot pressed the brake down as far as it would go.

Both girls were jolted forward, then sharply back.

The bright headlights vanished from the windshield, casting them in darkness.

The car made a half-spin and stopped at the snowbanked curb.

"Out of control," Karen murmured. "Out of control."

"Are you okay?" Micah asked in a trembling voice.

"Yeah, I guess," Karen managed to reply. "But the crash. I heard — "

"I — I thought — " Micah stammered. She tugged at the sides of her hair with both hands as if holding on for dear life.

Karen stared blankly at the dark windshield. "Did we crash? Is the car wrecked?"

Without waiting for an answer, she pushed open her door and took deep breaths of the cold air. "Oh. Look."

She pointed across the snowy street. Micah leaned over to follow her friend's gaze.

The other car had collided with a telephone pole.

The crash of metal. The shattering glass. It had come from the other car.

We're okay, Karen thought gratefully. We're perfectly okay.

But an inner voice kept her from rejoicing. You *wanted* to crash, the inner voice accused. You were so upset about Ethan, you *wanted* to crash.

Forcing away those thoughts, she wondered if the driver in the other car was okay.

She watched a large man climb out of the car. His boots crunched over the snow as he lumbered toward Karen. "Are you all right?" he called, shouting over the swirling wind.

Karen started to climb out, but the seat belt held her back. "Yeah. We're okay. Your car — "

"Headlight is smashed, that's all." The man stopped a few feet from Karen. He was wearing an enormous coat of some kind of shaggy fur. It made him look like a bear. Snowflakes clung to his glasses. "Sure you're okay?"

"Yeah. We didn't hit anything. Just slid," Karen replied, shivering. "I'm sorry — "

"Not really your fault," the man said. "I was going too fast." He motioned for her to close the door. "You can just leave. I'll get home okay. It's only a couple of blocks."

Karen watched the man walk back to his car, the big fur coat ballooning in the wind. Then she slammed her door shut and slowly backed the car from the curb.

"You want me to drive?" Micah asked.

Karen could feel Micah's eyes on her, studying her.

"I'm okay," Karen told her. "I'll go slow. Promise." Karen eased the car through a stop sign and made a careful left turn.

"This was a fun night," Micah muttered sarcastically.

"It's all Ethan's fault," Karen replied, surprised at her own bitterness.

"Huh?"

"It's all Ethan's fault," Karen repeated. "He can't *do* this to me!"

"Do you . . . want to talk about this?" Micah asked, her expression tight with concern.

"No. I don't think so," Karen replied softly,

her eyes straight ahead on the snow-covered road.

Karen dropped Micah at her house, then hurried home. The snow was turning to frozen sleet as she parked the car in the driveway and let herself in through the kitchen door.

The back of the house was dark. She stopped inside the doorway to pull off her wool cap and boots. Leaving them near the door, she brushed the cold snow from the front of her short, dark hair with one hand.

Then, with a shiver, she made her way to the front stairs. Her mother's bedroom door was closed. Mom must have gone to bed early, Karen decided.

Upstairs, Chris's door was closed, too. She could hear voices from the TV in there. Laughter. Probably *Saturday Night Live*.

Chris loved comedy shows. Sometimes he'd laugh till he had tears in his eyes and couldn't breathe, and Karen would just be sitting there blankly, wondering what he found so funny.

As she passed his bedroom, she suddenly remembered the mannequin stuffed in her trunk. What a dumb joke. She had an impulse to throw open his door and tell him how stupid he was.

Chris was on his winter break from school.

That meant he had a lot of time on his hands. Karen wasn't sure she could take two more weeks of his awful practical jokes.

She hesitated, shivering, her hands and feet nearly numb with cold. Should she go in and get on his case? I think I'd rather just get under the covers and warm up, she decided.

The sound of audience laughter on the TV followed her down the hall. It was warm in her room. Heat poured up from the floor register. Sleet pattered hard against the window. Karen hurried to pull the curtains.

She changed quickly into a long flannel nightshirt, tossing her sweaters and black leggings onto the chair beside her desk.

I'm never going to get warm, she thought, still shivering. Never.

She pulled back the quilt on top of her bed and was about to climb under the covers when the phone rang.

Startled, she jumped at the sound. And glanced at the clock radio beside her bed. Ten after twelve.

Who would call this late? she wondered.

She picked up the receiver midway through the second ring.

"Hello? Micah?"

"No," rasped a deep voice. "This is your worst nightmare calling."

Chapter 4

"Huh?" Karen gripped the receiver tightly in her cold hand. "*Who* is this?"

"Your worst nightmare," the deep voice repeated menacingly.

Karen laughed. "Oh. Hi! How are you?" she cried.

"Okay," the voice replied uncertainly.

"Adam — is your family all moved in? Are you in your new house?" Karen asked, carrying the phone over to the bed and tucking her cold feet under her as she sat on top of the quilt.

"Yeah. We're here," her cousin replied. "I can't believe we're back in Thompson Falls."

"I can't believe it, either," Karen said brightly. "Just like when we were kids. Mom and Dad used to — "

"Have you heard from your dad lately?" Adam interrupted.

"No. He doesn't write," Karen muttered, then quickly changed the subject. "So, how is everything, Adam? Do you like the new house?"

"I don't know," Adam replied. "It makes funny noises. Like groaning and moaning sounds. It's probably haunted. Or it was built on an Indian burial ground or something, and we're all going to be slaughtered in our sleep."

Karen snickered. "You're as cheerful as ever, Adam," she said sarcastically.

"Thanks. How's Chris? How does he like college?"

"You know Chris," Karen replied. "He's fine. He's always fine. He breezes right through everything."

"You still going with that long-haired freak?" Adam demanded.

Karen felt her face grow hot. She had momentarily forgotten how upset and angry she was at Ethan. "You mean Ethan? He isn't a long-haired freak," she said defensively. "Just because he has long hair doesn't mean — "

"Isn't he a little too good-looking for you?" Adam teased.

Karen didn't reply. She wasn't in the mood for her cousin's kidding around. And she especially wasn't in any mood for jokes about Ethan.

She and Adam were nearly the same age. They were both seniors. They had grown up together and had been fairly close, even though they didn't have much in common. They would study together and go to the movies when there was nothing better to do.

Then Adam and his family had moved away from Thompson Falls.

"Adam, it's really late," she said.

"Midnight is late?" Adam laughed scornfully. Then his tone suddenly changed. "Can you do me a favor, Karen?"

"Sure. What?"

"Monday will be my first day at school. I hate coming into a new school in the middle of the year. I mean, I won't know where anything is. I won't even be able to find the boys' room. Do you think if I get there early you could give me a quick tour Monday morning?"

"Sure. No problem," Karen replied. "Meet me a little after eight, okay? Just inside the front door."

"Hey, that's great," Adam told her. He sounded truly grateful.

Adam always was shy, Karen remembered. Moving to a new high school as a senior probably has him really stressed out. "I'll introduce you to some kids, too," Karen promised. "I want you to meet my friend Micah."

"Yeah. Okay. Everyone's probably forgotten me," Adam said with a trace of sadness. "I've been away so many years. Since sixth grade . . ."

He was always kind of a strange guy, Karen remembered. He never had many friends.

"See you Monday morning," she told him, yawning.

"Right. And thanks again, Karen. See you Monday morning." He clicked off.

Karen carried the phone back to her desk, then wearily climbed into bed. Yawning loudly, she forced herself not to think about Ethan.

Ethan and Wendy. Ethan and Wendy.

With their faces floating in her mind, she fell into a dreamless sleep.

She slept late on Sunday morning. It was a little after eleven o'clock when she came down for breakfast, dressed in gray sweats.

Chris was at the kitchen table, his back to Karen, starting his breakfast. He wore a maroon sweatshirt over faded jeans. Mrs. Masters was bent over the dishwasher, loading some dirty plates.

"Morning," Karen muttered. "You slept late, too," she said to her brother.

"Ohhh! My eye!" he cried. "My eye! It's — running!"

He whipped around to face her. He had placed an entire fried egg over his eye.

Karen laughed. She hated to encourage him, but it looked really funny. "You're sick," she told him. She slapped his shoulder really hard, making the egg fall into his lap.

"Chris, grow up," Mrs. Masters said sharply, her hands on her slender hips, a disapproving frown on her face. "I mean, really! How can you be nineteen years old and still be putting fried eggs on your face?"

"Easy," Chris replied, winking at Karen. He lifted the egg off his lap with one hand and plopped it back on the plate. "Want my egg?" he asked Karen. "Only slightly used."

"You want eggs, Karen?" her mother asked, closing the dishwasher.

"Um . . . no. Think I'll just make a Pop-Tart or something," Karen said.

"A Pop-Tart? Since when are you such a health nut?" Chris joked.

"Well, I'm going to run to the mall," Mrs. Masters said, drying her hands. She looked like she could be Karen's older sister. They had the same pale, delicate skin, the same dark brown eyes and brown hair; the same slender, almost frail, figures. "Sunday is my only day to do any shopping."

"Poor Mom." Chris grinned at her. He had yellow egg on his teeth.

"Don't make fun of me," Mrs. Masters scolded, giving the back of his head a playful slap as she passed the table.

Chris rubbed his head. "Hey! Sometimes I get tired of making fun of Karen, you know?" He turned to Karen. "Have you seen my dummy anywhere?"

"Oh, shut up, Chris!" Karen cried angrily. "You scared me to death with that thing last night!"

Chris laughed gleefully. "The body in the trunk!" he cried in his imitation of an eerie monster voice.

"You're not funny. Really. You're just a pain," Karen told him.

She ate her breakfast standing at the sink. Two strawberry-filled Pop-Tarts and a glass of cranberry juice. Then she settled down on the couch in the den, her father's old study, to call Micah.

They talked a little bit about the night before. Then Karen told her about her cousin Adam. "He moved into an old house on Monroe," she told Micah. "Yeah. Just three or four blocks from here. Isn't that weird? He hasn't lived in Thompson Falls since sixth grade. He's starting school on Monday."

"Ooh, he's so weird!" Micah exclaimed. Then she quickly caught herself. "No offense, Karen. I mean, I know Adam is your cousin. But he's definitely weird."

"He's not weird," Karen insisted. "He's just shy. He's terribly shy, Micah."

Micah was silent for a moment. "Does Adam still spend all his time reading those old horror comics and watching old horror movies?" she asked.

"I don't know," Karen told her. "I haven't seen him for ages. I know he used to collect all kinds of horror stuff. He was always really into it. Remember that creepy Halloween costume he made for himself when we were in fifth grade? The one with the green slime pouring out of his nose and mouth?"

"I always thought he was kind of creepy," Micah confessed. "But he's probably changed."

"I want you to be nice to him," Karen instructed, twisting the phone cord around her slender wrist. "He doesn't know anyone. Can you imagine? It's your senior year and you have to leave all your friends behind and move to a new place?"

"I still think he's weird," Micah replied. "But I'll try to be friendly. You know. Give him a break. Maybe he's gotten cute."

Karen suddenly heard a loud ringing sound. "What on earth is that?" she asked.

Micah let out a groan. "It's these hideous chimes my father bought. They go off every hour. They're really gross, but he loves them. Guess it must be twelve o'clock."

She shouted something to her mother. Then she returned her attention to Karen. "Have you heard from Ethan?"

Karen unwrapped the phone cord from her wrist. She had been lying over the arm of the couch. She sat up. "No. Not yet. You know Ethan. He'll probably sleep till noon."

"You're feeling better? I mean, about things?" Micah demanded.

"Yeah. I guess," Karen told her. "Yes. I do. Really."

She wasn't sure how she felt. She had been doing her best to shut Ethan out of her thoughts.

"I was really worried about you last night, Karen," Micah said with concern. "You — you really weren't acting like yourself. The whole idea of spying on Ethan — it was so crazy. And then the way you drove. I — I — "

"I'm feeling a lot better about things," Karen said. "You don't have to worry. I was thinking about it last night, before I fell asleep. You know what I decided, Micah?"

"What?"

"I decided that Ethan cares too much about me. He wouldn't go out with Wendy Talbot. I don't know what I was thinking of. But I know I'm right. I know how much Ethan and I mean to each other. And I know Ethan would never do that to me."

Karen glanced toward the doorway and cried out in surprise.

Ethan took a reluctant step into the room, a troubled expression on his face.

How long has he been listening? Karen wondered. She still held the phone to her ear. "Ethan, what are you doing here?" she asked, unable to hide her surprise.

He lowered his eyes, avoiding her stare. "Uh . . . Karen . . . we've got to talk."

Chapter 5

"Micah, I'll call you later," Karen said, staring hard at Ethan. She hung up the phone and climbed to her feet. "Ethan, hi."

"Hi." He shambled over to the couch, still avoiding her eyes.

He tossed down his jacket, then shoved his hands into the pockets of his baggy, faded jeans. He wore an oversized, pale blue V-necked sweater over a white T-shirt. His long, black hair fell over his shoulders. He had a slender silver ring through one earlobe.

"Chris let me in," he explained uncomfortably. He dropped down onto the big armchair across from the couch.

Karen lowered herself back onto the couch. She sat tensely on the cushion edge. "Where were you last night? I called you," she lied.

"I *told* you," he replied sharply. "I had to work. You know Ernie, that new busboy they

402

hired? He called in sick. So I had to take his shift." He ran a hand back through his long hair. "I didn't get home till after eleven."

"Eleven? I thought the shift ended at twelve," Karen said, trying to sound casual but not quite pulling it off. She fiddled tensely with the sleeves of her gray sweatshirt.

"The restaurant was empty," Ethan replied. "Because of the snow. So they let me go home." He sighed. "Wish I could quit that job. But with my dad laid off . . . you know how it is."

She nodded, studying the troubled expression on his face.

He's so good-looking, she thought. With those soulful, dark eyes. That broad forehead. I wish he'd smile. I love his smile so much.

Why is he here? Karen asked herself. Why does he look so upset? That isn't like him at all. What does he want to talk about?

Do I want to know? Maybe I don't want to hear it.

A heavy feeling of dread rose up from her stomach. She could feel her neck muscles tightening. Whenever she felt stressed out, she immediately got a stiff neck.

"What did you want to talk about?" she asked softly.

Ethan hesitated. He slowly raised his eyes to hers. "Well . . ."

The doorbell rang.

Ethan let out a nervous laugh.

Karen waited to see if Chris was going to answer it. When she didn't hear any footsteps, she hurried to the front door.

She pulled the door open. "Oh. Hi."

"How's it going, Karen?" Jake asked. She stepped aside so he could come in. Jake was Ethan's best friend. He was a tall, wiry, red-haired boy with long, gangly arms. He always reminded Karen of a grasshopper.

Ethan appeared in the front entranceway behind Karen. "Hey, there you are," Jake called to him. Jake had a funny, hoarse voice. A lot of kids called him Frog because of it.

"I've been trying to track you down, man," Jake told Ethan. "Your mom said you might be here."

"Jake, what's your problem?" Ethan asked, a startled expression on his face.

Jake pulled a worn, black leather wallet from his coat pocket. "Here, man. This is yours. You left it at my house last night."

Karen couldn't hold herself back. She turned angrily to Ethan. "Huh? You were at *Jake's* last night?" she demanded shrilly.

Ethan's face turned bright scarlet. "No . . .
uh . . ."

Jake held the wallet out to him.

Ethan grabbed it and jammed it into his back
jeans pocket. He was still blushing. Karen saw
him flash an angry glance at Jake.

What was Ethan doing at Jake's last night?
Karen wondered. Why would he break a date
with me and make up a lie about having to
work just to go over to Jake's?

"I . . . went over to Jake's on my way to
the Sizzler," Ethan said finally. His face turned
even brighter red.

Jake nodded, unconvincingly.

Ethan is such a terrible liar, Karen thought
miserably.

Why is he lying to me? He never lied to me
before!

She took a deep breath. She decided she
had to get the truth out of him.

"Hey, guys!" A voice interrupted from the
top of the stairs.

Chris hunched down so they could see him.
"How's it going?" Leaning against the banister,
he came halfway down the stairs.

Ethan and Jake greeted Chris warmly.

Ethan seems real glad for the interruption,
Karen thought unhappily.

"Hey, come upstairs," Chris urged, a devilish grin spreading across his face. "You can all listen in on this call I'm going to make. I'm calling this girl I met."

"Huh? You want us to listen in?" Jake demanded, confused.

"What are you going to do — call her up and make loud breathing sounds?" Karen asked, making a disgusted face. "That's your usual speed."

Chris looked hurt. "Hey, I wouldn't do that." He motioned for them to follow him, then started back up the stairs. "You'll see. It's going to be really funny. Come on. But don't laugh, okay? Don't let her hear you."

Ethan was the first one on the stairs. He hurried up after Chris, taking the stairs two at a time.

He's desperate to get away from me, Karen realized. He's been caught in a lie, and now he's so glad that my stupid brother got him out of trouble.

Jake started up the stairs after Ethan. He turned back to Karen. "You coming?" he called in his hoarse, raspy voice.

"I can't stand my brother's practical jokes," Karen told him, sighing. "But I guess I'll come."

Chris was already dialing the phone when Karen stepped into his room. Leaning over his desk, his sandy hair falling over his eyes, Chris grinned at her with the receiver to his ear.

Ethan dropped onto the edge of Chris's unmade bed. Jake leaned against the closet door. Karen stayed in the doorway, her eyes on Ethan.

These phone pranks Chris is always pulling are so dumb, Karen thought, frowning. Why does he think they're such a riot?

"Hello, is this Sara Martin?" Chris asked, disguising his voice, making it deeper. His devilish grin grew wider. "This is David Reston, your world literature instructor."

Jake let out a high-pitched giggle. Chris raised a finger to his lips, motioning for him to be silent.

"I'm glad you're enjoying the class, Sara," Chris said, keeping his voice as low as he could. "But I'm afraid I'm calling with some bad news."

Chris paused, listening to the girl's surprised reaction.

"Well, I'm afraid I caught you," Chris continued in his deep voice. "I know that you plagiarized your term report."

Jake slapped his forehead. He was struggling to keep from laughing out loud. Ethan had a big grin on his face.

I don't think this is funny, Karen thought,

standing stiffly in the doorway, her arms crossed over her chest. It's mean. Chris can be really mean.

"I'm sorry, Sara," Chris continued. "But I know where you copied your report from. You didn't really think you could get away with it, did you?"

That poor girl, Karen thought. She must be so upset.

"There's no point in denying it," Chris was telling the girl. "I know you copied your report from that genius in the class, Chris Masters."

"Oh, brother," Karen said aloud, rolling her eyes.

Chris burst out in laughter. "Yeah. It's me. Hi, Sara. You believed it was Reston — didn't you!"

Everyone in the room was laughing wildly. Everyone except Karen. Sara should hang up on him, she thought. Why is she being such a good sport?

Chris was waving his hand, motioning for Karen and the two boys to leave. Now that the joke was over, he wanted to talk to Sara in private.

Ethan and Jake followed Karen out of the room, still giggling about Chris's joke.

"Your brother is a riot," Jake told Karen.

"Ha-ha," Karen replied sarcastically. *"You*

don't have to live with him." They stopped at the bottom of the stairs. "Know what he did this morning?" Karen continued. "He put a fried egg over his eye."

Ethan and Jake both laughed.

"You think that's *funny*?" Karen demanded. "I think it's pitiful."

The boys laughed again. Then Ethan's expression turned serious. Karen saw the light fade from his brown eyes.

Jake reached for the door, intending to leave.

Karen decided she had no choice. She had to know what was troubling Ethan.

"Ethan, why did you come over?" she asked in a trembling voice. "What did you want to talk to me about?"

Chapter 6

Ethan tossed his long hair behind him with a flick of his head. Jake pulled open the front door. "Come on, Ethan." He tugged Ethan's sleeve. "You promised you'd help me shovel snow."

"Oh. Yeah," Ethan replied. He picked up his jacket. Then he raised his eyes to Karen. "I — I'll call you later, okay?"

"See you," Jake called back to her. He pushed the storm door open, and both boys headed out into the snow.

Karen stood and watched them from behind the glass door as they made their way to Ethan's red Bonneville. Jake reached down with his long, gangly arms and scooped up a handful of snow from beside the driveway. He heaved it at Ethan without bothering to form it into a snowball.

The snow made a white streak on the back of Ethan's jacket. To Karen's surprise, he just kept walking. He didn't bother to retaliate.

Something has really got Ethan upset, Karen knew. He didn't act like himself at all just now.

Did he come over to tell me he wants to go out with Wendy Talbot? Did he come over to break up with me, and then lose his nerve?

The cold seeped in from outside. She slammed the front door shut, but the white glare of the snow stayed in her eyes. She blinked, waiting for her eyes to adjust. Then she hurried to the kitchen to phone Micah and tell her to come over.

Micah obediently arrived about half an hour later. She had her thick, blonde hair pulled back in a loose ponytail. She wore a white sweater over black leggings.

Micah stretched out on her back on the couch in the den, holding one of the square couch pillows between her hands. Karen sat cross-legged on the carpet, her back against an armchair.

"Karen, lighten up," Micah scolded. "You're probably making the whole thing up."

"No, I'm not," Karen insisted glumly. She

rubbed her neck. The muscles had all tightened up.

"You really think he came over here to
tell you about him and Wendy?" Micah
tossed the pillow up and caught it in both
hands.

"He had the strangest look on his face, Micah," Karen said. "You know how laid back
Ethan always is. Not today. I could tell he was
upset."

Micah tossed the pillow up again. She let it
drop through her hands, onto her stomach.
"He was probably just tired, Karen. You know.
From working so late."

Karen sighed. She stared down at her
woolly white socks. When she finally spoke,
her voice came out shrill and angry. "If Wendy
tries to steal Ethan from me, I'll *kill* her. I
really will!"

"Whoa!" Micah sat up abruptly, lowering
her feet to the floor. She tossed the pillow at
Karen. It bounced off Karen's shoulder. "Stop
talking like that!"

"I mean it," Karen insisted. "If Ethan breaks
up with me because of her — "

"Listen to yourself," Micah interrupted, her
green eyes locked on Karen's. "Listen to how
crazy you sound."

"It's *not* crazy!" Karen protested in a shrill voice she didn't recognize.

"How old are you, Karen? You're seventeen, like me, right?"

Karen nodded.

"We're only seventeen," Micah continued emotionally. "We're both going to go out with *lots* of guys."

"No! I want Ethan!" Karen cried. She grabbed the pillow off the floor and heaved it against the wall. "I want Ethan — no one else. I'll kill Wendy. I mean it, Micah. I'll kill Wendy! I really will!"

On Monday morning, Karen woke up early. She pulled herself out of bed and made her way to the window. The sky had finally cleared. A red morning sun was lifting itself above the bare trees.

She dressed quickly, jeans and a sweater over two T-shirts. Then she gave her short, dark hair a quick brush, studying her pale face in the dresser mirror, and hurried downstairs.

Adam will be waiting for his tour of the school, she remembered. Then maybe she could catch Ethan and talk to him before homeroom.

She gulped down a tall glass of orange juice, her usual breakfast. She could hear her mother bustling about in her bedroom down the back hall, getting ready for work.

Karen spotted her boots by the kitchen door where she had left them to dry. Pulling a kitchen stool over, she sat down, pushed her left foot into the boot — and started to scream.

Chapter 7

"Chris — I hate you! *I hate you!*" Karen shrieked.

She let the boot fall to the floor and rubbed her wet sock.

Her brother had filled both her boots with snow.

"You creep! You stupid creep!" she cried. Before she realized it, she felt hot tears running down her cheeks.

Chris and their mother both appeared in the kitchen doorway at the same time.

"Karen — what on earth — !" Mrs. Masters cried, her dark eyes narrowed in concern.

Karen's shoulders were heaving up and down. She tried to stop crying, but she couldn't. "It's not funny! Not funny!" she choked out, pointing at the boots.

"Chris — you made your sister cry?" Mrs. Masters demanded sharply, turning to Chris.

"It was just a joke," Chris replied with a shrug. "She's unbalanced, Mom. Look at her. She's really unbalanced."

Karen found Adam waiting in the front hall at school. He greeted her with a smile, his dark eyes coming to life behind his black-framed glasses.

He seemed skinnier than the last time Karen had seen him. He wore his rust-colored hair very short. His chin was dotted with small red zits, she saw. He had a loose-fitting, hooded gray sweatshirt pulled over black denim jeans.

Karen dropped her coat at her locker, then led her cousin on a quick tour, starting with the gym and lunchroom in the basement, and ending up at the wood shop in back on the first floor.

"So? How do you like Franklin High so far?" Karen asked.

Adam shrugged. "So far so good."

He seems as shy and strange as ever, Karen thought. We've known each other our whole lives, but he's as awkward as if he had just met me.

"I just have to remember that the gym and lunchroom are downstairs, and the auditorium is upstairs," he said, scratching his bristly hair.

"I didn't have time to show you the science

lab or the computer room," Karen said, glancing at the clock above their heads. "They're on the third floor."

The hall had filled up with kids eager to stash their coats and get to homeroom. "I'll walk you to your homeroom," Karen offered, shouting over the sound of slamming lockers and loud voices. "Then maybe I'll see you later. I want you to meet my friend Micah."

Adam nodded solemnly.

"Your homeroom is right down here," Karen told him, starting down the hall.

She stopped when she saw Ethan.

He had his backpack slung over the shoulder of his blue-and-gray Franklin High jacket. He was talking to someone, Karen saw, struggling to see him through a crowd of kids.

He was talking to Wendy Talbot.

They were laughing together.

Wendy had her hand on the sleeve of his jacket.

So it's true, Karen thought, holding in a sob. *It's true.*

The crowded scene blurred. The kids shimmered away. The roar of laughing, shouting voices faded to silence.

Karen stood alone. Darkness fell over her like a heavy curtain descending.

I'm alone, she thought.

Everyone has disappeared.

Everyone.

The voices slowly returned, low at first, then as loud as before. The darkness lifted. Someone bumped Karen's shoulder. A girl was shouting, "Michael! Michael! Has anyone seen Michael?"

Karen could see only Ethan. He and Wendy turned away from her, walked side by side in the other direction. They disappeared around a corner.

"Karen — are you okay?" Adam was asking. "Karen?"

She stared down the blurred hallway.

Were those tears in her eyes that were making everything shimmer and bend?

"Karen — are you okay?" Adam demanded.

Staring straight ahead, unable to focus, her knees trembling with the walls, her heart thudding in her chest, the floor twirling beneath her, Karen knew the answer was no.

Micah had been flirting with two boys at the next table. Now she turned back to Karen. "You haven't touched your lunch," she said.

"I know. I can't eat," Karen replied. She crumpled the tinfoil over her sandwich, squeezing it into a tight ball.

"Wait a minute! What is it?" Micah asked. "Is it tuna fish?"

"I don't even know," Karen sighed. She jumped to her feet, the chair nearly falling over behind her.

"Karen — where are you going?" Micah asked, startled. "We still have twenty minutes. You — "

"I'm going to find Wendy," Karen replied in a flat, low voice. The room started to blur again as she said Wendy's name.

I'm not going to cry, Karen told herself, biting down hard on her lower lip. *I'm not going to cry in front of everyone in this crowded lunchroom.*

"Karen, sit down," Micah said sternly. She pointed to Karen's chair. "I mean it. Sit down. You're not going anywhere." Karen didn't budge.

Micah's firm tone turned pleading. "Let's talk, okay? Sit down. Let's talk."

"No, I'm going to find Wendy," Karen said softly, her voice revealing no emotion at all.

"But, Karen — you *can't*!" Micah cried. "She'll just laugh at you. You'll feel like a jerk, Karen. Karen — listen to me!"

Karen didn't reply. She turned and walked toward the lunchroom exit, taking long, determined strides. She could hear Micah calling to her, but she didn't turn around.

A group of cheerleaders were huddled outside the lunchroom, laughing loudly about something. From down the hall, Karen could hear the *thud* of basketballs from the gym.

Walking quickly, she passed several closed classrooms. Some kids didn't have lunch until the next period.

What would she say to Wendy?

The question jarred through her mind, made her slow her pace.

I'll tell her there's no way she can have Ethan, Karen quickly decided.

I'll just tell her.

She grabbed the metal railing and started up the stairs to the first floor. Two girls heading down the stairs called out hello to her as they passed.

Karen didn't reply.

Wendy, where will I find you? she thought.

To her astonishment, Wendy appeared at the top of the stairs.

She was carrying a huge sculpted head in both hands. Some kind of art project.

"Wendy, hi," Karen called breathlessly.

Karen's heart seemed to jump up into her throat. She could feel the blood pulsing at her temples.

She stepped up beside Wendy on the top step.

Wendy's straight red hair glowed in the sunlight from the window against the front wall. She turned her gray-green eyes on Karen. "How's it going?"

How's it going?

How's it going?

The words repeated in Karen's mind like an ugly, threatening chant.

How's it going? You *know* how it's going, Wendy! Karen thought, suddenly bursting with fury.

There was a flurry of motion.

A ripple.

And then thrashing arms.

And suddenly Wendy's sculpted head was flying in the air.

And Wendy was falling, falling backwards, her hands reaching for Karen, grabbing only air.

The papier-mâché head bounced down the hard steps.

Thud. Thud. Thud.

Wendy bounced beside it. Head first.

She let out a low cry each time her head hit a step.

Horrified low cries all the way down to the bottom.

Then she lay sprawled on her back, her arms outstretched, one leg bent under her, her red hair splayed around her unmoving head.

Karen stared down at her from the top step, her hands pressed tightly against her hot cheeks.

Have I killed her? Karen wondered.

Chapter 8

Did I kill her? Karen asked herself.

Did I push her?

Did she fall — or did I push her?

Karen couldn't remember.

The two girls who had been walking down the stairs were huddled over Wendy. Karen didn't move from the top step.

I didn't push her — did I? She fell. I'm sure she fell.

Down below, Wendy groaned, her eyes still shut.

The two girls suddenly raised their eyes accusingly at Karen.

"No, I didn't push her!" Karen shouted. "She fell. I didn't push her!"

And then, Karen was running. Running down the hall.

Her blue Doc Martens slapped the hard floor as she ran.

I didn't push her. I'm pretty sure I didn't push her.

I don't remember. I don't really remember.

Where was Karen running?

She wasn't sure. She just knew she wanted to run forever.

"Karen — could you come downstairs, please?"

Her mother's voice invaded Karen's room. Karen made her way to the bedroom door and opened it a crack. "Mom — I *told* you. I'm not hungry. I can't eat dinner."

Karen had hurried home from school and shut herself up in her room. She glanced at the clock radio. Nearly seven o'clock.

Her eyes moved to her backpack, lying unopened on the floor beside her desk.

What have I been doing all this time? she asked herself. I haven't done any homework. I was lying on the bed, I remember, staring up at the cracks in the ceiling.

Did I fall asleep?

"Karen — come down," her mother insisted. "Or shall I come up?"

Karen pressed her cheek against the bedroom door. "What do you want?" she called down warily.

"To talk," her mother shouted from the bottom of the stairs.

Karen sighed. She didn't want to talk. She *couldn't* talk.

What was she supposed to say to her mom?

"Guess what, Mom? Ethan got interested in another girl, so I pushed her down the stairs today and tried to kill her."

How would that go over?

She hesitated, her face still pressed against the door.

Her mother's footsteps were light and rapid on the stairs. Karen backed away from the door. Mrs. Masters entered, her dark eyes stopping on Karen, her birdlike features set with concern.

"Mom, I'm okay. I'm just not feeling well," Karen said, backing up.

"That was Micah on the phone," Mrs. Masters said, crossing her skinny arms over her chest. She wore a lime-green turtleneck over black corduroy slacks.

"Huh? Micah? She called?" Karen shook her head hard, as if trying to clear it. "Why didn't you tell me?"

"She called to speak to *me*," Mrs. Masters replied softly.

Karen wrinkled her forehead, bewildered.

She slumped down on top of the bed. "How come?"

Mrs. Masters took a few steps toward her, her arms still tightly crossed in front of her. "Micah told me you had a little trouble in school today." Her voice caught on the last word. She coughed and cleared her throat.

"She did?" Karen was confused. What had Micah said? Why had Micah called? What did Micah think she was doing?

"Do you want to tell me about it?" Mrs. Masters asked, her dark eyes piercing so deeply into Karen's that Karen had to look away.

"Not much to tell, really," Karen muttered. *Why don't you leave me alone? Just go away and leave me alone?*

"Micah said you made threats about some girl. A girl named Wendy," her mother said, clearing her throat again.

"Threats? Not really threats," Karen replied, staring down at the worn brown carpet.

"Micah said you made threats in the lunch-room. Then, a few minutes later, this girl fell down the stairs. Micah said the girl had to be taken to the hospital for X rays. That she has a concussion."

"Just a slight concussion," Karen muttered. "She's going to be okay."

"But some kids saw you there. Some kids think you pushed her," Mrs. Masters said softly, her eyes burning into Karen's. "That's what Micah told me."

"No!" Karen cried. "No! That's a lie! That's a stupid lie!" She had meant to stay calm, but her words burst out in a shrill screech.

Her mother's mouth dropped open for a second, revealing her surprise. Her dark eyes flashed, then quickly dimmed. "Karen, you can talk to me," she said with feeling.

She walked up to the bed and placed her hands on Karen's shoulders. "You know you can talk to me, don't you?" she repeated softly. "You can tell me what's troubling you."

"I know, Mom," Karen whispered.

Mrs. Masters leaned down to hug her. Karen sat stiffly, enduring the hug, not moving. Thinking about Micah.

"Well, whenever you're ready to talk, I'm here," Mrs. Masters said softly.

As her mother turned and walked slowly from the room, Karen began to tremble. It took her a while to realize she was trembling in anger. She leapt to her feet, closed her door, and began pacing rapidly back and forth, her hands clasped tightly in front of her.

How could Micah do this to me? she wondered.

How could Micah betray me like this?

I thought she was my friend. My best best friend. Someone I could trust.

So how could she rat on me to my mother?

Why did she call behind my back and tell my mother what happened today?

Karen reached for the phone. She grabbed it with such force, she knocked it onto the floor. The receiver bounced across the carpet. The dial tone buzzed angrily as she stooped to retrieve it.

Her heart pounding, she punched in Micah's number.

Micah picked up after the first ring. "Hello?"

"Micah — why?" Karen cried breathlessly. "I — I don't get it! Why did you do it? Why did you call her?"

"I thought I had to," Micah answered quietly, calmly. "Are you okay, Karen? You sound terrible."

"Why?" Karen repeated. "Why did you tell my mom?"

"For your own good," Micah told her. "I'm worried about you, Karen. Really worried. I thought your mother should know."

Karen could feel her anger rise up, take over. She was losing control —and she didn't care.

"You *betrayed* me!" she shrieked into the receiver.

"Now, wait — " Micah started to protest.

"You're not my friend! You're not! Don't ever talk to me again!" Karen slammed down the receiver.

She realized she was gasping for breath.

"Micah isn't my friend anymore," she said aloud in a choked voice. "Micah isn't my friend."

Ethan is the only one I have left, Karen thought, struggling to slow her racing heart, struggling to make the throbbing in her temples go away.

She rubbed her stiff neck with both hands.

Ethan is the only one left, she told herself.

Ethan squeezed the steering wheel with both hands. He shook his head bitterly. "I can't believe I missed those two foul shots," he sighed.

Karen reached across the seat and placed a comforting hand on the shoulder of his blue-and-gray school jacket. "We won, anyway, Ethan," she said softly. "So it really didn't matter."

"It mattered to *me*," he replied sharply.

They both stared out into the darkness. It was Friday night, and he had driven her home after the game. Parked in her driveway, Ethan left the lights on and the engine running, as if he were eager to leave.

"Want to come in?" Karen asked.

He scowled, still thinking about his missed foul shots.

"No one's home," Karen added. "My brother has a date. My mom is visiting her cousin."

"It was a bad night," Ethan murmured. "I didn't get any rebounds, either. The ball just didn't bounce my way."

"Come on, Ethan. We *won!*" Karen cried impatiently. She tugged his sleeve. "Are you coming in or not?"

His expression changed as he turned to her. He tossed his long hair behind him with a flick of his head. His hands tapped the wheel, pounding a nervous rhythm.

"Karen, there's something I have to tell you," he said in a strange, tight voice. "You're not going to like it. But I have to say it, anyway."

Chapter 9

Karen's breath caught in her throat. She suddenly felt cold all over.

"I — I think we should start seeing other people," Ethan blurted out, speaking quickly, slurring it all into one word. He stared straight ahead, avoiding her eyes.

"Huh?" Karen uttered.

She had been expecting it.

She had been expecting it — but now it came as a total shock.

Was he really breaking up with her?

"We could still go out," Ethan said, turning sheepishly to her. "I mean, we could go out a lot. I still really like you. I mean, we always have so much fun together. We could still go on our bike rides and everything. But — "

"Ethan, what are you *saying*?" Karen cried. She wanted to hold herself together, but her voice came out shrill and choked. And her shoulders were starting to tremble.

He slid his hands tensely over the wheel. "I just think we should see other people, too. There's no reason why we can't — "

"No reason?" Karen shrieked. "No reason?"

"Karen, calm down — okay?" Ethan said impatiently. "Can't we just talk?"

"Talk? What's there to talk about?" Karen cried. "I can see your mind is made up."

"Karen — please — we've always been able to talk to each other. That's one thing I really like about you."

"What's there to talk about?" Karen screamed. A wave of anger swept over her. She felt so angry, so hurt. She had a strong impulse to grab Ethan by the shoulders and shake him, shake him until he understood what he was doing to her.

"We can still go out some Saturday nights," Ethan offered weakly. "And we can still play chess. And — "

"Shut up!" Karen cried, surprised by the violence of her feelings. "Shut up! Just shut up, Ethan!" Tears rolled down her cheeks. "Are you breaking up with me or not?"

"No!" he replied instantly. "I mean . . . well . . ."

"I didn't push her!" Karen shrieked. *"I didn't push her! She fell!"*

Ethan gaped at her in shock.

Tears rolled down Karen's face, blurring her vision, putting Ethan behind a wet curtain, making him seem far, far away.

"Karen, calm down," he pleaded, grabbing her hand. "Calm down. I didn't mean — "

She jerked her hand away. "You can't break up with me! You *can't!*" she insisted, sobbing loudly.

Ethan shook his head helplessly. "I only said — "

"Shut up! I heard what you said!" Karen grabbed the door handle and pushed the door open. A gust of cold air brushed her hot face. Her tears blinded her, making the darkness appear to swim in front of her.

"You can't! You can't!" she screamed.

Without realizing it, she had stumbled out of the car.

Karen, you're totally out of control, a voice said inside her. *Karen, if you don't get control, you'll lose Ethan forever.*

But how can I? she asked herself.

Her legs felt weak. Her knees were quivering. Her chest heaved with each sob.

"I'll call you later," Ethan said, reaching to pull the passenger door shut. "Try to get yourself together, okay? I'll call you when I get home, and we can talk."

Karen turned and ran sobbing around to the back of the house. Ethan's headlights rolled over her as he backed down the drive.

Crazy thoughts jangled through her mind as she fumbled in her bag for her house key. Crazy, frantic thoughts.

I won't let him break up with me.

I'll kill him first. I really will.

Maybe I did push Wendy. I don't care.

What can I say to him? How can I make him change his mind?

Finally, she pulled out the key and managed to push it into the lock with a trembling hand on the third try. She pushed open the kitchen door and closed it quickly behind her.

The kitchen smelled of oranges. The house was dark. She ran to the stairs without turning on any lights. Her heart pounding, her eyes still blurred by tears, she ran up to her room and dropped face down on top of her bed.

"Doesn't Ethan realize how much I care about him?" she said aloud.

She buried her face in the pillow to stifle her sobs. Her crazy thoughts bounced through her mind. She gave in to them, made no attempt to stop them.

After a while, she realized she still had her

coat on. She climbed to her feet, breathing hard. She had stopped crying, but all the tears had given her a sharp headache at both temples.

Rubbing her temples, trying to rub the pain away, she made her way across the room. She clicked on the light — and cried out.

Her old teddy bear had been hung by the neck in the cord to the venetian blind. It drooped limply, its head tilted, its one remaining black eye staring across the room at her.

"Chris — you stupid jerk!" Karen shouted.

How can he be such a creep? she asked herself bitterly.

As she started across the room to rescue the old bear, the phone rang.

It's Ethan! she realized.

What am I going to say? What?

Got to think. Got to think clearly.

How can I make him see how much he means to me?

She picked the phone up in the middle of the second ring. "Hello?" Her voice came out a soft whisper.

"Karen, it's me." Ethan. "I just . . . uh . . . wanted to see how you were doing."

"I — I'm better," she stammered. "You just surprised me, that's all."

"I'm sorry," Ethan replied, but with little feeling. "This is hard, Karen. I hope — "

"I'm sorry I acted like such a jerk," Karen interrupted. She rubbed her throbbing temple with her free hand. "I didn't mean to scream at you like that. You must think — "

"No. Don't worry about it," Ethan said. "I'm just glad you're okay now. I mean, you sound calmer."

"Yeah. I guess," Karen replied. "It's just that — "

"Well, good night," Ethan said. He sounded very eager to hang up. "See you in school."

"Wait, Ethan — uh — I just want to say something to you. I just want to say — "

Karen was interrupted by a loud clicking sound.

"Oh. Hold on, Ethan," she pleaded. "There's a call on the other line. It might be my mother."

More clicking.

"I hate Call Waiting," Karen said. "It always interrupts at the wrong time. Hold on a sec, okay?"

"Okay," Ethan agreed.

More clicks. Then silence.

When Karen returned to Ethan a few seconds later, her voice was trembling and weak.

"Ethan, please — come over! Come over here right away!"

"Karen? What's wrong?" Ethan demanded.

"I'm all alone here, Ethan. Please — hurry! He said he was going to kill me!"

"Huh? Who?"

"The voice on the phone. It was so *horrible,* Ethan. He said he was going to kill me!"

Chapter 10

When Ethan's car pulled up the driveway, Karen ran out to meet him. As he stepped out, she threw herself into his arms, pressing her face against his.

"Ethan — it was so frightening!" she cried.

He kept his arms wrapped around her trembling shoulders.

She pressed her hot face against his. "He — he said such horrible things to me!" she told him.

His arm around Karen's shoulder, Ethan led her into the house. Their shoes crunched over the hard snow. "It was probably a joke," Ethan said softly.

"I — I don't think so," she stammered.

She clicked on the den light, and they sat close together on the couch. She shivered. "The voice — it was just so terrifying!"

She pressed her forehead against his cheek. His long hair tickled her face.

"It was a man?" Ethan asked softly.

"I think so, I couldn't really tell," Karen replied. "The voice was a whisper. Very hoarse. That's what made it so frightening. And then — the things he said. . . ."

"What did he say?" Ethan demanded, tenderly, soothingly stroking her dark hair.

Karen shivered again. "He said such ugly things, Ethan. He said he was going to kill me. He said he knew where I lived, and he was going to kill me. He said that first he would describe how he planned to do it, and then he would do it."

Ethan shook his head. He stroked her hair.

"I — I just kept screaming, 'Who *is* this?' " Karen continued, squeezing Ethan's hand. "I couldn't believe it was happening. I mean, you see stuff like this in movies and on TV. But I couldn't believe it was happening to me."

"It's got to be a joke," Ethan said thoughtfully. "Some kind of sick joke."

"Do you really think so?" Karen asked, holding on to him tightly.

"He'll never call again," Ethan assured her. "You can't let it frighten you. Just forget about it. Really."

Karen shuddered. "That weird, hoarse voice. I'll never forget it. Never! Who would play a joke like that? What kind of sick person?"

"Would you feel better if we called the police?" Ethan asked.

Karen pulled away from him and sat up. "The police? Maybe we should."

Ethan started to his feet. "I'll call them for you."

Karen pulled him back down. "No. Wait. They wouldn't do anything. What would they do? They'd just tell me it was someone's idea of a joke."

"Probably," Ethan replied, frowning.

"I hope it *is* a joke," Karen said, biting her lower lip. "I hope it is. It was so ugly, Ethan. So ugly. I — I'm still shaking."

"It's okay. I'm here now," he said softly. "It's okay, Karen."

He wrapped her in his arms. She leaned into him, raised her face to his, and kissed him until she stopped trembling.

Monday. Dreary Monday, Karen thought unhappily.

As she loaded her backpack to go home after school on Monday, Karen realized it had been a drearier day than most.

She had seen Micah at least a dozen times,

and neither of them had spoken to the other. Karen ate lunch by herself at a table in the corner of the lunchroom. Micah ate with some tenth-grade girls Karen didn't know.

All day Karen had the feeling that kids were staring at her. In the hall just before fifth period, a group of girls suddenly stopped talking as Karen passed.

Were they talking about me? Karen wondered.

Were they talking about me and Wendy?

When the final bell rang, Karen gratefully hurried to her locker, eager to leave. Hoisting her backpack onto the shoulder of her down coat, she stepped out the front exit, into a dark afternoon, the sky cloud-laden and charcoal-colored, nearly as dark as night.

Is it going to snow again? she wondered, lowering her head against the onrushing wind.

She had crossed the street and trudged halfway down the next block when she heard running footsteps behind her.

Was someone coming after her?

Before she could turn her head, two hands grabbed her roughly around the waist.

"It's me, Karen!" a hoarse voice whispered in her ear. "It's me!"

Chapter 11

"Let me go!"

Karen squirmed out of the grasping arms and spun around.

"Adam!" she cried. "Adam — you scared me to death!"

He laughed. He had a silent laugh that sounded more like coughing than laughing. His eyes flashed excitedly behind his glasses.

He shook his head. "You're too easy," he said, giving her arm a playful shove.

"Huh? What do you mean?" Karen demanded, waiting for her heartbeat to return to normal.

"You're too easy to scare. No challenge," Adam said.

What does he mean by that? Karen wondered.

Adam picked up his brown leather briefcase. They started walking, side by side.

Adam had a red-and-white-wool ski cap pulled down over his spiky, rust-colored hair. He wore a khaki-colored coat that was too short for him. His workboots clomped noisily against the sidewalk.

"What's with the briefcase?" Karen demanded. "Isn't that a little dorky? Why can't you carry a backpack like everyone else?"

"I don't like to be like everyone else," he replied. "I like to be different. I *can't* be like everyone else. You know that, Karen."

"But — a briefcase?" Karen cried, staring at it.

"I like it," he replied, swinging it as he walked.

"Well, how's it going?" Karen asked. "Your classes okay? You meet anybody?"

"Yeah. I guess I'm doing okay." They walked in silence for a while. "I thought you were going to introduce me to your friend. Micah."

"I'm not talking to her," Karen told him, feeling her face grow hot.

"Oh. Sorry," he replied.

They stopped at an intersection. A station wagon filled with four enormous barking dogs rumbled past. "Where do you think *they're* going?" Karen wondered.

"Anywhere they want to!" Adam joked. As

they started across the street, his expression turned serious. "You know, some kids think you pushed that girl Wendy down the stairs. I heard them talking today."

"I didn't push her," Karen replied quickly. "She fell."

Karen picked up her pace, keeping her eyes on the black, rolling clouds overhead.

"Wendy is telling everyone you pushed her," Adam reported. "She's trying to get witnesses. You know, kids who saw it. She says she wants to sue you or have you arrested for assault or something."

"That's stupid," Karen replied angrily, making a disgusted face. "There weren't any witnesses."

That remark made Adam stop. He shifted the heavy briefcase to his other hand. "How do you know there weren't any witnesses?"

"There were only two other girls on the stairs," Karen told him. "And they were looking the other way."

Adam studied her face suspiciously. "And Wendy just fell?"

"She slipped, I guess," Karen said uncomfortably.

The wind swirled around them. The sky grew even darker.

A car rolled slowly past. A red car. Karen

turned, thinking it might be Ethan. But it wasn't.

"She's very angry at you," Adam reported, scratching his hair through the wool ski cap. "You'd better stay away from her," he warned.

"No problem," Karen replied dryly. They started walking again, lowering their heads against the strong wind. "Maybe Wendy made the phone call," she added in a low, thoughtful voice.

"What? What phone call?" Adam asked.

She told him about the hoarse, whispering voice that threatened to kill her.

"Weird," Adam muttered, shaking his head. "Did you tell your mother?"

"Not yet," Karen replied. "Ethan said it was a joke. A one-time thing. And if it was just a one-time thing, I didn't want to tell my mom and get her all worried."

"Yeah. Right," Adam said thoughtfully, his eyes narrowed behind the black-rimmed glasses. "It's a one-time thing, Karen. I'm sure it's a one-time thing."

"So are we going to the new dance club Saturday night?" Karen asked. She sat on the edge of her desk chair, cradling the phone between her chin and shoulder as she brushed clear polish onto her nails.

It was a little after seven-thirty Monday evening. A frozen rain pattered against the bedroom window behind her.

On the other end of the phone line, Ethan hesitated. "I don't know. I may have to work."

Is he lying to me? Karen wondered.

Why does he sound as if he's lying? Am I just being paranoid?

"You worked *last* Saturday — remember?" she said crossly.

"I know," Ethan sighed. "I have to talk to Tony. At the Sizzler. If I can trade shifts with Tony, then you and I can go out Saturday."

He's lying, Karen decided.

He's definitely lying. He plans to go out with Wendy on Saturday night, and he's making up a story so he doesn't have to tell me the truth.

"I really want to see you," she cooed. "Last Saturday was so terrible."

"I know. I hope I can trade shifts," Ethan replied. "But if Tony — "

He was interrupted by loud clicks.

"Oh. Wait. That's the Call Waiting," Karen said, annoyed. "Hold on. It might be my mom. She's working late."

She clicked off.

A few seconds later, she returned to him. Once again, her voice was shrill and frightened. "Oh, Ethan — it was him again!"

Ethan groaned. "Oh, no."

"He — he said he was going to cut my throat!" Karen cried.

"Try to calm down," Ethan advised. "Did you recognize the voice? Could you tell who it was?"

"No," Karen told him. "He said he was closer than I knew. He said he could get into my house any time he wanted. Then he said he was going to cut my throat!"

She let out a frightened sob. "It was so horrible, Ethan! So horrible!"

"I'll be right over," Ethan said.

"Please — hurry!" she cried. "He said he could get into my house — any time he wanted!"

She hung up the phone.

Staring down at her wet nails, she saw a dark shadow move in the mirror.

She opened her mouth to scream, but no sound came out.

And then the dark figure lurched across the room and grabbed her.

Chapter 12

"Gotcha!" a voice shouted.

Karen gasped in terror and spun around.

"Chris!"

He tossed back his head and opened his mouth in a fiendish, horror-movie laugh. "Made you jump!" he cried triumphantly.

"Chris — you jerk!" Karen screeched. "You're not funny! You're not funny! Leave me alone!"

Karen leaned over the desk and buried her face in her hands. Her trembling shoulders revealed to Chris that she was crying.

"Hey — what's wrong?" he demanded. She felt his hand on her back. "What's your problem, Karen?"

She kept her face buried in her hands, wishing he would just go away.

"I'm sorry," Chris apologized. "It was just

a joke. I'm sorry. What's wrong, Karen? Why are you so upset?"

Ethan arrived a few minutes later, his long hair disheveled, his features set in a worried frown.

He tossed his jacket over the banister and followed Karen into the den. He was dressed all in black, a black sweater over black denim jeans. "Whose funeral is this?" Karen asked dryly.

"Don't be so morbid," Ethan replied.

Chris was already in the den, staring out the window. He turned when Ethan entered and greeted him with a grunt.

Ethan sat close beside Karen on the couch in the den. He kept clasping and unclasping his hands, cracking his knuckles.

Chris paced back and forth across the small room, shaking his head, glancing at his sister. "You should put cold water on your eyes," he advised her. "They're all red and bloodshot."

"I'm okay," Karen replied quietly, raising her eyes to Ethan.

Chris stopped in the middle of the room and leaned his weight on the back of the armchair. "You look worse than Karen does," he told Ethan. "You're as pale as a ghost."

Wind rattled the den window behind her. Karen felt cold air on the back of her neck. She tapped her fingers nervously on the soft arm of the couch.

"I'm just worried about Karen," Ethan told Chris, leaning forward tensely. "She told you about the calls, right?"

Chris nodded.

"What if this creep is serious?" Ethan demanded.

"Maybe we *should* call the police," Karen said thoughtfully.

Chris shook his head. "They'll say it's a dumb joke, which it is."

"How do you know for sure?" Ethan demanded.

"It's either a kid from school," Chris replied, "or it's some nut who just stays home and makes threatening calls. We studied these guys in a psychology unit last semester. I read all about them."

Karen let out an angry groan. "Chris — this is really happening," she said sharply. "It's not a case history in one of your psych textbooks."

She tugged at the sides of her short, brown hair. "I can't believe this is happening to me."

Another strong blast of wind outside made the window rattle again. Karen snuggled against the sleeve of Ethan's sweater.

"These guys never leave their houses," Chris continued, still leaning against the back of the chair. "Most of them are afraid to go out and face the real world. So they stay inside and make sick phone calls."

"But why me?" Karen cried shrilly. "Why did he choose me?"

"Are you sure it's a he?" Ethan asked, raising his arm and draping it around her shoulders.

"Yeah. Could you recognize the voice?" Chris demanded.

Karen shook her head. "I couldn't. Whoever it is just whispers. A very hoarse whisper. Like someone with really bad laryngitis."

"Well, next time, just tell him to drop dead, and then hang up," Chris advised. "Look at you." He shook his head disapprovingly, his sandy-colored hair falling over his forehead. "You're a total wreck."

"Chris is right," Ethan told her. "You can't let yourself get all upset. Just tell the creep to drop dead."

Karen started to reply, but the phone rang.

Chapter 13

Karen grabbed the couch arm. She raised her eyes to Ethan.

Ethan jumped to his feet, his hands balled into tight fists at his sides.

Chris hesitated, staring at the phone on the desk against the window. It rang twice. Then he moved quickly across the room and picked up the receiver in the middle of the third ring.

"Hello?" he shouted. "Who is this?"

Her eyes on her brother, Karen crossed her arms over her chest as if shielding herself. Ethan stood tensely beside the couch, also staring at Chris.

"Oh. Hi," Chris said. "How's it going?" His solemn expression gave way to a smile. "Hold on." He pointed the receiver toward Ethan. "It's for you. It's Jake."

"Huh? Jake?" Ethan's expression revealed relief and surprise. He glanced back at Karen as he made his way to the phone. "Now you've got *me* freaked!"

Ethan turned his back to Karen and began talking in low tones to Jake.

"You going to be okay?" Chris asked with genuine concern.

"Yeah. I'm feeling a lot better," Karen replied, forcing a smile. "Really. I'm sure you're right about the calls. Being harmless, I mean."

Chris glanced at the desk clock. "Mom is really putting in long hours," he muttered. "Well, okay. I'm meeting some friends. Tell Mom I said hi. Tell her I'll be in pretty late."

He gave her a little wave, glanced at Ethan, who still had his back turned, and disappeared from the room.

Karen rubbed her sleeves with both hands. The cold air was seeping right through her sweater. This den has always been the coldest room in the house, she thought.

She watched Ethan leaning over the desk. The light caught the silver ring in his ear and made it glow. She loved the way his hair flowed over his collar. She wanted to touch it, tug at it, pull it through her fingers.

When Ethan finally hung up the phone, she motioned for him to come sit beside her on the couch.

"I can't," he said, lingering by the desk.

"I've got to go help Jake. He can't get the math. He begged me to come over and do it with him."

"Oh." Karen sighed. She couldn't conceal her disappointment.

Ethan started to the door, then stopped. "You'll be okay, won't you?"

"Yeah. I guess," she replied uncertainly, her arms still wrapped around herself. She lowered them and climbed to her feet.

"You won't get any more weird calls tonight," Ethan told her.

She followed him to the front door. "Why don't you stay and help me with *my* math?" she asked teasingly, giving him her most inviting smile.

He smiled back at her. "Because you don't need any help with your math," he replied. "Jake is hopeless. Jake can't do long division."

He picked up his jacket and pulled it on. Then he kissed her, a short peck.

She reached to put her arms around his shoulders. But he turned and hurried out the door. "Later!" he called back to her as the storm door slammed behind him.

What's your hurry, Ethan? Karen thought sadly, staring out into the darkness.

Why are you in such a big rush to get away?

* * *

She didn't have a chance to talk to Ethan again until Thursday after school. He always seemed to be hurrying somewhere — to basketball practice, to work, or to Jake's.

Her heavy backpack slung over one shoulder of her down coat, Karen was on her way out of the building when she saw Ethan at his locker. "Hey — hi!" She called to him and went running over.

"What's up?" He greeted her with a quick smile. "You look great. What did you do to your hair?"

"Washed it!" Karen laughed. "You're not going to basketball practice?"

"Coach canceled it for today," Ethan replied. "He had to go somewhere."

"Good!" Karen declared. "Then you can come home with me, and we can study together." She brought her face close to his and whispered teasingly in his ear, "Or *not* study."

"Can't," he replied flatly. "They put me on the early shift tonight. At the Sizzler. I'm already late." He pulled his jacket out of the locker. A stack of books toppled out onto the floor. He bent down to retrieve them.

"You've been working a lot," Karen remarked, biting her lower lip.

"Yeah. We really need the money," Ethan replied, shoving books back onto the locker floor. "Oh. I'm sorry. I've got bad news. I meant to call you last night. I couldn't switch shifts with Tony."

She stared down at him. "You mean — ?"

"I can't take you to the dance club Saturday night," he said, avoiding her eyes. "I've got to work."

"Ethan!" Karen cried emotionally. "I'm really disappointed."

"Me, too," he replied softly. He still refused to look her in the eye.

Through gritted teeth, Karen asked Ethan to call her after work. He said he'd try.

Feeling really annoyed, she offered a curt good-bye and made her way toward the front exit, taking long, angry strides. She passed a group of laughing kids, heading to play rehearsal in the auditorium.

The building was quickly emptying out. Two blue-uniformed cleaning people were dragging mops and buckets from a small supply closet.

Karen turned another corner, headed down the hall, and nearly ran into Micah. Micah had her back to Karen. She was tugging at her tangles of blonde hair with one hand as she talked quietly to someone, standing very close.

Jake!

Karen was astonished to see Micah talking so cozily to Jake.

Sure, Micah would flirt with almost any boy. But she never could stand Jake, Karen thought, hesitating in the middle of the hall. So how come they're suddenly such good pals? Weird!

She watched them talking. Jake wore a black vest over a white T-shirt. Micah gave the vest a friendly pat.

Weird. Very weird, Karen thought.

Jake spotted Karen first. "Hi, Karen!" he called to her in his hoarse voice.

Micah spun around. "Karen!" Her green eyes opened wide with surprise.

Karen turned and started to jog in the other direction.

"Karen — come back!" she heard Micah call after her. "Karen — this is stupid! We've got to talk!"

Karen slowed her pace for a moment. Maybe I *should* stop and talk with her, she thought.

But she realized she'd be too embarrassed now. She'd already started to run away.

She turned the corner, ran past the two cleaners who had already started to mop the floor, past the auditorium where loud piano music came drifting out, around another corner

— where she nearly collided with Wendy.

"Oh!" Karen cried out, startled.

She gazed past Wendy down the long corridor. Empty. No one else in sight.

Wendy's eyes narrowed angrily. Something gleamed in Wendy's hand. She raised it toward Karen.

"Wendy — no!" Karen shrieked. "Put down the gun!"

Chapter 14

Karen's breath caught in her throat as Wendy lifted the gun higher.

The gun shimmered in front of Wendy's olive-green T-shirt. Wendy's straight, red hair caught the light from the ceiling.

"Wendy, please — !" Karen pleaded.

A strange smile formed on Wendy's face. "Karen, what's your problem?" she asked, her gray-green eyes narrowing as she studied Karen's alarmed face. "You *know* I'm the prop master for *Guys and Dolls*." She gestured toward the auditorium with the pistol. "They need this for the rehearsal."

Karen could feel her face grow hot. She knew she was blushing. She shifted her backpack to her other shoulder. "I thought — "

"Have you lost it totally?" Wendy asked scornfully, tossing her straight red hair back with a flick of her head. She laughed. "Did you think it was a real pistol? Did you really think I was going to shoot you?"

"No. Of course not," Karen lied. "I just thought — "

"Bang-bang," Wendy said, rolling her eyes. She pointed the prop gun at Karen's stomach.

Karen stared at her awkwardly, waiting for her normal breathing to return, waiting for her heart to stop pounding.

"I've got to go. I'm late. The rehearsal already started," Wendy said, starting past Karen.

"You know, I *didn't* push you!" Karen blurted out. She felt her face grow even hotter.

"I know," Wendy replied quickly, her face revealing no emotion at all.

"Huh?" Her words caught Karen by surprise.

"I know," Wendy repeated. "I was off balance. That stupid papier-mâché head started to slip out of my hands. I grabbed for it and fell."

"Oh," Karen replied, feeling foolish. "I — well — some kids were saying things. They said you thought I pushed you." She lowered her eyes from Wendy's stare.

"No. You didn't push me," Wendy said quietly. "But you didn't stay to help me, either."

Her expression turned hard. Her eyes burned into Karen's. "You didn't stay to see if I was okay. You didn't bother to come down the stairs. I saw you, just staring down at me from the top step."

"I — I know," Karen stammered, feeling her neck muscles tighten. "I was upset. I was scared. So . . . I ran. I just panicked, I guess."

Wendy sniffed, but didn't reply. "I've got to go." She gestured again with the silvery pistol.

"I know about you and Ethan," Karen said, letting the words spill out in a rush.

"What? What are you talking about?" Wendy asked scornfully.

"You can stop pretending," Karen said, staring down the long, empty hall. A jangle of piano music floated into the corridor as some-one opened the auditorium door. Someone was pounding the keyboard crazily.

"Karen, I really don't know what you're talk-ing about," Wendy said in a low, deliberate voice.

"It doesn't matter," Karen told her heat-edly. "It doesn't matter because Ethan is back with me now. That's the truth. He isn't break-ing up with me, Wendy. He isn't interested in you anymore."

Wendy rolled her gray-green eyes again.

"Wow, Karen — get a reality check!" she exclaimed.

"Wendy, I'm serious — " Karen insisted.

"I've got to go," Wendy said sharply. She brushed past Karen and disappeared around the corner.

Karen stood staring down the empty hallway, Wendy's footsteps fading behind her.

I confronted her, Karen thought. I said everything I wanted to say to her.

So why don't I feel better about things?

Why do I feel so much worse?

She slumped into the blue Corolla and drove aimlessly around Thompson Falls for a while. Sometimes cruising around town helped to calm her.

But not today.

As Karen made her way through the winter-gray streets, she kept seeing Wendy's sneering face.

I hate that smug look of hers, Karen thought. So smug and superior. Like she knows a secret that I don't.

A secret . . . a secret . . .

Karen stopped for a red light. She tapped the wheel tensely with both hands, picturing Wendy, her red hair, her laughing green eyes . . . the stupid prop pistol in her hand.

She deliberately scared me, Karen decided. I know she did.

She was waiting for me. She heard me coming. She raised the pistol to give me a scare.

"Whoa!" Karen murmured out loud, pushing her foot down on the gas as the light changed. She roared into the intersection. "Whoa, Karen. Let's not become a *total* paranoid! Let's not lose it completely here, girl!"

She drove past the school for the second time. A few kids had been let out of the *Guys and Dolls* rehearsal and were huddled on the front walk. A guy Karen knew was trying to balance on the metal railing beside the walk, flailing his arms in the air, finally leaping to the ground in defeat.

The back of Karen's neck ached. She rubbed it with one hand. The muscles were tight and hard.

She turned onto Jackson and kept driving. Houses and yards rolled by in a gray blur. Karen rolled through a stop sign without noticing.

She couldn't shake Wendy from her thoughts.

Why did she laugh at me and tell me to get a reality check? Is it because she and Ethan really are seeing each other?

No, Karen told herself. No, no, no.

The Sizzler suddenly came into view on the right.

Ethan is working in there, she realized.

On an impulse, Karen turned the wheel sharply, into the parking lot.

I've got to talk to Ethan, she decided. Ethan will cheer me up.

He didn't like for her to visit while he was working. The restaurant manager was really strict. She was always on Ethan's case for one thing or another.

I'll only stay for a few minutes, Karen decided, sliding the car into a parking space in front of the entrance.

There were only two other cars in the lot. She climbed out and stretched, straining to see into the restaurant through the glass doors. The aroma of charcoaled steak floated out to greet her.

Taking a deep breath, Karen pulled open the door and stepped inside. Bright white lights beamed down on the vast salad bar in the center of the room.

At first, she didn't see anyone in the restaurant at all. Then she spotted an elderly couple sitting across from each other in a blue vinyl booth against the far wall.

A waitress walked past the salad bar, a tray of water glasses tinkling in her hands. Two white-uniformed food servers stood behind the long counter to Karen's right.

It's so quiet in here, Karen thought, her eyes searching for Ethan. I guess it gets busier in a few hours at dinnertime.

I'll only stay a minute, she told herself.

Just seeing Ethan will cheer me up.

She took a few steps toward the rows of booths to get a better view.

No Ethan.

He must be in the kitchen, she decided.

"Would you like a table?" a young man with spiky black hair stepped up to her with an eager smile. "One for dinner?"

"No," Karen said, shaking her head. "I'm looking for someone. Ethan Parker. He works here."

"Ethan Parker?" the young man scratched his spiky hair and looked around. "Oh, wait. I just started. Here's the manager." He turned and called to a middle-aged woman at the end of the food counter. "Does an Ethan Parker work here?" he called.

The woman came walking over, her eyes trained on Karen. "Ethan? Are you looking for Ethan?" she asked.

Karen nodded. "I just need to see him for a minute."

"Well, Ethan doesn't work here anymore," the woman told her.

"Huh?" Karen gaped at her in surprise.

"Ethan quit two weeks ago," the woman said.

Chapter 15

Karen nervously pulled the hairbrush through her hair. She tossed the brush down. It bounced off the dresser top and onto the floor, but she made no attempt to pick it up.

I *hate* the way I look, she thought, frowning at herself in the oval dresser mirror.

Why do I keep my hair so short and ugly? Why don't I color it so it isn't so lifeless and dull? Why don't I wear a little makeup so I'm not always so ghastly pale?

Why can't I have big green eyes like Wendy?

Wendy. Wendy. Wendy.

Ethan and Wendy.

The names repeated in Karen's mind like an endless, mind-numbing chant.

Ethan quit his job at the restaurant so he could spend time with Wendy. He lied to me. He lied to me again and again.

What am I going to do?

She took a deep breath and held it.

Calm down, Karen, she instructed herself. Calm. Calm . . .

Letting the air out in a whoosh, she strode quickly to her desk. She picked up the phone receiver and punched in Ethan's number.

His mother picked up on the second ring.

"It's me. Karen. Can I speak to Ethan?"

"We're just finishing dinner, Karen," Mrs. Parker replied. "Can he call you later?"

"N-no," Karen stammered. "I'll only take a minute."

A few seconds later, Ethan was on the other end.

"Hi," Karen said uncertainly. Now that she had him on the phone, she began to lose her nerve. She was no longer sure she wanted to confront him.

"What's up?" Ethan asked brightly.

Something about the cheeriness of his voice strengthened her resolve. Ethan, you lied to me, she thought. And now you sound so cheerful because you think you're getting away with it.

"Ethan, I went to the Sizzler after school." The words tumbled out in a hard, tight voice. "I wanted to talk to you. But they told me you don't work there anymore."

Silence.

A long silence on Ethan's end.

Then, finally, he found his voice. "Yeah. I know. I quit. I've been meaning to tell you."

"Well, why didn't you?" Karen demanded shrilly.

"I . . . thought you'd be upset. I mean, I didn't want you to think I was a quitter."

Pretty lame, Karen thought, twisting the phone cord tightly around her wrist. Even I could come up with a better excuse than that.

"The job — it was interfering with my schoolwork. I was falling behind," Ethan continued. The more he talked, the less convincing he sounded. "So my parents said I should quit."

"Two weeks ago," Karen said through clenched teeth.

"Yeah. I've been meaning to tell you. Really," he insisted. "I mean, that's why I haven't been able to go out with you as often. Because I haven't had any money."

Liar! Liar! Karen thought bitterly.

"Well, I have a little money," she told him.

"Yeah, but — "

"If you're not working anymore, that means we can go out Saturday night, right? We can go to the dance club?"

Silence.

"Well, I'm not sure — " he started.

But they were interrupted by loud clicks.

"Oh, that's my Call Waiting!" Karen moaned. "Hold on, Ethan. Don't go away." Her voice trembled. "I hope it isn't that creep again. He really scares me so much!"

Another click. Nearly a minute of silence.

Then Karen returned to Ethan. "Ethan — can you come over?" she pleaded breathlessly. "It — it was him."

"Karen — try not to get upset," Ethan urged.

"I can't help it!" she cried. "He said the most ugly things, Ethan. Please — hurry over! He said he can see me! He said he can see me whenever he wants!"

"Karen, please. Take a deep breath," Ethan instructed.

"He said he was coming to cut my throat!" Karen cried frantically. "He said he's coming soon!"

"Karen — ?"

"Oh, please, Ethan — hurry over! You've got to help me! We've got to figure out who is doing this! We've got to stop him. It isn't a joke, Ethan. He — he really means it. I can tell!"

Karen uttered a tiny cry. "Oh — Ethan! The doorbell! I just heard the doorbell!"

Chapter 16

Karen hurried downstairs to answer the door. The front room was dark. She was the only one home. Her mother was working late. Chris was out with friends.

She stopped at the front door, breathing hard, and brought her face close to the wooden door. "Who is it?"

Silence. And then a deep, fiendish laugh.

Karen pulled the door open. "Adam? What are *you* doing here?"

"I've come to drink your blood!" Adam declared in a thick Bela Lugosi-vampire accent. His reddish eyebrows flew up over his black-rimmed eyeglasses, and he raised both hands as if to attack Karen.

"Adam, I'm a little stressed out right now," Karen sighed. "I'm really in no mood for kidding around."

"Who's kidding?" Adam insisted. He

stepped past her into the living room. He was wearing the too-short, khaki-colored jacket he always wore, zipped up to the neck. He had both hands buried in the pockets. "Is your mom home?" He peered through the dark room toward the den.

Karen shook her head. "No. Mom is working late, as always. And Chris is out somewhere, probably getting into trouble."

"How come you're so stressed out?" Adam demanded, his eyes studying her through his glasses.

Karen shrugged. "I just am." She really didn't feel like discussing the phone calls with Adam. She had told him about the first one. But she didn't feel like getting into it with him now.

Besides, what could *he* do to help?

"Adam, did you come over just to chitchat?" she asked impatiently.

He shook his head. "No. I wondered if I could borrow your history notes. The French Revolution notes from yesterday?"

"Yeah, I guess. I have them upstairs," Karen told him. "But I'll need them back for this weekend."

"I'll copy them over and bring them back tomorrow," Adam replied. "Promise."

She started up the stairs to her room to get

the notes. He followed close behind.

"I love the French Revolution," he said, a strange grin forming on his pale face. "All those beheadings."

"Yuck," Karen muttered, pulling her history notebook from her backpack.

"Slice!" Adam made a chopping motion with one hand.

"Stop!" Karen pleaded.

"Don't you wonder about all those heads?" he asked, still grinning. "I mean, what did they do with the heads after they cut them off? Just toss them aside? Or did they bury the head with the body? Do you think they sewed the head back on the person and then buried him? Or did they bury the head by itself? You know. In a square hat box or something."

"Adam, you really are making me sick," Karen murmured, rolling her eyes. She handed him the notebook.

"Can't you just imagine all the blood and guts pouring out of the neck, and the head rolling around on the guillotine platform? The history text really does a very poor job of describing it."

"Thank goodness!" Karen declared. "You really are weird — you know?"

"I'm just really into history," he replied.

She gave him a playful shove toward the door. "Go home, Adam."

His expression suddenly turned serious. "Have you gotten any more scary phone calls, Karen? Is that why you're so stressed out?"

"Yeah. I got another one," she confessed. "Just a few minutes before you showed up."

"Really?"

"It was very scary," Karen told him. "Very threatening."

She tried to read the expression on Adam's face. Was that a half-smile he was struggling to hide?

What *was* that frightening expression?

He started to the door. "I guess I was wrong about it being a one-time thing," he said softly. "Maybe you'd better take those calls seriously."

A few minutes after Adam left, the front doorbell rang again. Karen had returned to her room to study. She slammed the textbook shut at the sound of the bell and jumped to her feet.

"It must be Ethan!" she declared out loud.

She hurtled down the stairs two at a time and pulled the door open. "Ethan?"

No.

Peering out into the darkness, Karen gasped in shock.

Chapter 17

"Micah!" Karen cried in astonishment.

"I've got to talk to you," Micah called through the storm door. Her eyes burned into Karen's through the glass.

"No. We don't have anything to talk about," Karen said coldly.

"Karen, let me in," Micah called impatiently. She grabbed the storm door handle and pulled the door open.

"Micah, I'm busy," Karen insisted. But she stepped back so that Micah could enter.

Micah had her thick, blonde hair pulled back and tied loosely with a blue ribbon. She wore a pale blue down vest over a bulky yellow sweater, and faded denim jeans with a hole in one knee.

Karen led her into the living room and stood in front of the couch. She crossed her arms in front of her and didn't sit down.

Micah made a disgusted face. She stood awkwardly in the middle of the room. "I thought you and I were friends," she murmured.

"I thought so, too," Karen replied coldly. "But I guess not."

What is she doing here? Karen asked herself. She isn't my friend any longer. She's a traitor. A *traitor*!

"I'm really worried about you," Micah said, ignoring Karen's sneer.

"Worry about yourself," Karen snapped.

"No. Really," Micah continued. She stepped closer, her green eyes studying Karen. "Listen to me, Karen. You and I are friends, and — "

"We *were* friends," Karen interrupted, sadness creeping into her voice. She struggled to keep herself together.

Micah turned away. "I'm sorry you feel that way," she murmured.

"That's the way I feel," Karen insisted angrily.

Micah cleared her throat. Her charm bracelet jangled as she lowered her hands to her sides, balling them into tight, tense fists. "Ethan isn't worth it," she said, her voice barely above a whisper.

"Huh?" Karen wasn't sure she had heard correctly.

"I came here to tell you that Ethan isn't worth it," Micah repeated emotionally. "He really isn't."

"You know for sure about him and Wendy?" Karen asked.

Micah started to say something, but changed her mind.

"Come on, Micah — tell me what you know!" Karen demanded shrilly. "Tell me!"

Micah shook her head sadly. "He isn't worth it, Karen."

"Tell me!" Karen cried.

"I — I can't talk to you," Micah said, starting toward the door. "I can see that. I can't talk to you now." She made her way quickly to the front door, taking long strides.

Karen chased after her. "Tell me what you know!" she insisted. "Isn't that why you came here, Micah? To make sure I know the truth about Ethan and Wendy?"

Micah turned with her hand on the storm door handle. "I'm sorry," she said softly. "Really sorry." Micah hurried out the door.

Breathing hard, Karen leaned her back against the solid door and waited for her heart to stop pounding.

I really lost it, she realized. I totally lost it. Micah must think I'm crazy.

Why did Micah come? What did she want?

Karen's brain was spinning too wildly to figure it out.

Did Micah come to warn her? To tell her some news about Ethan and Wendy?

To help her?

No way to tell.

Maybe if Karen hadn't started screaming at her, Micah might have explained why she had come.

I've got to get control, Karen told herself. I'm just so stressed out. . . .

Karen made her way to the kitchen and put the kettle on. Some hot chocolate will help calm me down, she thought.

As she reached into the cabinet for a mug, the phone rang. She hurried over to the wallphone and picked it up. "Hello?"

"Hi, Karen. It's me."

Ethan.

"Oh, hi. I thought you'd be here by now," she told him.

"I can't come," Ethan said hesitantly. "I'm sorry, Karen. But my parents need the car. And they need me to stay here with my little cousin."

"Oh," Karen replied, unable to hide her disappointment. "Well — "

"Will you be okay? Do you think you should call the police?" Ethan asked.

"I don't know," she told him. "I don't know what to do."

"When is your mom getting home?"

"Soon," she replied, glancing over the sink at the kitchen clock. "Any minute, I guess."

"Good," Ethan said, sounding relieved. "Then you'll be okay?"

"I guess," she replied doubtfully.

"Oh — Saturday night. We can go to the dance club," Ethan told her. "If you still want to."

"Great!" she exclaimed, brightening. "That's excellent, Ethan!"

He's going out Saturday night with *me*! she thought happily. Me — not Wendy!

They chatted for a while longer. Ethan urged her to call the police about the creepy calls. She replied that she might.

When the kettle started to whistle, she said good night and hung up.

She was crossing the kitchen to the stove when she saw the broom closet door move.

It made a soft creaking sound as it slid open a fraction of an inch.

Karen gasped. She locked her eyes on the closet door.

Another soft creak.

The door edged open another fraction of an inch.

Karen raised her hands to her cheeks. "Who — who's there?" she managed to choke out.

The door creaked again, louder this time.

It swung open all the way.

And as Karen gaped in horror, Chris's body tumbled heavily to the floor.

Chapter 18

Karen cried out as Chris's body landed hard on its side. It bounced once, then lay still, one arm folded underneath it, one leg bent at an impossible angle.

"Chris — Chris — ?"

Had he been murdered and stuffed into the broom closet?

She took a reluctant step toward the unmoving body.

Was her brother lying dead on the floor in front of her?

Or was this another dumb practical joke?

Yes. Another dumb joke, she thought desperately. Please, please — make it another dumb joke.

Chris grinned at her. "I can't keep a straight face," he said. "You look so totally freaked, I can't keep a straight face."

"You didn't fool me," she lied. She breathed

a long sigh. "I knew you were faking."

"Liar. You're a liar, Karen. You fell for it. You should have seen your face. It was great!" Laughing in triumph, Chris pulled himself to his feet.

"When did you get home?" Karen demanded, ignoring his gloating grin.

"A few minutes ago," he told her. "I heard you heading for the kitchen. So I ducked into the closet. I couldn't resist."

"Your jokes are going to kill me, Chris," Karen said, shaking her head unhappily. "They really are."

Saturday night, Karen was drying her hair when she heard the doorbell ring downstairs. "Chris — could you answer it?" she called to her brother in the next room. "It's Ethan. Tell him I'm still getting dressed."

She listened for Chris's footsteps on the stairs, then returned to her hair.

Chris pulled open the door and greeted Ethan. "How's it going?"

Ethan stepped inside. He shook himself as if trying to shake off the cold. "It's brutal out there, man," he muttered to Chris.

The wind slammed the storm door against the side of the house. Ethan grabbed it and struggled to pull it shut.

"What a winter," Chris said, closing the front door behind Ethan. "Is that wind ever going to stop? It's almost like a hurricane out there."

"Tell me about it," Ethan muttered. He glanced up the stairs. "Is Karen ready?"

Chris shook his head. "I heard her hair dryer going."

"Is she okay?" Ethan asked tensely. "She didn't get any more scary phone calls, did she?"

"No. I don't think so," Chris replied. "I think she's just a little slow tonight." He led Ethan into the living room. "Take off your coat."

Ethan draped his coat over the back of an armchair.

"Nice shirt," Chris commented, staring at Ethan's loose-fitting silky, red-and-gold-patterned shirt. "Did somebody puke on it?"

"Ha-ha," Ethan replied, frowning. "We're going to that new dance club. You know — the one on the river? It's called River Club."

"Dumb name," Chris said, pulling a handful of cashews from a glass bowl on the coffee table. He pushed the bowl toward Ethan.

"Thanks," Ethan said, tossing several cashews into his mouth. "I didn't get any dinner tonight."

Chris glanced at the clock on the mantel. "You're early, man."

"I know," Ethan replied, grabbing another handful of cashews. "I wasn't sure what time Karen wanted me to pick her up. I was trying to call, but your Call Waiting is messed up."

"Huh?" Chris had started to drop some cashews into his mouth, but stopped.

"Your Call Waiting — it's messed up," Ethan said. "I kept getting a busy signal. I couldn't get through."

Chris lowered his hand with the cashews still in it and eyed Ethan suspiciously. "What are you talking about, Ethan?" he exclaimed, his expression puzzled. "We don't *have* Call Waiting."

Chapter 19

Karen made her way down the stairs a few minutes later. She wore a silky yellow blouse tucked into a very short suede skirt over dark green tights. "Hey, I'm ready!" she called cheerfully.

She stopped at the bottom of the stairs, surprised to see Chris, Ethan, and her mother huddled together on the living room couch. They were talking in hushed tones. They instantly stopped and stared at Karen as she entered the doorway.

"What's up?" she demanded brightly, flashing Ethan a smile.

Her smile faded as the three on the couch continued to stare across the living room at her.

"What's the problem? Is my skirt on backwards or something?" Karen asked with a short giggle. She moved into the room, studying their faces.

Her mother climbed to her feet. She chewed her lower lip. "Karen, Ethan and your brother have just told me a disturbing story. About Call Waiting."

"Huh?" Karen didn't catch on at first. "Call Waiting?"

"We don't *have* Call Waiting," Chris said vehemently. "You pretended — "

"Oh!" Karen cried out as she began to realize what they were talking about.

"Be quiet, Chris," Mrs. Masters said sharply. "Let me talk to her."

Karen could feel her face growing hot. She knew she must be red as a beet. She turned her gaze on Ethan. He avoided her eyes and appeared to shrink into the couch.

"What's the story with these frightening phone calls?" Mrs. Masters demanded, her hands clasped tensely in front of her.

"Well — " Karen took a deep breath.

"You told Ethan someone made threatening calls to you," her mother continued, her dark eyes burning into Karen's, as if searching for answers inside Karen's brain. "Each time, Ethan was on the line."

Mrs. Masters glanced back at Ethan. "Is that right?"

Ethan nodded uncomfortably and appeared to shrink even deeper into the couch.

"You told Ethan you had Call Waiting," Mrs. Masters accused. "But we don't have it, Karen. So how did you get these frightening phone calls?"

Her mother stared even harder at her, leaning forward tensely, her hands pressed firmly against her waist.

Chris shook his head, a tight frown on his face.

Ethan trained his eyes on Karen. She could see hurt and confusion in them.

"Okay, okay," she sighed, in a low voice just above a whisper. "Okay, okay."

She dropped heavily into the armchair across from the couch. Her shoulders were slumped. She lowered her head so she wouldn't have to face their staring eyes.

"Karen, how did you get the frightening calls?" her mother demanded softly.

"I didn't," Karen muttered.

"What?" Mrs. Masters asked.

"I didn't get any calls," Karen told them. "I made them all up."

Chapter 20

"I didn't get any calls. I only pretended," Karen said softly. She brushed a lock of dark hair off her forehead with a trembling hand.

"This is so . . . embarrassing," she murmured, keeping her eyes lowered, feeling her neck muscles tense.

"But why, Karen?" Mrs. Masters demanded. "Why on earth would you do such a thing?"

"You always say *my* jokes are the dumbest!" Chris exclaimed, shaking his head. "Well, this is the dumbest thing I ever heard of!"

"Chris — please!" Mrs. Masters scolded sharply. "Give your sister a chance to talk. This isn't a joke. It's serious." Her voice caught in her throat. She swallowed hard. And then she added quietly, "It's very serious."

"I really don't want to talk about it," Karen

told them, rubbing the back of her neck. "Chris is right. It was really dumb."

"I'm afraid we *have* to talk about it," her mother said. She crossed over to Karen and put a gentle hand on her shoulder. "I don't want to embarrass you, dear. I want to help you. I need to know why you thought you had to invent those frightening calls."

"To keep Ethan!" Karen blurted out shrilly. She felt tears glaze over her eyes. She sucked in her breath and held it, willing herself not to cry.

She felt her mother's hand squeeze her shoulder tenderly. "I don't understand," Mrs. Masters said, her voice barely above a whisper.

Two hot tears rolled down Karen's cheeks. She brushed them away with her fingers. "Ethan was going to break up with me. To go out with Wendy," she said, avoiding her mother's reproachful eyes.

"No way!" Ethan protested, pulling himself to the edge of the couch. "No way, Karen. That just isn't true."

"I . . . I made up the calls so he'd . . . stay with me," Karen reluctantly choked out. She raised her eyes, a pleading expression on her face. "Oh, Mom — this is so embarrassing!

Can't I just go to the dance club now?"

Mrs. Masters ran her hand through Karen's hair. Karen pulled her head away. "Can't Ethan and I go now?" she pleaded shrilly. "I've confessed, okay? I admit I was a jerk. So can I go now?"

"It's sick," she heard Chris mutter from the couch. "It's really sick."

"Shut up, Chris!" Karen snapped.

"Karen — " her mother said sharply. "You don't seem to understand how serious this is. You — "

"Yes I do!" Karen interrupted, jumping to her feet. "Yes, I do! But I said I'm sorry, okay? Haven't I been embarrassed enough for one night? Haven't I?"

"You don't need to be embarrassed," Mrs. Masters said softly, her dark eyes studying Karen with concern. "We all care about you, dear. I — I'm going to get you the help you need."

"Help? What do you mean *help*?" Karen screamed. She could feel herself losing control now. But she couldn't help it. Why was her mother talking about *help*? "I did a dumb thing, that's all," Karen muttered.

"But it's important to understand why," Mrs. Masters insisted.

"You mean you want to send me to a

shrink?" Karen cried, squeezing her hands tightly around her waist, staring angrily at her mother.

"Adam went to a very good doctor in town," Mrs. Masters said thoughtfully. "Before his family moved. He was upset about the move, and this doctor talked to him and helped him a lot. I'll call over there and get the doctor's name."

"Mother, I don't need a shrink," Karen uttered through clenched teeth.

"It wouldn't hurt to talk to someone," Mrs. Masters said.

"You're nuts!" Chris declared, stretching his arms above his head. "Totally nuts."

"Chris — I'm warning you!" Mrs. Masters cried angrily. "You're supposed to be the man in the family. Instead, you're acting like a two-year-old."

"Hey, *I'm* not the one who's nuts!" Chris protested.

Ethan was leaning forward on the couch, hands clasped tensely in front of him, staring toward the doorway.

"Can I go to the dance club or not?" Karen demanded, staring furiously at her mother.

Mrs. Masters hesitated, biting her lower lip. "Only if you promise you'll talk to the doctor," she said finally.

"Okay, okay," Karen muttered grudgingly. She turned to Ethan. "Let's go, okay?"

Ethan climbed to his feet. He had bright pink circles on his cheeks. He avoided her glance. Karen could see that he was totally embarrassed.

I've really blown it this time, Karen thought miserably.

Everyone thinks I'm a nut case. Ethan, too. He'll definitely break up with me now. Why should he hang around with a nut case?

Pretending to get the scary calls had seemed like a harmless way to keep Ethan interested in her. When she had seen him talking with Wendy, laughing with Wendy, standing so close to Wendy, Karen had realized that she would do *anything* to hold on to Ethan.

Anything.

But now her desperate plan had backfired.

If only she hadn't been caught. . . .

Ethan followed her to the front closet. Silently, he helped her on with her coat.

He's staring at me as if I'm some kind of sicko, Karen thought miserably. Ethan thinks I'm a nut case.

"Not too late!" Mrs. Masters called from the living room.

"Don't wait up!" Karen called back. She

forced a smile at Ethan, but he didn't smile back.

They stepped out into the windy, cold night. The seats in the red Bonneville were cold. Karen could feel the cold even through her skirt and tights.

Ethan drove to the club in silence, his eyes straight ahead on the road, a thoughtful expression on his face.

"I — I'm really sorry about . . . everything," Karen offered, putting her hand on his.

"It's okay," he replied without looking at her.

She forced a laugh. "It's actually kind of funny, don't you think?"

He hesitated. "I guess," he replied.

At the River Club, Ethan seemed to cheer up a little. They began to dance as soon as they arrived, moving to the loud, throbbing rhythms under flashing red-and-blue lights.

Karen was beginning to feel better, just starting to relax, when Ethan led her to the tables at the side of the dance floor. "I'll be right back," he told her, shouting over the pounding music.

Before Karen could protest, he disappeared toward the front of the club.

Where is he going in such a hurry? Karen

wondered. She stood uncomfortably against the wall, watching the red-and-blue forms of the swaying, bobbing dancers under the swirl of lights.

When Ethan hadn't returned five minutes later, Karen took a seat at one of the tiny tables. Elbows on the table, she rested her head in her hands, her eyes searching eagerly for Ethan.

Where is he? What can he be doing?

She jumped up as a frightening thought flashed into her mind: Has he left me here?

No. Of course not, she assured herself.

There I go being crazy again.

She decided to follow him. She made her way across the dance floor, pushing and bumping her way through the dancing couples.

They all seem so happy, she thought. Why can't Ethan and I be happy, too?

She stopped when she saw him. He was leaning against the wall, talking into a pay phone, a hand over his free ear, trying to block out the loud music.

Who can he be talking to now? she wondered, feeling her neck muscles tighten.

Ethan glanced up and saw Karen. He gave her a quick wave, then turned his back as he continued his call.

Karen stood at the edge of the dance floor.

The red-and-blue lights swirled over her. The floor appeared to tilt and sway in time to the steady, relentless rhythm.

She shut her eyes, but the flashing, rolling colors didn't go away.

When she opened her eyes, Ethan was standing in front of her.

"Did you just call Wendy?" The words burst out of her.

"Huh?" He swept a hand back through his long hair and leaned forward to hear her over the music.

"Did you just call Wendy?" Karen repeated, shouting into his ear.

"No way," Ethan replied, frowning.

"Swear to me you're not going out with Wendy!" Karen cried.

"Huh? I can't hear!" He brought his face close to hers. His long hair brushed her cheek.

"Swear to me!" Karen screamed. "Swear to me you're not interested in Wendy!"

Ethan solemnly raised a hand as if taking an oath. "I swear it," he shouted.

Did she believe him?

She wasn't sure.

As they began to dance, a slow, soft dance, she held on to Ethan so tightly, so tightly, he couldn't get away if he wanted to.

*　*　*

Nearly two weeks later, on a snowy Thursday night, Ethan arrived at Karen's house after dinner for a study date. Mrs. Masters greeted him at the front door and ushered him inside.

"Is the snow sticking?" she asked, peering over his shoulder as Ethan stamped his wet boots on the rubber floor mat.

"It's starting to," he told her. He brushed some wet snowflakes from his long, black hair.

"Before you go up to study with Karen, I want to thank you," Mrs. Masters said quietly.

"Huh? Thank me?" Ethan reacted with surprise. He pulled off his backpack and followed her away from the front stairs.

"You've been so considerate," Mrs. Masters whispered, glancing to the stairs, not wanting Karen to hear. "You've been so attentive to Karen. I really appreciate it, Ethan."

Pink circles formed on his cheeks. He shook his head hard as if trying to shake away the compliment.

"It's been so good of you to come over every night and to see Karen every weekend," Mrs. Masters continued, not noticing his embarrassment. "You've really been so good for her. You have no idea. You really have made the difference, seeing her through this bad time."

"That's good," Ethan replied awkwardly. "I'm glad."

"Dr. Rudman says that he's had some very good sessions with Karen," Mrs. Masters continued, shoving her hands into her jeans pockets. "He says he's very encouraged by Karen's progress."

"Great," Ethan murmured.

"Well, I didn't mean to embarrass you," Mrs. Masters said, smiling warmly at him. "I just wanted to thank you for being there for Karen. Go on upstairs."

"Okay. Thanks," Ethan replied. Hoisting his backpack over one shoulder, he eagerly made his way up to Karen's room.

She glanced up from the open book on her desk as he entered. "What were you and Mom talking about?" she demanded.

"Nothing much. Just the weather," Ethan told her.

Karen started to say something, but the telephone rang. She picked up the receiver after the first ring. "Hello?"

"Karen, this is your imagination calling," a harsh, throaty voice whispered in her ear. *"I'm inside your brain. I'm going to kill you. I'm really going to kill you."*

Chapter 21

"No!" Karen screamed.

The phone dropped from her hand, clattering onto the desk.

"What *is* it?" Ethan demanded, his eyes wide with surprise.

"It's real!" Karen choked out. "Ethan, it's real this time! The call — "

He grabbed the receiver. "Let me hear!" He raised it to his ear. "Hello? Hello? Who's there?"

Karen stared at him as he listened intently. He turned to her, a bewildered expression on his face. "Just a dial tone," he murmured. He replaced the receiver.

Karen threw her arms around him and pressed her face against his chest. "It was so horrible, Ethan! Such an ugly, raspy voice. He said he was my imagination. He said he was inside my brain and he was going to kill me!"

Ethan didn't reply.

Karen pulled back and studied his face. "You believe me — don't you?"

"Yeah. Of course," Ethan replied automatically.

Karen caught the doubt in his eyes.

He doesn't believe me.

Ethan doesn't believe me.

She shoved him angrily away with both fists. "It's real this time!" she cried. "It was a real call, Ethan!"

"I believe you," he insisted. "Really, Karen. I believe you."

But she could see in his eyes that he didn't. She could see in his tight-lipped expression that he thought she was inventing another drama.

Late that night, Karen lay wide awake, unable to fall asleep, staring at the rectangle of light on her ceiling from the streetlight outside her bedroom window.

The whispered voice repeated its harsh threat in her mind again and again. *"I'm inside your brain. I'm going to kill you. I'm really going to kill you."*

Ethan didn't believe me, she thought miserably.

He had made an excuse and hurried home.

He didn't believe me. Even though this time it was real.

Real. Real. Real.

Was someone *really* going to kill her?

She shut her eyes, trying to force the harsh whisper from her mind, trying to will herself asleep.

When she reopened her eyes, she became aware of darting shadows.

Movement. The creak of the floorboards.

A nearly silent footstep.

Someone is here, Karen realized. Someone is in my room.

She struggled to sit up, but was held down by a hidden force, a heavy weight.

Paralyzed. I'm paralyzed.

What is happening to me? Why can't I sit up?

The floorboards groaned again, closer this time to her bed.

Shadows bent and shifted.

She stared into the darkness, still struggling to sit up.

But the heavy weight pressed against her chest, held her head flat on the pillow. Her hair felt wet and sticky under her head.

Shadows moved.

She heard a muffled cough.

"I'm inside your brain. I'm going to kill you. I'm really going to kill you."

Black shadows slid over gray shadows.

The floorboards creaked and groaned.

"Who — who's there?" Karen's voice came out harsh and raspy. *She had the same voice as the caller on the phone!*

"Who's in my room?" she called in the throaty whisper.

Silence. Sliding shadows close to the bed.

And then a figure moved out of the shadows. And a face lowered itself right above hers.

"Chris!" Karen cried.

He grinned down at her, his face half in shadow, half in light.

"Chris — what are you doing in my room?" she cried.

His face floated over hers. His grin grew wider. His eyes burned down into hers. "It isn't a joke," he said.

"Huh? Chris? What do you want?" Karen cried.

"It isn't a joke," Chris repeated.

And then Karen saw the gleaming blade — and recognized the big kitchen knife her brother raised slowly in his hand.

Chapter 22

"Chris — please!" Karen pleaded.

The knife blade gleamed, lowering toward her throat.

If only she could move. If only she could sit up, slide away.

But the weight pressed down on her, holding her there beneath the gleaming blade, beneath her brother's frightening, unwavering grin.

"Chris — ?"

He backed away suddenly, his face fading into the shadows.

And Karen suddenly realized to her horror that he wasn't alone. Shadows moved silently. Other faces appeared.

"Adam!" she whispered. "Adam — are you here, too?"

Beside Adam she saw Ethan. Then Jake. She saw Micah's tangles of blonde hair next, and then Micah was there. Chris, and Adam, and Ethan, and Jake, and Micah — and Wendy!

Their faces were illuminated by a silvery glow. The glow of broad knife blades.

They all held kitchen knives. The gleaming blades rose above Karen, shining brighter and brighter, until she had to turn away, had to shut her eyes from the shimmering white glare.

"Have you *all* come to kill me?" she wondered.

"It isn't a joke," Chris said. "It isn't a joke this time."

No. It's a dream, Karen suddenly knew.

She knew when she opened her eyes, the faces, the knives, the shadows would all be gone.

Just a dream. A frightening dream, she told herself.

She opened her eyes.

She sat up.

She had been right. She stared into the silent darkness.

Just a horrible dream.

She stared at the ceiling for the rest of the night, afraid the dream might continue if she fell back to sleep.

* * *

A few days later, Ethan met her outside the lunchroom in school. "How's it going?" he asked cheerfully. "Did you ace Carver's midterm?"

"Think so," Karen replied, bending down to pick up a penny. "Hey, look what I found. Isn't finding a penny supposed to be good luck?"

Ethan had turned away, she realized. Tucking the penny into her jeans pocket, she saw that Jake had appeared.

"Where've you been, man?" Jake demanded in his raspy voice, after slapping Ethan a high-five in greeting. "I haven't seen you in days."

Ethan's cheeks turned pink. "Well, I've been spending a lot of time with Karen," he explained.

Karen turned to see Jake glaring at her coldly.

Jake doesn't like me! Karen suddenly realized. The discovery caught her by surprise. She had known Jake even longer than she had known Ethan.

But until this moment, she had never realized that Jake didn't like her.

"You want to grab some lunch?" Jake asked Ethan.

Ethan turned to Karen. "No. Not today. Karen and I — "

"Okay. Later," Jake said, shrugging. He

shambled away, his long grasshopper legs taking unhurried strides.

"If you'd rather have lunch with Jake — " Karen started.

Ethan shook his head. "No. Come on. Did you bring your lunch, or do you want to buy something?"

Before Karen could answer, she felt someone tap the back of her sweater. She turned around to see Jessica Forrest, a girl she knew.

"Karen, there's a call for you," Jessica informed her. "In the principal's office."

"Huh? A call? Who is it?" Karen demanded.

Jessica shook her head. "I don't know. I work in the office at lunchtime. They just told me to try to find you."

Karen felt her heart start to thud in her chest. Blood pulsed at her temples.

Who would call her at the office? Was something wrong with her mom? Was there an accident? Had something terrible happened?

"I'll save you a seat," Ethan said, pointing to the lunchroom.

Karen barely heard him. Her mind whirring with frightening thoughts of what the call could be, she followed Jessica to the office, half-walking, half-jogging.

Jessica stopped to talk to some kids. Karen hurried past her.

She ran into the principal's office and breathlessly grabbed up the phone at the end of the long counter. "Hello?"

"I can see you, Karen," the throaty voice rasped into her ear. *"I'm in your mind. I'm your worst nightmare. I'm going to kill you."*

Karen's mouth dropped open, but no sound came out.

The phone receiver trembled in her hand.

Who is doing this to me? she asked herself.

Do they just want to frighten me? Or do they really plan to kill me?

Who is it? *Who?*

She tried again to say something. But the phone had gone dead.

The dial tone buzzed in her ear.

"Don't use that phone," a woman's voice called.

"Huh?" Karen dropped the receiver onto the phone.

"Don't use that phone, Karen."

Karen turned, her heart pounding, to see Mrs. Ferguson, the office secretary, pointing at her. "Huh? What's wrong, Mrs. Ferguson?" Karen asked in a quivering voice.

"You'll have to use a different phone," Mrs. Ferguson instructed. "That phone isn't working at all, Karen. It's out of order."

Chapter 23

How can the phone be broken? Karen asked herself, staring hard at it. I just heard that frightening voice. He talked to me on that phone!

I didn't imagine it! I *didn't*! Karen told herself.

With a cry of despair, she turned and bolted from the office. She could hear Mrs. Ferguson's alarmed voice calling after her. But Karen ignored it and kept running.

Out into the crowded hall, filled with kids returning from lunch, getting ready for fifth-period classes. Karen turned first left, then right, unsure of where she wanted to go — and stumbled right into Adam.

"Hey — !" he cried out, startled, and dropped his brown leather briefcase on his foot.

"Adam?" His surprised face blurred in front

of her. The floor appeared to rise up beneath her. Karen backed up against the wall, breathing hard, and waited for her head to clear. "Adam, what are you doing here?"

"I go to school here, remember?" he shot back, staring at her hard through his black-framed glasses. "What's your problem, Karen? You look terrible!"

"I — don't feel well," she told him, rubbing her throbbing temples with both hands. "I really feel sick, I think."

"I have my mom's car," Adam said, leaning toward her, trying to make himself heard over the slamming lockers and shouting voices. "Want me to drive you home?"

"Uh . . . yeah," Karen replied impulsively. "Thanks, Adam. I really do feel sick." She glanced up at him, trying to make his face come into focus. But it remained a fuzzy blur. "Won't you get into trouble?"

He shook his head. "I'll drive you home and be back in five minutes. I only have study hall next period, anyway."

Karen made her way unsteadily down the hall to her locker, where she collected her coat and books. Then she hurried out to the student parking lot.

A few seconds later, she was sitting next to Adam in his mother's old Honda Civic. It was a wet, gray day. Most of the snow had melted, but a few large patches dotted the ground.

The tires spun on a small square of ice as Adam pulled out of the student parking lot. He was tapping the wheel with both hands, nervously rapping out a rapid rhythm.

"Feeling any better?" he asked, eyes straight ahead on the road.

"A little," Karen replied, pressing her hot forehead against the cool window. "I have to call Dr. Rudman."

Adam thought about her answer for a while before replying. "What's the problem?"

"Phone calls," Karen said under her breath. "I — I've been getting these horrible, threatening calls. For real."

Adam didn't react. He turned onto Fairfield.

"I just got a call. In the office. This frightening voice. I don't know who it could be. He said he could see me. He said he was going to kill me."

Adam glanced over at her, then quickly returned his eyes to the windshield.

"But then Mrs. Ferguson said the phone was out of order, that it wasn't working," Karen continued with a sigh.

Adam hummed under his breath. "Wow."

"You don't believe me, do you?" Karen accused.

"Well . . ."

"No one believes me," Karen said angrily. "You think I'm crazy, don't you, Adam."

"No. Of course not," he replied.

"I'm not making up these calls," Karen told him. "I'm not. They're real. Someone is really trying to scare me. I made up the other calls. I admit that. It was a really stupid thing to do. But these calls are real, Adam."

"On a busted phone?" Adam exclaimed.

Karen sank back in her seat.

Adam thinks I'm crazy. He thinks I'm hallucinating or hearing things or something.

I'm not. I'm *not*!

She realized she was desperately trying to convince *herself*!

"Well, as soon as I get home, I'm going to call Dr. Rudman," she said, more to herself than to Adam.

"Good idea," Adam muttered.

"Why are we stopping?" Karen cried, suddenly frightened. She stared hard at her cousin.

"Because you're home," he replied, gesturing out the window.

"Oh!" Karen could feel her cheeks growing red. "Sorry. I really am a basket case today."

She pushed open the car door. "Thanks for the lift, Adam. I really appreciate it."

"Hope you're okay," Adam said.

"You don't believe me — do you!" Karen blurted out, suddenly feeling very sorry for herself. "You think I'm making up these calls."

Adam shrugged his slender shoulders. "I don't know, Karen." And then his eyes narrowed behind his glasses as he added, "Sometimes I hear voices, too."

"Adam — "

"Sometimes I hear them late at night," he continued, his expression solemn.

"Adam, please — " Karen pleaded. "I'd better get inside, okay? Thanks again." She climbed out and slammed the door shut behind her.

He's totally weird, she thought as she ran around to the back door. Totally weird.

Karen let herself into the house. The kitchen smelled of stale eggs and bacon. The breakfast dishes were still in the sink.

"Anybody home?" she called.

Of course not. Chris was at school. Her mother was at work.

She let her backpack fall to the floor, crossed the room to the refrigerator, and pulled out a can of Coke.

It felt strange being home in the middle of

the day, walking through the silent, empty house. She felt like an intruder. She felt as if she didn't belong here.

Crazy thoughts.

I'd better call Dr. Rudman, she thought unhappily.

As she started toward the kitchen phone on the wall, it rang.

The sound burst through the heavy silence.

Startled, Karen nearly dropped the Coke can.

A second ring.

She stood frozen in the center of the floor, staring in horror at the red wallphone.

Was it the frightening caller?

Was he really watching her? Had he followed her home?

Should she answer it?

Chapter 24

After the third ring, Karen grabbed the receiver and pressed it to her ear. "Hello?" Her voice came out tight and frightened.

"Karen? You went home?"

"Ethan!" she exclaimed, sighing with relief. "Ethan, I'm sorry. I — "

"I waited for you," he said. "By the lunchroom. What happened?"

Karen could hear loud voices in the background. She heard lockers slamming, kids laughing. She knew Ethan was using the pay phone outside the library.

"I — I got another call," she stammered into the phone. "It was really frightening, Ethan. The same hoarse voice. He said he was going to kill me."

"That's terrible," Ethan murmured without any feeling.

"You don't believe me — do you!" Karen

accused, her voice trembling. "It was a real call, Ethan. A real threat. Do you believe me? *Do* you?"

He didn't reply.

The kids' voices in the background seemed to grow louder.

She heard a long bell ring.

"I've got to go," Ethan told her. "That's the bell. I was worried about you, so — "

"But do you believe me?" Karen demanded, not intending to sound so desperate.

"I'll call you later. I've got to run," he said. "Call Dr. Rudman, okay?"

He hung up.

Karen remained with the phone pressed to her ear, leaning against the kitchen wall, the steady buzz of the dial tone drilling into her brain.

He thinks I'm making it up, she thought bitterly.

The next morning Karen dreaded returning to school. Would the kids be gossiping about her? Would word have gotten around that she had left school in the middle of the day because she was hearing weird voices on broken phones?

Her mind whirring with troubled thoughts, Karen was halfway down the driveway when she realized she had forgotten her coat.

"I really *am* losing it!" she said out loud, hurrying back to the house.

She arrived at school a few minutes before the final bell and hurried to the office to deliver the absence excuse note her mom had written.

The two secretaries were arguing about pencils as Karen stepped up to the long counter. "The Number Two pencil is softer than the Number Three," Mrs. Ferguson was insisting.

"They're not numbered for softness," the other secretary insisted. "They're numbered for darkness."

"Mrs. Ferguson?" Karen called, holding the folded-up excuse note over the counter. "Sorry to interrupt — "

Mrs. Ferguson made her way to the counter. "Good morning, Karen."

"My absence excuse," Karen muttered, handing her the note.

Mrs. Ferguson unfolded the note and glanced at it quickly. Then she raised her eyes to Karen. "I owe you an apology," she said, folding the note up again.

"Huh? For what?"

"For yesterday," Mrs. Ferguson replied. She pointed to the phone at the end of the counter. "The phone *wasn't* out of order. It had been broken for three days. But the guy came to fix it yesterday morning, and nobody told me." She smiled at Karen. "Sorry."

"Uh . . . that's okay," Karen replied.

The bell rang. Karen turned and hurried out the door.

So the phone had been working after all.

Knowing that fact didn't cheer her up at all.

That only meant one thing: *The call was real!*

The threat was real.

Someone who knows me is trying to scare me, Karen realized.

Someone wants to scare me — or kill me!

But who?

The halls were empty. She was late.

Her footsteps echoed in the long, silent hall. A classroom door slammed hard, startling her.

She turned a corner, heading to her locker to deposit her coat — and someone grabbed her from behind.

Chapter 25

Karen cried out, her voice echoing down the long, empty hall.

An evil laugh invaded her ears.

She spun around. "Chris! You creep!"

Her brother grinned at her, pleased that he had scared her.

"Chris — what are you *doing* here?" she cried angrily.

"Thought you might need this," he said, still grinning. He held up her backpack.

"Oh, no," Karen moaned. "I left without my coat this morning. Did I forget that, too?" She grabbed the backpack away from him.

"Getting a teensy bit absentminded, are we?" he teased.

"Thanks for bringing it," Karen said. Then she added, "You didn't have to scare me to death."

"Why not?" he replied, laughing. He gave

her a quick wave, then headed toward the exit.

Karen stood watching him leave, shaking her head.

Why does he enjoy scaring me so much? He really never misses an opportunity. . . .

A door slammed, stirring her from her thoughts.

She dropped her coat in her locker and, lugging the backpack on one shoulder, ran down the hall to homeroom.

Karen slipped her hands around Ethan's neck and pulled his face close.

They kissed. A long, sweet kiss.

She moved her hands up to his long black hair and stroked his head as she kissed him.

When the kiss ended, she sighed breathlessly and lowered her forehead to his chest.

They sat in silence for a long while.

I've never felt so close to him, Karen thought happily.

She snuggled against him, wondering what he was thinking.

They were at one end of the den couch. A single lamp cast an orange glow over the room.

Wish we had a fireplace, Karen thought dreamily.

She raised her face for another kiss. But Ethan climbed quickly to his feet.

"Where are you going?" she asked, surprised.

"Jake's," Ethan muttered. "I told him I'd come over." He glanced across the room to the desk clock.

"Jake's? How come you're spending so much time with Jake these days?" Karen demanded, unable to keep the hurt from her voice.

"He's my friend — remember?" Ethan replied sharply.

Karen jumped up and threw her arms around Ethan's waist. She hugged him, pressing her face against his long, soft hair. "Don't go," she whispered.

Ethan turned to face her, gently removing her arms from around him. "I promised Jake. Really."

"I — I really don't feel like being alone here tonight," Karen said shakily.

"Sorry," he replied, lowering his eyes.

"Can I call you at Jake's?" she asked.

He hesitated. "Well . . . we might go out."

"Ethan — do you believe me about the phone calls?" The words tumbled from her mouth. She hadn't planned to talk about the calls. But the fact that Ethan doubted her had been troubling her mind the entire evening.

"Um . . . yeah," he replied, tugging at the

tiny silver ring in his earlobe. "I do."

Karen wasn't sure she believed him.

"Do you have any idea who might be making the calls?" she asked.

He started toward the front door. "Some creep, I guess," he replied.

"Some creep?" She followed him across the living room.

Halfway to the door, he turned back to her. "What makes you think it's someone we know?" he demanded. "It's probably a total stranger, Karen. You know. Someone who just punched your number at random."

"No," she insisted, crossing her arms over the front of her purple sweater. "No. No way. Whoever it is knows my name, Ethan. They didn't dial it at random. They reached me at school, remember? They asked for me at school. They *know* me, Ethan."

"Yeah. I guess you're right," he said softly. He picked up his jacket from the stairway. "Call me if you need me," he told her.

She came forward to give him a good-night kiss. But he hurried out the door.

Upstairs in her room, Karen tried to study. But the words in the government text became a dark blur on the page.

I feel so alone, Karen thought, bent over

the desk, supporting her chin on her fists. I really need a friend.

Maybe it's time I made up with Micah, she told herself.

Actually, Dr. Rudman had suggested it.

She and Micah had been close friends all year. They had so much in common. They had always been able to talk about their problems together.

"Micah." Karen said her name out loud. "Micah. Micah." Such a pretty name.

She glanced at the desk clock. Almost ten. Not too late to call.

I'll phone her and apologize, Karen decided.

But before she could reach for the phone, it rang.

She reached across the desk and picked it up before the first ring had ended. "Hello?"

"This is your imagination, Karen."

The hoarse, whispered voice in her ear.

"I'm inside your brain. Can you feel me in there?"

"No!" Karen cried angrily. "Leave me alone! Leave me alone! Do you hear me?"

"But I'm inside your brain, Karen," the frightening voice rasped. *"I can't leave you alone. I'm going to kill you. Maybe tonight!"*

Karen started to cry out again — but she muffled herself when she heard a sound.

A sound behind the rasping voice.

One sound.

Karen listened to the sound. Heard it again clearly.

And knew who the caller was.

Chapter 26

Her heart pounding, Karen grabbed her coat and hurried out to the car. It was a clear, cold night. A pale half-moon shimmered in a dark purple sky. Small patches of snow dotted the dark ground.

The blue Corolla started easily. But the windshield was frosted over with a thin layer of ice.

Karen impatiently tried brushing it away with the wipers, but it didn't work. With a loud groan, she climbed out of the car and scraped the windshield with a plastic scraper.

"I hate winter!" she cried aloud.

Tossing the scraper onto the back seat, she climbed back into the car, switched on the headlights, and headed away.

I can't believe this, she thought.

I really can't believe this.

But she knew she was right. She knew who

had been calling her. She knew who had been threatening her, frightening her.

Now she had to find out *why*.

Her foot pressed down all the way on the gas pedal, Karen drove through a stop sign without even noticing.

"I can't believe that someone so close to me would do that!" she cried aloud.

She suddenly realized she was gripping the wheel so tightly, her hands ached.

With a furious cry, she made a sharp turn onto Jefferson.

Most of the houses were already dark, she saw, even though it was only ten-fifteen.

The houses, the front yards, the winter-bare trees rolled past the window in a dark blur.

A few moments later, from the top of the hill where she had spied on him, Ethan's low, ranch-style house came into view.

Feeling her anger rise in her chest, Karen lowered her foot on the brake to slow the car.

Chapter 27

Karen stared out at Ethan's house, stretching darkly over the flat lawn.

The car slowed nearly to a halt. She realized her legs were trembling.

Her entire body was shaking.

Shaking with anger. With hurt.

How could somebody so close to me want to frighten me like that?

It was a question she knew she had to answer.

The light was on in Ethan's bedroom in the far corner of the house.

Is he home from Jake's already? Karen wondered. Is he in there right now?

Ethan. Ethan. Ethan. The name repeated in her mind.

But the horrifying question pushed Ethan's name aside:

How could somebody so close to me want to frighten me like that?

Taking a deep breath and holding it, Karen drove the car past Ethan's house. Past the house next to it. Past the empty lot beside that.

Then she made a sharp right turn into the long driveway across the street.

The wide yard was still covered by a thin layer of snow. A light over the porch cast pale white light over the gray-shingled front of the house.

The bare trees shifted in a slight wind. What were they whispering to her? Karen wondered.

Were they telling her to go back?

Karen closed the car door quietly behind her and then raced up to the front door.

What am I doing here? she asked herself, running on trembling legs.

What am I going to do?

What am I going to say?

She leaned against the glass storm door, pressing both hands against the glass, struggling to catch her breath.

The front door, she saw, was open a crack. A line of bright yellow light seeped through the opening.

She grabbed the handle of the storm door and pulled the door open.

She listened.

Silence.

Behind her on the street, a car rumbled past.

Karen pushed open the wooden front door just wide enough to slip inside.

Now what?

What do I say? What do I do?

The living room was brightly lit. A fire crackled in the fireplace. All of the lamps were on. The chrome-and-white-leather couches appeared to glow in the bright light.

An enormous, framed movie poster of Clark Gable and Vivien Leigh from *Gone With the Wind* hung on the wall opposite the window.

Karen had always loved that poster, loved the strength of Clark Gable as he carried Vivien Leigh up the tall staircase.

But now it filled her with revulsion.

She hated the poster, hated the modern white couches and chairs, hated the room, the whole house.

Why am I here?

What will I say? What will I do?

Karen gasped and froze against the wall as Micah came into view.

Micah had her back to Karen. She was

dressed in loose-fitting gray sweats.

She sat on a square, white leather ottoman in front of the window. One hand held a cordless phone to her ear. The other hand toyed with strands of her thick, blonde hair.

Her back pressed against the wall, her knees shaking so hard she could barely stand, Karen stared across the brightly lit room at her old friend.

What should I say to her?

What should I do?

"Micah — !" Karen screamed before she even realized it. "Micah — I know it's you!"

Micah gasped and dropped the phone to the plush white carpet. She jumped up unsteadily from the ottoman, her green eyes wide with shock.

"How did you get in?" Micah cried.

Karen stepped toward her. "I know it was you!" she repeated in a tight, angry voice she didn't recognize. "Why, Micah? Why did you do that to me?"

"Huh? How do you know it was me?" Micah snapped back, her shocked expression turning to anger. "How do you know, Karen?"

"Oh, Micah," Karen sobbed. "I heard the chimes. It was ten o'clock. I heard the stupid chimes behind your whispering voice."

Micah's mouth dropped open, but no sound came out.

"Oops." Micah shrugged. Her expression remained hard, her eyes trained warily on Karen.

"Why?" Karen demanded again, taking a few steps closer. "Tell me why."

Micah backed toward the fire, her hands tensed at her sides. "You're so dumb, Karen," she murmured scornfully.

"No name-calling," Karen said sharply. "Just explain, Micah. Just explain why."

"For Ethan, of course," Micah replied with a sneer. She tossed her hair behind her shoulder with one hand.

"Huh? Ethan?"

Micah let out a scornful laugh. "You mean you didn't *know* about Ethan and me? You didn't know that Ethan planned to break up with you so that he and I — "

"But I thought it was Wendy — " Karen interrupted.

Micah shook her head. "He was never interested in Wendy," she said softly. She picked up the iron poker from its stand and turned to jab at the fire. "Why do you think I was spending so much time with Jake, Karen? So that I could see Ethan. Ethan and I met at

Jake's. You couldn't possibly think I was interested in Jake — could you?"

"I — I didn't know," Karen replied weakly.

"But you ruined it. You ruined everything," Micah said with emotion, poking harder at the fire.

"Ruined it?"

"With those stupid phone calls you made up," Micah said bitterly, her green eyes glowing angrily in the darting orange firelight.

"But, Micah — " Karen started.

"Shut up!" Micah screamed. "You ruined everything. When you started the routine with the phone calls, Ethan suddenly felt so sorry for you, so guilty. He couldn't bring himself to break up with you in your hour of need."

"I know — " Karen said.

But again Micah cut her off. "Shut up, I said! Shut up, Karen!" Micah poked the fire furiously, sending up waves of sparkling cinders. "When you started inventing those stupid phone calls, I never saw Ethan. He was spending all his time with you. Every night. Every weekend. He felt so sorry for you."

Micah twisted her features in disgust. "And all the while, you were a total fraud, Karen. A total fraud. You made up the calls to hold on to Ethan. You ruined everything for me! Everything!"

"But, Micah — you were my friend!" Karen protested breathlessly. "You were supposed to be my *friend*!"

"I tried to warn you," Micah told her. "I came to your house. I tried to warn you that Ethan wasn't worth it." She shook her head bitterly. "But of course you wouldn't listen to me."

"And then you started making those awful calls?" Karen cried.

"You're crazy, anyway," Micah said coldly. "I figured a few *real* calls would send you over the edge. I wanted Ethan to see how crazy you were. I wanted him to realize that he belongs with me — not you."

"No!" Karen cried, her entire body shuddering. "No! No! No!"

Her anger took over. She couldn't hold it back any longer.

Karen opened her mouth in a loud cry of fury.

Then, before she even realized what she was doing, she was plunging across the room, rushing at Micah, ready to hit her, to tear at her, to *hurt* her.

Micah's eyes went wide. She turned from the fire and raised the hot poker.

Karen tried to stop. But her anger was like

a tidal wave, out of control, pushing her, pushing her, carrying her forward.

"No — please!" Karen cried.

But it was too late.

"Ethan is mine now!" Micah screamed.

And she shoved the burning hot poker through Karen's heart.

Chapter 28

Karen dropped to her knees as the pain burned through her chest.

It took her a short while to realize that she hadn't been stabbed with the poker.

A hot cinder had leapt from the fire and burned through her sweater.

Micah stood over her with the black iron poker poised in one hand. In the bright firelight, her hair glowed as if aflame.

"Give up, Karen," she muttered, narrowing her eyes in hatred.

"No!" Karen shrieked.

Her anger swept her forward again.

She drove blindly with her arms outstretched and tackled Micah around the knees.

Micah cried out as the poker sailed out of her hand and bounced across the carpet.

Karen pulled her down, and the two girls began wrestling furiously on the floor in front of the fire. Uttering breathless cries, they tugged and punched at each other.

This is crazy! This is crazy! Karen realized as she struggled.

But she couldn't stop herself.

She cried out as Micah slipped out from under her and, panting loudly, climbed to her feet.

Karen reached to tackle her again. But Micah dodged away.

And then Karen saw Micah pick up a heavy white lamp from an end table.

Karen struggled to roll out of the way.

But Micah was too quick.

With an anguished groan, Micah raised the lamp above her, preparing to swing it down on Karen's head.

"Please — " Karen managed to cry out, raising her hands and shutting her eyes.

She waited for the lamp to crash down on her. Waited for the pain.

When it didn't come, Karen opened her eyes — to see Ethan pulling the lamp from Micah's hands.

Micah released the lamp without a struggle and took a step back.

"Ethan!" Karen cried joyfully.

"I'm so glad you're here!" Micah declared, throwing herself into Ethan's arms. She pointed down at Karen. "She — she was going to kill me!"

"No — !" Karen protested, struggling to her feet.

"She's crazy!" Micah told Ethan, still pointing at Karen with one hand and holding on to Ethan with the other. "Karen told me she hears voices, Ethan. She said her voices ordered her to kill me! She's so crazy, Ethan! Karen came here to kill me! Because of her voices! We — we have to help her! We have to get her to a hospital right away!"

"Okay," Ethan said softly.

Chapter 29

"Okay, Micah," Ethan repeated softly. "You can stop lying to me."

"Huh?" Micah's mouth dropped open in surprise. Ethan pushed her away from him and helped Karen to her feet. Then he slipped his arm around Karen's waist, holding her tight.

"She's crazy!" Micah insisted weakly. "She hears voices, Ethan. She — "

"Enough," Ethan said softly. "I heard everything, Micah." He pointed to the cordless phone on the carpet. "I was on the phone with you, remember? You didn't turn it off when Karen came in. I heard your whole conversation. That's why I came running over."

Micah sighed. Her shoulders slumped. The light seemed to fade from her green eyes. "But, Ethan, you and I — ?"

Ethan shook his head. "Micah, didn't it ever occur to you that I stayed with Karen through all this because I *care* about her? Sure, you've been after me to break up with her. And I was tempted for a while. But I came to my senses. I realized how much Karen means to me."

Micah let out an anguished sob of defeat. Then she turned away, her features twisted in sadness and dismay.

The room became silent except for the crackling of the fire.

Karen leaned her head against Ethan's shoulder. She felt his arm tighten around her waist.

"Am I hearing voices now?" she asked. "Or did you really say that?"

"*I'm* hearing voices, telling us to leave," he replied softly. Holding her close, he led her to the door.